To my loves:
Maggie, Jonah, and Leah
'*the best is yet to come*'

CALEB ROCKE

AS SEEN IN A MIRROR

BEGINNING OF THE END

Black Rose Writing | Texas

ISBN: 978-1-68433-420-9
PUBLISHED BY BLACK ROSE WRITING
www.blackrosewriting.com

Printed in the United States of America
Suggested Retail Price (SRP) $21.95

As Seen In A Mirror is printed in Baskerville

*As a planet-friendly publisher, Black Rose Writing does its best to eliminate unnecessary waste to reduce paper usage and energy costs, while never compromising the reading experience. As a result, the final word count vs. page count may not meet common expectations.

AS
SEEN
IN
A
MIRROR

A chance meeting deemed worthless. A pamphlet discarded as a waste of reading. A conversation thought to be frivolous. If only we would peer outside our own small-mindedness and take in that we considered insignificant. To see it in its truest form would astound us. What we thought lost was time for us to gain. What we consider an irrelevant twist of mundane, instead an elaborate weave in a pattern more significant than anything we could have imagined. What narrow mind of humans. What degeneration of a society that looks only within itself and does not seek to know all that can be revealed.

~ Anonymous ~

BEGINNING OF THE END

July – Future

"Amazing!" the fat man exclaimed.

Fat was the correct term. Ugly would be another. The man was generously overweight, and his baldness and heavy whiskers did not improve his overall appearance. Standing near the large display window at the front of a small knick-knack souvenir shop, of which he was the sole owner and proprietor, he stared – observing the crowds of people walking the cobbled sidewalks.

"It's simply amazing," he repeated again.

"You literally just said that," a sarcastic female voice came from the back of the room.

The bald fat man turned and regarded the young woman, barely out of girlhood, who was not only his employee, but also his niece. He nodded conciliatorily, affirming her presence more than her words.

"But it's inconceivable! Everybody is wearing them."

"Inconceivable? Really? It's July, which means summer, which means *lots* of sunshine. And in case your thinker didn't remember," the girl condescendingly pointed to her brain. "This is Savannah, Georgia, not some faraway town in Minne*sota*!" The girl sneered as she accented the 'sota'. She put her hands on her hips and with a look of disgust added, "What's the big deal already?"

The fat man exercised patience and merely raised his hands as if protesting an argument. "I'm not going there, Anna."

The girl shrugged her shoulders and in a mocking voice retorted, "Who said I was going anywhere, old man?"

The overweight gentleman merely snorted and turned his back to her; the flavor of the exchange not uncommon. Besides, the crowds of milling people beckoned to him. He transfixed his gaze once again out of the shop window.

.   .   .   .   .

The young man sauntered across the marble floor. He glanced around, more out of habit than anything else. Nobody minded him. Little about him would attract their attention anyway. His attire was that of a hipster. Dark metal-rimmed glasses made his face look smaller than it really was. Naturally curled chestnut brown hair covered his head. What could not be seen was the fact he had earned a Ph.D. in Biological Sciences using brilliant, yet daring research.

The marble seemed to stretch on forever, but finally, the hipster scientist reached the granite slab hanging against the wall on the opposite side of the room. Stopping a few feet away, he pulled a wad of chewing gum from his mouth and tossed it into the nearby garbage bin. He then began reading the inscription hanging above.

WHO CAN PREDICT WHEN MANKIND'S HISTORY IS ABOUT TO CHANGE? WHO CAN PREDICT THE CATASTROPHIC EVENTS THAT RESULT FROM THIS CHANGE? WHO CAN ANTICIPATE THE UTTER AGONY AND HEARTBREAK THAT COMES WITH LOSING ONE'S SELF? WHO CAN KNOW?

The young man had to admit it looked elegant. The dark chiseled sentences were etched into beautiful granite, easily visible, suspended high on the building's side. With a sigh, he ran his hand through the curled chestnut hair. Elegant or not, he could not help but feel a bit of resentment as he scanned around the area. What was he doing here? And why would one bear the utter agony and heartbreak that came with losing one's self?

Turning his eyes, he contemplated the inscription once more. A sudden, strong sense of déjà vu came over him. Rolling his tongue, his lips pursed. "I wish the skies of high heaven you were still here. Maybe then we'd have a clue on how to beat this."

.   .   .   .   .

"We're a go," the radio crackled. "Delta-6 is in position."

"Copy." The passenger in the front seat turned and nodded to the person riding alone in the back. "All set, sir."

The rider in the back did not respond to the statement. Instead, he took a deep breath and collected himself. The meetings with the World Council would be both strenuous and stressful, packed with pressure. Protestors would be there too, he was sure of it. His left eye instinctively blinked. The movement felt weird, so he tried opening it wide. The optic instrument rebelled and fluttered open and shut a couple more times.

"Are you okay, sir?" It was the passenger in the front seat again.

The man in the back nodded. "Perfect. Just another day in paradise."

■　　　■　　　■　　　■　　　■

The lone car made its way along the deserted highway. The car's sleek, glossy blue paint rippled in the hot heat of summer and its shiny hubcaps glistened from the bright sunshine. It was a newer car, the model from the previous year. It sped along smoothly on the interstate highway.

The windows were down and the driver, a young man in his late twenties, bobbed his head in time with hip-hop music blaring from the sound system.

"I just *wanna go* back, *wanna go* back; just wanna see you – *one more time*," he punctuated the words as he sang. "Why, oh why, did you *choose to* leave? I just wanna go *back!*"

He was handsome. Black-haired, smooth-chinned; about six-foot-tall; his frame average though athletically toned. The smile on his face was friendly and reflected at him as he glanced at the side mirror, singing carefree to the world. Skillfully maneuvering the car around a large pothole, he headed towards the far right lane and the off-ramp ahead.

The young man glanced about as he exited the main highway. From all appearances, the area was once a prominent shopping district – stores, restaurants, and eateries – removed by just ten miles from the hustle and bustle of downtown Minneapolis. However, now the area seemed to be all but abandoned. In one parking lot, a slew of shopping carts were jammed together in a corner. Another lot had weeds growing between the empty car stalls. The entire quarter was devoid of people.

Who would've thought I'd be the only one on I-35? The young man thought grimly.

He checked his rearview mirror, more out of habit than anything else. Behind him, nothing was to be seen but road. His eyes traveled around the empty stores and parking lots.

Of course, there's nobody. Why would there be? Haven't seen a soul for miles.

The automobile neared the end of the off-ramp and approached a toll booth.

"Another great, failed idea." The driver scoffed out loud this time, speaking to no one but himself. "Why would you put a toll here? What a waste…"

Continuing to mutter to himself, he swerved through the booth taking the middle lane. There was no gate. It was lying in pieces on the pavement about twenty feet away having been smashed off long ago by a speeding driver.

The black-haired man looked left and right as the automobile moved towards the intersection. No cars were present. In fact, there was not a single car or person to be seen in either direction. Turning the wheel counter-clockwise, he accelerated and proceeded to drive through the intersection.

Above the hanging stoplights glared a bright red.

ONE

March – Present

It was hot. There was no denying that. Even for the last day in March, it was hot. On this particular early spring morning, the sun shone brightly, sending waves of shimmering heat towards Earth. This had been a season, for many years, when the Arctic would still be sneaking down and blasting freezing temperatures while unwelcomed snowfall would abruptly descend and cover the ground. But that was yesteryear.

With the effects of what had initially been called global warming, it was now warm every day – unless it was unseasonably cool. The paradox was the new paradigm. The issue had been a heavily debated topic for decades, but the earth-shattering realization that climate change *was* real and *was* happening could not be ignored by skeptics any longer.

Ocean temperatures were rising along with sea levels, and polar ice caps were melting at an alarming rate. Forget about the polar bears or their southern friends the penguins – catastrophic calamity was going to befall Earth's citizens. It was no laughing matter, yet some joker cracked Greenland would finally be green.

After centuries of polluting the environment, the ozone layer had been mutilated beyond recognition. Each day passed with increased harmful rays and gases entering the hemisphere. Scientists were left to wildly guess the harm it would cause humanity. Few made any actual predictions.

One of those to do so was Dr. Charles Grafton, a brilliant biophysicist, and chemist who had discovered the cure to melanoma. The discovery of the treatment was groundbreaking, and few could have anticipated the effect it would have. No one rejoiced or celebrated the cure to one of the most common forms of cancer by basking in the sun. Instead, there was much public outcry and visible withdrawal of human activity during daylight.

It was then Dr. Grafton issued his famous thesis on the overall condition of humanity due to the state of the atmosphere. The argument contained many hypotheses and scientific theorems with little supporting evidence. But in the modern world, the feeling of fact always dictated the reality of fact.

The initial argument Grafton made was overexposure to sunlight triggered a biochemical reaction in the body, which could cause migraines, skin cancer, outbursts of fury, and general discomfort. It morphed from that into *exposure* to sunlight would cause migraines, death through cancer, violent outbursts of wrath, and constant pain. If one presents something as truth and tells oneself long enough, eventually it is believed. They told themselves, and they believed it.

Amid this ever-developing phobia, on a quiet residential street in the outskirts of Minneapolis, Minnesota, a shiny new, glossy blue sedan convertible, its make from the previous year, was parked alongside a curb bordering a small yard. Situated in the middle of the yard was a small, white and brick two-story house. It was modern, in the sense of yesteryear, but now was considered outdated and in need of TLC.

The front lawn was robust and healthy. Thick, green grass – fulfilling its vital role in photosynthesis for all of life – ran from the curb up to the front of the home. Splitting the yard unevenly in half was a driveway traveling from the edge of the curbing to the front stoop of the house. Why the convertible was parked on the street and not in the driveway, only the owner of the car could say.

A couple houses further down, the road curved left and moving away from the street was an abandoned rail track for the old freight trains that used to run. A gurgling brook – which had once been a knee-high creek, an offshoot of Vadnais Lake – ran under the rail, through a large culvert, and continued on. On either side of the tracks, majestic trees stood tall. Lustrous, vibrant leaves filled their branches.

It was late morning, and most of the neighborhood residents were off to work or at school, so the typical busyness one might find in a sprawling suburban community was absent. It was so still, the gentle stream of water at the brook could be heard anywhere on the street.

Inside the white and brick home, a young man in his late twenties was reclining on a propped up futon, next to an open window. The heat did not bother him, nor did he seem aware of the air conditioner softly humming in the background. He was sitting silently, cocking his head to one side. His eyes were closed as he focused – concentrating on something from without.

The man suddenly smiled. There it was! He could hear it now – the gentle ambient noise of water running over stones down at the creek. Yet, a familiar cry for help swiftly jarred the peaceful calm, and the man opened his eyes and glanced out the front window.

In the corner of the lush green yard, a killdeer mother was trying to protect her young from a couple of crows that kept swooping in and taunting her. She sent up her warning cry, and the male killdeer responded as he flew in and landed about ten feet from her. He started to play as if he had a broken wing and flopped on the ground.

This fooled the crows, and they moved from harassing the mother and her young to chasing the father and his broken wing. But just as they were about to snatch him, the male killdeer's wing miraculously healed and off he went. Climbing higher and higher into the sky; the crows followed.

Josh Cunningham, the man on the futon, smiled. Picking up a beer from the side table next to the futon, he took a swig. He watched as the killdeers continued to fool the crows with the charade another two or three times.

"Stupid crows," he said to no one in particular. "How can they not see they're being played? All the while, what they really want is out there, vulnerable for the taking?"

Bemused by his logic, Josh laughed and stretched out even further on the futon. He was about six-foot-tall, his build average though athletically toned. Both the home and sedan convertible outside were his. While he loved the peace and quiet, it was a rare experience.

Glancing out of the window again, Josh searched for the killdeer family. The male bird and crows were nowhere to be found. Obviously, the trick had paid off, and the crows left dissatisfied – fooled by the ingenious methods of the killdeers.

Josh chuckled out loud. "Crows are idiots. What a beautiful impressionist that male killdeer. Selling a perfect fake; bought by the mighty crow…"

He continued to talk to himself. It was a bad habit. Years ago, he had been told by his psychology professor that it was a sign of his inner self trying to connect with a world he had subconsciously shunned.

"Baloney" was Josh's answer to the professor. A straightforward man, Josh believed in the abstract, but only to a certain degree. "If I can't see it, if I can't touch it, then I don't wanna hear about it."

A buzzing noise cut short the one-sided conversation, and Josh glimpsed at the small table to his right. His handheld vibrated with an incoming call. The number was more than familiar.

Tipping back the bottle, he took another swig, and then set the bottle on the table. Grabbing the vibrating device, he swept his thumb across the screen.

"Hello?"

"Josh, it's Sam. Where are you?"

Of course, it would be Sam Walters, field coordinator from SEH – Morphing Division. Who else would bother calling while he was supposed to be off?

"Dude, I'm at home. Relaxing. Having a beer. What are you doing?"

"Knock it off," Sam was exasperated. "We need you here – now! The place is going bonkers. Some feed just came in with a really bizarre video. It's already being purported as an 'outbreak' of the Disease."

Josh listened as Sam talked. How that boy could talk! Grabbing the beer from the side table, he took another quick sip. Then he thought of something.

"What disease?"

"Exactly. That's what I mean. What disease are people talking about? This thing has already morphed into a national spot on News Weekly."

"I really don't know much about diseases, dude." Josh pushed back as he swished down another swallow of lager.

"Pony up then! This isn't just a science story for SEH, it's being requested by Pharma Group. Jacobi himself sent the request to John."

Pharma Group – the pharmaceutical mega-division of SEH – of course, they would be the ones to trample his tranquility! It must be something big, though. Mark Jacobi was the founder and CEO of SEH. John Stevens was the director of the Morphing Division. Anytime there was something afoot that required the origin story, it would be assigned it to SEH's truth verification team – the Morphing Division. If the assignment came to them directly from Jacobi, the CEO…

"Are you still there?" Sam interrupted Josh's thoughts.

"Hmm? Yeah. Am I supposed to be flattered?" Josh's voice was flat. The nearly empty bottle twirled in his left hand as he glowered savagely out of the window.

"Look man, I know you were promised a vacation after the last trip. And I know two or three days off at home is hardly a vacation, but…"

"But what?" Josh was agitated. The peace and solitude, that place of zen he had just moments before – he felt it slipping away. "For the last six months, we've been chasing phantom sightings. Most of which were in Kentucky!" he said ferociously; leaving just what he had against Kentucky unspoken. "Do we actually have anything concrete this time? Or is this just another pet project John thinks can win him brownie points?"

There was a slight noise on the other end of the line. Josh heard some muffled talk, and then Sam's voice came back clear and even.

"You want proof? I'm sending over the report we received from the Public Health Agency of Canada. You have your i-Beam toggle?"

Josh nodded.

Taking another quick sip from the bottle, he again placed it back on the table. His mind no longer quiet and calm. He began thinking about all those trips to Kentucky and also Tokyo and London. They had received feeds of strange phantom sightings in these regions. The first thought was aliens. The loss of an entire power grid in Kentucky furthered suspicions. Talk of alien intervention was as active as always, but as Mark Jacobi would say, "aside from comic books or play toys, aliens don't exist."

The answer had to be something else. Something more human, more fundamental; it was definitely from Earth. Naturally, Jacobi had assigned it to the crack team in his truth verification department. After all, they were truthseekers, and if there was something to be found – Sam, Josh, and the rest would root it out. Yet, after months, they had found nothing.

"Are you there?" Sam's impatient voice cut in again.

"Hang on."

Fishing around on the floor, Josh picked up his traveling bag. Reaching inside, he pulled his i-Beam toggle from it and paired it to the handheld. A 3D holographic display leapt in front of his eyes.

Cradling the handheld in his left hand, he set the i-Beam with its 3D holograph on the small table. Reaching out with his right hand in a fist, he pushed forward until it disappeared inside the huddled mass of pixels floating in front of him. With one quick motion, he opened his hand and simultaneously flicked the display ahead. The visual expanded to full size.

"Speaker option," Josh said, setting the handheld down. The device would provide the audio feed the i-Beam could not.

Leaning forward, he used his thumb and forefinger to pinch this and that – minimizing and maximizing windows of data as he saw fit. Standing behind the windows, a distinct, though somewhat fuzzy around the edges, image of Sam Walters smiled at him.

"Hey, pretty boy."

"Shut up," said Josh tersely. He cocked his head to one side and scowled at Sam. "The ante's gone up. I'm getting a *real* vacation. A beach. Say Cancun."

"I'll do what I can, but first, we find out what's going on here."

Josh snorted, knowing the "but first" could take weeks, if not months. Nonetheless, his attention was back on the streaming media in front of him.

"Any live feeds?" he asked.

"That's the cool part. There *is* a video from two days ago."

"That's old," he was going to add more, but Sam shot him a look of exasperation. "Okay, throw it on."

The field coordinator nodded and turned to his left. Part of his body disappeared from Josh's view. The latter chuckled to himself as he stared at the half-body of Sam Walters. Sometimes holograph video conferences were amusing.

Sam's whole body came back to the frame. "Just sent it; you should see it in a minute."

A chirp sounded from the handheld's speaker.

"Got it."

Josh flicked his wrist, and the message moved into the holograph display. He pressed his forefinger into the holograph's colored pixels and touched the link. The video loaded, and Josh stretched out his hands. The feed went full screen, all other data disappeared, aside from the interposed image of Sam Walters in the background.

At first, blurry images appeared, but then the video camera refocused, and the picture became sharp.

A handful of people were milling on the sidewalks of what was clearly a busy street. A hotdog vendor manned his stand on the corner, a tattered umbrella hung droopily over it. A couple of food carts were further up the block – trying to sell cheap, greasy food. A street musician was banging away on some five-gallon pails; there was a dog running loose; loud noises from a couple over-anxious street merchants as they yelled – trying to hawk their wares. And of course, the shoppers who didn't belong – carrying bags filled with expensive accessories and over-priced garments – as they passed through the neighborhood.

The buildings were unsightly. Graffiti donned most of the exteriors. A smashed window could be seen in the top right corner of the camera's screen and the housing apartment on the left side – there were bars on the front door, and three windows missing completely.

"Seems like a street, in a dubious part of town, in a big city. Nothing unusual," Josh remarked, observing all of this in just a few seconds.

"Keep watching," Sam replied.

Josh's eyes drifted over the moving frame – taking in every detail. Something unusual did catch his eye. He leaned in closer and stared intently at the middle of the screen.

"Is that blood?"

Sam nodded from the other side of the video.

"Where is it coming from?" Josh followed it up the frame. The blood came slowly dripping into the image from the top-center of the picture. It dawned on him. "It's from the person recording."

The camera swung around. A man's face appeared. It was haggard; deprived of sleep. Pinched with hunger; the man appeared to have not eaten for days. His shoulder-length hair was blotted together. Most disturbing were his eyes – a stream of blood trickled down from the corners of both, and dropped onto his hands holding the camera.

The man was saying something, but Josh could not understand it. It was in Canadian French. Cocking his head, Josh glanced at Sam for an explanation.

"He's telling us his eyes have been itching, terribly itching for the last few weeks. The blood just started yesterday. He's making a movie so that everyone can see the world that will soon envelop all of us."

"Why would he say that?"

"Keep watching."

The camera swung from the man's face and panned the room. It was hard to see at first as it was quite dark, but the camera auto-refocused. Josh gasped.

Seven bodies lay on the floor, neatly arranged next to one another. The bodies were oozing blood; visible marks from a violent beating before death. The clothes they were wearing, though soaked in blood, were freshly pressed and otherwise unscathed.

"The man killed them. In a fit of rage, he killed them. They are his wife and six children." Sam explained.

The man's voice began shouting, and the camera swung wildly upward, then back down again towards the street. There were shouts from outside– some in English, some in French. Faces from below looked up at the camera. People began to point and excitedly gesture. Josh figured the man must have climbed out the window and was now standing on the ledge.

"Danger! Beware!" The man's voice said in English. "Do not trust anyone! Watch out for your own fate."

With that, the picture suddenly flew downward. In less than two seconds, there was a burst of noise, and the screen snapped off. Josh needed no explanation as to what had happened.

Sam's body pushed through the distorted image, and the field coordinator stepped closer to Josh.

"You know what the Canadian government is saying? They are saying he died of epilepsy. That he was psychotic and shot his family in a fit of rage. They say it was mental illness."

"What about his bleeding eyes?"

"Oh, that was left off their report. This video was leaked by someone who either must live around there or paid a lot of money to get the chip this was on. Just how they got it is a guess, but that's why it's two days old."

"Something isn't right."

"What do you mean?" Sam eyed Josh through the holograph lens.

Josh pulled his left hand across his chin, massaging his jaw. He looked out of the window – he could see the killdeer mother sitting on her nest. She seemed so confident. As if she knew, no matter what, she could handle her responsibility – the nest which she and the male had so carefully and meticulously prepared.

Straining his ears, he could hear the bubbling brook beckoning to him. The neighborhood was quiet and in order – a contrast to that which he had seen on the video. Josh looked back at Sam. That was it.

"The bodies – they are lined up neat and tidy, yet bloody and viciously beaten. Inside, despite being horrific, there is a sense of order. Outside is chaotic and messy. It's almost pitch dark in the house, yet outside abundant sunshine. Maybe I'm over-analyzing, but these are poignant contrasts. Why would this guy kill his family and then try to protect others by warning them? Sure he could be mentally ill, but his behavior seems to be on a different dimension. Yeah," Josh nodded his head. "The contrasts are telling."

"You're worth your weight in beer," said Sam. "We've found reports that said sunlight made this guy flip out. The sun caused a man to go bat crazy. What do you think?"

Josh swore. "Idiots – to think sunlight caused this. I tell you, people take the first thing that pops in their head and use it as an excuse for everything. Seeing *is* believing."

"Sure, sure," Sam was impatient. "But if he didn't kill them, someone else did. And why? *#TheDisease* is already trending on social media. People are claiming this is a cover-up. But for what and why? I have a flight coming to Blaine. It'll be there in two hours."

Josh growled in acknowledgment. *So much for being 'off,'* he scoffed to himself.

"You see why I'm concerned?" Sam's face was earnest.

Josh mulled the situation and realized if he was working irregular, long and hard hours, then Sam, as the field coordinator for these assignments, must also be exhausted.

"Talk of a cover-up is interesting. This does have obvious half-truths, assumption, presumption – the usual signs of a morph," he agreed.

"Always on the same wavelength, but I do think this might be different. I can explain when you get here. Say, here's a question: if there is a cover-up, how other incidents like this do you think have happened?

"It's an isolated incident, Sam."

"Is it?"

Josh shrugged at his coworker and stood up. He grabbed the beer. With one gulp, the bottle was finally empty. Straightening himself, he gave a quick nod.

"You are right about one thing, Sam. We've got work to do. I'll be there in a few hours."

TWO

Josh rearranged himself on the black leather seat. Chartered flights were one of the privileges that came with working for a large corporation like SEH.

"Are you okay, sir? Do you need anything?"

Despite being chartered solely to pick up Josh, the airline company still provided a flight attendant. 'Kevin' was the attendant's name as displayed on the breast pocket ID badge.

"I'm good, Kevin, but if I need anything, I'll let you know."

Kevin nodded and moved on towards the rear of the plane. Josh smiled to himself. Traveling was a nice perk, even if he did it more than he would like. Except he wished he had a companion to travel with, someone like Amanda.

His brow furrowed as the thought crossed his mind. Biting his lip, he gently sucked his teeth. He did not want to think about *her*. Not now.

It was the crazy world of chasing the next morph that propelled Josh on the journey which took Amanda away, at least according to him. Irregardless if she had died from an automobile accident, when a young child darted into the road and she swerved to avoid hitting the boy. In doing so, her car crossed the dividing line and straight into the path of a semi-tractor. Authorities said the vehicle had turned 360-degrees twice before coming to a halt a hundred and fifty feet from the point of impact.

A garbled message burst from the overhead speaker. Josh was happy for the abrupt interruption into his unpleasant reverie. He leaned back and bounced his head against the headrest. It was plushy.

The engines on the small jet grew louder as the plane taxied for takeoff. Flying was exhilarating. He could see the world up high. Not a limited area, as one might see if standing at an elevated point on Earth's surface, but rather an encompassing view that seemed to stretch on forever. It made Josh feel like a god – if such a thing existed.

Which doesn't exist, he thought dryly. Then he laughed to himself. The idea of a god existing in a world where humans shot and killed their own; where natural sunlight was a vicious enemy to the people. Earth was being eviscerated faster than it was populating. The levels of suffering and depravity so much, a man beat his own family before killing them. No, such a thing as a god couldn't exist.

The plane slowed as it made the turn at the end of the runway. Josh knew almost to the second how long they would wait. He had made the flight many times.

His head fell back onto the plush cushion, and he looked out of the window. The outside world slightly distorted by the thick acrylic pane. *It always is, though, isn't it?*

He glumly thought of the injustices and superficial culture which had embedded itself in society. Even the airport had its own history. The site of a massive shootout a few years earlier – before Josh lived there. It started with a lovers' quarrel. One man shooting his boyfriend after finding out the latter was cheating on him. Next thing, the FBI, Minnesota State Police, and ACSO were involved in a high-speed chase that culminated with gunfire exchanges near the airport. Three police officers were shot, two of them died. The man who had started it all was found dead – his body riddled by fifty-two bullets.

Josh pondered the violence – senseless killings – such as the man in Canada. What *was* going on? Mind control? A government drill? Maybe an overdose? *Heck, even the ridiculous morphing that the sun could do this,* he thought of the purported theory by a famous scientist.

His eyes closed. He pictured the world on the other side of the plane's window. In his mind, he could create any world he wanted – one free of killing and death. A world where a twelve-year-old boy stepped up to the plate with a shiny new bat and knocked the dirt from his cleats. A farmer tilled his fields while crooning along to country music. A baby laughing as mother tickled her belly. It was a happy place; a place where life abounded. There were no mysteries, no unknowns; everything was predictable. Naysayers were not allowed. Dissenters disbursed. Haters done away with; peace achieved. There was no suffering.

Josh's eyes fluttered open. The most frustrating thing of all, as a society, they had reached a point where diseases were explained and cured. Dr. Charles Grafton's cure for melanoma had proved that. Wars were a thing of yesteryear. The War in Asia seemed far more distant than just a few years removed. Education and knowledge had reached a pinnacle never achieved before. In no previous time as now, could one feel as complacent and apathetic while still maintaining a high quality of life and enjoyment.

Yet, everything was changing whether as a byproduct or subset to the achievements. The world had been polluted and abused for years. The environmental factor could not be ignored, it loomed obvious. People turned on their neighbors; hating the sight of people they had known their entire lives. Impatience and intolerance had reached a feverish pitch. Josh swore to himself as he snapped back towards the cabin and drew in his breath.

If he were not careful, he would suck himself into a negative brood, exaggerating everything around him. *And that's not conducive for a truthseeker*.

The small jet thrust forward and gathered speed. The change in the engine's pitch reminded him that while nothing remained the same, still, the world would always suffer. First, it was his mother, then Amanda, and now…who knew what social media's *#TheDisease* really was or what it might be.

The plane climbed higher and higher into the stratosphere. Josh felt sleepy. His eyes closed. Maybe sleep would be the answer. After all, it felt so peaceful to slip off to a quiet land where no one could harm him. Where disease and suffering did not reign supreme; a world he alone created and controlled. His eyelids vibrated slightly, unable to focus on his dreams; crazy thoughts kept rushing in. He sighed and shifted to his left as best as possible. *Please come, sleep. Please come.*

Ever so slightly, he dozed off. His breathing became more rhythmic and steady. He perceived his eyes opened dreamily and observed a rushing brook – vibrant and free. Birds were soaring in the air. A mountain range spread as far the hazy blue sky ran. The view morphed and he was staring at a woman seated in a chair. He knew this woman. It was his mother.

.   .   .   .   .

"So what's it like in Washington?"

Josh smiled at his mom's words. She was always so curious about his life. He remembered the first time he went to school. When he had come home, she had asked more questions and took longer doing so than the four hours of kindergarten.

He turned and looked at her.

"Busy, hectic, and crazy all the time. You see a limousine caravan on one street, and then find another in the next. If I had a dollar every time I saw a foreign ambassador…well," he took a seat next to his mother. "I'd have enough to buy a sandwich from Polly's."

His mother merrily laughed out loud. "I never imagined you going to work in Washington."

"Well, it's just for three months. I won't be there permanently – or even regularly – I suppose." Josh stretched his hands above his head and yawned. "Sure does make a man hungry though."

"There are freshly made sandwiches in the fridge – tuna and pickle – just like you always want," his mother said, laughing again.

"You are the best."

In two quick strides, Josh was at the refrigerator opening its door. He placed the carefully prepared sandwiches on the counter. In another motion, he grabbed a plate and unwrapped the cellophane from the sandwich.

"And what about your girl, Amanda?"

Josh blushed. "Aw, come on, Mom. Let it go. I haven't even seen her in a couple weeks."

"Because you've been in Washington," his mother remonstrated. "You are so cute."

"Stop it," Josh mumbled between bites of sandwich. He opened the fridge again and took out a container of milk. Generously filling a glass, he swished down the last morsel with a gulp.

It was quiet then. Josh loved these moments. When everything was so still one could hear anything a thousand yards away; he listened intently. The river's rushing water was heard. He loved the flow of water –

something so calming, so soothing about it. His cell vibrated in his pocket. He pulled it out and the screen illuminated. *Dang*.

"I have to go, mom." His visit cut short.

"So soon?"

"Work calls. It never stops."

"Come here, Josh. Give me a goodbye kiss."

Obediently walking over his mom, Josh leaned down and gave her forehead a peck.

"Tell me, what does it look like today?"

Josh turned and observed the river. Even though his mom's house sat removed from its banks, with another house impeding much of the view, he could still see enough.

"It's beautiful. Bright, sunny – I see a couple boats out there today. There is a guy fishing on the other side – not sure if he's in a canoe or... And on this side, a couple yahoos are trying to kayak. Mr. Macgregor is out hoeing in his garden. I see Mrs. McReedy watering her plants. And old man Thornhill is yelling at some kids...again."

Josh looked back at his mom. Her mouth curved in a gentle smile, her eyes closed as she listened. Then she opened her eyes slightly and reached her hands forward – searching for his, yet grasping in vain. He gently grabbed ahold of hers and gazed into her empty eyes.

"They are all happy though, Josh," she commented.

"Really? How do you know that?"

"Just because I'm blind doesn't mean I can't see. Blind will always be blind. Not seeing is another matter."

It was an oft-spoken phrase of hers. Josh repeated the last part in unison. Turning away, he strolled to the door, stopping when he reached the threshold. He looked back. His mom's head was turned slightly – facing the corner of the room – yet searching for something. He could tell she was listening for the shutting of the door.

"You know what you get when you have all these bloody Scottish names out here in the Rockies?" he quipped.

"Scotch on the rocks."

The grin on Josh's face was ear to ear. "I love you, mom."

"I love you too."

. . . . .

A jolt of the plane caused Josh to wake from his pleasant memory. A tear trickled down his cheek; he brushed it away. The last three years had brought too much pain, he was over it already. Nobody needed that much suffering.

While the dream was frequent, it still haunted him. *Seeing is believing. How can a blind person truly see?* His mother's words beckoned to him. He could not figure out why. *And why today?* Josh inwardly glowered. There was enough to raise his anxiety already without painful memories.

What was the truth of the Canadian shooting? What was the story behind the video chip? Who discovered it? Who had leaked it? Was it the same person or was someone else involved? Perhaps an organized group of dissenters or maybe even conspirators?

Closing his eyes, Josh vainly attempted to recreate the dream, to change the conversation. His eyes flickered open. It was pointless. The vision was gone, a remnant of his past. Another sigh escaped him, longer this time.

"Everything okay, sir?" Kevin stopped next to Josh's seat with a concerned expression on his face.

"Yes. I'm fine. Thank you."

■　　■　　■　　■　　■

The rental care was far from impressive. Josh eyed it with disgust.

"Just like SEH to set me up with an economy. Why I put up with this crap…"

His annoyed voice broke as he continued to mumble and swear under his breath. Reaching down, he opened the front door and slid into the front seat. At least it was leather. With one smooth motion, he pulled his sunglasses off the top of his head and slid them over his eyes. Using his other hand, he pressed the ignition button.

Bzzz, bzzz.

Josh reached into his pocket and pulled out his handheld. It buzzed in his hand as he glanced at the caller ID. The number was unknown. He chose not to answer and tossed the phone onto the empty passenger seat.

Putting the car into gear, he slowly steered towards the exit. The smell of the freshly cleaned interior of the rental subconsciously reminded him of the trip to California with Amanda. He preferred not to think about it, but as usual, could not help himself.

"Things are crazy enough without thinking about *her*," Josh spoke out loud – his voice tinged with bitterness. "Why do I have to keep being reminded of these painful things? My mom, Amanda – what are you telling me, Universe?" He raised his voice, and lifted his eyes heavenward. He then fell silent and began brooding over the mission ahead.

Thinking of the assignment did not improve his soured mood. Of course, life would not be getting better. The sequence seemed natural – more death following death. A heavy sighed escaped. He flicked the left marker on and merged the car onto the freeway.

He was frustrated. It had been just about four years since he had been advanced to the role of field agent. SEH held a contract with the government in their pharmaceutical mega-division – Pharma Group. The Group handled quite a variety of cases and projects. One of their specialties was to identify biological and chemical attacks that initially cloaked as natural-borne illnesses. If the outbreak was indeed a naturally occurring illness, they would work on a vaccine or antidote. If it was viewed as a biological terrorist threat, they would hand it off to the military. The Morphing Division, where Josh worked, played a crucial role in being SEH's in-house truth verification team on the origins of these episodes.

The team was formed shortly before the War in Asia and was critically involved during the aftermath. Next came complex cases involving alien technology and interfacing. Some people thought the stories were restricted to the mythological bunker called Area 51. But in reality, extensive research and studies on extraterrestrial life and their encounters with Earth not only existed, but were very much active. The ever-constant degradation of the planet only augmented matters.

Josh thought most of it was bunk. He had yet to see an alien or any concrete evidence of their existence.

"They have as much of a chance existing," he would say, "As a god or supreme-being. The universe is our guide, and until I see otherwise, I'll stick with what I can see and experience."

It was not a bad logic to have – especially in his field. More often than not, morphing was just that – a concocted pseudo-reality spinning an entirely different story than what actually occurred. Being passionate about truth, as well as a person who would never quit until his curiosity was satisfied, Josh found the job suited him well.

Everything was going swell until he noticed he was spending vast amounts of time in the field. Personal life ceased to exist. Tragedy struck with his mother, and then Amanda, and he found himself wishing an alien would appear. Or that the phantom sightings on his last assignment had paid off and they found a Superior Being. Surprisingly, it would make life more simplistic and easy to understand. It would take away the questions of *why*?

The study of the deterioration in the universe and mankind was challenging – and had a lengthy history. Ever since the early days of the millennium (and even before) when global warming and the eradication of the ozone layer became topics of political and social culture, scientists had been scrambling for answers to prevent the "next big thing"…to be ready for catastrophic calamity.

It took months of prodding before Congress had approved funding to SEH's Pharma Group. One could hardly question the delay. What would a company that relied heavily upon scientific modeling and methodology be able to do in regards to solving biological and chemical outbreaks? There were pharmaceutical and medically-based research companies across the globe who were better qualified – Tachi Yin Merger (TYM) – for one. Regardless of the lingering questions, the contract was executed.

It took another generation (or so it seemed) to assemble a group of the smartest and most innovative research analysts the world over. Apparently, once money was involved, the initial lofty ideals took a back seat to scientific development on the drug front. That is where the money was at.

How Josh came to work for SEH's Morphing Division was a story itself. He did not apply for a job, but instead was contacted and offered the position by John Stevens. Shocked but excited, Josh accepted. The chance to work for one of the most prestigious companies in the world did not come twice.

If he had been told he was handpicked by the founder and CEO of SEH – Mark Jacobi – Josh would have laughed it off. But it was the truth. Jacobi had stumbled across a published report Josh had written years earlier while in college. The authentic truth-seeking desire and raw tenacity displayed by Josh in the paper resonated strongly with Jacobi's vision for the Morphing Division. It was an easy call in the CEO's mind.

Jacobi was first and foremost, a businessman. Second, a scientist. He was under no delusions that a person could crack the mysteries of the modern world with the snap of the fingers. Yet, ever since an infamous election and the consequential events that followed, mainstream news had been ostracized by the lesser-known reporting faculties. Morphing had become so common it was hard to know what was fact-based and what was based on fabrication. A fine line existed between reality and fantasy.

Out of this murky mess, Jacobi created his own truth verification team. Their sole focus was to find the origin story and set it straight. The Morphing Division had several field agents, but it was Josh Cunningham who set the standard.

"He's a truthseeker if I've ever seen one," Jacobi declared more than once.

Finding truth, however, knew no timetable. Yet, the world was always spinning, so it was best to be efficient. One never knew how much time was left, before darkness all but set in.

Josh felt the strain of this timetable and often complained life was too short and sweet to be worried by alternative facts. His line of work merely cemented his belief. Constant analysis and research; compiling deep-dive reports; data takes. Technically, his title was Field Agent – Level Four. When he was in a bad mood, Josh referred to himself as a Data Master – Level Forget.

Today was no different. He wished he were far away. For instance, the vacation to Cancun that Sam Walters had promised.

Boy, hot sandy beaches sure sound appealing right now! Propped up in a chair, beautiful women in bikinis, have some martinis...

A 'ding-dong' from his handheld, jerked him out of his daydreaming. The alert was notification of a voice message. It was from the unknown caller. That was odd. Josh gave no self-identification in his voicemail greeting. Whoever called either knew him or had gotten his number from someone. In either case, since they used an unknown interface, it was troubling.

Picking up the handheld, Josh pressed the screen and listened to the unknown caller's message. His face clouded, eyes narrowed, and his lips became tight.

Somebody's gotta be pulling a sick joke.

THREE

The lime-green economy hatchback pulled to an abrupt stop at the entrance gate of SEH headquarters. The driver's side window rolled down, and Josh pulled out his badge for identification. The security guard sauntered over, sunglasses gleaming, and jerked his head in welcome as he took the offered ID.

Josh glimpsed ahead, bored by the usual proceedings. The contents of the voicemail he had listened to on the way over still bothered him. Slightly shaking his head to clear the thoughts, he glanced up at the guard and gave a faint smile.

"Nice day, isn't it?"

"Humph." The guard made a guttural sound in his throat. "You're clear."

Stepping back, the guard motioned with his arm. The gate opened, and Josh focused his attention ahead as he passed through. Once the car cleared the entrance, the gates quickly closed shut.

The SEH headquarters was located near Washington, D.C., in northern Virginia. Some would like to think it was near the CIA, but Langley – home of the Central Intelligence Agency –was a good twenty-five miles away.

The complex seemed a second home to Josh. His feet retraced the familiar path to the elevators in the atrium and he pressed the call button. He was in the main building on the grounds, yet the structure did little to boast of SEH's massive worth or influence. A loud breath escaped Josh as he observed the sterile environment. It resembled closer the interior of a department store than a high-security clearance center for the operational arm of a multi-billion dollar company. Even the magnificent atrium was little adorned, and felt cold and uninviting rather than warm and welcoming.

Not exactly my version of a second home. A scowl set upon his brow. The constant back and forth trips as Sam Walters summoned him. *If I'd known I'd become nothing more than a courier...* the furrow deepened. In truth, his mind was troubled, and the drab interior was really the least of his worries.

For one, there was the leaked video. The irony that it was the Public Health Agency of Canada trying to cover up an incident rather than the United States Department of Health was of no small significance.

Josh was also bothered by the mysterious voicemail on his phone. *I need to talk to Sam...* his train of thought lost as a gong sounded – notification the elevator had arrived.

Inside, Josh selected the fifth floor. The Briefing Center was located there. Sam had messaged to report there instead of his office. The elevator door began to shut.

"Wait!"

A hand caught the right side of the door just before it closed. The light ray safety activated and the doors re-opened. Into the elevator, stepped a man wearing a harried look. His brown hair was slightly disheveled; five-day shave grew on his face. He looked as if he had not slept in days. The man slumped against the back wall of the elevator cab and nodded at Josh.

"Oh man, have I been waiting for you!"

It was Sam Walters, a man of medium stature and built compactly. The disheveled brown hair was starting to recede from his forehead and equally dark-rimmed glasses perched upon his nose. Together, they gave his face a somewhat owlish look.

"Things have been hopping since we talked."

"I'm sure," Josh replied. He leaned against the side handrail as the car started its ascent. "You look terrible."

"It's insane man," Sam forced a small smile. "The amount of activity since the video popped up – insane. For instance, the Public Health Agency of Canada has completely redacted the video – only after it went crazy viral. Heck, even some of the big networks are spinning a story. And the peculiar part?"

Sam was interrupted as the elevator gong sound again. The doors opened – they had arrived at their destination. The two men proceeded towards the security checkpoint.

"It's the stories coming in from all over the world," Sam did not skip a beat.

"Of people jumping off buildings and murdering their families?"

"No," Sam gave a short laugh. "Don't be ridiculous. Stories about the Disease. People bleeding blood from their eye sockets. Mood swings, becoming extremely violent – almost barbaric. A crazy, itchy, burning sensation from the temples…"

Sam broke off as the two men stopped and raised their hands. A guard waved an electronic sensor over them. He motioned the okay to continue on through the checkpoint. Sam began again, keeping his voice low.

"Truth is, Josh, I think we might be entering the apocalypse. Zo…"

"Don't say what I think you are going to. Zombies? Really? What is this? A movie made for teenagers? Or thirsty crowds needing an 'end-times' fix? You can get that from street corner preachers where I come from. Look, you have been studying this for too long without a break, Sam. There is no way this is a doomsday illness or madness, or whatever you might want to call it."

"Really? Then why are you here?" Sam challenged Josh as the two stopped and faced each other. "I mean, really, what are you doing if you don't truly believe, deep down, that this is something *big*. Bigger than anything we could've imagined? And you know it has to be all connected. I know *you do*." Sam put his hand on Josh, looking straight into his eyes. "Man, this is creepy, scary stuff. I mean," he looked about wildly as if unsure who might be listening. His eyes refocused on Josh's perplexed face. "Maybe today we'll find some answers. Maybe today we'll see if I'm truly going crazy or if there is something *bigger* happening here."

"Maybe," Josh answered. "But the reason I'm here is that it's my job; nothing else. Now, what's this meeting?"

The bespectacled field coordinator looked at Josh with a big, toothy grin. "That's the kicker."

"What?" Josh was exasperated.

"Follow me."

·   ·   ·   ·   ·

The two men walked further away from the security checkpoint and down a hall. They passed through a large room that was buzzing with activity – web conversations, holographic meetings, and large 3D monitors displaying rhythmic patterns of information. Then they went left and took a quick stroll along a dark hallway.

When the third door on the right came, they pushed it open to another corridor. After ten paces, they confronted a set of steel security doors. Sam punched in a code on the keypad, and the doors opened. They had arrived at the Briefing Center.

Three other people were in the main meeting room. A woman stood near one of the tables and looked up as Josh and Sam entered. Another man stood looking out of the tinted reflective window. The third person, lounging in one of the chairs, uncoiled his tall frame as they approached.

"Great timing, Sam, just like a high-priced hooker!"

"I try my best," Sam forced a laugh, ignoring the crude comment from his boss.

Of course, Josh knew John Stevens, the person who had just addressed them. The other two were strangers though. He waited to be introduced.

"You must be Josh Cunningham."

The unknown woman spoke and flashed a friendly smile towards Josh. It was a sweet smile.

"Yes, ma'am."

A hearty, beautiful laugh came from the woman. "Don't ma'am me, Josh. That sort of behavior isn't complimentary anymore. I'm Lieut. Rhianna Adams, assigned to this project by Admiral Connors. "

"Please to meet you," Josh recognized the admiral's name as the Deputy Secretary of the Department of Homeland Security. *Why is someone from DHS present?*

"Take a seat." The unknown man standing by the tinted window turned to face them.

Without a word, Josh casually took a seat in one of the large, oversized chairs. Sam slid into another.

"An agent of ours has been following the activities of the Public Health Agency. They say they have a cure – well, a vaccine they believe will be the cure."

"Cure?" Sam asked.

The man by the window was clearly annoyed. "Yes, I said *cure*."

"I don't understand…"

The man's dark eyes glinted angrily. "Until I ask if there are any questions, you'll refrain from interrupting me."

Sam nodded, and without thinking about it, sat up straight in the chair. Josh bemusedly looked at the man by the window and opened his mouth to say something. Thinking better of it, he stopped himself. This yet-to-be-introduced speaker clearly was not one to be trifled with.

"The thing is, if they *do* have a cure, we need to get our hands on it. The damn video they could not keep secret has been getting more views than Mikaela Waters' sex tape!"

A few small chuckles broke out at the reference. Ms. Waters was an actress who had become instantly famous via social media six months earlier for a leaked video – providing oral sex to a small group of men at a nightclub.

"I don't think I need to stress the importance of the situation. If we fail to obtain a cure, or even more, broadcast we *have* a cure – pandemonium will break out. I don't think that is something I want to deal with – or you!" the man shot a cold stare at Sam, who in turn, nodded as he shrunk back from the glare.

"I scarcely think Sam meant we should *not* find out if they have the cure, Blair. But I think he's confident in his team's ability to find information and as of yet, no evidence for a cure has been uncovered."

Ah! Josh quietly sucked his teeth. The unknown man was Blair Leshief, Director of Pharma Group, the mega-division of SEH. While organizationally Pharma reported to SEH with Mark Jacobi as CEO, Josh knew Pharma Group pretty much pulled their own punches. Blair Leshief indeed carried himself that way.

"It doesn't matter," Leshief snapped back. "Mr. Walters, you did your job bringing Josh here. You are free to leave."

It took a moment for the words to sink into Sam. He looked quizzically at John Stevens, who merely shrugged his shoulders. The field coordinator abruptly stood up and nodded.

"Of course, I'll go. Good luck, Josh. Whatever is planned, you'll come through." Sam turned towards Josh and mouthed *'call me'* as he walked away.

The steel doors swung silently shut behind Sam. Josh pursed his lips and studied the three remaining in the room. He was uncertain of what was to happen next.

"We have arranged a meeting for you, Josh," said Leshief.

"I figured as much."

"We will be meeting an agent – they are bringing something to us. It will be at 900 hours tomorrow morning. You'll be meeting here."

The man flashed a pulse to the wall, and the holographic display lit up with a 3D model of a location some thirty-odd miles from the Canadian border in upstate New York. Josh was unfamiliar with the area.

"Lieut. Adams will accompany you. Until we ensure this cure is neither a biological or chemical weapon, we will be working in cooperation with the Department of Homeland Security."

That was curious. While Pharma Group held a government contract, and would track the origin to ensure it was neither a biological or chemical threat, as far as Josh knew they never involved an accompanying liaison from the Department of Homeland Security. *Just what exactly are we dealing with here?*

Suddenly, for a reason he did not even know, Josh blurted: "We aren't stealing the formula, are we?

"Steal?" Blair Leshief stared coldly at him. "No. We are not going to *steal* it. We are just going to copy it! What kind of team is this?" The Pharma Group director looked at John Stevens. "They question everything we do?"

"It's the very best team."

The two men stared at each other for a moment longer. There was a silent, weird conversation going on between the two. Tension rose in the room. Josh felt uncomfortable and shifted uneasily in his chair. Finally, Lieut. Rhianna Adams cleared her throat, and the two men broke their macho staredown.

"It appears we are in agreement. Josh, you can follow me," the lieutenant said. "I will brief you on the mission's details."

Josh rose from the oversized chair, bewildered by the meeting – both in the people present and the details shared. Where would this assignment lead? Curosity set in. He followed Lieut. Adams out of the Briefing Center.

■　　■　　■　　■　　■

WHO CAN PREDICT WHEN MANKIND'S HISTORY IS ABOUT TO CHANGE? WHO CAN PREDICT THE CATASTROPHIC EVENTS THAT RESULT FROM THIS CHANGE? WHO CAN ANTICIPATE THE UTTER AGONY AND HEARTBREAK THAT COMES WITH LOSING ONE'S SELF? WHO CAN KNOW?

IN HONOR OF DR. CHARLES GRAFTON, FATHER OF TWO AND BELOVED HUSBAND, A BIOPHYSICIST EMPLOYED BY THE STATE OF PENNSYLVANIA. HIS SPECIALTY: BIOCHEMISTRY – STUDYING: HIS PASSION. DR. GRAFTON'S WORK FOUND THE CURE TO MELANOMA

AND GARNERED THE NOBEL PRIZE. THE STATE DEPARTMENT DEEMED HIS RESEARCH WITH REGARDS TO 'HUMAN RESPONSE TO SUNLIGHT' TO BE OF GREAT SIGNIFICANCE. THE THESIS 'ATOMS AND THE REGENERATION OF LIVING ORGANISMS FROM THE NUCLEUS OF NOTHING', IS A SCIENTIFIC MASTERPIECE.

SCIENCE WILL ALWAYS KNOW DR. GRAFTON AS A MAN OF AMBITION. TO HIS FRIENDS: CHUCK, THE FUN-LOVING GUY. TO HIS FAMILY: A FATHER, HUSBAND, AND CLOSE CONFIDANT. THE REST OF HUMANITY WILL FOREVER BE INDEBTED FOR THE CURE AND KNOW HIM AS AN INNOVATOR AND MONUMENTAL FIGURE IN HISTORY.

Luke Baer stood, reading the inscription to himself. He had to admit it looked elegant – etched into the granite slab high upon the building's side. Running a hand over his head and through curled chestnut hair, he exhaled. Using his left index finger, he pushed the dark metal-rimmed glasses back up his nose.

He gazed introspectively at the inscription. The first paragraph was Dr. Grafton's own words, delivered while accepting the Nobel Prize. It sounded mystical then, and the eeriness had not evaporated over time. It was as if the man could see into the future, predicting patterns of medical code that would trigger an outbreak, and then assisting with the cause and effect analysis of said outbreak. Dr. Grafton had discovered the cure to cancer after all! But that was yesterday and today, seemingly with new reports each day of strange epidemics across the globe, Dr. Grafton's foresight would go a long way.

Another sigh escaped Luke.

"Maybe then we'd have a clue about what we're even looking for," he muttered to himself, pondering the predicament of Pittsburgh University.

One of the two lead researchers for Pittsburgh's Research Team, a non-scholar program embedded in the Department of Immunology and Infectious Diseases (IID), Luke was among the best in his field and excelled in his work. The Research Team though was not without competition.

Both TYM and SEH's Pharma Group were strenuously working around the clock in the same pursuit – finding the "next" cure. Forget about the billion-dollar pharmaceutical companies and their clever bypasses of the elongated process for FDA-approval; the race for the newest and best drug was always on. Yet, with each new outbreak, Luke could not help but have a feeling all of them were somehow connected, a metamorphosis of something bigger. It could not just be another vicious flu outbreak; it had to be something else, didn't it?

A video had appeared online that morning. It showed a man in Canada committing suicide after presumably slaughtering his family. It was horrific, and from all appearances, the man was suffering from an infection. #TheDisease trended whilst the video went viral.

Luke was enough a scientist to not get caught up with every new rage, but something about the video intrigued him, tugged at his heartstrings. In his mind, the spikes he had been noticing on the daily readings over the last couple months could not be ignored any longer. It coincided with what was happening around the world. In fact, each week, a new drug was being announced as a new cure for a new disease.

"What good is immunological engineering if it's discarded by the wayside for a newbie drug by some young upstart looking to impress?" He was again talking to no one.

Why won't people work together? Isn't it for all of humanity we're fighting? Maybe the video going viral is a good thing – though rarely that's the case.

Luke glanced at his right wrist and saw the time. He was running late for a video conference with the people in London. He would hear about it from the other lead researcher at Pittsburgh – Melinda Gore. She did not like him.

Enrolled at Pittsburgh the same year, they stayed on postgraduate, and both finished their doctorates while working at the University. And all that time, ever since he could remember, she did not like him. Luke had no idea why. Sure, he was a bit more driven to test a theory than wait; to assume the anomaly rather than discard it. Meanwhile, Melinda was not just patient, but always vigilant for outside help to the fast lane.

Tugging his backpack a little closer, Luke started heading for the exit. He was so engrossed in his thoughts, he did not notice the pretty redhead walking towards him until he crashed headlong into her.

"I'm so sorry," he mumbled as he casually glanced at her. He did a double-take. "Man am I sorry!"

The redhead's smile deepened at Luke's words. She was beautiful. A loose strand of hair fell down her cheek, caressing it. Her hazel eyes glistened with mirth, and her face glowed angelically. She stood with hands on hips, accentuating her curves, and stared at Luke.

"I'm Tess, short for Tessa."

She winked. Luke's face colored. He was embarrassed. The girl was hitting on him.

"I'm Luke."

"Hi, Luke. How are you?"

Luke shook the young woman's outstretched hand and merely nodded. Tessa giggled.

"That's all you've got to say?"

"Um, yeah, I…"

The woman laughed again. Luke liked it when she laughed. Her whole face lit up, and her smile broadened, showing faint dimples at the corners of her perfectly formed mouth and soft lips.

"Ok, then. Well, here." She leaned against the wall and reached into her purse.

Luke watched as she wrote upon a piece of paper. He was dumbstruck by her beauty. His eyes moved over her body. She was wearing a lavender blouse; a short black skirt hugged her hips. Black heel boots came midway to the kneecap. She definitely was not an intern. He casually glimpsed at her left hand. There was no ring.

Tessa turned back to him. "Here you go."

Luke was petrified. He stared at the piece of paper offered to him.

"Take it. I promise it won't bite."

Slowly reaching out, he accepted it, and stared at the numbers written down.

"It's my number," Tessa said matter-of-factly. Lowering her voice, she dipped her head as she tried to look into his eyes. "Seriously now, don't go broadcast it to the world."

Luke grasped her meaning. She was challenging him, daring him to succumb to her flirtations. He straightened himself and attempted to put on a boldface

"Yes, of course. Definitely."

Tessa stepped back with a look of shock. She put a hand to her mouth.

"My god, it talks!" She batted her eyes and began walking away. "Nice meeting you, Luke. Call me, maybe."

"Yeah, nice meeting you…Tessa." He wanted to smack himself. He had nearly forgotten her name already.

The redhead smiled and waved.

Luke muttered a mild obscenity. The girl, she was something else, caught him by complete surprise. *Made a fool of me,* he silently cursed again. He reminisced on Tessa's smile, her gorgeous face, vivacious personality – sexy and wonderfully dreamy all at once. And her laugh! That was something he could live with for an eternity.

Notwithstanding the mesmerizing image and tempting visuals Tessa possessed, she faded from Luke's mind as he hurried down the building's exterior staircase to the sidewalk below. Tugging his backpack close, his thoughts returned once more to Charles Grafton and the mission that lay ahead for Pittsburgh's Research Team.

What is the nucleus of nothing?

Luke squinted, suddenly wondering why his glasses had not shadowed. The self-tinting function was off. Then he saw the clouds rolling in and did not wonder anymore. Darkness was coming.

FOUR

The early morning sun gleamed off the silver wingtips. The small plane was parked outside a hangar at Dulles International Airport, and Josh stood patiently outside, waiting to board.

"You slept well?"

"Sure," he volunteered.

Lieut. Rhianna Adams' right eyebrow lifted at his response. "That's interesting. Usually, civilians don't sleep very well before a mission."

"I've been around. A meeting – however top-secret and mysterious – isn't going to upset the apple cart."

"Let's set one thing straight, this isn't some field trip we're going on. This is an authorized US government operation. Is that clear?"

"Yes, lieutenant," Josh answered in a respectful tone.

"Good."

Rhianna Adams snapped her wrist, and in one fluid motion, drew her sidearm out and then back into its holster. She tugged on the end of the earpiece in her right ear and waggled her head back and forth. Everything was settled, and she gave a thumbs up to the pilot.

The small plane taxied and lifted quickly into the air. The flaps moved up and down as the pilot pulled back on the controls and the plane climbed higher into the morning sky. The firing of the prop motor was the only noise heard in the cabin.

It was a two-hour flight to the secure location of the mysterious meeting. Josh figured he might as well be comfortable. He adjusted himself in the seat, wiggling his tall frame to maximize the legroom. The propeller plane was not tiny, but neither was it a flying bus. A yawn escaped him. He became aware of Lieut. Adams watching.

"I wonder why you would ever work for an organization like SEH?"

Josh gave a short laugh. He had heard the question before, but it struck him funny coming from a US soldier.

"We all have our passions. Mine is finding out what's truth."

"You can hardly call the garbage SEH Pharma Group spins to be truth. Paid contractors to process whatever the government shovels down your throat is more like it."

"And what are you?" Josh shot back. "A paid soldier licensed to kill whomever the government tells you to."

Lieut. Adams brown eyes glinted with a hint of anger, and she stared back at Josh, who eventually broke his gaze and looked away.

"Look, sometimes I'm paid to escort high-profile people around too. Speaking of which, what exactly do you do?"

"I'm a field agent."

"Of what exactly?"

"Morphing."

"Of science?" Rhianna spoke sarcastically. "I heard Pharma is struggling to meet FDA standards. They've been accused of cutting corners."

Josh held up his hands. "Seriously, I told you I work in the Morphing Division – truth verification. Accurate statements don't bother me. Truce?"

He did not know why his DHS liaison was being so cold, but he extended a hand in a show of good faith. After a moment's hesitation, Lieut. Adams reached out and shook it.

"My job is to find the origin," Josh continued. "Trace the report back to a source and follow it through. It's too hard in today's fast-paced world for a person to know where truth ends and legend begins. That's why we have a truth verification team at SEH."

"So you're a journalist?"

"Haha," Josh's laughter was sincere, though probably louder than he realized. "Heck no. I hate reports and writing. I'm more of an analytical researcher. A truthseeker. Please do not confuse me with a journalist."

"My apologies, I've never met someone who worked *in* morphing. I have watched the videos and heard talk of morphing; I just thought they were referring to special effects."

Josh did not know if she was serious or not. He chose to keep the conversation moving.

"You met Sam Walters at the briefing room, he's the one who runs point on our assignments. There's some support personnel with him too. I tackle the field side – solo," he added. "We're a good team. But things have been strange this year. Like this incident in Canada."

"Bizarre. Murder-suicide, as common as the day, yet cloaked in double meaning," said Rhianna cryptically. "Tell me, an anomaly is something that exists when it shouldn't, but you can't really know if this incident is an anomaly now, can you? I mean, people have feared zombies forever and…"

"Zombies?" Josh turned, and incredulously stared at his liaison, not believing his ears. "This is not some fantasy thriller, lieutenant. With all due respect, the video showed something extremely unheard of and unpredictable in every way. If this is a medical outbreak, an antidote can't be developed without knowing the source of contamination."

"How do you know it's contaminated? What if it's viral? Even cyber? What if it's a cover-up for something dastardly?"

"That's ridiculous."

Josh was starting to think his liaison was a conspirator. They were people who doubted everything shown or revealed to them. They lived in great fear and suspicion of their fellow human beings. Unlike the public outcasts – dissenters and haters – conspirators lived in the shadows and lurked in the abyss of the darknet.

"How so, Josh? What gives you such assurance that this incident is something you can quantify and source? What if it is the Disease?"

"Well, first, the assumption this is the Disease, is not something proven. Second, what a morbid thought. Are you my liaison or a negative dose of energy?"

Lieut. Adams's brown eyes lightened slightly as she smiled.

"You presume too much. I'm not trying to be negative. These are just questions I think you should consider."

"Well, I don't know the answers."

"Ah, and that is why you work in morphing. You want to know the truth."

"Precisely."

Josh was surprised. Strangeness and sarcasm aside, Rhianna Adams had hit the nail on the head. It was the primary reason he had joined the team – even after Jacobi himself had followed up on John Steven's offer. Truth mattered to Josh, and all the negative energy in the world would not stop him from fulfilling the universe's plan. He looked out of the window. Dark clouds were rolling in from the west. A storm was brewing.

"Well, perhaps you will discover some of those answers today." The lieutenant broke in, her voice was again cryptic. She leaned back in her seat. "We have a ways to go, Mr. Cunningham, hold tight. The pilot says the ride is about to get bumpy."

. . . . .

Customers were not to be found in the nearly empty Georgia knickknack shop, *Savannah Souvenirs*. It was early morning, and tourists to the historic city were either peacefully slumbering or enjoying hot breakfasts. As the sun rose, traffic would increase to the wharf district, but now, the only people in the store were the proprietor – a bald, fat man – and a local pub owner, who also the shopkeeper's most trusted friend.

"What do ya think, mate? Will they have answers?"

It was the pub owner asking the question as he eyed the shop's heavyset proprietor, who was standing behind the front counter.

Jim Burillo ran a fat hand over his heavy whiskers and contemplatively shook his bald head. "No, Patrick, it's the government. Do they ever have answers?"

"Depends who ya ask," responded Patrick Flannigan as he sauntered to the front door. Leaning out, he spat a stream of tobacco juice onto the cobbled walks, and then returned to his position by the display case.

"It's all China's fault. Ever since them and the Russians joined the summit, things have been weird. I swear they listen in on our conversations."

"No, Jimmy," Patrick remonstrated. "It's simpler than that. Uncle Sam listens and sells the recordings to them."

The two men continued to banter back and forth. The video leak from Canada the day before had spooked them plenty. Each man prayed and hoped answers would come out of Washington that day. Both knew those prayers would likely go unanswered.

"Well, I'd hate to be up there," Patrick spoke again. A veteran of the military he had done two tours in Afghanistan. "DC will be crawling with security. Some joker will probably try something. Or the protesters – always can count on some knucklehead from that group."

"They *should* protest," said Jim. He was angry with the current president. "What good has Turouning done? Stirred up controversy by erecting that demon idol in the Mall."

"Demon idol?" Patrick was puzzled.

"The totem pole."

"Ya think that's a demon idol?" the pub owner was incredulous.

"Well, it sure ain't Christian!"

"Look, Jimmy," Patrick rebutted. "I'm Irish and more Catholic than ya, and I most assuredly can tell ya, that ain't no demon idol!"

The conversation went on, and eventually, returned to the G9 summit being held that week in Washington, D.C.. It was, in fact, the subject of conversations across the globe. The US was hosting the event for the first time since China and Russia had been admitted into the group – thanks to no small effort by a former US president. The magnate had promised to make America great again. If including the two foremost world superpowers into a formerly elite group of negotiating countries was making the nation great again – he succeeded.

"Give the president some time," Patrick urged as he consoled his friend.

Jim skeptically waved his hand. He was wary of much these days. Especially the stories passed down from the government and spread through the mainstream media. Being a nominal Catholic, he believed in God, but also in common sense. Morphing was the new norm, and one never knew what story was morphed or what was original. Just once Jim wished someone would look him in the eye and tell the truth.

"Stop by the pub later. We can watch the briefs of the day's meetings." Patrick offered over his shoulder as he left the small shop.

"Fair enough," Jim replied.

There was no harm in at least staying informed of the Summit's proceedings. The president better watch out though. He was not making any friends.

■   ■   ■   ■   ■

"Prism is arriving."

Pres. William Turouning heard the radio chatter from the front of the long car. He sighed. It was going to be a long three days. A world that very much wanted and needed answers would be watching their every move. Nervously, he reached up, and tugged on a ruby red necklace.

The limousine rolled to a stop in front of the plaza. A black SUV was following and it also stopped. Two men in black coats exited the SUV and walked to the limousine's right passenger door. Scattered throughout the area were another twenty to thirty men in black suits. Black sunglasses covered their eyes.

Large crowds were thronging against the police horses and militia dressed in riot gear. Even the Marines were present. The nation's capital was holding nothing back in preventing any outbursts of violence or displays of dissension during the summit.

Pres. Turouning stepped from the long car and waved to the supporters gathered on both sides of the building leading up the marble steps to the giant doors. He smiled. His handsomely cut Native American features were accentuated by the grin. The president was a pleasant man, but disliked from his first day in office.

Maybe it was the embracement of his native religion. Perhaps it was erecting the totem pole to celebrate the influence of Native American generations from yesterday, today, and tomorrow. It could have been the fact his ability to manage national security was under constant scrutiny. Just two weeks ago, a terrorist had killed twenty-three people with an explosive-rigged vehicle, crashing it into the side of a famous mall in Florida.

A month before that was the stabbing that left four people dead in California. And then, of course, the cyberattacks that had stolen not only the identities, but also the entire life savings and retirement accounts, for over a hundred thousand people across the country.

To say he was behooved would be an understatement.

Pres. Turouning turned and smiled at the people assembled behind him. The smile slowly faded. While throngs of supporters were gathered around the staircase to the G9 building, behind the presidential caravan, were the thousands of protesters. Some were waving signs with nasty words and phrases, others carried skulls and pitchforks. A few even wore masks. The world was demanding answers. Suddenly, his left eye fluttered, and he felt a sharp, stabbing pain.

Quickly, he turned and motioned to his escorts. He could not show weakness.

One of the agents, eyes shaded by black sunglasses, lifted a hand to her mouth, and spoke tersely.

"We're coming in."

■   ■   ■   ■   ■

"What exactly is a master set? Have you ever seen one?"

The woman speaking had her hands on hips, her head cocked quizzically as she looked at Luke Baer. He perceived others in the room turning their eyes towards him too.

The Pittsburgh Research Team convened daily before tackling their assignments on various projects. They would share the newest findings and reports; collaborate on any essential items. Today Luke had been excited to share his theory on the latest batch of samples retrieved from the IID lab. Since the Canadian video of a man jumping from a ledge had leaked, *#TheDisease* was madly trending. Luke was a scientist and not prone to believe social media alarmists who broadcast every new outbreak as *the* outbreak. Still, something about this episode seemed more sinister, more genuine, a threat to be taken seriously.

Luke was one of the leads on the Research Team, the woman who had just asked the question was the other. The way she addressed him, scornfully asking the question as if he were an impudent child, infuriated him. He felt more an intern than a lead.

"Uh, no," Luke remonstrated, stammering as he tried to stand tall. "But it's been proven the brain has a trigger, a master set that controls far more of our core mental functions than previously realized."

"An unproven theory, not tested evidence. Certainly, you know the difference between the two. Chem-Lab, anyone?" The woman looked patronizingly around the room. Bits of laughter broke out among those gathered.

Immediately, Luke's face flushed.

"Ms. Gore, you may be correct in what you are saying. But I think it naïve of the University to ignore this spike. The numbers make sense, the hypothesis adds up! We are not Tachi Yin Merger or Pharma Group. We are a learned group of scientists working for the greater state of Pennsylvania to find an answer to this new outbreak. We cannot ignore this despite *any* collection of prior data findings we might have. Dr. Grafton certainly would not do that."

Ms. Gore stared at Luke. She was visibly fighting back words she wanted to spit out. Forcing her eyes away, she focused on the display board.

"Fine," she snapped her fingers, and the projector went dark. "You win, Luke. Have it your way. But please remember, we have an entire program riding on our research. I do not think the Chairs of IID or Research Operations are going to want to hear that we are taking an unproven and quite bold theory in our path to a cure, instead of relying on our historical markers. We will be deviating from centuries-old methodology in biological and medical code, and instead, forging our own."

Luke sensed the eyes of everyone in the room turning towards him again. He was only concerned with one person though – Melinda Gore. She had long stood opposite him on research findings. Sometimes he felt it was like Congress – people opposing people for the sake of political identification.

He knew he was right, though. He knew the answer had to be somewhere in the anomalies – hidden, but painfully obvious. The spiking was derivative of that. Calmly exhaling, Luke slowly blinked his eyes.

"You may be right, Ms. Gore. But I cannot back any idea that ignores such precipitous spikes. We must sacrifice methodology for the sake of efficiency and to claim first-finder privileges on a cure. Because of this, I cannot keep silent."

"Well, this wouldn't be the first time. Again," Melinda cavalierly ventured, glancing around the assembled group. "Chem-Lab, anyone?"

The whispers of laughter grew louder as chuckling swelled and rippled across the room. Luke winced. She was poking at him; driving the wedge further into his ribs. He did not need any reminders about Chem-Lab.

Suddenly, the door to the room flew open.

"Hey! Look what just came in." A man rushed into the room, excitedly waving his arms as he ran over to where Melinda and Luke stood. "This feed was just leaked on one of the portals we access to find information on incidents. Same portals we gather most of our information on." The man was speaking so fast, the words tumbled out one over the other.

"Slow down," Luke said as he took the tablet.

Melinda leaned in to look. Luke swiped the screen, and the video began playing.

It was from India. A woman stood clutching something in her hand. The item was oozing blood, and the blood dripped onto two bodies lying on the ground beneath the woman. Both were small children. Both wore freshly washed clothes. Both had been beaten before death. It was a gruesome scene and reminiscent of the Canadian video that surfaced just the day before.

"Well," Melinda softly murmured. "Appears this might not be an anomaly. Maybe we start exploring all solutions regardless of methodology."

She gave a cold smile to Luke. He could not believe it. She was acknowledging his position as being correct. She pulled away.

"Please turn that off. It's sick and horrible. How could someone do that to their own kids?"

Clearing her throat, she looked about the room of interns, their faces troubled by what they had just seen. Her lower lip quivered. Luke shuffled his feet, unsure of where to begin.

Melinda was not though. Recomposing herself, she began issuing directives to those assembled. The room soon began to buzz with activity.

The analyst who had burst in with the news, whisked the tablet from Luke's hands, and disappeared into the throng of interns starting their work. Luke remained quiet and thoughtful as he observed the bustling movement.

That's a second video now. It's so similar – a copycat perhaps? But yet, it's so genuine and not staged. Our only option is to keep moving forward. Aetatis progressu.

Though numb from what he had just seen, Luke was not overly concerned with Melinda Gore issuing directions to the team. He had his own plans. Ancient methodologies would not stand in the way of progress. Soon, very soon.

Stick to the plan, Luke. Stick to the plan.

FIVE

The sun beat down mercilessly. For the first day of April, it was hot. The expansive storm clouds encountered a few hundred miles away had stayed south. Here in upstate New York, there was scarcely a cloud to be seen.

The small propeller plane sat parked on the tarmac at the end of the runway. The pilot was still in the plane. He had his handheld out and was streaming movies. The bulky headset worn during flight had been traded for a lighter pair of earbuds.

The location was secure all right. Josh had no idea where they were, and there was not anyone else there either. He figured it must be a national forest, given all the trees. Whomever they were meeting was not very prompt.

Josh surveyed the field in front of them. One could not see it from even a few hundred yards back. Who would expect to find a cleared path in the middle of the forest? Let alone a runway. Its smooth blacktop ran straight down the middle, splitting the field in a clean swath. There were no hangers. It was not an airport, rather a secret landing strip for covert meetings like this.

It was hot enough, even without the abundant sunshine. To make matters worse, the wind had gone the same direction as the storm clouds before – east – and there was not so much as a gentle breeze left behind.

Wiping his hand across his forehead, Josh flicked away the beads of sweat forming and trickling down his face. He was in shirt-sleeves, but that did little to alleviate the warmth generated by the glistening morning sun.

He felt someone watching and turning, saw Rhianna Adams curiously observing him.

"Two years ago, someone reports a blinding light caused them to crash into oncoming traffic – killing one person. Twenty months ago, a person goes on a rampage and slaughters – skins – his entire family. When the suspect is apprehended, he's missing one eye. Fifteen months ago, NASA reports unusual cosmic activity – talk of a massive alien intervention, but there is no follow-up. The EPA reports the ozone layer has completely evaporated and puts strict guidelines on any mining, forestry, or harvesting operations. Earth geologists release data showing unusual tremors. You've had a busy year."

The news-heavy monologue from the lieutenant, which recapped many events from the last year, surprised Josh. Rhianna had been relatively quiet ever since their conversation on the airplane. Unsure how to answer her observation, he merely shook his head.

"Twenty-five percent."

"What's that?" he asked, puzzled by her words.

"They say twenty-five percent of the world is infected."

Josh bit his lower lip to keep from laughing – or maybe crying – he was not sure which. The theory seemed ludicrous. He had heard of the hullabaloo trending on social media – where people claimed the illness had been prevalent for years, and how much of the world was infected. Twenty-five percent seemed to be the going rate used in the morphed statistics.

"Once again," Josh patiently asked. "How do you so brazenly assume this is part of a global conspiracy? If twenty-five percent of the world was infected, don't you think it'd be in more of the news feeds?"

"If they let it," said Rhianna cryptically, casting a knowing look at Josh.

He shrugged his shoulders. While displaying little reaction externally, the lieutenant's words troubled him. What if there was a cover-up of that magnitude going on? Who was responsible for it? What were they hoping to accomplish? Would someone downplay a pandemic instead of broadcasting it?

"If there is a cover-up going on…" he articulated his thoughts.

"There is," Lieut. Adams interrupted.

Josh held up a hand. "Even so, *if* there is…why?"

"Preservation," she paused, sensing his doubt. "You don't believe me?"

"No, I don't."

Rhianna was wearing large black sunglasses, and her brown skin glistened in the afternoon sunlight. She gave a small smile at Josh, and he could not tell if she was mocking him or showing genuine friendliness. She did seem quite interested in conspirator ideologies for a liaison from the Department of Homeland Security.

A whirling of blades broke in, interrupting any further conversation. The sound of beating air descended upon the pair. Josh tilted his head up, and his eyes searched the blue skies above. First, he caught the glare of the sun, but then he made out the distinct outline of a military helicopter.

"Looks like they decided to show," Rhianna said, her voice terse.

Josh nodded in silent agreement. He was trying to shake the echoing of her shadowy words just spoken. He watched as the heavily armed helicopter slowly lowered itself to the ground on the east side of the runway. It was about thirty or forty paces from the prop plane, yet, Josh could still feel the rushing air caused by the jet turbines of the giant propeller. He felt his hair rise, and his cheeks push back as he struggled to remain fully upright.

Lieut. Adams straightened herself from the relaxed position she had been in.

"Let's go."

Walking became easier as the swishing of the blades slowed and the engine whine quieted. Two men stepped from the helicopter. On one of them, shoulder bars signifying a colonel, gleamed brightly in the sunshine.

"I am Josh Cunningham," Josh warmly greeted. "This is my associate, Lieut. Rhianna Adams."

The colonel gave a slight inclination of his head.

"I presume you have the package?" Josh continued.

"Ah." The colonel's words were terse. "No."

"Excuse me?" Rhianna's dark eyes flashed in surprise as she stepped forward in front of Josh and confronted the Canadian entourage.

"The formula doesn't exist."

Josh was puzzled. His eyes furrowed as he processed the colonel's words.

"Wait. What do you mean there isn't a formula?"

Rhianna held up her right hand, and Josh stopped talking. She looked back at the colonel.

"We are under orders from the Pentagon to meet you. Our intelligence said Canada had developed a formula that might be the cure."

The colonel pursed his lips. "I didn't say there *wasn't* a formula. I said it doesn't exist."

"Stop talking in riddles, colonel. Just what do you mean?" Rhianna Adams' right arm fell naturally to her waist where her weapon was holstered.

The other man from the chopper raised his hand. "I wouldn't, lieutenant."

"No need for guns or violence." The colonel was impatient with the proceedings. "Lieut. Adams, Mr. Cunningham," he spoke while individually nodding to each of them. "I am Col. Javier Bordeau of the Canadian Air Force. This is Chief Warrant Officer Leon Martin. Martin is special forces…I wouldn't mess with him." The colonel added as an afterthought.

"Now that the pleasantries are out of the way, would you mind telling me what you mean: the formula doesn't exist?" said Rhianna brusquely, her eyes flashing indignantly.

Javier Bordeau stared coolly at the lieutenant. "The formula *did* exist – it was being tested and seemed to be working. Jordan MacDonald is a brilliant biochemist, and we were sure we had found a cure. But then…"

Col. Bordeau stopped speaking. He licked his lips and nervously glanced at Leon Martin. The CWO's face was passive, but his eyes were grave.

"Sir, what happened?" asked Josh.

His stomach was sinking, his mouth going dry. These secrets he did not know – formulas, cures, global mass infection – the ominous words of Col. Bordeau did not bode good tidings.

"I said Jordan MacDonald is a biochemist, I meant *was*. Last week, Jordan was assassinated. I say assassinated because it was not murder; it was an attempt to eradicate a man and his chemical formula from saving this planet. We're conducting investigations right now as to who killed or had him killed and what happened with the formula."

"It went missing?" Rhianna barely contained her anger.

"Yes and no. The hard drives with the chemical makeup have been erased, but they didn't disappear, they are still at the lab. However, they are completely empty."

Josh listened in disbelief. His eyes mindlessly moved over the landing strip. None of it seemed real. It was if in a dream.

"Wait," he suddenly stammered. "MacDonald was murdered last week? The video *just* came out."

Leon Martin glanced incredulously at Josh with a look that asked, 'Are you serious?'

"What don't I know?" Josh demanded. His eyes searched the three other's faces, stopping on Col. Bordeau.

The colonel shrugged his shoulders and sighed. "Corporate monkeys."

Josh's eyes narrowed. Rhianna Adams and Leon Martin both snickered.

"Back to Square One," Javier Bordeau ignored Josh's exasperated look. "We don't have any drives that weren't wiped. Any trace of the formula is gone. The mainframe was hacked remotely, and all known copies have been erased. It was a professional job. Maybe another country, another pharmaceutical firm – no one knows yet."

"This sucks." Rhianna snapped; then cursed. "It's like someone knew and planned this whole thing."

Josh cast a warning glance at the lieutenant. She was starting to sound crazy again.

"We aren't dead, though, not yet." The colonel's voice was even-keeled. "I don't know what you plan on doing with this new information, lieutenant, but if I were you, I'd go back to Admiral Connors and tell him that he might want to advise evacuation from major metropolitan areas."

Evacuation? The word stunned Josh,

"This is crazy," he muttered out loud.

"Think it's crazy?" Leon Martin exclaimed. "Believe me, I've seen crazy – things you *never* want to see. People pulling their eyes out; attacking and *biting* people who just happen to be strolling by. Most activity is at night. You can't find a single soul out in the day. It's like light repels them, but dark attracts."

Josh studied the Chief Warrant Officer's face while he spoke. It was grave and formal, yet showed traces of fear.

"What branch of special forces are you?"

"The branch that investigates these incidents," Col. Bordeau offered. "Martin is on a task force handling the reports."

"Reports?"

"Yes. The attacks. Crazy behavior, rabid even, and it does get worse at night."

"Bull," Josh said. First, Rhianna Adam's cryptic conspirator words and now this bunk from the Canadians. He had enough. "This isn't some movie."

"No," Leon Martin glowered. "It's not. And that is precisely what has us concerned."

Javier Bordeau glanced at his mobile device. "We have to go. I am sorry I've brought bad news."

"It's not your fault," Rhianna said. "It seems there is little good news these days."

"Indeed."

The colonel straightened and saluted. Pivoting about, he walked back to the chopper with Leon Martin. The two men boarded the craft as the engine began to fire again – blades swishing through the air.

Rhianna swore and continued muttering obscenities as she and Josh began retracing their steps back to the plane. Lifting her foot, she kicked at a pebble on the tarmac.

Suddenly, a blurred swoosh noise was heard. A deafening boom! Flames leapt forth as fire engulfed the chopper. Barely forty feet into the air, the helicopter exploded as a missile crashed into its side.

"Down!" Lieut. Adams screamed.

Smoke enveloped them. Something went flying over their heads as they hit the pavement. Debris filled the air. The smell of burning flooded Josh's nostrils. He lay still, pinned down by the lieutenant.

"Oh my – oh my," Josh shouted, shaking with fear. "Are they – what was – how?" His heart was racing; temples pounding. He could not breathe.

"Come on, Josh," Rhianna violently pulled on his arm. "They are dead. We aren't. We've got to move."

"Why? Who did this?" Josh screamed curses at the blazing fire.

The noise of an engine accelerating caused them both to turn their heads. From a prone position on the pavement, Josh watched as their prop plane pilot gunned the small craft forward. He was leaving!

Rhianna Adams jumped up and waved both hands. The pilot did not look back. Reaching down, she pulled her sidearm out and fired it into the air. The plane jettisoned forward and roared down the small runway. In a matter of seconds, the aircraft was off the ground, disappearing into the horizon.

Josh shakily pulled himself to his knees and then buckled over. He gagged and vomit spilled from his mouth. He stared paralyzed as the fire consumed the helicopter and its passengers. While seeing it all happen, none of it felt real.

"C'mon, Josh," Rhianna was at his side again. "We have to go. We've waited too long already."

Breaking his stare from the burning pile of metal, Josh realized the little intel on what really happened in Canada died with it. *Now what?* The familiar feeling of arriving at a dead end started and then suddenly stopped. Something was different this time. *There's more to this than meets the eye.*

Josh struggled to his feet. He could not stop shaking. A warm hand touched his shoulder, and he looked into the reassuring eyes of Rhianna. For the first time, he saw authenticity.

"We gotta get out of here, Josh. Whatever hit them, knew they were here, and us too. We could be next!"

SIX

When William Turouning was a young boy, he used to dream about being president of the United States. The dream's fulfillment came on the most important day of his life – when he was sworn into the highest office of the nation. Now, in the middle of the most prominent summit the country had ever hosted, enthusiasm had ebbed and given way to feelings of embattlement. He was fighting for his reputation. His legacy was at stake. Forget about a second term – it was highly improbable. The aftermath of the War in Asia, then the earthquake, and then the ever-increasing terrorist attacks in his own country had seen to that.

Pres. Turouning leaned forward as the Chinese Premier continued to drone on. *Who invited him in the first place?* The angry thought crossed William's mind, though he very well knew how China and Russia came into being part of the G9. He daily cursed the former US president who had facilitated the additions.

Leaning back, William rubbed his left temple. It had been hurting for the last few days, and he was beginning to worry. He was scared to ask his doctor to take a look though. Ever since Dr. Charles Grafton had published his expose on the dangers of natural sunlight and the potential risk of rabid behavior due to infection of the eye – people were paranoid. No reason to feed the provocateurs on social media something they could trend on him.

A yawn tried to escape. He caught it just in time, using his right hand rolled into a fist and pushing ever so slightly against his open mouth. He felt another one coming when suddenly, a commotion broke out.

"Grab Prism!" one of the agents yelled, and William felt himself being lifted from his seat and rushed out of the room.

The group traveled along a dark hallway and suddenly, a door opened. They swerved into a room and the door slammed shut behind. William heard the sound of a combination lock sealing the entrance. His eyes refocused and he realized the room was filled with other foreign power leaders as well as many secret service and security personnel.

"What the hell is going on?" demanded the Prime Minister of the United Kingdom.

"A helicopter carrying a high ranking official was just shot down in upstate New York!" Prime Minister Harrison of Canada answered as he stepped forward, shoving an accusatory finger towards William. "What do you have to say, Mr. President?"

William was confused and turned to one of his aides. They leaned close and muttered in his ear. Whatever was whispered caused the president to vulgarly curse. He then looked back at Prime Minister Harrison.

"My sincere condolences, Prime Minister, I wasn't aware of this tragedy. If I had been, I would've interrupted the summit immediately and responded appropriately."

"What was a high ranking Canadian official doing in the wild wilderness of north New York?" asked the Premier of the People's Republic of China.

Of course, it would be that rat asking such a question! Bitterness filled William's mind.

"It was a confidential meeting between the Public Health Agency and SEH regarding the Disease. The outbreak has been spreading, but until recently, was contained to a whisper on social media. That is, until one of our citizens decided to broadcast his own insanity to the entire world," Prime Minister Harrison snarled.

"If it was such a confidential meeting, how did the helicopter get shot down?" Again it was the Chinese Premier.

"I believe I just asked that question," Prime Minister Harrison shot back. He turned towards Pres. Turouning, his dark eyes burning with anger. "William, I asked a question."

"I honestly have no idea," the president answered, slumping back in his chair. Yet, another terrorist attack in his beloved country, on *his* watch.

"The meeting was supposed to be a handoff of highly classified research information on the cure. Last week though, before that imbecile recorded himself, one of our brightest biochemists was found dead – an apparent suicide. Except it wasn't, it was murder."

Several gasps erupted from the small party of world leaders. Each of them represented the most powerful nations on the planet. At that moment, all of them felt insufficient for what was happening on Earth.

"A cure?" William questioned Prime Minister Harrison, a hopeful look upon his face.

A sigh escaped the Canadian leader. "Well, we aren't sure. Not only was Jordan MacDonald murdered, but all his research was destroyed as well."

Additiona gasps were heard.

"Damn the cure," the Russian president spoke up. "How did this happen?"

The American and Canadian looked at each other, both hoping the other had answers, both realizing neither did.

"We'll hold a presser," William finally said. He sighed, and then in an attempt to have courage, lifted his shoulders. "We'll spin a story that will appease the dissenters and assure the fearful, while we wait for our better tomorrow."

Pres. Turouning looked at Harrison as he spoke. The Canadian Prime Minister thoughtfully scratched his beard and nodded in agreement.

■   ■   ■   ■   ■

The lights were pointed to the front of the room, illuminating the area more than sufficient for the cameras directed at Pres. Turouning and Prime Minister Harrison. The two men stepped to the podiums assembled next to one another and solemnly shook hands. The Prime Minister spoke first, and William watched as hundreds of press agents thrust their cameras and handhelds forward – broadcasting the news of the Canadian helicopter attack to the world.

He wished the lights were not so bright. The need to rub his eye permeated his mind. It took every ounce of strength to resist the temptation. His turn came to speak.

"Thank you, Prime Minister Harrison. America expresses our deepest condolences regarding the horrific attack on a Canadian helicopter in New York. The helicopter was part of the Canadian air fleet. I'm sure many are worried and wondering what has happened, and want to know what our response will be."

He paused. The only sound audible was that of camera shutters. Not real ones, but sound effects one could choose on the digital or holographic options.

"I'm here alongside Prime Minister Harrison to assure you that we are working *together* to figure out the source of today's attack. Despite what some broadcasts have claimed, I want to assure both Americans and Canadians that this *was* a terrorist attack and in no ways an act of war by the United States of America."

"Today we are just as united as we were yesterday," chimed in the Canadian Prime Minister. He flashed a smile to his American counterpart. "We *will* hunt down those responsible and bring them to justice!"

"Are there any questions?" the press secretary asked.

Hands shot up all over the room. One distinguished member of the press corps, renowned for her piece regarding the atrocities committed during the War in Asia, had the first question.

"Who was on the helicopter?

Pres. Turouning thought the question should be answered by the Canadian leader, and acquiesced with an inclination of his hand.

"I believe Prime Minister Harrison has that information."

■　　■　　■　　■　　■

Luke's thumbs flew over the keypad. He tried hard not to jab. Anger flowed through his veins. He kept brooding over Melinda Gore and what she said. *How dare she bring up Chem-Lab! That's so like her.*

He had spent three years working on the Chem-Lab project and had nearly perfected his prognosis, when she pointed out the historical trends in the medical code misaligned with the anomalistic spike discovered in the last batch of research. He thought the anomalies were proof enough to proceed. She disagreed, and said they needed to be cautious and analyze further.

Luke brushed her opinion aside and presented his theory to the University's Immunology and Infectious Diseases panel. They bought into his plan. It was aggressive, but showed promise at capturing first-finder privileges.

The theory turned out to be overly aggressive. The biomedical invention failed. His mentor and head of the department, Dr. Grafton, graciously swept the debacle under the proverbial rug. Melinda was not so kind.

Luke took a deep breath and glanced at the screen one last time. He unconsciously nodded. A tap of his right thumb and a quiet *swoosh* was heard. Message sent.

"Today, just a short while ago, a Royal Canadian helicopter was shot down in upstate New York."

Luke glanced at the screen hanging on the wall, and read the 3D titling as the prime minister of Canada held a joint press conference with the US president. He was intrigued by the news of the blown-up helicopter, especially given the two videos released in the last forty-eight hours.

Watching as the press conference continued to unfold, Luke scrolled through his social media. Talks of protest and "Bring it home!" – a popular catchphrase given the drastic increase of terrorist attacks on American soil over the past three years – were trending. Suddenly, his ears picked up another conversation in the room where he was sitting, and he could not help but listen in.

"Do you think the professor is really going to die?"

It was a female voice, and he turned and looked sideways at the speaker. She was talking to another person; both were seated at a table several feet away. Luke looked down, pretending to be browsing his handheld as he eavesdropped.

"Dr. Grafton has pulled through many things. I doubt he'd leave us now. Somewhere inside his soul, he'll find the strength and healing to go on."

"This isn't sci-fi," the girl spoke again. "This is real life. Stuff happens."

Luke's peeking eyes caught the backend of a shoulder shrug.

"I don't know what to tell you, I think positive thinking is the best thing we can offer the universe at this point. Nature will run its course. Hopefully, Dr. Grafton remains positive enough to give himself a chance."

"Ugh," the girl said. "I'm so sick of the bs. Positive this, positive that. You'd think the whole world was made up of positive energy. Since the start of the century, we've continued to evolve with our environment; continued to pollute our world and dump toxic waste into our atmosphere. We don't give a crap what happens. We assume as long as we remain positive, things will somehow improve. Which isn't true," she was exasperated. "Our dying planet is proof enough. And look at the freaking news! Another terrorist attack – and this one way closer than LA."

Her friend tried to reassure her. Luke's lips drew into a thin smile. He had heard the argument before. Someone who believed in mind over matter, trying to discuss their wild theories with a physicist. Such a person could maybe sway philosophers and psychologists, but real scientists – they knew the truth.

The two started to argue. Luke turned his attention back to the news conference. He read the titling of the closed captions.

"Who was on the helicopter?" someone in the press corps asked the question.

Luke recognized her as a lead reporter for a well-known news agency in Washington, D.C. One of the few, real news agencies left. She had won a Pulitzer for her work during the War in Asia.

"The persons aboard the craft were not members of the Canadian government, despite it being an aircraft issued by the Royal Fleet. It was a private contractor who had flown in for a meeting with some of their US contacts in rural New York."

Luke scowled as he read the captioned response of the Canadian Prime Minister. That did not sound right. Why would a private contractor be flying in a government-issued helicopter? Someone else in the press corps asked the same question. Luke smiled. He often thought about becoming an investigative journalist before he had settled on research scientist.

The president answered this question.

"I believe that's a standard perk for being a government contractor; we do the same for many contractors of ours. We are trying to identify *why* this craft was targeted, more so, the persons on board. We will not rest until we have found them. As Prime Minister Harrison said, we will bring them to justice!"

A chirp sounded. Luke glanced at his handheld. A new message had arrived. Swiping the screen, he put the phone to his ear. A female's voice was on the other end.

Luke's face became ashen gray; a troubled expression appeared. He slowly nodded; oblivious to the fact the speaker could not see him. Tapping his thumb on the front screen, he slowly laid the handheld down onto the table.

Leaning back in his chair, he blinked as he surveyed the room. Suddenly, the destroyed helicopter, the Canadian man and Indian woman with their slaughtered families, they all seemed more distant, less relevant. Here, his world was crumbling. Melinda Gore had shoved him out of the way – even as they pursued an assignment of his own – and now...

A groan escaped. He did not realize how loud it was until he became conscious of the couple seated a few tables away. They were no longer arguing, but instead, staring at him.

Realizing this, Luke stood up. He took a step towards the exit, and stopped. He looked back at the students. They were still curiously looking at him.

"That was a loud sigh," the first girl spoke.

Luke gave a short laugh. "My bad. I didn't realize it was so loud until it came out."

He scrutinized both of them, contemplating their future. Two promising students who were trying to forge ahead in their lives and shape their future – seize their destiny, whatever that might be. He felt compelled to give some unsolicited advice.

"About that power of positive thinking, mind over matter – I've heard that crap before. Here's what you need to know. Life happens. People live. People die. Things come up, things go down. But no matter what religion you claim to believe in – faith, spiritual reasoning, meditation, the boogeyman, or Santa Claus – it won't have one iota effect on life."

The physicist student was visibly impressed by Luke's speech and nodded. Whether it was in agreement or merely acknowledging his opinion, Luke did not care. Instead, he turned his eyes towards the first girl.

"And just so you know, Prof. Grafton is dead. He died a few minutes ago." Luke pirouetted and started to leave again, but once again hesitated and stopped. He glanced back over his shoulder. "Aetatis progressu."

With that, he strode ahead and exited the room.

SEVEN

Clutching the side of the luxurious car, Josh leaned against its comfy leather interior. His shaking had subsided, but he still felt sick. He turned and looked at Lieut. Rhianna Adams. She gave a small smile of encouragement.

"Your first time is the worst. The shakes will leave. Always do. Takes a few hours, but you'll be fine."

Nodding in reply, he contemplated his liaison's words and considered what he knew of her. In the last hour, he had gone from skeptical to not knowing what he made of the lieutenant. For one, she was resourceful.

They had picked up the car when they had emerged from the forest. A country highway ran alongside the woods, a small gas station next to it. The vehicle was parked away from the fuel pumps in a side parking spot; the owner apparently inside the convenience store or otherwise not visible.

Josh was surprised when Rhianna calmly walked over, and pressing the numbers on the side of the car, entered a code.

"This doesn't belong here," she quipped. "It's time to move."

The car unlocked, and reaching down, Rhianna yanked a panel off to access the electrical wiring. Seconds later, the car roared to life and they had a ride.

For another, she had remained perfectly calm during the last hour while he cowered and trembled. She displayed confidence in knowing what she should do as she led Josh away from the exploded chopper. *She is a soldier*, he told himself, *but still…*

"What just happened?" he muttered out loud. "Tell me what you know," sudden anger flashed in his eyes. "You've been holding out on me!"

Rhianna calmly observed him. Callously holding the steering wheel with her knee, she reached into her top right breast-pocket and pulled out a pack of cigarettes. She inclined her palm forward, offering one to him. Josh shook his head. She proceeded to pull out a smoke, and tapped the end of it against the carton before stuffing the pack back into her shirt. Fishing around her pants pocket, she produced a lighter. In a few seconds, the exotic smell of cherry tobacco filled the glossy interior of the car.

"Damn," Adams said. "I'm sure glad they stopped loading artificial ingredients into these things. That stuff kills the effect."

"Everything," Josh remonstrated, refusing to let Rhianna get sidetracked. "I'm playing with a short deck."

Rhianna rolled down the driver's side front window and blew a tunnel of smoke out of her mouth. She cocked her head to one side as she looked at Josh. An audible noise escaped her as she relented and put one hand back on the wheel.

"You, more than most, should know we are rarely dealt anything *but* a short deck." She spoke as if explaining a problem to a child. "If I had told you about the complexities of this meeting before – you would've been nervous and worried. There is no need for that."

"Don't talk to me that way," Josh was steaming. "I'm not a stupid cheesehead sticking my head where the sun doesn't shine! My job is to find out the origin story, not some alternative fact just because that's what's convenient."

"And then what," Rhianna snapped back. "You would have had the perfect solution to *prevent* what happened back there?"

"I'm no time changer, but not warning me was unprofessional."

Rhianna did not answer. Instead, she flicked the butt of the cigarette out of the window. With a press of a button, the glass rolled back up. Her mouth drew a tight line as she mulled the situation.

Josh leaned back in his seat and exhaled. *Slow down, Josh. Keep it together.*

"Look, I truly do *not* know what happened. It was supposed to be a highly classified meeting. We were obviously compromised." said Rhianna matter-of-fact.

Josh knew she was telling him the truth. She pulled her handheld out, and spoke a number into the microphone.

"Identify." A robotic voice said from the other end.

"Lieut. Rhianna Adams, Password: Northern Lights."

There was slight static on the other end. That was unusual, in an age when everything was crystal clear – perhaps even too digital.

Suddenly, a man's voice came on. "Lieut. Adams, you are to report back immediately to control."

"On my way, sir," she hesitated. "Requesting confirmation of what just happened."

"I'm not authorized to say so."

Rhianna swore. "That doesn't cut it. My associate and I were nearly killed in an attack, and I want to know who the hell authorized that strike!"

It was silent for a minute, the small buzz of static returned, and then the man's voice.

"Return to control, lieutenant. That's an order."

Rhianna cursed and tossed her handheld into the backseat. She pressed her foot down further onto the accelerator. Josh did not see how they could safely travel much faster. However, he figured it was not worth agitating Lieut. Adams more, so he didn't mention it.

Instead, he gazed of the window and watched as the countryside swiftly passed by. He was confused by the whole situation. Who did she just speak to? Was it someone in DC? Why was there static on the line? Was the helicopter attack related to the murdered biochemist and the Canadian video leak? He numbly reached into his pocket. Maybe Sam would know. His hands were shaking. He sensed Rhianna watching him.

"What are you doing?"

"Sending a message to my field coordinator; maybe he knows something."

"Do *not* send that message. Until we know who's behind this, you tell no one. Do you understand?"

"No, I do not understand," Josh shouted as he punched the air with a clenched fist. "Why were we sent on this mission when the evidence had already been destroyed? And why would your command center not answer your questions? Do you think they don't know about the explosion?"

"It's the 21st century, Josh, and the US military. Of course, they know," clipped Rhianna.

"Do you think they are watching us?"

"Who?"

"The people who sent the missile, whoever is behind this – trying to thwart our efforts!"

Lieut. Adams laughed out loud. Maybe it was just because it contrasted to the gravity of the situation, but her laugh had a merry ring to it.

"You're starting to doubt and rightly so. I mean, why would someone send a missile out here to blow up a helicopter?"

"Hold on!" Josh forgot his fear as he expostulated. "I'm not claiming a cover-up or a conspiracy. I'm a truthseeker. My entire identity is founded in finding out what's true – establishing the baseline of reality. But if you think I'm going to believe that a missile was fired by accident, and randomly destroyed the only link to a story – well, you don't know me."

Rhianna looked quizzically at Josh. "You aren't concerned about the cure? The medical profits? I thought that was Jacobi's angle – getting out in front of any outbreak that might have a 'cure' to make a few billion?"

"I already told you. I work for SEH's Morphing Division, not Pharma Group. My job is exploring stories as they morph and discovering the truth behind them. I do not know why they assigned this outbreak to us, but they did, and that's why I'm here." Josh evenly replied.

He was not angry at Rhianna. He was used to this – the dead ends. His job involved a lot of disappointment; ninety-five percent of the time, things did not work out, and he would reach the end. He was used to it.

"My apologies, Mr. Cunningham. I meant no offense. I've been doing this job long enough to know sometimes the good intentions of others get hidden by our own preconceived opinions based on the vast majority of bad intentions by others."

Josh nodded as he rubbed his eyes. The morning's tumultuous events had worn him out. He was tired and drained of energy.

"It has to be connected though. The man in Canada, the lab exploding, MacDonald getting killed, the chopper – that's what you call it, right?" Josh glanced at Rhianna.

A small smile appeared on her countenance. "Sure. Chopper, bird, helo – whatever works. So you want to know why? By your own admission, it would appear someone or something is trying to extinguish evidence of what this man *had* and what MacDonald found. For that matter, anyone who might've been in contact with him."

"Like Javier Bordeau."

"Exactly. I even suggest the hypothetical blends into reality. That while the government of this country and dozens of others across the world are working together to keep wraps on the Disease, there is an organization operating without any governments' knowledge. This organization is working on finding out the real answers behind the mysterious Disease, and why everyone else is being so quiet."

Josh carefully paused before answering. "Well first, you keep referring to *the* Disease, as an established fact. We don't know that yet. And second, I would say such an organization doesn't have a chance without the government's knowledge or permission."

"Permission!" the lieutenant snapped. "This is America – the *US of A* – people don't need the government's permission to do anything."

"No," Josh retorted, his feelings hurt by Rhianna's outburst. "They don't, except when the matter relates to national security and puts to risk the overall safety and health of this country's residents."

"Spoken like a true government contractor."

"I am *not* a government contractor."

"No, just an employee for the largest pharmaceutical group employed by Uncle Sam."

"I am in the Morphing Division, remember?"

"Right."

Josh's phone chirped with a notification. He glanced at it.

"The president is holding a press conference on this."

"That was fast," remarked Lieut. Adams.

Josh looked at her questioningly.

"What?" she retorted. "You don't think that's a little soon?"

He ignored her. Swiping his thumb, he watched as Pres. Turouning addressed the world with Prime Minister Harrison.

A few minutes passed by. The car kept up its dangerous high speed. Reaching a plateau and crossing over, the landscape began changing from countrified to suburban. All of a sudden, Josh exclaimed, "What? Why would you say that?"

He caught Rhianna staring at him, and he pressed the broadcast feed on his i-Beam. Immediately, a holographic image of Pres. Turouning jumped in between them. The sound of the president's voice was loud and clear, as if he were in the car with them.

"As Prime Minister Harrison said, there were no members of the Canadian government aboard the craft. It appears it was a private contractor who had a meeting with some of its US-based contacts."

"Does he really not know who was on board?" Josh realized the question was stupid, even as it left his mouth. "Of course he does, but why deny it?"

"His job is to protect people, to assure a fearful nation. How many attacks is that in the last few weeks? Once this video hits the net, you'll have plenty of morphing going on, yeah," Rhianna smiled knowingly at Josh. "I learn quick."

"Something doesn't add up," Josh replied. "Something is off."

Rhianna jerked the steering wheel to the left and pulled into a private drive. They were in a somewhat abandoned area, and that is when Josh realized they had entered a military outpost of sorts. The sedan hurried along and rolled to a stop alongside a rectangular-shaped building. By its appearance, Josh guessed it was an aviation hub. He noticed a small helicopter, much like the one a news crew would use, sitting next to the building with its blades already swishing through the air. Josh warily looked at it.

"It's okay, Josh. We're safe." Rhianna said, putting the car in park. "We'll take this bird to control in Maryland. Don't believe me?" she added as she saw the look of uncertainty on his face. "No. It's right, you shouldn't. You have to see something to believe it. Which is all the more ironic, because what *have* you seen except data from other sources that have shaped your thinking and research up to this point. You are a smart man," she nodded as Josh shook his head, confused by her words.

They climbed out of the car and walked towards the small helicopter. A passenger was sitting up front with the pilot. Lieut. Adams and Josh boarded, and sat down in the two back seats. Once they were buckled in, the small craft started its ascent into the air.

"Smart and persistent, Josh," Rhianna looked over at him. "You may or may not believe what I've suggested. So take a little bit of advice – check the tabloids."

With that, she swung her microphone boom down and started to chat with the pilot and passenger in front.

The tabloids?

Josh was confused. Sucking his teeth, he sighed and leaned back. The day had gone beyond crazy, and he still could not get over the fact the president had lied about who was onboard.

Cover-up? Twenty-five percent of the world is infected? He reflected on what Rhianna had said earlier. *Something's wrong here, I know it. I need to talk to Sam.*

EIGHT

The limousine rolled to a stop alongside the curb. Pres. Turouning took a deep breath and stepped from the long car. Raising his left hand, he waved at the press and crowds gathered to the right of his door. His handsomely cut Native American features were accentuated by a big smile; a large pair of black shades hid his eyes. He turned to his left and swore.

Protestors were on the left side. Large black signs, crossbones, and skulls; some were carrying cardboard pitchfork cutouts. William's smile faded, not so much from the pitchforks as something else. Every single person wore them. Black heavy shades covered their eyes.

He glared at the protesters; the pounding in his heart not from anger but fear. *There are so many of them! It can't be. Has the Disease spread so quickly?*

"This way, Mr. President."

William was hurriedly moved towards the entrance of the building. The protesters screamed louder – it was a haunting, horrifying guttural sound. More like that of an animal than a human.

The thick, steel doors swung open. A couple of local SWAT team members stood next to them holding shields, protecting the entrance.

"Incoming!" one of them yelled.

There was a clank, and an old, useless grenade bounced harmlessly off the shields. Regardless, there was a quick retort of fire. The crowd screamed, but backed up. Two bodies were lying motionless in the street.

"That'll show the animals," a secret service agent chuckled.

The doors closed behind the presidential detail.

. . . . .

"Quickly! Get those people out of here!" a man shouted to his companions.

They rushed forward and grabbed the two lifeless bodies. The protests would continue, but it was demoralizing and bad taste to do so while fallen comrades laid in the street.

The man who had spoken was clothed in military garb – typical for the protesters. Camouflage pants and a dark green shirt; a snake tattoo barely visible on his left arm. His face was covered with a skeleton mask, and in his hand, he held a wooden pitchfork. His voice was gruff and bore the resemblance of a drill sergeant.

"I'd love to show those animals," a woman standing next to the man said. She was also dressed in camouflage, though only as a top; she wore black pants.

"Revers, hold it steady!" said the man, placing a firm, yet gentle hand on his comrade's arm.

"I don't know how you can keep so still, Danny. The president is an ape letting the secret service and police treat us with such brutality. The secrets have to stop!"

Danny Graves nodded as the former corporal spoke. Danny had toured during the War in Asia. That is when an IED took off his right arm. He had spent nearly fourteen months in rehabilitation. The result was a perfectly useful prosthetic that he manipulated practically as well as his left limb. The former corporal – Kelly Revers – had served two tours in Syria. Fire was in her belly, and he liked that. Still, the delicate situation they found themselves in, demanded restraint and control.

"Two attacks in two weeks and they do nothing. Every day people talk about some new outbreak – whether the source be chemical or other life forces – and what does Prispuss do?" Danny used the derogatory version of Pres. Turouning's code name. "Heck, what did the last one do?"

"Ha," Kelly spat. "Nothing! Unless you count inviting every alien and terrorist with open arms while spouting off and destroying our relationships abroad. Made us damn vulnerable. I didn't serve 12 years just to watch a rube and blowhard destroy my country!"

"You and me both," said Danny, again touching Revers arm. "Patience. We'll get our chance soon enough. Ha, what rich irony. Nearly a trillion dollars spent on spying – mostly US citizens – and still can't prevent a terrorist attack. Good investment. Remind me to call my financial advisor to get a piece of that action!"

The former soldiers laughed. It was hollow.

Around them swarmed the other protesters. Most were dressed in some sort of military garb. It was a sign of their hatred and disagreement towards the current administration. More than one carried a poster. 'Dissenters' was the common word used to describe them.

Danny Graves and Kelly Revers fit the bill. George W. Bush seemed awfully eager to attack Saddam Hussein over the pretense of "terrorism." Did anyone actually watch the footage of those planes hitting the Twin Towers? No way those did not come down without internal ballistics.

FDR's speech lived in greater infamy than the loss of 3,000 soldiers. Of course, there was another shooter in Dallas. Did someone really think a potshot killed JFK? And all those mass school shootings? Seemed far greater emphasis by the "victims" families to push gun control than time spent mourning the loss of their "child."

There was no question, the term Dissenter fit. In the shadows of the gathered protestors, even some conspirators lurked, and that is what separated Danny Graves and Kelly Revers from the rest of the assembly.

The signs bobbed up and down as the dissenters weaved back and forth along Pennsylvania Avenue. It was a familiar sight, although it sometimes took a different route. One day they chose to protest along the Mall. Another time they had stationed themselves on the steps of Lincoln Memorial. Danny himself gave a rousing speech at the top of Jefferson's Monument as they stared across the Potomac. He vowed to bring the truth to light. His words rang true; his guise intact.

Of course, haters and dissenters were detained regularly, but only would conspirators be prosecuted. They were "too dangerous" to exist with the rest of society. The danger excited Danny, but in reality, the risk was minimal. Aside from his fellow conspirators, no one could conclusively say that he was involved in *any* shadow operation. He lived his life so covertly, there was hardly a trace of his actual existence. He liked it that way.

Rain began to fall. Danny slowly swayed back and forth, thinking. Something about the way Pres. Turouning appeared during the press conference with the Canadian Prime Minister, and then, even more so, the president's harried expression as the motorcade arrived. Danny was sure. He pulled his handheld out and started to thumb a message.

"Well?" Kelly looked at him.

Danny shook his head. "He doesn't know anything. This might – just might – be for real." Swiping his thumb, he looked up. There was no reason to loiter any longer. "Round 'em up, Revers. Our work here is done."

∎   ∎   ∎   ∎   ∎

The rotor blades swished evenly through the air as the helicopter started its descent to the helipad. Josh leaned against the side of the craft and scrutinized the military base below. They were in northeast Maryland. The lieutenant had told him it was close to an outpost Admiral Connors, the deputy secretary for the Department of Homeland Security, frequently visited. "It's best to return to my home base and find out what they know," she had said. He did not disagree.

A grim look was on Josh's face. Things were not adding up. The strange conversations he had with Rhianna Adams brought an uneasy feeling. Something about her, he did not entirely trust. The leaked video from Canada was appearing less a singular event, and increasingly part of something bigger.

"Think you'll find answers?" Rhianna asked, glancing over at him.

He nodded in reply to the DHS liaison and cocked his head sideways.

"You might doubt it, but I will find out the truth."

"I don't doubt your desire or ability. I doubt the character of others."

The small helicopter landed without so much as a bump. Josh unbuckled and prepared to leap out, when suddenly, sirens blasted in the distance. Confused, he observed military police vehicles scrambling from the other side of the tarmac. They were scurrying towards the helicopter.

"What's going on?" he asked, looking at Rhianna.

She did not answer. Instead, she glared at the pilot and passenger in the front seat.

"Sergeant?"

The passenger sitting next to the pilot turned and pulled his heavy black shades off.

"I'm sorry, ma'am, Admiral's orders."

Scrambling out of his seat, the sergeant disembarked. The pilot too also hastily exited the craft. Josh watched in astonishment as the approaching military vehicles circled – surrounding the chopper completely. A black SUV emerged from the back of the caravan and drove forward until it was just ten yards away, then the doors opened, and three officers got out.

The trio drew near. The other soldiers, who had emptied from the vehicles, clutched their military weapons. Josh's shoulders started to tighten, and a knot formed in his stomach. Something was amiss.

"Lieut. Adams, you are under arrest for treason and for the assassination of Col. Javier Bordeau and Chief Warrant Officer Leon Martin. You will stand trial by court-martial."

Two of the officers stepped forward and grabbed Lieut. Adam's arms.

"What about him?" one of them nodded towards Josh.

"He's free to go."

"What are you doing?" Josh could not believe what was going on.

"Arresting someone. You are free to go."

Befuddled, Josh looked at Rhianna. He was astonished. Her words of dissent and conspiracy aside, she had not done anything to the Canadian military officials. Or had she? Someone had to know about the meeting. And they *did* survive the attack. She could have died, though. While self-sacrifice was commonplace in the Middle East, it was not in the US.

Rhianna saw his troubled expression. She forced a smile.

"Think about what I said, Josh. It's a free country."

"I've had enough crazy for one day," he muttered in reply. He turned and impulsively addressed the arresting officer. "Why are you taking her? I was there, our pilot *left* us."

"Fled for his life, you mean," the officer held up a tablet.

A shaky video began playing, and Josh gasped. He was in the video, walking towards the camera. Rhianna was located behind him in the picture, and he suddenly noticed her hand at her side. His eyes grew big. Was she holding something? He could not tell because the image suddenly became very bright and obscure.

"That's the explosion," the officer explained.

The video started to normalize. Josh saw himself on the ground and Rhianna a little further back, her face turned towards the blown up helicopter.

"This video was sent to us by your pilot. He was handpicked for this mission to keep an eye on Lieut. Adams. A recent review of her network use found illegal communication between her and an unknown agent. Coupled with this video, it is more than incriminating. But as I said before, Josh Cunningham, you are free to go. I strongly advise you to leave *now*."

■ ■ ■ ■

"Prism is in the building."

The secret service agent spoke into his left wrist as he pulled his shades a tad closer and relaxed his stance, surveying the surroundings. Despite the throngs of protesters located outside the gates, all was calm directly in front of the White House. There was no movement on the lawn, save a squirrel darting back and forth. The agent glanced left and upwards –a squad of snipers were positioned on the roof, holding their automatics close in case of danger.

"We're clear."

Inside the House, frustration simmered to a boil. Pres. Turouning sighed as he walked into the Oval Office, stopping in front of his desk. His black hair was badly ruffled, and his shoulders sagged underneath a spiffy, dark blue suit. He bent forward and placed both hands on the front edge of the desk. Looking down towards his left breast, where an emblem of the American flag adorned his coat, he closed his eyes. He shook his head, overwrought with thought and emotion. The president turned wearily and addressed the party standing in the room with him. His tone was not one of resignation, but rather defiance.

"Many presidents have served in this office. Why is it on my watch, we keep having disaster after disaster befall us? Hmm? It was an embarrassment to hear breaking news of the attack in a room full of dignitaries!"

The sadness and weight of the situation became one of anger and frustration. The Native American jabbed his long finger at the group of cabinet members, aides, and agents.

"Am I to understand that not even *one* of my esteemed aides was privy to the attack before I was hauled into a room of my peers? Charley," the president snapped. A woman looked up from near the back of the room. "Tell me, you're the Secretary of State. and you couldn't give me a heads-up on this?"

Charley Conners opened her mouth to speak, but the president did not let her.

"Bill, how long have you been serving as Secretary of Defense? Hmm? I held you over from the previous administration, and you did not have a clue about this attack before it's blabbed all over the G9 room?"

Bill O'Leary did not bother to answer. He merely shook his head.

"You know Russia and China are going to use this as leverage. Call the hangman already."

It was quiet for a minute. The monotonous tick of the clock on the president's desk could be heard. An audible groan escaped Turouning.

"Did you see those protesters? Once again they came in droves. Bearing skulls and crossbones no less! Is this the 18th century that I'm to be tarred and feathered for these attacks? There isn't a single person in my administration who had intel on this one? Or the man flipping out in Quebec? We all know how strained our relationship has been with our friends to the north this past decade! What kind of team have I assembled that doesn't have the *foresight* to tell me this?"

William suddenly felt a sharp pain in his eye. He leaned forward on the desk, and rubbed it hard with his right hand while he muttered, "And those stupid protesters…I thought we had outlawed dissension."

"Protesters can hardly be accounted for, sir…"

The president snapped his fingers, interrupting the speaker, and held up a long finger. His face twisted in anger.

"Did I ask you for excuses? I don't recall asking for excuses. Maria, did you hear me ask for excuses?"

William addressed an unimportant aide standing near the outer circle of the small assembly. She took an apprehensive half-step back as she slowly shook her head in reply.

"See, John? Maria didn't hear me ask for excuses. So why in the world did you give me an excuse? And why do you bother talking when I am? I don't think that's acceptable. In fact, I don't think that's justifiable. In fact, I'm going to fire you. Get out."

The deputy officer who oversaw logistics and reported on fluctuations, stood still as the president finished his tirade. William walked to his desk and pushed a few items around. When he looked up, he saw the officer was still in the room.

"What? Do I not even have control over *my own* office? Get out of here, sir!"

The deputy officer's face turned red, and he abruptly left the room, slamming the door behind him. The tension was thick as the president warily eyed the remaining people. A sudden glint of satisfaction crossed his features.

"There. More rubbish from the previous administration thrown out. If we didn't have this ridiculous wave of nonsense – Republicans and Democrats trying to get along – I would never have had John on my staff in the first place."

The president emphatically spoke as he walked around the desk, positioned in the rear center of the room. He flopped into the oversized leather chair stationed behind it.

"Okay. Let's get down to business. Charley, Bill, what's our next move?"

The two cabinet members looked at each other momentarily, and then Charley Conners began talking, as Bill O'Leary started messaging his command team at the Pentagon.

William was not paying attention. He stared out the oval office windows and thought back to the eerie scene he had experienced that morning for the umpteenth time.

Skulls and crossbones, pitchforks – insinuating I'm the devil! How dare they. Who do they think they are? Why am I responsible? Am I a god that I can dictate what happens to our world? Ach – the president shook his head. *What is happening to people? Everything is changing.*

The attack on the chopper – Prime Minister Harrison said everyone on board had died. William planned on calling Mark Jacobi to inquire if SEH had lost anyone. He would have to handle that conversation delicately, he did not want to raise suspicion or divulge details – even to a confidant like Jacobi.

William's mind went to the purpose of the G9 summit and the alarming details shared by the World Council's delegate, Ambassador Derrick Omach. More trouble was brewing. *Will it never end? Will we never have world peace?* He anxiously rubbed his chin.

Secretary Bill O'Leary was addressing the assembled group. Fighters were already scrambled, patrolling the DC skies. The DoD would not rest until the radar issue was resolved. The missile that struck the chopper in upstate New York had not even registered.

Suddenly, William rubbed his eye again. The itch was back; unmistakable and intensely fierce.

.   .   .   .   .

"What in the world is going on, Sam?" yelled Josh as the digital face of his field coordinator appeared in the holograph conference.

"Slow down, man. Where are you?"

Josh tried to take a breath. Adrenaline was pumping through him, and he struggled to calm himself. Moments before, he had fled the base where Lieut. Adams had been arrested. After the military police officer's threatening words and manner, he left before another second past. Grabbing the sides of his head, he tried to think – his mind was a whirl.

"I'm outside a military outpost in Maryland. Lucky to be out. My DHS liaison was just arrested!"

"What? Again, slow down, man. Start from the beginning."

Sam held out both of his hands and motioned down with them. Similar to the way a catcher communicated with a pitcher when trying to calm the hurler or keep the ball low.

"How about this? We get an assignment, supposedly to obtain a formula for a Disease infecting a lunatic who killed himself and his family. When I arrive, with my now arrested liaison, to a covert and *secure* meeting – Canadian government officials tell a dark story of an assassinated biochemist and his destroyed research. Their narrative grows twisted, and one of them shares how he is specifically tasked with investigating reports – attacks of crazy, even rabid behavior. You saw the news – the helicopter they came on was blown to bits as it was leaving."

"Yeah, all over the news."

"So Rhianna – Lieut. Adams – brings me here as we run from the attack and on the way we happen to hear a press conference by the president denying the attack. When we land, the lieutenant is arrested for treason and murder of the officials we had just met. How could she murder someone if I was with her the whole time? I mean, did she pre-plan the attack before we went? Tell me you know something, Sam. What's going on?"

Josh was breathing heavily. His words coming faster and faster, yet as he finished, he began to feel calmer, more regulated.

"Wow," said Sam. "Obviously, I heard the news, and your insight doesn't help clear it up any better either."

"Brilliant. The one person I trusted and hoped could tell me something – knows nothing."

"I didn't say that. There was another video released."

"Another video?" Josh was surprised. "You mean like the Canadian one?"

"Yeah, but I think it's a copycat. Someone in India staged a video where she seemed to have killed her children."

"Why do you think it's a copycat?"

Sam ran a hand over his head and pulled off his glasses. The field coordinator was thinking about how to answer the question.

"Call it a gut reaction."

"Oh, great! I just got done with someone like that."

"What?"

Josh proceeded to tell Sam what Rhianna Adams had said during the day – including the hypothetical organization running counterintelligence to find out what was really going on with the latest events, and more specifically, the trending #TheDisease.

"What did she mean by that?" Sam was both perturbed and interested.

"I don't know."

"Tell you what, man. Stay up there for a bit and see if you can find anything that supports what she told you."

"I'm not a spy or reporter, Sam," Josh was insulted by the request. "We're only on this assignment because of Pharma Group."

"Don't you want to know if there's any truth to her words?"

Leaning back against a tree, Josh considered Sam's proposal. It was true. He was curious if there was more to what Rhianna said. She had hinted at conspiracy by suggesting her hypothetical organization "blended into reality."

A few hours can't hurt, especially if I find anything.

"Fine," he relented.

Sam smiled from the other side.

"But only for the rest of today. Probably a waste of time and I'd like to get back home."

"Sure, sure," Sam nodded and put his glasses back on. "Stop back here before you do, though. See you tomorrow."

NINE

The fat man snorted as he stared at his TV, watching the replaying footage of the burning helicopter in New York. The G9 summit had taken an unexpected twist with the terrorist attack. Unfortunately, Patrick Flannigan had canceled the planned hangout the night before, so the two of them could not talk about it. Jim Burillo wished they could have met.

There was so much to talk about these days. Everything was becoming so strange and foreign. The man in Canada who shot and killed his family, then the mother in India who murdered her own children with her bare hands. Jim shook his head.

There's too much bad news back here, he blamed the small room where the TV was located. Struggling up out of the rocking chair, he hit the mute button on the remote, and walked from the backroom towards the front of his store.

"Holy Toledo! There's a lot of 'em today," Jim turned and looked at his niece.

Anna was sitting on the counter, legs freely swinging and banging into the counter's wooden side. She scowled at her uncle in annoyance.

"You said that yesterday; and the day before."

Jim smiled. At least he got her to respond.

The passing crowds presented greater interest to him than usual these days. Savannah, Georgia always had its fair share of tourists; that was common knowledge. If it were not for tourists, *Savannah Souvenirs* would not exist.

After all, Jim admitted to himself, he had a pretty good set up. It was hard to get real estate near the Downtown and Historic Districts of town. Initially, the shop was located further than most tourists traversed, but with the opening of Wharf ONE, business had gradually increased over the years.

Gazing out of the window, Jim sat, his fat chin quivering with excitement, as he counted the number of people. Some might say he was slow of mind. Nothing could be further from the truth. His fascination with the demise of humanity clearly showed more brain than the most intelligent minds trying to sort through the science behind what was happening.

Perhaps there was some truth though because, after a few additional minutes of crowd watching, Jim slowly began pushing the broom he was holding back and forth – moving more than sweeping. His brow was knit together in deep thought. Much troubled him lately. The scores of people wearing dark glasses had grown the past few weeks.

One could not doubt Jim's worth ethic, though. The small store he owned was a testament to it. He was the sole owner, proprietor, and provided the general upkeep for the store. It was a small outfit – sandwiched between a candy shoppe and a t-shirt merchandising store – initially owned by Jim's father.

Jose Burillo was the first American citizen in his family. He had married a young Hispanic American woman who insisted that all their children be raised as American, be given "proper" American names, and speak English. For the firstborn son, Jim seemed a logical choice.

Jim's childhood was far from pleasant. His father worked long and hard hours to provide for his family – and still came up short. Yet, Jose would not look for "outside" help. He refused government assistance, and even in his older years when welfare and healthcare expanded to provide coverage for most Americans, Jose declined.

"No man owns me," he boasted to his friends.

Growing up, Jose's philosophy was embedded in Jim's environment. His father vowed to never let the family starve. He promised no one would have him up against the wall. Then at the young age of fifteen, Jim's mother died.

The death of his wife greatly affected the mental stability of Jose. He hit the bottle, and never stopped running. When Jim was twenty-five, police authorities fished his father's body out of an ocean inlet near Hilton Head Island.

The firstborn son and second oldest of four, Jim was suddenly the head of the household. The oldest Burillo girl had run off with a wealthy Mexican never to be seen again. After his younger brother was arrested for trafficking cocaine, Jim had only his little sister left in his care. The little Burillo sister had a boyfriend who Jim never liked. He liked the boyfriend even less when he found out his sister was pregnant.

And that is when Anna became part of the story. She never knew her father, and when she was eight, her mother died from poor health – or so went Uncle Jim's story.

Anna came to live with her uncle, and for the first few years, aside from one terrifying incident, things went all right. They got along fine; one might even suggest they were close. Jim did his best to take care of her.

When Anna turned thirteen, something changed though. She tired of living with her uncle. She wanted a "normal" life and not to be tied to a "dirty little shop in a city that's nothing more than a whorehouse for tourists" – or at least, that's how she described it.

Jim saw the change in Anna as natural growth for any girl blossoming into womanhood. But as Anna became more surly and rebellious – hanging out with boys much older than herself – he found a reason for concern. Then he discovered a bag of rocks. The curse of the Burillos was chasing Anna. Drug use.

That was three years ago. Now, Anna was eighteen. A groan came out as Jim leaned heavily upon the broom, lost in the buried memories of the past. He barely managed taking care of the young woman. She had become so unruly, he never knew when she would snap at him.

It's not like I haven't done anything for her, he wiped a tear away from his eye with one of his chubby hands. He stared at the extremity. *Maybe Anna is right. I'm a worthless pig. But at least, I give her a safe place to live, and she'll never starve!* Jim's eyes lit up with defiance, and he felt a sudden rush of adrenaline. It dropped.

"Probably going to starve herself first," he muttered to no one in particular.

Eventually, he came around to the front of the store, and glanced at his skinny niece who was perched on the counter holding her phone. He watched her longer than he meant. Becoming conscious of his gaze, Anna looked up. Jim hurriedly resumed pushing the broom. She gave an exasperated sigh, and rolled her eyes.

"Whatever, old man. I'm just texting."

That worried Jim. Texting – sending inappropriate pictures and messages to a boyfriend who mistreated her; used her for sex and drugs. At least, that was Jim's worry. He began moving back towards the rear of the store again.

The phone chirped. Anna swiped her thumb across the screen. A smile crept across her face. She bit her lip, and her thumb touched the screen, writing her response.

Jim watched, eyes crinkling with concern. He gave a long sigh, his fat belly heaving up and then back down. Inventory had to be completed today and entered into his electronic storage device. Most people called it a computer, an ancient and outdated one at that. The shopkeeper said that was not the name of it anymore – merely an electronic storage device.

"A computer," he would say, "was a device created in the 50s and elaborated in the 90s by Bill Gates. Extricated by the wealthy as a cheap gimmick for both man and beast, they so manipulated society and made a butt-load of money in the process!"

That, of course, was utter nonsense and equally made no sense. But one enjoyed listening to the fat man talk. His fleshy lips would "spit" on the P's and T's in such a way that if a snake could talk and was hoarse on top of it – that is how the fat man sounded.

He could care less what people thought. Jim was not prepossessed, nor self-conscious. To him, as long as people got along in peace and harmony, all was well.

The tourist season was just starting in Savannah, and already crowds of people were rising with the temperature. It was a balmy 86-degrees on this particular day. Beaded sweat formed on Jim's brow and then dripped, without hesitation, down his face. The shop did not have air conditioning. With tourists coming in and out, it did not make sense to run it – according to Jim.

A loud sigh, and he resumed his inventory counts. The crowds of people would have to wait. He needed to count all the beer and soda in his cooler. It would take him a little while. Mathematics did not come easily.

Completed with that task, he slid the door shut, and turned to walk back to the front. So preoccupied with his duties and task at hand, he did not notice Anna. No longer sitting on the counter, she was walking along in the aisle.

"God! Watch out."

The Styrofoam cup filled with hot coffee pushed up against Anna's pink tank top as he walked into her. Without a cover, the contents of the mug swirled furiously – threatening to spill over.

"I'm sorry," Jim mumbled. "I thought you were sitting on the counter. I didn't see you."

"No, you didn't." The girl's tone was sharp and unkind. "Why did you think I was sitting on the counter? Because I'm a lazy ass like you're always telling me? Maybe if you weren't so busy trying to watch your *fat* as you bounced along the aisles, actually doing physical work for once, you would've seen me."

Jim stumbled up against one of the display racks. His eyes smarted and hurt; his countenance like one who had just been slapped. Pulling a white kerchief from his breast-pocket, he furiously blew his nose into it.

Anna stared at him, her eyes crackling with intense anger. It was a stark contrast. The generously overweight bald man collapsed next to the upright skinny blonde girl. Like David and Goliath.

"I can't help it, Anna."

A snort of disgust, quite unwomanly, came from the girl's throat. She cast a sharp, disapproving scowl at her uncle.

"Can't help it? Can't help the fact you weigh over three hundred pounds? Can't help the fact all you do is slob around and eat 24/7? Can't help the fact you sweat like a pig when you do something as easy as counting a few cans of Coke? Can't help the fact you have the maturity of a five-year-old with the curiosity of a two-year-old? God, you get off watching crowds of people wearing *sunglasses,* and think the government is always listening to you! You are constantly stuffing your face with crap. You know, Jim," her tirade paused as she inserted her uncle's name with resounding disgust. "You remind me of a slug. Someone who exists only to eat, sleep, and eat more."

The abusive dialogue was unwarranted and it crushed him. Meekly covering his head with his hands, Jim slumped to the floor. His fat belly began heaving as hot tears streamed down his face. The energy he had to hustle and bustle was zapped. Any desire to accomplish further work gone. He felt worthless, like an outcast mutt who had no future except one of misery and extermination. At the moment, either option seemed viable and somewhat comforting.

Staring at her uncle, Anna's face bore a wrathful expression of utter contempt compounded with disgust. Vulgarly snorting once more, she stepped over him, and walked away.

Jim's tears continued to flow as he contemplated himself. Large clumps of fat hung to him like a tick, going nowhere, devouring both health and image. He watched the retreating figure of Anna and sighed – deeply and heavily. She *was* thin and good looking. It did not matter if she was thinner than she should be. He was fat – plain and simple. They were a picture of extremes, and he felt the worse half.

■ ■ ■ ■ ■

A young woman stood in the doorway, staring at Luke as he furiously typed away on a keyboard. A sorrowful look amalgamated with pride was upon her face. Brenda was in her mid-twenties and had just finished graduate studies the year before. Upon completion, she stayed on to intern for the Pittsburgh Research Team. Her passion was immunology, and many said she could be one of the smartest interns the University ever had, but she had a weakness. Luke Baer.

Most found Luke to be overly aggressive and self-confident in his theories – Chem-Lab had been proof of that. Because of this, working with him brought a certain stigma. However, Brenda found Luke's work to be refreshingly ahead of the times, perhaps even prophetic – it made for both excitement and fulfillment. And besides, she looked to Luke as an older brother, and dearly loved him.

"Melinda Gore has it out for you," she said, walking over to Luke's desk.

"Tell me something I don't know," Luke growled.

Just that morning, he had been excluded from Pittsburgh Research Team's daily morning huddle. It had been 24 hours since he recommended taking the bold and audacious approach to the outbreak of the Disease. Melinda Gore had realized the importance of pursuing it, and then promptly disposed of his involvement. Her reference to Chem-Lab in front of their colleagues offered her the chance.

Luke felt the magnitude of a week's amount of stress condensed and packed in the last day. It was one thing to lose his position as a lead on an assignment. It was quite another when his own ideology was usurped and used against him.

Dang woman! Why does she hate me?

"If you don't find something soon, she's going to silence your voice. Right now, I believe we *need* your voice."

"And why would she do that?" The typing stopped as Luke snapped back, ignoring Brenda's affirmation of his work.

The intern instinctively pulled away. "Whoa, cowboy. I'm on your side."

"Sorry," Luke mumbled. The typing resumed, though it was less intense and seemed even distracted. "Crap. This is pointless. What do you have?"

"Nothing. That's the problem," Brenda motioned with her hands. "Unless you want the intel from TYM or Pharma, we have to wait. Melinda's put a clamp on all information coming in and going out. Oh, and she put a stay on your clearance level."

"What?"

Luke tossed the touchpad aside and stood up. He began pacing the floor, back and forth. It was a nervous habit of his and fit the occasion. This was the first he heard about the stay on his clearance.

"She said she did not want you jeopardizing the department's future. People are going rabid enough over the leaked videos without a doomsday science prognosis."

"And I would have that, would I? What about the Department's future?" he fumed. "How exactly would securing first-finder privileges *not* help our future?"

"It's what she said," Brenda shrugged. "Do you want the research TYM did?"

"No," Luke shook his head. "Those money-grabbing idiots do not have any idea what they are doing. I'll just take Prof. Bradley's."

Brenda nodded and stood up. Walking out of the room, she disappeared through the doorway.

Using his right forefinger, Luke pushed his glasses back up his nose. Beads of perspiration formed on a furrowed brow as he gazed at the piles of test information lying on the desk in front of him. He was unaware of anything in the vicinity save that pile of papers.

The work left behind by Dr. Charles Grafton was of no small consequence. Nor was the mess it was in. While Grafton was a brilliant researcher and scientist, as an individual, the doctor was the epitome of disorganization. Luke saw an irony in this and of course, had good-naturedly mocked Dr. Grafton while the latter was still alive. Today, however, Luke found himself cursing the man while concurrently breathing silent praises.

TYM! Luke's brow furrowed as he thought of the enormous pharmaceutical company based in Japan. Tachi Yin Merger was aptly named after Tachi Medicine was purchased by Yin Mill. *Take Your Money* was Luke's own acronym. The group had some well qualified and even brilliant scientists, chemists, and engineers. But the group also had several young, ambitious individuals with barely any experience and whose sole purpose was the financial reward – or so claimed Luke.

Pittsburgh University was not working in direct competition with TYM, but Luke preferred to think of his work on the Research Team as being more grounded in practical science and medical thought. At least until Melinda Gore started preaching overly patient practices. It collided with his burning desire to secure first-finder privileges on each assignment. He became more rash and daring. He did not feel like his original self anymore.

The unknown diseases which were popping up always hit suddenly and spread rapidly. Fear of the unknown led to little truth. Every outbreak morphed into something more dangerous than it probably was. So far, there had been few theories – at least good ones – on what caused the outbreaks and what might cure them. While some were concerned about the international ramifications and potential threats, Luke's own mind was wrapped up in the cause of the disease and the immediate effects thereof.

Dr. Grafton's work had the comparative breakthrough of $E=mc^2$ with regards to how humans viewed sunlight and interaction with its harmful rays. Global warming theorists were celebrated for speaking the truth, despite the many naysayers who simply argued climate change was continually evolving and happening.

Regardless of the theories, the last few months had not been easy. And now, the crazy reports of a Disease – a growing epidemic that assaulted the human mind – transforming normal behaviors into unpredictable terrors. The two recent murder-suicide videos proved something terrible was afoot, and if there was a cure to be had, by gum, Luke wanted to find it.

"Which is why my work is more substantial and important than TYM!" Luke said out loud.

His mind regularly thrashed both coherent and incoherent theories on what he was researching. The anxiety and stress of the past several months were felt. He sighed. He had been keenly aware of this nagging feeling since – well, at least, the past few weeks.

Staring abstractly at a notebook in front of him, he smiled.

Funny. Here we are in a paperless world, and perhaps the most critical research item is still – the notebook.

"Prof. Bradley won't allow anyone outside his lab to view the panels."

Brenda's breathless voice cut in as she popped her head around the door. Luke presumed she had been running.

"What? That's ridiculous. How can he do that? His research should be open access to anyone at the university!"

Luke knew this was not true. A few years ago, the University had passed an information access exception for its faculty. Ongoing research by a professor or department could remain under full or limited protection as long as they chose. Much piracy had invaded the college classroom and campus. Pittsburgh was taking a step to curb the trend. And besides, much of the work done by the Research Team remained confidential even when in active assignment.

Knowing this did not make Luke any less furious. He jumped to his feet again, and once more strode back and forth in an effort to calm himself. Brenda watched as he pushed his arms out, and leaned his palms against the desk.

"This is crazy," Luke shook his head at Brenda. "It's almost as if they don't want us to know anything."

"Professor Bradley?" Brenda was confused.

"Maybe..." Luke paused. "No, I mean all the research. Like the media portals we get our information from. Seriously, why would you restrict your deep dive probe report to one group? One segment of the people?"

Brenda gave a short laugh. "It's just one person, and he has a legal right."

"Humph," Luke snorted, expressing his opinion on the legal right.

"Isn't there anything here?" Brenda motioned to the piles of papers and electronic devices on Luke's desk.

"Sure. There's plenty of information. Dr. Grafton was a brilliant man. He discovered a lot of things. But he did an abysmal job of capturing that information. Dr. Grafton forgot we live in the 21st century and not the 19th. He forgot we sometimes use electronic devices to enter information so that at some point, a poor schmuck – such as myself – can later retrieve said information."

Brenda was laughing by the time Luke finished. He tried to suppress a grin. It felt good to make light of the situation.

"And of course, this is just part of his research files," Brenda smiled. "Well, let me know if you need me on anything else."

"Sure." Luke returned the smile, and Brenda left.

Rocking forward on his palms and pushing himself up, Luke took a deep breath. *Why is Bradley refusing to let us see his research? Privacy rights be damned!* He had heard a theory on an independent radio talk show – he stumbled across it on his podcast feed a few weeks ago – it suggested reasons as to why all this was happening. Luke did not know what to think of their theories.

"Oh to hell with this!" he was impatient. "What are they hiding?"

"What?" Brenda's head popped around the corner.

"Nothing, I was speaking to myself. I don't understand why Melinda fails to realize the danger that comes with ignoring the anomalies. Or maybe she does, but just doesn't care. I know the mistakes in my past. But I *have* to believe for every wrong calculation like Chem-Lab, there's a reality of Hiroshima waiting to happen."

"You know, I could listen to you all day, Luke. There's a reason I'm still here. But the reality is you aren't going to get the support you need from the rest of the staff. They say it was more guess than calculated theory. But hey," Brenda added at the sight of Luke's miffed expression. "I *am* the only one here. I'm on your side."

Luke sighed and plopped into his office chair. He was being surly, and he knew it. Inside his gentlemanly etiquette scolded him.

"I appreciate it, Brenda. I realize there's a stigma one gets working with me, I'm sorry about that." He tried to collect his thoughts. "Speaking of calculated theory, do you know what happened with the file regarding that outbreak in China. The one which had the dead cells – only they weren't actually dead?"

Brenda eyed him curiously. "Yes, but I'm not sure how that's related."

"Just a hunch."

"Those would probably be with the rest of Dr. Grafton's research. I'll be back," the intern went to retrieve the file.

Might as well start with a hypothesis – at square one, Luke seized the sudden idea that had come to him. *I will let it dictate my research, and we shall see what we find.*

Waving his hand, he then remembered the holograph projector was broken. He would have to manually key it in. He was not in a position with the Department to request new equipment purchases.

Brenda was back.

That was fast.

"You have a visitor."

"Seriously?" he was incredulous.

"When have you ever known me to kid?"

"He can come in," Luke half-heartedly motioned with his hand.

"I'll let *her* know."

Luke's eyebrows rose. *Her?*

"Ms. Tessa..." Brenda stopped, and looked at the smiling redhead tailing her. "I'm sorry. I don't know your last name."

"It's all right. He knows me," Tessa Morgan laughed, and winked at Luke.

He sat up straight in his chair. His face felt hot, and he struggled to maintain his composure. A knot hit his stomach, and he swallowed hard a couple times.

"It...it is fine, Brenda. Thanks!"

Brenda smirked, and left the two alone.

"My, my! Quite the office you have," Tessa said, running a finger along the edge of his desk. "No projector?"

"It broke," said Luke nervously. "Two months ago. Apparently, we don't have the 'budget' for a new one. Especially now," he added as an afterthought.

"Oh?" Tessa looked at him curiously. "It does seem there is never a budget for the people who are actually *doing* the work, right?"

She laughed, and Luke cracked a smile. She was beautiful.

"Well, I didn't stop by because I wanted to see your office."

"No. Why did you?" he stopped. "Wait, how did you know where I worked or who I worked for?"

"Shhh," Tessa came around the desk and put a finger against his lips. "Know where you worked?" She tossed her hair flirtatiously. "You are a silly man. You may be working on some secret science project, but it isn't that hard for an intelligent woman like me to track down a handsome man like you."

Luke smiled back. He could not help, but enjoy the tingling exchange of pleasantries. Her beauty and charm were intoxicating. She was dressed in a simple purple blouse, loosely fitting around her breasts and curves, showing the perfect amount of cleavage. A black skirt hugged her hourglass hips and fell to her knees. Her red hair was curled at the ends, and the way she could fling it from side to side mesmerized him.

Brenda smiled from outside Luke's office. She had been trying to set him up for a long time with various girlfriends. She liked how Tessa commanded the room. Maybe there was some potential here. It would have to wait; she had other things to attend to like that incident in China.

Walking over to the filing cabinets, she opened a drawer and shuddered as she pulled the file. Looking down at the photograph taken of the incident, a chill ran up her spine.

A man lay in the street. His eye sockets empty; blood pooled on the ground next to him. Two or three paces away was a body, neatly set face down, arms tucked to the side. The head had been severed, but carefully placed where it should have been. The body was that of a little girl, not more than eight, maybe nine. There was a single word written on the photograph, a filing note when it had first come in.

DIABOLUS.

Suddenly, Brenda felt sick.

．　　■　　■　　■　　■　　■

"Uncle Jim, you'd better come here!"

Jim woke from his slumber, surprised at hearing his name called. Scarcely an hour had passed since Anna had maliciously attacked him with her words. The verbal abuse had taken its toll, and caused him to take a short refresher snooze on the rocker in the backroom of *Savannah Souvenirs*. Now though, his niece's words arrested his attention.

Anna never addressed him as uncle; something was wrong. Struggling to his feet, he clumsily kicked over a box containing small packages of chips.

"Hurry, old man!" Anna's voice quivered.

Jim shuffled towards the front, and became aware of yelling. Hurrying forward through the store as fast as he could run, he pushed open the front door, and stepped out onto the cobbled street. He was nearly bowled over.

Hundreds of people were running all around him down the street. Shouts and yells filled the air. The chaos dazed him momentarily. He held his hand up.

"Stay inside, Anna," he yelled over his shoulder, venturing into the crowd.

At first, Jim could not tell what the commotion was about. Too many people were pushing and shoving for him to have a clear view. He decided it was time to use his weight as an advantage. Barreling forward, he began bumping people out of the way, his belly swaying with each step.

Nearing the front of the assembled crowd, he saw a woman running up and down the riverfront. She was screaming and yelling, but Jim could not distinguish her actual words. Pressing himself to the front of the crowd, he stopped, transfixed by the scene.

Blood oozed from the woman's face. She held a knife and slashed it wildly through the air. Then she turned and stared at the gawking onlookers. Opening her mouth, the woman screamed and menacingly wielded the knife through the air.

"Danger!" she yelled. "Beware!"

"What is going on?" Jim asked, addressing no one in particular.

A boy standing next to Jim heard him, though, and looked up at the shopkeeper. The lad's eyes were big with excitement.

"She just started yelling and wailing. Came out from the hotel over there," the boy pointed to a prominent looking building on the far corner of the street. It was about a block away, but Jim was familiar with the place of lodging. It had been erected a few years earlier and brought in a good number of tourists.

"What is she yelling about?" Jim asked the boy, figuring he might know that as well.

"Who knows?" the kid excitedly shouted. Feverishly clapping his hands, he let out a whoop. "This is the most exciting thing I've ever seen!"

Jim cast a reproachful eye upon the youngster. *Probably plays video games all day and his brain is filled with nonsensical dribble.*

Suddenly, there were screams from somewhere in the throng of people and heads turned to look. Out of the corner of Jim's eye, moving between the thronging bodies of onlookers, he saw a man slipping through the crowd. Something about the man riveted his attention. It appeared no one else noticed the man, as they were still trying to ascertain who was screaming. This man was dressed in black and wearing dark shades. He pulled something from his pocket.

Jim's eyes widened as he saw the glint of a barrel. Adrenaline rose, and he started forward, but he could not move. His knees buckled in place.

"Do not trust anyone," the woman warned in a high pitched voice. She was swaying uncontrollably; the knife slashing wildly. "Watch out for…"

The man in black raised the barrel; his finger squeezed the trigger. There was no sound, but Jim watched horror-stricken as the woman crumpled to the ground. Blood spurted forth from the headshot wound.

The crowd went into a frenzy! Screaming and yelling, people tried to get away. Jim craned his neck to see what the man in black was doing. But the man was not there. Shoving his way forward, Jim vainly tried to locate the shooter. But the silent assassin could not be found.

Heading back towards the place where the woman had crumpled, Jim saw blood pooling around her body. The knife had fallen harmlessly onto the wooden planks of the wharf. And there, next to her dead body, was a pistol. Smoke streamed from its barrel.

His mind felt like it was going to explode. He could not comprehend the last few minutes. Who was this lady? Who was the shooter? Everything had come and gone as fast as lighting, leaving behind a deadly trail marked in red.

Sirens sounded, and the size of the crowd increased as people came flocking to see what had happened. Jim was in a daze and did not know what to do.

Suddenly, someone shouted. "She had the Disease!"

That pushed the crowd back a bit. No one wanted to get to close to the body or catch something contagious.

She was a victim of the Disease. What is this new illness? Is it connected to the G9 summit? Or the blown up helicopter? The Canadian video? It might all be related, by St. Christopher!

Jim was blown away by the idea. He turned and started walking back towards his shop. On the way, he heard snatches of conversation.

"She had the Disease all right!" "Just like the man in Canada!" "Crazy as a bat!" "Just came running out of that hotel like a madwoman!" "Don't go near her, you don't wanna catch it!" "Has anyone called the police? Where are they?"

He neared the intersection of wooden planks and cobbled sidewalks. A news van pulled up, and the crew jumped out and started holographic live streams to social media. Jim stopped at the shop's entrance and pivoted to observe the hysteria going on around him. Scratching his bald head, he slowly rubbed a hand back over it as he listened to the fear in people's voices. Even with all the conversations buzzing around him, Jim did not hear anybody mention the shooter – the man in black.

Was I the only person who saw him? he was amazed.

He noticed the boy he had stood next to on the wharf. The lad was now standing in front of *Savannah Souvenirs*. A reporter and camera operator from the news crew were interviewing him. The boy was trembling, fear etched across his face, as he recounted the incident.

"She had the Disease all right. She was acting crazy, running around with a knife, screaming a bunch of stuff."

The boy was trembling so much the reporter reached out and touched the youngster's shoulder to help calm him. The next words the boy uttered caused Jim's mouth to drop open in disbelief and astonishment.

"Then suddenly, she has a gun! She puts it to her head and pulls the trigger."

The kid broke down sobbing. His head dropped, and tears fell freely. The lad cursed and batted his arms. His head shot back up, and he stared past the reporter, straight into the camera's lens.

"Do you understand me? One minute, she's normal. The next, she transforms and shoots her own frickin head right in front of us!"

TEN

"I got your text. Came as fast as I could. What's up?" Josh was breathless from the quick scamper over. His eyes squinted, trying to adjust to the abundant light in the room.

It was late morning, and bright sunshine was streaming in through the large windows in Sam's office. No attempt had been made to lower the tinting. Being a corner office, there were windows on two sides of the room. Thus it was illuminated better than any other room or corridor in the entire SEH campus.

"Find anything last night?"

"No. A dead end, just like I thought," Josh answered, recalling the conversation he and Sam had the night before. "But what's so urgent? You said something's popping?"

"Yeah, yeah," Sam nodded and walked around the massive desk.

Four display panels were centered on the desk, another four were elevated – two on each end of the workspace – with extender arms. Two more monitors still were behind Sam's chair, which Josh doubted the man actually ever sat in.

"I don't know what to say…" Sam cryptically paused. "We got another video."

"So you told me."

"No, no, not the Indian one. This one is *new* – from this morning – down in Georgia. A woman blew her brains out in the Historic District. All over social media, but I doubt you saw it."

Josh gave a faint smile. It was well-known to his close friend and colleague that he never went on social media unless absolutely necessary. Josh preferred to engage in news broadcasts, sports, or TV shows when he had spare time; or perhaps read. Social media apps used very little of his device's battery or data.

"Well, this last incident has me thinking. You mentioned Lieut. Adams suggested widespread sinister actions were going on. I've found something that suggests it's real and bigger than I thought possible. I'm talking conspiracy big," Sam lowered his voice. "Like, why would the president deny who was aboard the helicopter? We all saw the presser. And then, as you said," Sam motioned towards Josh. "The lieutenant was arrested as you landed for the assassination of the same officials our president and the Canadian Prime Minister lied about."

"Seriously, dude? Don't start. Rhianna Adams maybe or maybe did not orchestrate the missile attack, but she was speaking sedition – conspiracy. And I told you, I found nothing."

"C'mon, man, you know better. Do you really think you could crack something so deeply hidden in a few hours last night?"

"Well…" Josh started, and then stopped as he saw Sam incredulously looking at him. Shaking his head, he acquiesced.

"You couldn't, but I could – with the help of these –" A grim look was on Sam's features and he waved his hand towards the desk and the ten panels, all of which were streaming data.

"What'd you find?" Josh studied Sam's face. *He knows something. Is it all connected somehow?* "What did I miss?"

"Nothing. It wasn't in New York or Maryland. It was in Georgia."

With that, Sam leaned back, snapped his fingers, and moved them in a circular motion. A projector, sitting on the edge of the desk, fired up, and came to life. Josh stepped back as the holograph image surrounded him. It was a riverfront, there was a wharf. Crowds of milling people and a crazy lady screaming near the water's edge.

"Where is this?"

"Savannah."

"Right. And this morning?"

"Just two hours ago."

Josh watched the streaming video. A bald, generously overweight man was pushing his way towards the front. Josh chuckled. Sam saw it and laughed too. Then they stopped. The woman crumpled to the ground, blood spurting from her left temple.

"What the…" Josh took an instinctive step forward.

"Exactly. And listen to this. If I scrub the audio…"

"Danger! Beware." The lady yelled in an eerie, otherworldly voice.

"Is that the scrub?" Josh asked, turning to face Sam.

Walters slowly shook his head and mouthed 'no.' He pointed back at the holograph.

Swiveling back, Josh watched the replaying clip as the woman crumpled.

"What was that she said just before?"

Sam flipped his fingers, and the feed rewound ten seconds. He cranked the audio.

"Do not trust anyone. Watch out for…" Then blood shot forth, and there was silence.

"My gosh," Josh stepped back, amazed. "It's exactly like the man in Quebec!"

"Precisely," Sam said. His hands shook. "But that's still not the scrub."

The audio started again.

"Delta in position."

There was static.

"On your mark, Player 18."

More static. A low guffaw.

"They'll never know what hit them."

"What is this?" Josh leapt forward and peered closer at the holograph display. Straining his ears, while staring at the video, vainly hoping he could discern who was speaking.

"That is exactly what I want to know," Sam folded his arms, his eyes clouded in mystery as he looked questioningly at Josh.

"Ah. You are here!"

An angry voice cut into the conversation. John Stevens, director of the Morphing Division, strode into the room. Both men turned and greeted John. The man's face was red and drops of perspiration beaded on his forehead. He was waving a digital file in his right hand and motioned with his left.

"See this? Hmm? Makes two accounts of the same story – three if you count India – in the last seventy-two hours and my crack research team is standing around chit-chatting about God knows what."

"John, we're hardly chit-chatting," Sam replied, holding up a hand in protest. "We're talking about the Georgia video."

"Ah, I see." John looked Josh up and down, ignoring Sam's presence. "And then why are you still here, Josh? Hmm? Waiting for something?"

Sometimes John's sarcastic attitude and biting words would get to Josh. It was moments like these he would try to remember something his mom taught him – or maybe it was Thumper. 'If you can't say something nice, don't say anything at all.' Josh bit his tongue and counted to five.

John Stevens was still staring, when Josh glanced up and evenly met his gaze.

"Yes, I am waiting for something. Answers."

"Oh?" John's arms dropped, and he walked to the side of Sam's desk. Nervously knocking on the wooden frame twice, he then turned. "Answers regarding what?"

"New York. What happened up there?"

"Ha. You tell me. You were the one there."

"Don't give me that, John. I've worked here too long and too hard to be told answers like that."

"Just what sort of answer do you want, Mr. Cunningham?"

John stepped closer and jabbed a long finger towards Josh. The informal and casual working atmosphere suddenly changed to a frosty formality.

"I want answers on why the president lied. Why my escort from the DHS was arrested immediately once we landed. What happened with the research on the guy who killed himself and his family? The contact we met said the scientist studying it had been assassinated?"

The chief of the Morphing Division clicked his tongue a couple times, another nervous habit of his. Licking his lips, he cocked his head sideways while giving a small, condescending smile.

"The president did not lie, and I would be cautious in accusing him of that. I don't know the story about the lieutenant, except," John paused for dramatic effect. "Why did she fly to another base on your return? What do we really know about her or DHS's involvement? Regarding the research – it's not gone. Apparently, the people aboard that craft were undercover from *Daily Spin*," John referenced a popular Canadian news site. "They were trying to solicit fear-mongering about a new 'Disease.' The real Public Health Agency of Canada contacted us while you were gone and provided the results of the autopsy. Turns out the man was perfectly healthy, aside from his mental instability."

"Well," Josh was surprised at the calm in his voice. "That's complete crap, John. And if you don't know it, at least I do. Something terrible happened up there, and nobody wants the truth to be heard. Why is that? Even if you are right, that still contradicts what Turouning said at the presser."

Sam nodded his approval behind the scowling figure of John Stevens. He gave a supportive thumbs-up to his coworker. Josh saw it and gave a quick flick of his head in appreciation.

It was quiet in the room. Josh could feel John sizing the situation up, contemplating what to say in response. The director chose to move on.

"So what about it, Josh? Are you taking that assignment to Georgia?"

Josh felt like throwing his hands in the air and saying words that should not be spoken to a boss. Instead, he took a deep breath, and nodded.

"Good. Then let's stop dillydallying and get a move on it. Sam?"

Sam was staring at Josh, amazed at the restraint his colleague had demonstrated. He gave a visible jump as he realized John had addressed him.

"I got travel passes here, hotel reservation, photos of the area from the satellite feeds, and even the medical tags from the woman who killed herself."

Stevens listened to Sam and nodded. He said the plan sounded great and he looked forward to an update. The Morphing chief then exited the office. Josh stood still after the departure, trying to digest the new information John had just shared. None of it made any sense – the last three days were a cluster, a conundrum of conundrums. Sam walked over, and put a hand on Josh's shoulder.

"You okay, man?"

"Yeah," Josh replied. He paused. "I'll find out what's going on, Sam."

A smile cracked the field coordinator's serious countenance.

"I know, Josh. We'll give 'em hell."

Josh pulled his handheld from his pocket and held it over the transmitter sitting on Sam's desk. The device chirped, notifying him the transfer of data was complete. He would look over the dossier on the flight to Georgia.

Is this all connected? If those were real undercover reporters, why would someone kill them? And the Daily Spin? They are more gossip than fact; any casual viewer knows that. They pose no threat to a narrative. The lieutenant arrested for treason? Her words might be seditious, but she did mention a mass cover-up. Still, why would she be guilty of treason if the Canadians were actually from a gossip site? None of this makes any sense. His brain hurt.

"Time for tequila," Josh spoke out loud as he left the room.

Outside of Sam's office, sat a woman busily engaged on a portable workstation. She overheard Josh's words, and glanced at him with a smile, as he passed by.

"Have some for me too," she said with a soft drawl.

"From Georgia?" Josh asked.

The woman blushed. "Wow! It's that noticeable?"

Josh laughed. "I get around a lot. And it's on my mind. I'm heading there next."

"I know," she responded. "Makes sense seeing you are the lead field agent for SEH, Josh Cunningham."

Now, Josh blushed. "Aw, whatever, I'm just part of the Morphing team, same as you…though I haven't had the pleasure of meeting you yet, Miss…?" he held out his hand.

"Carrie Haselow," the Southern belle replied, shaking his hand. "So you're heading to Georgia – for the wharf incident?"

"Yeah," he answered. "How'd you know?"

"Who doesn't? It's all the rage on social media."

"Of course. Say, while I'm there, anything you want me to grab?"

His question was not in earnest, he merely enjoyed talking to this woman. Whether the Georgia brunette was aware of his feigned earnestness or not, she played along anyway.

"Ah, that's sweet of you to offer! Since you ask –" she flashed a smile that melted his heart. The smile turned into a mischievous grin. "There's a shop down there, run by an old family friend. The place is called *Savannah Souvenirs*. He sells the cutest, daintiest little boxes of tea. Chamomile Cinnamon – it's the best."

Another laugh came from Josh. "Chamomile Cinnamon. Got it."

"Thank you," the heart-melting smile flashed again. "Say hi for me. His name is Jim."

■　　■　　■　　■　　■

There was a storm coming. Josh could feel the change in the wind as he approached the commuter jet. It was going to be a bumpy flight to Savannah. Kevin, the flight attendant, smiled as Josh climbed the stairs.

"Seems we're flying all over the place these days."

"Ha, you don't know the half of it," Josh replied.

Kevin simply nodded and kept smiling. The plane door closed. Josh flopped into one of the leather cushion seats and shut his eyes.

.　　.　　.　　.　　.

"He was a good man. He loved you, he loved me," Ellen spoke softly, caressing the little boy's curly hair.

Josh's young eyes gazed up at his mom's face.

"Why, mommy? Why did he leave us?"

The child was barely six years old, and yet, he could recite the story from memory. He just preferred to listen to his mom tell it. It seemed less scary then.

He leaned back in her arms as she recounted the story. A father who loved the outdoors, the hunting season was his favorite time. One of his best friends was hunting with him and failed to check his blind spot. Tears fell from Ellen's eyes, and ran down Josh's little head. He choked back his own hot tears.

"I wish daddy was still here. I hate Bryce!"

Bryce was the other hunter.

"No, no," Ellen kissed her little boy's hair. "We mustn't hate."

"Why did it happen? Why was my daddy killed?" Josh looked pleadingly at his mother.

Ellen did not know how to answer. How does one explain the loss of a father to a six-year-old boy? How would she explain the heartache she felt every day thinking about the memories her son would never get to enjoy?

Throwing the ball in the backyard; buying a bag of peanut M&Ms to share while running errands; eating ice cream cones on a casual trip to the hardware store. How he would never get to experience the thrill of hearing his dad say, 'I'm proud of you, son'? His father would never see him graduate; never see him marry. Her son had been robbed of all these and more by a .308 caliber round of ammunition.

"No one knows, Josh," Ellen clutched him, hugging him close. "But everything has a purpose. Absolutely everything."

"How do you know, mommy? How is losing daddy a purpose?"

She gave a soft, sad smile while she answered, confidence ringing in her voice. "We have to trust and believe. Never stop believing."

.　　.　　.　　.　　.

Josh woke as the plane hit turbulence. He blankly stared out of the plane's window. They were up high – clouds blocked his ability to see anything else. They also lured him, casting a net of drowsiness. He slowly shut his eyes. His eyelids flittered a couple times, then nothing.

·   ·   ·

The dreams returned – but this time, he was older. He was standing in his mom's house. She was older too, gray hairs starting to show on the corners of her head. Josh stepped towards her and put his hands over hers.

"It's going to be okay, mom. We'll beat this!"

"Oh, Josh," she gave a soft laugh. "You've become an optimist."

"The doctor said nothing was for sure."

"Yes, but he also said to realize the chances of beating this are nearly impossible."

"You can't go blind, mom. You just can't!"

"Blindness isn't death, my son," Ellen smiled at Josh, squinting ever so slightly to focus on him. She lifted her hands and placed them gently on his face. "Never to have seen would've been the pity. But I have seen so much, and I will continue to see more! Just because I'll be blind, doesn't mean I can't see."

"Why?" Josh cursed, moving away from his mom. "Why do bad things always happen to me?"

"They happen to everyone, Josh. There is purpose…"

His mom's voice faded, and Josh became acutely aware of sirens wailing. Someone was panting. Feet were hitting the pavement in rapid stride – running as fast as they could. He suddenly realized it was himself running, and he was no longer in Colorado. It was a familiar area, though. He rounded the corner and saw the car. He felt sick to his stomach.

■   ■   ■   ■

Josh's eyes fluttered open again. He had enough of the nightmares. He was not going to think about *that*. It was bad enough he had been dreaming about his mom.

Leaning back, he moodily stared out of the small plane window. The clouds broke, and below he could see a packed highway – tourists jammed in like canned sardines. *Feel bad for those suckers. I hate parking lot driving.* Traffic was overly congested in any major metropolitan area. Overpopulation was no longer a liberal ideology spouted off by mad scientists. It was a sad reality.

Another bump as the plane hit a pocket of air. *So much for the "no-turbulence" marketing trends.* Airlines and charters both claimed that one could enjoy a perfectly safe, smooth flight. They were even allowing people to bring their own beverages on board.

Josh had heard the tall tales of flying before September 11, 2001 – years ago – when people brought practically anything on board. Then things changed. Flying became different. One could only take certain items, only say certain things. Forget about threats of hijacking; even whispers of bombs, guns, or knives would detain a person. Yesterday's world had certainly been different.

The engine cut to half-power as the jet prepared to land. The mission ahead: he would find out the truth, regardless of the obstacles. Whether there was a purpose in everything or not, one thing was fundamentally clear – bad things happen. And he would be damned if he did not figure out just why.

ELEVEN

Josh wore dark shades over his eyes as he walked the riverfront. It was hot. The sun was beating down mercilessly. He wondered how people tolerated it – living in this type of heat for so many months. Minnesota – just like Colorado – suited him perfectly.

He had arrived the afternoon before and uncovered nothing. Very few people shared details other than the already widely circulated story. The woman had the Disease. She was screaming and waving a knife. She was threatening to kill people. Nobody mentioned anything that helped clue him in on the disturbing conversation Sam had scrubbed from the audio file.

The hotel where Josh was staying was the same one where the deceased woman had stayed. The place of lodging was crawling with police, detectives, reporters, and social media purveyors. *#TheDisease* was trending – there were dollars to be made. The entire circumstance maddened him. New outbreaks in society were not uncommon, and despite the bizarre symptoms now surfacing, they scarcely provided a strong reason to instantly label it *the Disease*.

Why name it so quickly? With such authority? There is so little we know. But few people are exerting an abundance of common sense these days, so… A wry smile crept over him.

The trending increased the difficulty and challenged Josh in finding the morph. Yesterday ended without so much as a glimmer of the origin story. So today, he had set out with renewed purpose.

"I might be fighting every morph possible, but at some point, the legend dissolves, and the truth emerges," he muttered out loud, trying to self inspire. It was a tall order.

Social media had changed the world a decade ago. The Canadian murder-suicide video already had more views than the population of China. And as Carrie Haselow had said, the live footage broadcast via InstaStream of the Georgia lady's death was the rage. It was dominating the internet. Still, were they linked? And if so, how?

The shades gleamed from bright sunlight as Josh's eyes slowly moved, scrutinizing the crowds of people. Did any of them have an idea of what was going on? What was happening? He doubted it. One thing he knew was bona fide. *Fear grips them. I can feel it. That's all morphing is anyway: fear-mongering.*

Josh began walking again, his feet silently moving along the cobbled walks. He would have to send his report over to Sam. The man was waiting for it. And John Stevens, he was probably already having conniptions – Josh had not sent a thing the day before.

■   ■   ■   ■   ■

"Ain't a word of truth," the homeless man covered in dirt and grime spoke with a knowing air. He cast a sullied look at Josh. "That ladey was jest sitting thar when – whamo! She bolted like a darn cat. Started screaming sumthing fierce. I 'spect she being manippelated by aliens or sumthing like dat."

Josh nodded as he carefully listened. The filthy man wiped a torn shirt sleeve across his nose, a streak of snot trailing behind it. Inwardly, Josh winced. He tried to maintain a clean lifestyle.

"You think she had the Disease?" he asked. Maybe asking obvious questions was a better way of rooting out the truth.

"What else wud she have? Gumnabbit boy. Don't ask such stuuupid questions!" The poorly-clad man looked irritated and ambled away at a snail's pace.

Nothing but complete and absolute belief in the Disease, Josh sighed. He should have wrapped his report already. *Perhaps I am over-analyzing. Maybe the Disease is the origin story.*

It felt like all the interviews had been a complete waste of time. They all seemed so similar – joined in proclaiming a new terrifying disease that would exterminate humanity. Something of that caliber, of such severity –

just popping up? It seemed unlikely. He shot a quick text to Sam and waited. The handheld chirped. It was not from Sam.

WHAT DO YOU KNOW?

The number was unknown. Josh was intrigued.

ABOUT WHAT?

He waited for the response, a few seconds went by.

YOU KNOW WHAT.

"Haha," Josh laughed out loud. "I'm too old for games."

Pocketing the handheld, he walked ten yards then stopped. A shop sign caught his attention. The name of the store in large script across the front window: *Savannah Souvenirs*. Carrie Haselow, the woman he had met outside Sam's office, mentioned that place. A smile spread across his features. Walking over to the door, he opened it.

. . . . .

The interior of the shop was unassuming enough. On the left side, was a random assortment of postcards, coffee mugs, beer coolers, key fobs for entry systems, and even a small section of ball caps. On the right side, 3D printed tee shirts boasted tourist catchphrases and attractions from the greater Savannah area.

A soda cooler was located near the back of the store and directly in front of Josh there was a vast assortment of pita chips, Fit & Health bars, dried fruit, nuts, pouches of avocado, and a single bag of classic potato chips. Josh smiled. He did not eat fried food that often. Grabbing the bag of chips, he moved toward the shop's front counter. A bald, fat man stood behind it, wearing a pleasant smile.

"Will that be all?"

Josh examined the contents of the wall behind the counter, and suddenly clapped his head.

"Man, I almost forgot. I'd like some chamomile tea – chamomile cinnamon."

"Of course, yes," Jim Burillo turned and grabbed one of the decorative tins. Turning back towards his customer, he winked. "For a lady friend?"

"My god, Jim, all you think about is sex!" a female voice barked rudely. Anna came from behind the chip display, and dropped a box of avocado pouches on the sales counter. "You embarrass me."

Josh blinked, surprised by the sudden, harsh outburst. The shopkeeper held back tears as he licked his dry lips.

"You can ignore her. She doesn't mean to be so rude."

Josh nodded as he watched the retreating slim figure of Anna.

"Yours?" he asked.

"No," Jim sighed. He started to wipe down the shop counter, which was perfectly clean. "My niece."

"Works for you?"

Jim smiled to himself. He liked the questions. It was not every day a stranger would pop in and ask personal questions.

"Of sorts. She lives with me, and this is my shop."

"Ah."

Josh was content with the information, the shop owner was not finished.

"Came to live with me after her mom died – overdose. Took a double eightball."

"Holy cow." Josh's eyes widened.

"It runs in the family. My mom, brother, sister – her mom," Jim nodded in the direction where Anna had gone.

The longer the shopkeeper rambled, the more intrigued Josh grew listening. He wondered if this was the man Carrie Haselow had mentioned back at SEH headquarters. It was easy to see why she would remember him. He appeared to be a likable guy.

Jim would not stop talking. The floodgates had opened. He shared the story of how his mom had died, then his brother, and lastly his little sister – Anna's mom. Drugs were the driving force behind all three. It was a sad tale. With the heavy sadness in his own past, Josh empathized with the man. He did not have any interest in sharing his stories, though, so he asked a question.

"Tell me, how did you recover from these sudden deaths? How did you handle the grief of losing three loved ones?"

"It wasn't so sudden, not with my family," Jim replied. "I saw it coming."

"Right. That's what I'm struggling with," said Josh. "All the rage today seems to be talk of the disease. Yet, a disease is an illness; it has to run its course. How could it just suddenly pop up? And where are the families of these victims? There does not seem to be any voice or statements from relatives or close friends. Almost like they didn't exist," Josh's voice faded; the thought fascinated him. Why weren't there any surviving family or friends?

Scowling, Jim spun away. He tossed the towel aside; unintentionally being rude to his guest. The shopkeeper did not want to talk about these types of things, especially with someone he scarcely knew. Yet, as always, he could not help himself.

"Crisis actors," he blurted out.

Josh's eyebrows lifted. His plan was working.

"You seem like a smart guy. I need to send a report back to my team. What do you know?"

There was a pause, then the short fat man spoke, his back to Josh. "What I know is the woman didn't kill herself."

The truthseeker's eyes opened wider. *This is a new twist! What else does he know?* His mind started racing. He took a quick small breath, tempering his eagerness. *Patience, Josh.*

"I know, I know," Jim slightly turned his head, so his voice would carry better to his customer. "The reports all say that. They claim she killed herself and was threatening other people. But that ain't the truth." Jim turned all the way around, and leaned over the counter, getting as close as he could to Josh's face. He then whispered. "Someone shot her."

Josh did not blink. This was his chance. Without skipping a beat, "Who?"

"I don't know," Jim exhaled. He pulled back and placed his hands on the front counter. "Someone in a dark suit with dark glasses; everyone wears 'em nowadays, so who knows." Biting down on his lower lip, he cut his eyes at Josh. "But I tell you, she was shot by that man. Clear as day."

There was no reason for the shopkeeper to lie, Josh surmised. He seemed truthful enough. He had been open about his past; there was no reason to suspect he would make the story up. Was the alleged shooter from the government? Josh recalled the audio scrub. It certainly seemed to imply military involvement. Then he remembered the seditious words of Lieut. Rhianna Adams. Was there a kernel of truth in them? Suddenly, he realized the shopkeeper was still talking.

"I tell you, sir, something is going on. Just the other day, I heard on the broadcast that there's some strange building happening. Construction of a massive city, and not just one, but several!"

"A city?"

"Yeah, but underground."

Josh checked his audible scoff. This was not the first time he'd heard the rumor. There was, in fact, an underground bunker not far from SEH's headquarters in northern Virginia. It had been promoted among vast conspiracy theories to be a secret city, a holding cell for the real rulers of America – the theories were wide and far. In reality, it was just an old safe house left over from the Cold War days.

"What broadcast?" Josh attempted to act interested.

"TruthX."

Hiding his smile, Josh took a half-step away from the counter. The notorious talk show was a hit among those who aligned with the alt-movements in America. They had little evidence and much conjecture in all of their "news briefings."

"And that isn't all," Jim was oblivious to Josh's skepticism. "I was online the other day, and saw that in Africa there have been entire villages overrun with the Disease. People killing their own families; drinking their blood!"

"Gross." Josh was mildly amused. His job was to find the origin story, he was a truthseeker. He knew a farce when he saw one. Yet, something kept him listening to the outgoing shopkeeper.

"It may seem it's all new with Canada, India, and what's happened here the last few days, but I tell you, there's more happening than they let on."

"Who's they?"

"The media, the government, everyone!" Jim's fat fingers shook with excitement. He had not felt this much energy in ages. Coming around the counter, he put a hand on Josh's shoulder. "Do you have time for me to show you something?"

"All day." Josh smiled in response.

This is fun. I really shouldn't be egging him on. He felt a tinge of reproach. He ignored it.

Jim led him over to a small TV projector, and Josh whistled. He had not seen anything so old since he visited a thrift store back in St. Paul. Those places always had outdated tech available for cheap dollars. Jim noticed his expression.

"It's a hobby of mine," the shopkeeper explained, motioning at the old TV. "I love old technology. Besides, they can't hear us then," he whispered, pointing upwards.

Josh nodded, and silently gave a thumbs-up.

The screen flickered on, and Jim adjusted the antenna.

"Give it a second."

Suddenly, vivid images burst onto the small screen. It was mayhem. People were running in a street, not just a handful but an entire crowd!

They were pushing and shoving others as they ran. Jim pressed a fat thumb to the volume button. The noise grew louder.

"Here *they* come," he pointed excitedly at the top of the screen.

Josh peered closer, wondering what 'they' were. He saw a swarm of people, running a few paces behind the rest of the fleeing crowd; bumping into and jumping over each other. Something looked different about them. Their body movements were loose – as if disconnected. One of them bounced off a moving truck like a rubber ball. Another suddenly grabbed the camera and screamed into it.

Both men instinctively jumped back. Josh's heart was beating fast. He looked at the older man.

"What was that?"

"A zombie."

Josh gave a short laugh. "No, seriously, what?"

Jim stared back without blinking. The younger man realized his new acquaintance was serious.

"You think those were zombies?" Josh tried to keep the incredulous out of his voice.

"What else could they be? What else is the Disease? Even sick human beings don't behave like that. I know there's some newfangled theory that this is caused by sunlight. But this isn't new. There have been reports of this for some time now."

Fear-mongering. Josh was angry. *The number one way to spread propaganda.* Harnessing his anger, he smiled pleasantly at Jim.

"Perhaps, but that's why I have a job. I need to find the origin of these stories."

"Oh! I can help with that," Jim offered proudly.

He walked back to the front of his store, Josh trailing behind. The shopkeeper stopped at the counter, and reached down. On one side, the magazines were neatly sorted into various rows. Picking up a few copies of the leading tabloid magazines, he turned around and handed the magazines to Josh. By this time, Jim was breathing heavily from the exertion.

"You'll find everything you need here. It's on the house," he tried to wink.

"Thank you, that is very generous." Josh was genuinely appreciative. He turned to leave the store, but then thought of something. "The TV – was that a live stream?"

"Oh no," Jim shook his head. "They loop it."

"They?"

Jim shook his head again. "I don't know. It's been playing for a few weeks now."

"Do you know where it happened?"

"Nope, don't know that either."

Josh gave a small grin, and nodded. "It's nice meeting you. I'm Josh by the way."

"Jim – Jim Burillo." The bald, fat man extended a warm hand.

Josh shook the offered hand in farewell. Clutching the magazines close, he tipped them towards the shopkeeper as he walked out the door.

"Thanks for these, Jim."

Once outside, he gave a low whistle and slid his shades back over his eyes.

"Wow," he quietly muttered. "That shopkeeper is nice and friendly – but bat crazy. What's this world coming to?"

TWELVE

Tabloids. Years ago, they had been rejected by mainstream media as nothing more than gossip mills. Such as the time they proudly broke a story saying a former president and first lady were getting divorced; or when they claimed to reveal the truth behind a disgraced actor's lifestyle. The flashy pages spewed forth provocative photos and sensationalized writing. Regardless of their story, much was left to be desired in the way of substance.

In the digital age, not much changed. The stories – still sensationalized – focused on driving clicks, rather than truth. Respected journalists rejected anything produced by the publications as exaggeration or fabrication.

While Josh was not a journalist, skepticism flowed freely as he opened the magazines. He wondered if anything resembling truth would materialize. At least it would provide him with some entertainment on the flight back to SEH.

Flipping through the magazines' pages, he began to notice the content was filled with whisperings of strange happenings. They were crazy, to be sure. But they were framed as absolute, and not conjecture. A few months ago, Josh would not have wasted a second of his time reading them. Today was different though, because of yesterday.

A chirp on his handheld pulled his attention away from the tabloids. Tossing them aside, he pulled out the device.

BE CAREFUL WHAT YOU READ

It was the unknown number again. He thumbed a hasty response.

LIKE THIS TEXT?

For a moment, Josh thought maybe someone was pulling a distasteful joke. Sam crossed his mind, but his colleague was too serious about this assignment to goof off.

YOU KNOW WHAT I MEAN

The reply piqued his curiosity. He looked about the cabin.

Kevin was nowhere to be seen. The door to the cockpit was closed, as was the rear entry to the galley. Whoever was sending these messages probably wasn't on the plane, but he didn't know for sure.

Picking up the magazines, Josh stashed them in his briefcase. He would read them later. Pulling out his i-Beam, he dragged his fingers right. The device powered on. A snap of his thumb and forefinger, and there was a flicker, then a bright red keyboard appeared.

For ten seconds, he considered altering his report on Savannah. Sam probably already knew it was nothing – the source material was going to be elsewhere. *John Stevens won't be happy. Screw him.* Josh knew what he should do.

He tapped send.

■　　■　　■　　■　　■

Luke's brow furrowed in concentration as he poured over the stash of folders in front of him. The papers summed up all the information Brenda had found on *Diabolus*. The incident in China had been buried, and he was not aware of any science or medical department that had examined it. It was too bizarre to be considered an actual illness. It was an anomaly. A spike. A grin appeared on his face. *It will hold some answers then.*

Brenda stood in the doorway. He saw her out of the corner of his eye.

"Well, nothing beats a pile of crap to dig through."

A smile flashed across the intern's face. "Metaphoric and literal too."

"*Diabolus* first appeared in China, and I found Dr. Grafton referenced it once more in Africa, some 18 months later. Is this a coincidence or are they somehow linked?" Luke spoke out loud, not directly to Brenda, but as he thought it. "And if they are linked, then how?"

He drummed his fingers on the edge of the desk. A frown appeared on his face. Brenda walked further into the room, stepping close to the folders.

"Genetics?"

"Thought of that, and already checked. No. Honestly, couldn't be more different."

"Location?"

Luke shook his head. *China and Africa are literally thousands of miles apart. Sometimes the questions Brenda poses...*

"Shared interest?" she broke into his musing.

"That's interesting. Like what?" the scientist glanced quizzically at Brenda.

"I don't know," the girl shrugged her shoulders. "Maybe a mutual interest in astronomy or a hobby like quilting..." her voice faded.

"You're kidding me. What would astronomy or quilting have to do with this?" Luke was flabbergasted at the idea.

"You don't have to look at me like that," said Brenda, her shoulders dropping. She looked to Luke as an older brother, and his harsh tone hurt her. "It's just an idea. Obviously, I didn't mean *those* two things specifically."

"Fair enough. I mean if the two are linked – we're going to have to get pretty weird."

They stood still, concentrating on the papers scattered about. The only sound was a gentle whir of the solar-powered clock on Luke's desk. Its small gears rhythmically moved as the seconds passed. Rubbing a hand over his chin, Luke contemplated the situation. Somehow, someway, these two events had to be connected. The particulars in the incident, even down to the gruesome details of the death, were all too similar.

Suddenly, Brenda's face brightened.

"You know what you should do, Luke?"

He looked at her, and could not help but smile when he saw her countenance. Sometimes Brenda looked so cute. He did not think this in a romantic way, but rather appreciating the girl for who she was.

"You should call her."

"Call her?" he asked, unsure of Brenda's meaning.

"Call that girl – Tessa."

His face went red, and he bit down on his lower lip. *That girl. Of course, Brenda would want me to see her; always trying to set me up.*

"I think we have more important things to do, than find a date for Luke."

"Haha," giggled Brenda. "I love when you get all flustered, and speak in the third person."

An intercom buzz sounded from the room outside the office. Brenda began retracing her steps towards the door.

"Call her," she yelled back at him, extending her pinky and thumb while pressing them against her face like an old-fashioned telephone.

Luke sighed. There was no reason to call the woman, he had too much to do. Solving the *Diabolus* puzzle was going to take time. *Then again, I've already spent two days, and it's going to take much longer. No harm can come in taking a break.*

His mind was made up.

．　　．　　．　　．　　．

The elevator was broken. It seemed it was broken more days than not. Forced to take the stairs, Josh bounded up to the floor where the Morphing Division was located inside SEH headquarters.

Fresh off the plane that landed forty-five minutes ago, he was ready to tie up loose ends and head home. It seemed like ages since he had slept in his own bed, though the reality was it had been only a few days.

"Here you are!" the excited voice of Sam Walters corralled Josh's attention.

Emerging from another hallway, Sam grabbed his arm and steered Josh off to the side of the corridor. Holding up a drive, he waggled it in front of the truthseeker's unblinking eyes

"Have you seen this yet, man?"

"No. Should I have?"

"Well, you couldn't, anyway. There's nothing on here."

"And that should matter, because?" Josh was at a loss for what Sam was talking about.

"Because that means it has been deleted!" Sam continued talking, and Josh held up an interrupting hand.

"Slow down, dude. I have no idea what you're talking about. What's been deleted?"

"Like I was saying, this drive had the data from those Phantom sightings we investigated earlier this year. All that info is gone! And the report from those incidents in London – I can't find it anymore either."

Josh had forgotten about London. There had been two unrelated incidents involving mentally ill people smashing windows and beating up folks. He had not thought much of it at the time because the team was preoccupied with the Phantom sightings in Kentucky. He shrugged.

"Well, who cares about Kentucky anyway? That proved to be nothing more than a dead end. And just because you can't find the London report, doesn't mean it's gone. Why does it matter?"

Before Sam could answer, a grating voice cut in.

"Welcome back, Josh," John Stevens was strolling down the same corridor where Sam had pulled Josh. "What's going on, Sam?" he added, seeing the field coordinator's agitated countenance.

"I was just telling Josh about the missing data."

"Ah!" John nodded knowingly as he looked at Josh. "I told Sam earlier, I'm sure it's nothing. Most likely, just misplaced."

"I *know* this is the drive, John," Sam waved the device he was holding. "I handled it every day during that project."

For a moment, there was an awkward silence. Josh hated the feeling. He knew Sam probably was not wrong. He also knew John Stevens was pigheaded and always had to be right. Of course, this dynamic had the potential to create situations filled with high tension. This moment was one of those times.

"Kentucky was nothing, London proved to be unrelated to what we were actually dispatched on. I mean some poor schmucks escaped from a psych ward? C'mon, Sam, you are supposed to find the morph – not create one! That's all I have to say, regardless of where the actual drive is." John spoke dismissively and with a tone of finality. Finished, he resumed his stroll down the corridor.

Josh watched their department chief go, and then turned to Sam. He wore an expression that asked, 'well?'

"I know this is it, Josh. Why would John deny it? Somehow the data on here has been wiped. Couple the last two incidents, and our missing reports from London and Kentucky, I am beginning to question what's going on."

There were very few people in the world Josh trusted. Sam was one of them. Not only had the man been his field coordinator ever since he came to SEH, but Sam was also one of the only people who had met both his mother and Amanda. He was the only person who had stood by Josh's side at the funerals.

"Rabid people," Sam mused as he bit his fingernails, a stress habit Josh abhorred. "The behavior..."

"Look, I don't know what to say, Sam. You've been questioning the narrative this entire time. And to be honest, I too have been asking myself questions about these recent assignments. Like what happened with the helicopter in New York? I mean that almost killed me! And then in Georgia, even India – copycat or not – something just doesn't add up."

He motioned Sam to draw closer and lowered his voice.

"In Savannah, I met this crazy old guy. Very friendly, very nice, but crazy. He showed me a looped video of an attack that he claimed were zombies – they weren't. I did recognize something in the video, though. A mechanism that we came across before – synchronized actions."

Synchronized actions. The Achilles heel of morphed stories. A truthseeker could spot the difference between spontaneous movement and synchronized actions in a moment's glance. Some people focused on the subjects in an incident – hence the term crisis actor. Josh thought that was a farce. The victims were always real, but the perpetrators? The agitations which caused the reaction? That's where truth separated from fiction. To be sure, a truthseeker might have to study it for a while, but the facts would not stay hidden for long. Synchronized actions.

"What's the point of looping a video like that except to spread fear," Sam began as if asking a question, but he ended up making a statement. The two men nodded their heads in agreement. "But why spread the fear? And fear of what?"

"That's what we'll find out, Sam. I'm not sold this is some mass hysteria cover-up, or that someone has an agenda," he thought of Rhianna Adam's words. "But I don't like seeing or experiencing one thing, and then be told it's something else. They aren't peddling alternative facts, but rather direct contradictions to what happened. Like New York, Canada, or your missing file drives."

"Shh," Sam motioned with his finger. "Not so loud, Josh. You don't know who might be listening."

Josh shrugged. Despite his brilliance and critical thinking, Sam was starting to sound paranoid. The truthseeker thought his coworker too smart for that.

"I'll take my chances."

"Crap, I entirely forgot why this all mattered," Sam exclaimed.

"Aside from rabid people?" Josh asked, a hint of snarkiness in his voice.

"It wasn't," Sam was defensive. "It's about the missing files on Kentucky – which is what I meant to say all along. There was another phantom sighting. I asked if we should send a team out, I was told under no circumstances."

"Where was it?" Josh's curiosity was aroused.

Sam's eagerness ebbed. "Kentucky."

"What makes you think this is anything different? Probably a good call, since it'd be a waste of resources."

"Maybe…" Sam was distracted. He reached out, and grabbed Josh's arm again, starting forward down the hall. "C'mon, I wanna show you something."

The two made their way along the corridor, and then turned and went down another hallway. They passed by various departments. Applied sciences, mechanical engineering, even a food test lab. Pharma Group was the conspicuous missing division. They had their own headquarters in San Francisco.

Hurrying through the building, they neared a corner; Sam pushed open the door to his office. Snapping his fingers, a bright holograph light appeared.

"Display." Sam's voice was clear and crisp.

A blue and red light came on, and immediately half the room was canvassed by a projection displaying all sorts of information. Geographic and atmospheric maps, research reports, streaming video clips, news broadcasts, even social media posts. Sam's personalized filter was sorting through millions of posts as they occurred. Meanwhile, the ten panels around his desk began feeding mass quantities of data into a queue. It was as if a media player merged with a search engine. The result was mind-blowing.

"Sometimes, I forget how cool your office is."

"I know, right?" Sam breathed exuberantly. "Most processing power in the building."

He thumbed a few things aside, and then pinching his fingers, gradually spread them out, zooming in on a particular feed.

"This is a report I've been working on. I've been tracking power grids across the country."

"Why?"

"Because if something doesn't make sense, you look for the anomalies."

Sam's behavior was beginning to worry Josh. He knew the man was skeptical and questioning the purpose – the origination of their missions. Despite his own questions though, this covert research conflicted with Josh. Skepticism was not tolerated anymore. It was one thing to dismiss a morphed story, but to actually disbelieve the official record was another thing.

"Did you find one?" Josh asked.

Sam responded by merely waving his hand towards the projector.

"What am I looking at?"

"A power grid in Kentucky. The phantom sighting just reported was in this area – and I know the last ones were too. Only this time," Sam emphasized his words. "The entire grid lost power, yet, *nothing* actually lost power."

The confused expression on Josh's face caused Sam to elaborate.

"It should've been a blackout. Nothing should've been working, yet...*everything* continued to run normally as if nothing had happened. That doesn't make sense." Sam's voice began to go faster as his excitement grew. "Nor does the fact that the grid *we're* located on – has been drawing three even four times the amount of normal power. I've also located several other pockets of extraordinary power draws across the globe – places like Russia, Syria, the United Kingdom – as well as other regions here in the States."

Josh stared at the display as Sam spoke. He could not deny the facts being presented. The new information did raise questions. Why would the power grid in northern Virginia be drawing so much? It was not even summer.

"How long has this been going on for?"

"Several months, I just found a way to hack the grid's record database though, so..."

"You need a break, Sam." Josh was surprised at how assured his voice sounded. "You're right, this doesn't seem to make much sense, but I do know one thing," he stepped next to Sam and looked him in the eye. "You've been working your tail off, and you are going to burn out. I do not want to see that."

"Sure, sure," Sam brushed off his friend's concern, and moved his hand quickly to the left. The display shut off. "Why won't they give us an answer? Why is everyone ignoring this?"

"They aren't ignoring the events, just some of the details. It might mean nothing."

"What if the discards – worthless, useless events that we categorize away – are in actuality part of something much bigger? Like sewing – or quilting! One small weave in the fabric can be so significant to the pattern."

It was a good question, and in all fairness, demanded an answer. Josh did not have one.

"I don't know," he said, staring into his friend's troubled eyes. He was worried about his colleague. He had so many questions of his own these last few days, but Sam's words overshadowed them. "I have to believe there's more to all of this than meets the eye, but..."

"Okay," Sam's demeanor suddenly and strangely changed, and he became upbeat again. "I didn't mean to drag you into the crazy whirling brain of mine, Josh. Go home, get some rest. You've been killing it lately, man. I'll let you know if I hear anything else on this." Sam waved his hand at where the holograph display had been.

Surprised by the sudden mood change, Josh merely nodded in reply and walked out of the office. He could hear Sam muttering to himself.

"Maybe I still have that old report from China? Gruesome outbreak. Man, what did I name that again?"

THIRTEEN

July

The lone car made its way along the deserted highway. The car's sleek, glossy blue paint rippled in the hot heat of summer and its shiny hubcaps glistened from the bright sunshine. It was a newer car, the make from the previous year. It rolled smoothly down the interstate highway.

The windows on the car were down, and Josh bobbed his head along in time with the hip-hop music blaring from the sound system.

"I just *wanna go* back, *wanna go* back; just wanna see you – *one more time!*" He punctuated the words as he sang. "Why, oh why, did you choose *to* leave! I just wanna go *back*."

Looking about as he exited the main highway, Josh shook his head. The area was once a prominent shopping district – stores, restaurants, and eateries – removed just ten miles from the hustle and bustle of downtown Minneapolis. Now though, it was an abandoned area. In one parking lot, a slew of shopping carts were jammed together in one corner. Another lot had weeds starting to grow through the cracks in the asphalt.

He checked his rearview mirror, more out of habit than anything else. Behind him, nothing was to be seen but road. His eyes traveled around the empty stores and parking lots.

Of course, there's nobody. Why would there be? Haven't seen a soul for miles.

Nearing the intersection of the off-ramp and main road, Josh quickly glanced left and then right. No one was coming. Turning the wheel counterclockwise, he accelerated and proceeded to drive through the intersection. The hanging stoplights above glared a bright red.

The blue sedan was now on a less-traveled side road. The surrounding area had a sprawling suburban feel. Traffic conditions remained the same as the major highway though, devoid of any vehicles save the blue one.

Josh whistled along with the satellite feed – playing Beethoven's *5th Symphony*. Slowly applying pressure to the brakes, he nonchalantly turned the automobile onto a side street. A few more blocks, a quick swerve onto another street, and he pulled alongside the curb and stopped. A lush green lawn ran from the curbing, up to the front of the small, white and brick home.

Stepping from the car, Josh stretched his arms and legs. "Don't much feel like," a yawned escaped him, and whatever else he was going to say remained unspoken.

The car door shut, and he started up the driveway towards the entrance to his house. The sky was cloudless. Green leaves covered the trees. Somewhere in the distance, a bird chirped. Reaching the front door, he fumbled with his keys, trying to find the right one. Suddenly, he stopped, and became aware of the ambient noises in the atmosphere. The air seemed soundless.

Pirouetting about, he surveyed the neighborhood. Its appearance quite different from when he had first moved to the home a few years ago.

For one, there very few people outside, and those who were, busily engaged in particular activities. Like mowing their lawn or walking the dog. A young teenage girl was jogging on the street, an earpiece carefully hidden, just visible in the middle of her left ear. Large sunglasses completely hid her eyes and much of her face.

Looks like Mickey Mouse.

Josh looked down at his right hand; the front door key still firmly clasped between his thumb and forefinger. Shifting his feet, he pivoted, and slid the key into the lock. With a twist of the handle, he pushed it open.

He stared at his living room. The small table where he would set his beer; the faded futon where he would so often recline while trying to relax. The fireplace on the opposite wall.

Life's a joy.

Forcefully smiling to himself, Josh threw his jacket onto the futon, and walked into the kitchen. Dishes piled the sink, the floor had not been scrubbed in ages, and the smell coming from the corner told him he forgotten to take out the trash before he left on his trip. To top it off, the beer bottle he had finished the day before he left, was still sitting on the counter.

Gotta get a grip on this, dude.

He grabbed the hanging pull strings, and yanked the garbage bag from the trash can. It burst open, spilling its rotting contents all over the floor.

He cursed out loud. "Why? What have I done?"

Wearily setting the remaining shreds of the garbage bag down, Josh rested against the counter. The bright morning sun snuck but a few drops of golden rays in through the slits on the drawn shutters.

"Need some light in here," he said to himself.

He flipped on the kitchen light. There was a brilliant flash, and then darkness.

"Could things get any worse? Really?"

Frustrated, he muttered a stream of profanities as he stumbled forward in the darkness. He just wanted to rest and not think about *life*. Jerking open one of the kitchen cupboards, he clumsily pawed about until he located a spare bulb.

Pulling a chair up to the fixture, he climbed on top of it, and slowly unscrewed the burnt-out light. Carefully installing the new one, a slight glow emitted at first, and then a bright beam burst forth.

That's better.

Josh stepped from the chair, sighing as he examined the mess below. Sluggishly bending over, he started to retrieve the spilled contents of the garbage bag.

That trip was a complete waste of time! Only positive was the drive home.

He chuckled out loud. It struck him funny that the drive home would be the best part. Then he remembered something. The smile faded.

■   ■   ■   ■   ■

The water fountains were not the primary attraction at Station Square, but they were definitely the featured one. Many long nights had been spent by families, couples, and lonely singles watching as the lights below the fountains illuminated and danced through the spraying water – changing colors and synchronized to music. The atmosphere could be festive, reflective, happy, sad, inspirational, or hypnotic. It was the perfect place to have a date, and that is why this particular afternoon found Luke sitting on a bench with a female companion.

"You seriously tried chasing him away?"

"Yes," Luke answered sheepishly.

He was mesmerized by the redhead's beauty. She took away his stress, made him forget about the complications and nightmare of finding a cure. She caused him to relax and let go. He was so happy he had called her that day long ago in April. When he told Brenda as much, she had thrown her arms around him, and told him it was the happiest day of her life.

"A squirrel? You tried chasing a squirrel?"

The merry laughter from Tessa Morgan broke Luke's trance, and sent warm chills down his chest. He liked the girl a lot. She was smart, friendly, and beautiful. She was worth the call.

"So did you catch him?" Tessa's long lashes complimented her glistening hazel eyes.

"C'mon," Luke was embarrassed. "Be real."

"I am," The woman laughed again. The smile on her face grew as she leaned back and tossed her long hair.

It was a pleasant day. The sun was mostly hidden behind clouds, and what few people were strolling through Station Square, kept to themselves and their electronic devices.

"I'm thrilled we ran into each other that day in the hall."

Luke spoke impulsively. He regretted it. He wanted to say it differently, sound as educated as he was and less like high school. Still, he had just come from the hall, and the memory waxed strong.

"So am I."

"My life…can be very boring."

"So you've said," she giggled again. She looked away, and watched a couple pigeons fighting over a scrap of sandwich. "But you don't talk about it much," she added demurely, as if anticipating a shutdown response.

"Well, it's pretty lame. My job is just a bunch of boring science stuff."

"C'mon. That is so cliché."

Luke chuckled. "Maybe, but isn't that most of life? Cliché sayings packaged in marketing bits, greeting cards, and even art?"

"Wow, aren't you the philosopher."

Tessa was mocking him. He knew it. However, the rush he received when they verbally sparred made for stupendous flirting. He could not help himself. The last three months had been busy, stressful, and ever-changing. The University's Department of IID took a significant blow with Dr. Grafton's passing. Melinda Gore had challenged the Research Team to strength their resolve and dedication in finding a cure for the Disease.

Luke himself was doubtful. By abandoning their aggression, he figured the University did not stand a chance against TYM or Pharma Group for first-finder privileges. The Research Team operated separate of IID – as well as Research Operations – but the rippling effect of losing Dr. Grafton coupled with the onslaught of the Disease, caused the senior leadership of those departments to turn to one of its brightest alumni – Melinda Gore. They promoted her to head of the Team and charged her to take control and forge ahead.

If Luke was not at such odds with the woman, he knew he would marvel at her tenacity and leadership qualities. He might disagree with her, and find her to be difficult and blasted methodical, but he could not overlook her scientific capabilities. The rest of the Research Team naturally gravitated to her leadership, and Luke was left on the outside, looking in.

Brenda had stuck by his side, though. "Through thick and thin, I'll be here, Luke Baer," she often said. Thinking of Brenda made him smile, and it reminded him of his date.

What an incredible thing love is – it had been years since love had crossed Luke's mind. High school, he figured. In college, he was always learning, studying harder, and achieving better results. Graduate school was more of the same. His doctorate field demanded complete dedication and resolve. Love had been put on a back burner – until now.

He smiled at Tessa. Her eyes danced. Leaning forward, their lips locked. She had a sweet taste – like strawberries. It was a taste not uncommon to Luke. Her scent like a lily of the field; her bedsheets smelled like morning dew. These aroused senses he had enjoyed quite often the last few months. Even that very morning, he had woken up next to her.

Tessa pulled out of the kiss and smiled. He grinned back. He basked in the feeling that rushed over him; enraptured by her charm. He lost himself to the glorious dreamy world he lived in when he was with her. She made him forget everything terrible going on – Dr. Grafton's death, being kicked off the team by Melinda Gore, even the Disease which had changed the face of the globe.

"I think so."

"Beg pardon?" Luke pulled himself out of his fantasies; unsure what Tessa meant.

"Thinking out loud," she answered.

"C'mon," he prodded, knowing that wasn't the case. "We've been together long enough, you can tell me."

"Oh, really?"

"Yes."

There was a pause. Tessa looked at him, and batted her eyes. She leaned in, wet lips parting ever so slightly, and softly kissed Luke again.

"I love you," she said.

"I love you too."

"I know," the girl was unfazed. Standing up, she winked at him.

Luke blinked. Had he just said that? He could not believe it. No hesitation on his part. No consideration.

Is this for reals?

He watched as Tessa straightened herself, running her hands down the side of the tight skirt that hugged her hips. Her light blouse rippled in the soft summer breeze, it highlighted her perfectly shaped bosom.

She's so sexy, smart, and she said 'I love you,' he was lost in love. It was a glorious thing.

"I have to get back to work," Tessa said. "See you tonight!"

Luke nodded, and watched as she walked away. He did not know much about her job or personal life. She had not divulged many details, and he had not pressed her either. Originally from Ohio, she had moved to Pittsburgh after college, and worked downtown in the Heinz Tower doing market analysis and research. He thought she had said it was for a recruiting firm, but could not remember, nor did he care. Her mysteriousness only enticed him all the more. And besides, she was his lover – what else mattered?

Walking away from Luke, Tessa consciously put one foot in front of the other. She knew he would watch – enthralled by her swaying hips, her butt accentuated by the tight skirt. She knew he could not help it. She also knew when he had said 'I love you,' he truly meant it.

Tessa did not look back. Pulling out her handheld, she casually swiped her thumb. A message was written. She tapped the screen. A quiet swoosh emitted from the speaker.

MISSION COMPLETE. TALENT SECURE.

FOURTEEN

Home – Josh had practically forgotten where that was or what it felt like. Ever since the last day in March, when the Disease broke national headlines, it had been non-stop activity for the Morphing Division. Each day felt shorter than the one before – as if someone were manipulating the hours on a watch by turning the small knob round and round. The changes in the world and the environment had become evident in stark ways.

Although he had replaced the burnt-out bulb, the kitchen was still dimly lit. Opening the fridge, he reached in and grabbed a beer. He dragged his feet across the floor, walking back to the living room. Plopping into the futon, he audibly commanded the 3D TV to turn on. The screen momentarily flickered and then the image became sharp. Josh stared blankly at the program, oblivious of what he was watching. The volume had been previously muted, so he was sitting in silence.

A few minutes passed. Lazily turning his head, he stared out of the window. The neighborhood was as still as the living room. It was as if everything had paused, but yet time continued to flash by. Nobody was outside. *Everybody stays in now*, he mused. It was keeping with the times. The national health bulletins all communicated the same message – "Stay inside, avoid contact as much as possible with others."

He sighed. He never felt more alone in his life than he did now.

There is no longer such a thing as community. The new game is isolation.

After taking another swig of beer, Josh set the bottle down on the small table. Lying on the table's surface was a spread of magazines. They were the tabloids he had received from the *Savannah Souvenirs* shopkeeper months ago. He had read them all, and should have recycled them, but for some reason, he refrained from doing so. Picking one up now, he stared at the provocative front cover. It spewed eye-popping titling, begging people to read it.

Whoever developed this marketing scheme did a great job.

While mainstream media had portrayed the events in Canada and Georgia as the start of the Disease, the tabloids spoke a different story. They claimed the Disease had been active for months, maybe even years. Story after story, "eyewitness" accounts spoke grizzly tales of murder, suicide, and "zombie-like" behavior. One article talked about seeing Jesus Christ, and he had told her this was punishment for allowing gays and queers into normal society.

That is where they lost Josh. He could buy into murder-suicides but bring in aliens, zombies, or Jesus Christ, that is where logic ended, and sci-fi began. Suddenly, as if waking from a deep sleep, Josh shook himself and pulled his handheld out of his jeans' front pocket.

Using his thumb, he scrolled along the screen. Emails, the latest news headlines, weather, even the sporting news – what was left of it, that is. The Twins had moved a couple years back; basketball and soccer had both lived their moment and faded away. The NFL was gone – ravaged by lawsuit after lawsuit.

MAN DIES JUMPING OFF CLIFF. RESURRECTS NEXT DAY; CLAIMS THE CURE.

The headline and link jumped out to Josh. His thumb pressed down.

He was immediately disappointed. Right away, he recognized the story had been significantly morphed. Something in the story did attract his attention. The details – impeccably described. The sound bites – superbly scripted. He checked the site's address. While nearly every news outlet ran morphed stories, some were more reliable than others. The link was from a major broadcast provider.

"What's happened with truth verification these days?" he wondered out loud as he glanced down at the tabloids in front of him. The stories filling their pages were not unlike the one he had just read online.

Slowly reaching up, he thoughtfully rubbed his chin. Biting his lip, he sucked his teeth. His mother had tried breaking that habit when he was a kid. She failed miserably.

"Why are some of these stories reported, while others get buried in the exaggeration and fabrication? It's as if certain stories fit a narrative, while others don't, so they get promoted and shared. That isn't right; it doesn't make any sense."

Leaning back on the futon, he closed his eyes. He saw himself standing on a runway in the middle of a forest, Lieut. Rhianna Adams not far from him.

The lieutenant turned and looked at Josh. "What if there's a cover-up? A secret organization working to find the real answers behind this."

Her words, spoken that day, were abstract enough. The past few months, Josh heard them playinig over and over again in his mind, haunting him.

Who is this secret organization? What is their end game? If there's a cover-up, why? What's the purpose of it? A selective narrative, while doubtful, isn't outside the realm of possibility. But a global conspiracy? That's mere fantasy.

INTERESTING, ISN'T IT?

A text popped up onto his handheld. Simultaneously, the device dinged with notification an email had arrived.

"JOSH, I'VE FINISHED A PRELIMINARY SUMMARY. I WASN'T SURE IF I SHOULD EVEN SEND IT. GIVE A LOOK AND LET ME KNOW WHAT YOU THINK. – SAM"

Josh toggled back and reread the text – three times. It was an unknown number, but he doubted Sam was using a burner phone. Yet, how else to explain the text and simultaneous email? A gnawing, nagging feeling started.

First, it had been Lieut. Rhianna Adams, then Sam Walters had confided his own doubts back in April. They were daring to suggest something was off about the broadcast stories. Did they not know conspirators were ridiculed and even outlawed in Europe? Nobody thought the Disease was a laughing matter. That much was clear. But where Ground Zero was and the spreading cause behind it – that was another thing.

Who to trust? He trusted Sam; that he knew. The man could be impulsive, but he was one of Josh's best friends. So, maybe something was going on at SEH. And with SEH's Pharma Group holding a government contract, then perhaps there was some truth in Rhianna's words.

But remember, she was arrested for treason, and you still don't know what involvement she had with the chopper attack.

The questions permeating his mind pulled him, enticing him to look at the email from Sam. His thumb edged towards the attachment link, hovering over it for what seemed an eternity. Sweat pooled on his brow. Josh became aware of the device shaking. He held up his empty left hand

and spread it out, his five fingers pointing in the air. It was he that was shaking.

At that moment, he became aware of the rapid pulse, the quickening of his breathing, his eyes not being able to focus. He sensed what the link might hold. Was he ready?

Josh turned, and looked out the small, front window. Despite it being late morning, dark moving clouds hovered overhead. The sun was gone, that was a good thing. His neighbors were starting their day. Kids' happy voices began to ring across the block.

Community, not isolation.

His thumb moved. The attachment loaded.

∎　　∎　　∎　　∎　　∎

"Mr. President, Ambassador Omach is online."

William Turouning pirouetted on his right foot, and nodded to his aide. Quickly slipping into the comfy padded chair, he propped his elbows on the desk. The World Council meetings would resume soon, and it was best if he got up to speed on the latest developments from the Ambassador. William's steely gray eyes stared ahead of him – at the large holographic display portraying the live feed from Uganda.

"Mr. President," Ambassador Derrick Omach spoke with an accent, but in perfect English. "It is an honor to talk with you."

William casually waved his hand.

"Of course, my friend. What news do you bring?"

"We've been progressing ahead of schedule," the African carefully hesitated before his next words. "But the Disease has worsened."

"How? I thought it already quite bad," Pres. Turouning's voice cracked with fear.

"Calm, we must remain calm, William." Derrick dropped formality. "If we panic, the results would be far more catastrophic."

"I know, I know," the president sputtered. He stood up, stepped away from his desk, and began pacing the floor.

"You know, Derrick, it's enough we have to worry about extremists blowing the world up, or shooters killing kids, or starvation in Africa – without a disease that is eliminating people faster than the rebel forces in Nigeria!"

Both men politely chuckled. The turmoil in Nigeria was well known. Ever since radical Islamic extremists had taken out the Nigerian government, the dominating rule of control had tossed from one group to the next. Rebel forces had controlled the country for the last five years, and the death toll of innocent people grew each day. First, it had been Nigeria, but the instability spread to neighboring countries as well. Chad, Cameroon, and Niger all battled internal strife and politics. The president's brief brevity was needed amidst their tense conversation.

"How is it on your side of the continent?" asked William as he ran a hand across his forehead. It felt hot.

"Good good! My country has found ways to sustain itself. Kenya has battled the illness more than politics, thank God, and piracy has been nearly wiped off the Somalia coast."

The president was listening, but his head dropped into his sweaty palms, and he slouched back into the plush easy chair. His eyes moved around and settled on a faraway object – too far to be discernible.

"Are you okay, Mr. President?" Derrick's voice sounded distant.

The cacophonous noise of an ever-busy capital city faded. It was as if all were standing frozen in place like silent statues.

The president quietly arose, distracted by something, and stared out a window. He became oblivious of the African ambassador, who was standing in the holographic display, watching with a puzzled expression. William's only conscious thought was the faraway object. It seemed a pleasant sort of glow.

Indeed, it was nothing as bright or as treacherous as the sun. And it was addicting. Like a drug that, once consumed, becomes one's entire passion and thought of being.

His left eye started to twitch. The irritating itch behind his eye was beginning again. He focused on the faraway spot and stood still.

"Mr. President, are you okay?" The cloudy voice of the ambassador sounded somewhere behind him.

William did not answer, spellbound by what he was observing. Suddenly, as if shot by a stun gun, he recoiled and fell back a step. Turning around, he began rubbing his right hand across his neck and sighed. He was aware of his tightly clenched left fist. Sweat beads had formed on his forehead, and slowly trickled downward. Inhaling deeply, he faced the ambassador.

"Um, ah, where were we?"

Derrick stared at the American president.

"Sir, I think we can postpone this meeting until later. It appears you are not feeling well."

William tried to nod in response.

"In a few weeks, I'll be coming back to the States anyway. We can continue our conversation then, Mr. President."

Pres. Turouning waved his hand in acknowledgement. The display flickered, and the image of Ambassador Omach vanished. Stumbling back a couple steps, William began violently shaking. Something was on his cheek. Unclenching his left hand, he reached up and dabbed at the moisture. He pulled his finger away.

It was blood.

.　　.　　.　　.　　.

"The last few months, you might have seen videos such as these, of people killing themselves while speaking an ominous message, warning us of an impending disaster. Perhaps, that disaster has arrived."

The narration was spoken cleanly, without dramatic emphasis, and matter-of-fact as someone reading a news broadcast. The videos being shown were the Canadian man and the Georgian woman.

Josh took a draught of his beer, and watched the unfolding video. It was more or less typical morphing – fear-mongering of a "deadly virus sweeping the world and to beware of people who complained about light or didn't wear their sunglasses."

He laughed out loud as the narration told him this last part. Grabbing his handheld, his thumb scurried about. The text sent.

Chirp.

"That was fast," he said, glancing at his device.

DO YOU REALLY THINK THAT?

Josh became aware of his hand shaking, and his grip on the handheld suddenly gave way. It dropped to the floor with a loud clatter.

His text had been sent to Sam. The text just arrived, came from the unknown number.

The device chirped again. Leaning over, he picked it up, his hand still shaking. It was Sam.

I KNOW IT SEEMS IMPLAUSIBLE, BUT MAYBE IT'S TRUE? WORTH A SHOT AT LEAST.

For some time now, Sam had been chipping away at him. His colleague had seemingly become convinced there was a cover-up of some variety going on. Whether that originated from a government agency or a media outlet – Sam refrained from saying. He only doubted what was being presented.

What if something malevolent is going on? What if the events are not only connected but coordinated? Man, that takes a lot of crazy to believe.

WHY DON'T YOU BELIEVE?

The text came from the unknown number. Chills ran down Josh's back as he broke out into a cold sweat.

Who is this? What do they want? How do they know my thoughts?

Josh swallowed hard. He had enough on his plate without random solicitors challenging him, and asking questions. He was also worried about Sam. The man was starting to sound like a conspirator – spitting in the very face of what they did.

The device suddenly rang. He nearly fell off the futon. Laughing off his startled nerves, Josh swiped.

"Hello?"

"I'm not trying to freak you out, man."

"Sure, but c'mon, Sam. Our job is to identify what is true or false. How can you send me something that mimics common dissenter material? Our credibility would be stripped if someone knew."

There was a pause. The ticking of the clock on the fireplace mantel could be heard.

"Sorry. It's just..." Sam sighed as he struggled to formulate his thought. "It's just your report from Georgia said those things."

Josh was in the middle of taking a sip of beer, and the liquid spewed back out of his mouth as he heard this. Hurriedly setting the bottle down, he pulled the device closer to his ear.

"That's a lie, and you know it!"

"Right, right," Sam said quickly. "I saw your original report when it came in too. It was just like you texted me. The incident, while unfortunate and weird, couldn't link to anything else." Sam took a quick breath. "Well today, when I happened to open it up to cross-reference something, I saw this."

There was a swishing sound, and Josh pulled the handheld away from his ear, holding it up. The screen lit up as the message arrived. Opening the document, his eyes darted back and forth as he quickly scanned the contents.

"Bogus. These are complete lies! I didn't say this!"

GA INCIDENT FORETELLS OF IMPENDING DOOM. REPORT THOSE WHO DON'T WEAR. COMPLAINTS OF LIGHT OR SUSPECT BEHAVIOR SHOULD BE TAKEN SERIOUSLY. TELL SOMEONE.

The phrases leapt off his screen, and shook him to the core. The entire file was a bald-faced falsehood.

"They are going to release this to all media outlets claiming SEH's truth verification team had identified as early as April, the wide-ranging effects of the Disease. That it's more than just an illness, but a virus with complete takeover of the human mind. They sent this for an initial viewing to several health agencies across the world like CDC, WHO, and PHE. Their response? Anyone with light sensitivity or suspect behavior – whatever that is – should be reported. Do you see why I'm worried?"

Sam's voice pleaded with Josh's emotions; hoping his friend would no longer think him crazy. Slowly exhaling, Josh counted to five. His eyes locked on the fireplace, drawn to the dark, mysterious cavern where, when lit, a bright light would dance upon burning logs.

"This is typical morphing. Have we've been hacked? I can't see anyone in the department releasing crap like this."

It was quiet for a moment, and after with a deep breath, Sam said, "John Stevens signed off on it two hours ago."

■   ■   ■   ■   ■

"I can manage myself!"

The president snapped at the secret service agent standing outside the car door. The agent had tried opening the door. Pres. Turouning kicked his left leg out, and pushed it open himself. He staggered to his feet.

"I hate these galas. Why do we have them? If being cooped up all day at the damn Council meetings wasn't bad enough, they have to hold these great big 'international' galas."

The president swore again as he shut the door. He accidentally clipped his hand in the process. The pain was tremendous, but he shook it off. It was nothing compared to the searing agony in his left eye.

"Out of my way! Nobody is going to shoot me, fool."

The president waved the converging agents back. They stopped advancing, but kept a tight ring around their protectee. Despite Prism being an absolute ass at times, it was their sworn duty to protect and keep him safe. Lately, the protests had been heating up.

Stumbling across the passageway, William opened the door to *Lugar Perfecto*. He stepped inside. It was calm. Soft music floated down the corridor from another room. He did not care.

The eye's searing agony intensified. Closing it shut, he put his left hand over it. Setting two fingers against the eyelid, he pushed back as hard as he could. Somehow by inflicting more pain, it dulled the intensity. Perhaps that defied logic, but it worked.

Clumsily tugging on the handle of a restroom door, he opened it. Stepping in front of the mirror, he turned both faucet knobs on. After letting the water run for a few minutes, he abruptly turned the left knob off. The cold water still ran. He felt it rush over his fingers, soothing them. Lifting his hands, he furiously dabbed his eyes and face.

After a moment, William turned the cold water knob counterclockwise. The stream ceased, and a few loose drops fell into the sink bowl. Picking up the towel lying on the edge of the counter, he wiped his face, blotting the cloth on the sides of his forehead. He stopped, and stared at himself in the mirror.

A grim, frustrated, worn-out man reflected at him. Red patches encircled his entire left eye; his retina was visibly scratched across the surface. The itching pain had become too much. Sitting there today at the meetings, and then having to endure a boring gala with over-enthusiastic supporters was too much.

He glanced down at the sink. Droplets of blood still clung to its sides. Holding his hands out, he examined them. There were still smudges of blood on the fingertips. Choking back a sob, he stared, defeated into the mirror.

"The gods be damned. This can't be happening to me!"

Uncontrollable tears began streaming down his cheeks. He raised a shaking hand, and wiped the back of it across his brow, which was dripping with sweat.

The Native American's shoulders sagged as he first cursed, then started to pray in his mother tongue. The rote memory of the words from when he was a child, came rushing over him like a waterfall. The hot tears flowed freely . He felt helpless. And like he did when he was a child, he felt alone.

His breathing grew rapid as if he were an injured soldier – shot through the chest. Suddenly, without any hesitation, he started to claw at his eye. He shrieked with pain as his nails dug deep into the socket. He screamed as the agonies of hell descended.

William's arms began to flail about. His right hand smashed one of the lights above the vanity mirror. Blood gushed from the cut. He looked up at the remaining lights, and screamed again. It sounded more a howl than a scream. Like a savage animal dying to break loose.

Without fear or knowledge of what possessed him, he could no longer fight back. He swore, cursing every entity he knew, even his dead ancestors. He swung both hands madly above his head, smashing and punching out at anything. The restroom's remaining light bulbs shattered and went out. The room fell into total darkness.

There was silence. The calming quiet of darkness enveloped William. His tears dried; numbness set in. A balmy sense of relief flooded over.

His hands were strangely composed as he extended his right hand. *It laid there* – clutched in his right fist. *Finally,* he silently breathed with empty hopelessness, *some relief from this misery!*

The fist unclenched. What he held rolled off his hand, and onto the tiled restroom floor. In a trance, he stared at it, and then suddenly, he felt sick. Leaning over the sink, he vomited. The contents of his stomach emptied into the bowl. Once finished, he reached over, took a paper towel, and dabbed his mouth.

With a small sigh, he straightened himself as he gazed into the mirror. He blinked, and then dropped to a knee. The emergency lighting had gradually illuminated, dimly lighting the restroom. It cast heavy shadows upon the wall. A strange aurora – ominous and eerie, yet darkly inviting – enveloped the room.

On his knees, he could see it – barely visible in the dimness. It had stopped rolling, and now just laid there. It was his left eye.

FIFTEEN

"What are you so happy about?"

"Can't a fellow just be happy?" Luke stopped whistling, and looked at Brenda with a sheepish grin.

"Sure," she replied. "Only you're more than happy. You're looking better than I've ever seen you – well-kept, healthy, and emanating a sparkle. I know why."

Luke gave her a glance that asked, 'oh, really?'

"You're twitterpated."

He tried to laugh off her pointed statement. Deep down, though, he could not help but think she was right. He was sleeping better than ever, which made no sense given the turmoil of the last few months. His appetite was strong. He did feel happy, and furthermore, he felt *alive* – all because of Tessa Morgan.

That morning he had woken up in her bed. Obviously, he made her breakfast. It was the least he could do. He loved being with her. He loved everything about her. She was intoxicating; aloof and mysterious, yet, sexy and charming. What wasn't there to be in love with?

Brenda was chatting happily away, her voice merely an ambiance in the background. He could not focus on what she was saying. Inside, an inner battle had started.

I admitted I loved her. That's ridiculous! I hardly know her. She did tell me first, though. That scarcely matters, she knows that I do. That I meant it.

"Are you happy, Brenda?" Luke spoke out loud, hoping to quell the inner voices.

"I'm happy for you. I've been waiting a long time for this day." The intern looked Luke straight in the eyes as she answered.

Deep, genuine laughter spilled from the research scientist. Brenda was as a sister to him. The fact his assistant was so hell-bent on matchmaking was hilarious. The fact she was giddy over his current relationship – meant the world to him.

Brenda left the room as she went to her own desk. Luke flopped into his office chair with a plop. Exhaling loudly, he bit his lower lip. He half thought of sending a text to Tessa, but then thought better of it. He did not want to come off as needy or attached.

Moving his hand, he grabbed the digital mouse. He began his daily routine and started scanning his inbox. Suddenly, he stopped. On the left side of his holographic display was an icon he had never seen before.

That's curious. I wonder if IT installed new spyware on the network.

Such installations would require him to sign in. Without a second thought, he tapped the icon with the digital mouse. There was no sign-in box.

"Hello? What's this," he muttered out loud.

The icon opened to a window, which contained many rows and columns. Suddenly, it started to scroll. Luke quickly tried to double-tap. That did nothing. He then put his hand into the display, and manually attempted to override the operation. That did not work either.

Numbers and names began to move by his frantic eyes; sentences containing medical jargon. He happened to notice what appeared to be a watermark in the background of the document.

Using careful precision, he was able to grab and pinch the backdrop, as the file continued to scroll. He flicked his fingers, and the watermark expanded.

"CDV," Luke read slowly.

It was a monogram with the initials etched into what appeared to be a drop of water hitting a pond. *Quite the sophisticated watermark*, he was curious and started to pay better attention to the data flashing by. It took him a couple minutes to realize what he was looking at.

"Brenda, come in here, please," his tried to remain calm, but his voice quivered.

Dammit, so caught up with that girl, I stopped thinking clearly.

Brenda appeared in his office, her eyebrows lifted in a questioning manner.

"Look at this. Do you see what I think I see?"

The girl carefully watched the scrolling file for a moment and then simply said, "It's study results; appears to be..." She raised her head with a horrified expression. "Oh my gosh, Luke, this can't be!"

She ran from the room.

He knew where she was going. There was a cabinet in her office which stored all the old paper files. He rubbed his forehead with a nervous hand, and then his chin.

Brenda was back in a flash, holding a physical folder and waving it in the air.

"Got it!"

She laid it down on his desk.

"*Diabolus*?" He looked away from Brenda and back at the holograph display. "I – we extracted everything we had in this file when crap hit the fan back in April. We hit a dead end. But," he paused, and pointed at the colorful pixels displayed in front of them. "This file here seems to have additional insight into that incident." A harried look came over him. "I thought Grafton was the only one who documented *Diabolus*?"

"Apparently not," Brenda inclined her head towards the display. "And this is so much more than Dr. Grafton had. Genetic screenings, brain scans, autopsies, even the biometrics – which are highly classified."

The two of them studied the notes in front of them. Suddenly, Luke lifted his head and cocked it sideways.

"Holy cow, there's a quadratic formula used here in the digital file. The categorization gives that away. Something else is here. If we can decipher the algorithm, we might find the hidden files."

"I see!" Brenda excitedly nodded. She glanced sideways at Luke. "Where did you get this?"

His mouth partially opened, as if caught stealing from a cookie jar. He remained paralyzed for a moment, and then shook his head.

"I don't know. It was here when I got in this morning."

"Luke, nobody is just going to send highly classified research on a massive disease outbreak with secret details from *two* years ago to you on accident."

"I know, I know."

Luke began pacing his office. His brow furrowed as he ran a hand through his chestnut brown hair. His feet led him to the window, and he gazed out, down at the campus below.

Hundreds of people were roaming around the University, unaware of the information he had just seen. Further to the southwest, in downtown

Pittsburgh, thousands more were carrying on their day, oblivious to the fact a single research scientist had life-altering information regarding the Disease that once bore the name *Diabolus*. A cataclysmic intersection was fast approaching. Did the file really hold the answers to what might save them?

"What are you going to do?"

Luke sighed. "Truthfully, I don't know. How this got here, why me, who sent it? These are questions I do not know the answers too. Brenda, please don't tell anyone about this."

"Of course not, Luke. You know we're a team."

Luke nodded, his mind was elsewhere though. *What do I do now?*

. . . . .

A hushed electronic beeping alerted the young college kid sitting at the desk. He tapped on his keyboard and opened a new window. His eyes lit up, and he swiveled his chair.

"Ma'am, he's opened it. File is scrolling as we speak."

"Excellent," the woman replied. "I knew he would."

"What's next?" Another woman who was dressed in military garb, sauntered over to where the first woman stood.

"Well, now we wait, Revers. He may not be the current head of the Pittsburgh Research Team, but that's not because of his smarts. He's going to reach out, and try to contact us for more information. We'll be ready."

"Sounds like a plan, I'll let Danny know." Kelly Revers pivoted on her right heel, and walked away.

The redhead crossed her arms as she continued to monitor the incoming feed. A loose strand of hair caressed her cheek. A whisper escaped her lips.

"Soon we'll know, Luke, very soon."

. . . . .

"They say the number of wearers increases every day, Patrick. Why I even said the same thing to Anna yesterday," Jim leaned against the back wall of his shop counter, and shook his head.

"I'll never let them stick me with anything," said Patrick Flannigan vehemently.

"I just wonder when the real story is going to be told."

"Ha!" Patrick snorted in response, and spat a stream of tobacco juice onto the shop's wooden floor.

Jim did not care, or if he did, one could not tell. The day was passing uneventfully, hardly a half-dozen customers. Business had been getting slower and slower. Patrick Flannigan had come over, and the two spent most of the time in the backroom watching TruthX. Now, however, they were standing in the shop's front, and viewing another broadcast via the small portable TV Patrick had brought over.

It was streaming a 'breaking news' story out of the Congo. Apparently, the villages were receiving care packages from the WHO that contained special medicine in an attempt to fight the Disease. Jim was not one to keep up with all the new technology; he preferred older tech. That said, doing a quick search on the interwebs yielded no results for the Congo story.

Anna watched the two men from her spot on the far side of the shop, and rolled her eyes. Her boyfriend was due to pick her up any minute. She could care less if Rome was about to burn. At least, she would not be an idiot 'dissenter' like her uncle.

Jim turned and saw Anna watching them. He smiled. She scowled in response.

"Hey, Jimmy, look at this!" Patrick said eagerly as he motioned to the mini-screen.

The shopkeeper's attention returned to the TV, and his eyes widened.

"What did I say!" he practically shouted. "This is what I predicted!"

SIXTEEN

Josh grabbed his keys, and headed to the front door. It had been two days since he arrived home. Two days of inactivity. Two days of brooding over the files Sam had sent. Enough was enough. He had to get out of the house, and go for a drive.

Pulling the door shut, he scanned the neighborhood. The sun was brightly shining. The leaves on the trees were a radiant green. Nobody was outside to enjoy the weather. Josh glanced at his neighbors' houses.

Everyone had their shades pulled, shutters closed, and drapes loosened, covering the windows from the natural light. There was no visible movement.

"Like a flea-bit scene from *I Am Legend*," he angrily scoffed as he walked to the car at the curb. Jerking open the driver's door, he tossed a water bottle, and his handheld onto the front passenger seat. Then he stopped, and looked at his house again.

The building had once been a home. And for a while, he had loved, even cherished the small St. Paul suburb where it was located. The people were friendly, the air was clean, and his world peaceful. That had all changed.

Josh pulled his sunglasses off the top of his head, and in one smooth motion, slid them over his eyes. With his other hand, he reached down, and pressed the ignition button.

Putting the car into gear, he swiftly accelerated away from the curb. Everything was so different now than five years ago, when he first moved to Minnesota. But then…he preferred not to think about Amanda.

"It's crazy enough without thinking about of her," Josh said to no one in particular.

The research Sam sent over had unnerved him. It prompted him to go back, and read some of the referenced past incidents – including diving back into the scandalous tabloids. During his research, he discovered a series of unrelated events that all had the same uncanny details. Tried as he might, he was unable to distinguish any pattern in the circumstances though. They were all random.

"But…what if that's the real caveat – the spindle moving things." The idea bothered him, and he did not know the answer.

Easing up on the accelerator, the car neared a four-way stop. They were infamous in St. Paul. It seemed the state of Minnesota had once been commited to becoming the first state in the country where the modern traffic circles were discarded, and instead, the ever-trusty four-way stop was put to use.

The car rolled to a halt. Suddenly, his handheld started buzzing. The loud vibration startled him. Reaching over, he picked it up.

"How long are you going to ignore us, Josh?"

The voice sounded robotic, yet its tone was human. The cryptic delivery of the words chilled him.

"Who is this?" Josh demanded firmly, his tone even-keeled.

"What does it matter?" the voice replied. "SEH will soon be dissolved, and you will be left without a job. Why do you ignore reality?"

"So you're calling to offer me a job? How sweet of you," he pulled the device away, preparing to hang up, but the voice spoke again.

"We're calling to warn you…beware, danger is near."

All of a sudden, a loud horn sounded, which caused Josh to lose his grip on the steering wheel. Dropping the handheld, he clutched the wheel tighter, swerving out of the way as a semi-truck – horn blaring loudly – bore down from the opposite direction. The semi had seemingly appeared out of nowhere.

Josh swore and anxiously exhaled. Regaining control of the wheel, he straightened it, and drove into Minnehaha Falls Park. His insides jangled by the sudden near-death experience.

"What was a semi doing out here on a small side street? This isn't I-35!" he thought out loud. "Who called me? Is it the same person who's been texting me? And how did they know to warn me? How did they know where I was? Or that a truck was going to collide with me? Too many questions!"

Shaking, Josh opened the sedan door, and stumbled out. He had stopped near the main north entrance to the Park. The Falls was just a short walk away. Water always calmed him; he needed to go take a look.

Green leaves filled the shrubs, and red leaves the maple tree branches alongside the walking path to the Falls. A bridge overlooked the small yet magnificent waterfall, and the trail ended as it emptied onto this bridge. The stream of water moving downstream ran under the bridge, and then slipped forthwith over a precipitous edge, cascading some fifty feet to the basin below. It was not Niagara, but the park was a favorite destination in the area.

Josh leaned on the bridge railing, and deeply breathed the sweet air around him. It had been a smart decision, he already felt less discombobulated. Then he noticed someone watching him, standing high on the bluff above the opposite side.

"Does that person have...a camera?" he muttered curiously.

Without warning, without knowing why, a feeling of terror seized him. His eyes darted around, and he noticed another person standing at the top of the west staircase leading to the bridge he was on. It was another entrance to the park. The terror swiftly changed to paranoia. He had to *leave* and quickly.

Backing up two steps, he turned, and fled up the path. The car was close, and as he neared it, he pressed the ignition key on the remote. The sedan's engine started. Josh grabbed the door handle, and violently opened it. Sliding into the driver's seat, he slammed the door shut. In one second, his right hand slid the car into gear, and his right foot pushed down on the accelerator.

The vehicle swerved back onto the side street. Behind him, a black car turned and started to follow. Josh's breathing became heavy. His hands began to sweat. Slowly, he applied the brakes and cut his speed. The car behind him responded in likewise manner. Speeding up, he turned onto another boulevard.

He glanced around. He had not driven in this area much, and was not quite sure where to go. Looking ahead, he saw a bridge, and some of his anxiety left. It was for Highway 5, he could take that back to I-35, and then head home.

Converging onto the onramp, he slammed his foot to the floor. The car bolted! Checking the rearview mirror, he saw the black car still behind him. His breathing quickened, and his heart pounded.

The blue convertible passed over the bridge, and started its way towards the city of St. Paul. The tailing sedan kept its distance, but still followed. Josh gave a hard swallow.

Is my mind playing tricks on me? Is this just a coincidence?

The next several miles were traversed, and he occasionally peeked in his mirror to see the black car still following. It was not until he suddenly spun the wheel, and exited onto the ramp for his street, that full-on panic set in. The black car also exited.

I can't go home. They can't follow me there. Who are they? What do they want? Is it the person who called me before? The same who's been texting? Keep driving, just keep driving.

His mind was made up. His street was next, but he did not want to give away his destination, so he continued on. After another mile or so, without signaling, he quickly whipped the wheel, and spun into a big-box store parking lot. He glanced in his rearview mirror. The black car never slowed, and continued on its way.

Josh gave a loud sigh. Pulling into a space, he put the car in park, and just sat there. Cold sweat ran up and down his body. His shirt was soaked. His hands hurt from the pressure with which he had been gripping the steering wheel. He swallowed hard.

After a few minutes, Josh put the car in gear and started back towards his own street. No one was following him this time. Pulling into his driveway, he pressed the opener for his garage. He did not know why, he never parked in the garage, but given what had just happened, it seemed the natural thing to do.

At that moment, he became aware of someone standing in the yard of the house across the street. He did not recognize them. While he was not overly friendly with his neighbors, he did know who they were. The person standing outside did not live there. The anxious feelings returned.

The blue car rolled into the garage, Josh hit the opener again for the door to shut. He continued staring in his rearview mirror, watching the stranger as the door settled behind him. Pressing the ignition, he finally turned off the car.

He crawled out of the seat. He felt weak and tired. He reached for the doorknob to go into his house, when his handheld suddenly went off.

"Dang it!" he jumped into the air.

Hastily pulling the device out, he was ready to throw it against the garage wall when he realized the number was familiar. A long, slow exhale followed.

"Hello?"

"Josh, how is my favorite truthseeker?"

It was Mark Jacobi. The call must be urgent. Josh could not remember the last time he had talked to Jacobi.

"Hey now," another voice chimed in, unmistakably John Stevens. "Let's not get too carried away! I run the team."

"So you do," Mark gave a courteous laugh, acknowledging John's role as director of the Morphing Division. "But anyway, how has the time off been, Josh?"

The truthseeker listened to the other two men talking. He closed his eyes, and counted to five; his heart still beating fast. The call had startled him. For that matter, the info from Sam, repeated cryptic calls and texts, maybe being under surveillance, being followed from the park – the weight of it all overwhelmed him.

"Doing well," he lied. "Nothing like time away from work."

All three men politely chuckled. Obviously, Jacobi and Stevens were not calling for social reasons. Jacobi made that clear as he spoke again.

"We have an assignment for you. It involves your alma mater."

"Pittsburgh?" Josh's ears picked up at this intriguing development. What did his old school have going on that he needed to be involved?

"Yes. We have yet to announce it publicly, but Pharma Group will be partnering with Pittsburgh's Department of Immunology and Infectious Diseases – IID. Together we can pass TYM or any other competing organization for first-finder privileges on the cure for the Disease. Melinda Gore has been running the Research Team since Grafton passed. She's been doing some nice work, and approached us with the offer. It's a good one."

"A very good one!" chimed in John Stevens.

"And I think we all know time is of the essence if Pharma Group is to get control of the market on this."

Josh nodded, forgetting the other two could not see him.

"That makes sense, but how do I fit in? I work truth verification, not biomed."

"This is why I like you, Josh," said Jacobi. "You're observant and forthright. You're a big part of the team. We depend on you."

Josh was honored and said so.

"This will be a win-win situation," John said, seizing the chance to hear himself talk. "SEH will be able to funnel resources to Pittsburgh, and in exchange, we will have exclusive access to their research records – which means Pharma Group will be able to produce a cure much faster than anyone else. And of course," he gleefully gloated. "That means more money and prestige – for all of us!"

"Sure, but it also means better resources," Jacobi emphasized, amused at his associate's words.

"Sure, sure," John replied.

"So," Josh interjected. "How exactly does this involve me again?"

"Because it's your alma mater – didn't Mark say that already?" John was irritated.

"I did," Jacobi cut in, trying to rectify the sudden change in the tone of the conversation. "Josh, you will be a good *presence* for our first interaction with the IID department. Both in Pittsburgh and also – in San Francisco."

"San Francisco?" Josh was puzzled.

"Yes," Jacobi carefully replied. "As you know, our Pharma Group division is headquartered out in the Bay area. What you might not know is they are hosting a summit for the leading biomed science divisions. There is some big news that they are preparing to share, in partnership with our new ally Pittsburgh University. This is top-secret and confidential. It's by invite only and your presence will be helpful."

That's curious, Josh pondered. *He's said that word twice now.*

Out loud, he asked, "This summit is an in-person conference not via i-Beam?"

It was a good question. In-person conferences were a thing of the past. Nearly everything was given via i-Beam or holograph broadcast.

John answered. "Sam can get you the specifics, but from what we understand, due to Pentcom's massive cybersecurity breach, Blair Leshief said a live event was best. Not sure why this matters?" Stevens added as an afterthought, questioning Josh's motives.

"Oh, believe me," Josh replied. "I'm not opposed to a trip back to Pittsburgh or going to San Francisco. This actually sounds quite good given everything that's happened the last several months – phantom sightings, people gruesomely killing themselves, missiles blowing crap up in front of me…" Josh broke off with a dry laugh. The other two joined in.

Jacobi and Stevens wrapped the call by telling him that Sam would be in touch with all the particulars.

"Keep your eyes open," Jacobi closed, his tone strange. "Don't stop working while you are out there. Your presence is appreciated."

Three times now. That's weird.

"Will do, Mark" he responded. "I'll let you guys know the moment I have something to report."

"Spectacular. Take care of yourself, Josh."

.　　.　　.　　.　　.

The small TV illuminated the otherwise dim and drab backroom of *Savannah Souvenirs*. Jim sat in his rocking chair, but he was not moving back and forth. Instead, he sat leaning forward, with his feet planted firmly on the floor, his eyes wide. Patrick was perched on a small stool next to him, also watching the screen, eyes transfixed.

"The conference begins in two days, and runs for two days. A cure is supposedly going to emerge from this convention, but our sources say something else could be at play. Pharma Group's director Blair Leshief gave a rousing and inspirational speech ahead of the convention, but interestingly enough, the convention was absent from his actual words. It appears the event is being held under tight security, and most media outlets have not shared a *single* word that it's even happening. We at TruthX saw fit to inform our viewers about the conference as it once again confirms our worst fears: something is going on, and we the people are being lied to."

Jim shook his head as the broadcast continued. He looked over at Patrick.

"Do you believe this? A conference is going to find a cure for the Disease?"

"Doubtful," Patrick stood up, and straightened himself. There were kinks to get out after hunching on a stool.

"Why are they lying to us again? Why not just tell us the truth?"

"I suppose TruthX, as much as they might say otherwise, like it that way themselves. They wouldn't have a business otherwise."

Jim could not believe his friend's words. He started to speak and then stopped. When he did begin again, he was stammering.

"Are – are you suggesting they aren't being honest?"

Patrick shrugged his shoulders. "All I know is some bloke has to be making big bucks on the Disease. Whenever there is something big happening – a War in Asia, an earthquake in Chile, a Disease around the world – somebody is harvesting the money."

Jim nodded thoughtfully. He could not argue with this observation and besides, the TV broadcast was ending.

"We shall see what happens in San Francisco but know this – what happens there will *not* stay there."

SEVENTEEN

"Welcome to CDV." The receptionist warmly smiled at Luke as he entered the building.

The decision to visit the CDV building in downtown Pittsburgh was not a flippant one. After discovering the monogram on his computer, he had struggled with it the rest of the day. By evening, he had clicked on the '?' in the lower right of the monogram, and found an address. It was downtown and not far from the campus. His mind was made up; he would visit them in the morning.

But now, he was less sure, and had butterflies in his stomach. Pushing the feeling away, Luke smiled in response to the friendly greeting, and said hello.

The woman was dressed in a navy blue outfit – a skirt ran mid-length, with a buttoned blouse that hugged her curves. She was pleasant looking, and her warm, friendly voice sounded sweet.

"May I get you something to drink?"

"Um," Luke did not know what he wanted. "I'm fine."

"You sure? I can get you a beer or maybe something on the rocks?"

"Gin then. Thanks for offering."

Luke was surprised she had offered alcohol. Quite the operation they must be running if they were giving away free liquor.

The girl disappeared behind the counter as she fished out a glass. She reappeared, and filled a glass with ice. She generously poured the blue bottle of gin; ice crackling as the liquid hit the cubes. She then handed the glass to Luke.

"Now that we've taken care of that – how may I help you?"

"I have an appointment with Mr. Graves."

"Ah, yes. Please take a seat. I'll page him."

■　　■　　■　　■　　■

"Are you sure this will work?" Danny Graves peered at Tessa as he adjusted the tie on his white collared shirt.

"It's my job to recruit, Danny. I've been working this case for three months."

"Literally working it," Kelly Revers sneered as she made an obscene gesture.

Tessa rolled her eyes. "I did not say it *wasn't* enjoyable, but trust me on this one. He's perfect for us."

"If you say so," Danny turned away and looked in the mirror, inspecting his appearance.

"You look magnificent." Tessa nodded in approval.

"Well, I need to look good. First thing he'll see is the prosthetic."

"Well, you are right. But you got hurt during your service time before your job as a scientist. How is that so implausible?"

"Humph," Disgruntled, the former sergeant stepped away from the mirror and exhaled. "Maybe so; I just hope the kid doesn't put two and two together until we say so. Otherwise, things will get messy."

Tessa put her hands on her hips. She was annoyed with the idea Danny suggested. It did cause her to wonder if she had read the situation correctly. But that was her job as a recruiter. She was never wrong.

"If he bolts, that's what you're here for – and Kelly."

Tessa motioned towards Kelly Revers, who nodded in response. For dramatic effect, Kelly pulled her sidearm, and twirled it in the air. In one fluid motion, she popped the magazine out, shoved it back in, and racked the slide.

Tessa cut her eyes and gave a stern look at Danny.

"Go easy on him, you're supposed to be a nerdy scientist. Leave the guns to Revers," she jerked her head towards the former corporal who had resumed her reclining pose against the back wall.

"Fair enough," the big man growled. "I just didn't anticipate playing actor so much when the cause began."

"So what is the gamma reading?"

Luke popped the question to his interviewee, a big, muscular man who clearly felt uncomfortable in a suit. The prosthetic arm was unusual, but a Purple Heart did not disqualify one from pursuing a career as a scientist.

"Ah, well, the gamma reading was off the charts."

"Off the charts? That's bad."

"No, no," Danny Graves tried to recover. "Off the charts in a good way."

Luke was already feeling quite skeptical of the man and CDV. Based on the interview, he felt as if they were just a bunch of jokesters pretending to be scientists. Yet, he knew that the results from the research study were not wrong.

"So then, you did not actually have a reading. Let me illustrate," Luke was exasperated, and standing up, walked to the center of the room.

Pulling a small device, with a stubby knob at the end, from his pocket, he rotated it, and a bright light flickered forth. It was a mini-projector holograph. Setting it down on the floor, Luke clapped while spreading his arms wide. Instantly, the beam burst forth a hundred times the span it had been, and practically encapsulated the entire room with moving images.

Danny's mouth opened slightly in awe of the tech and amazed at Luke's decisiveness.

"I know the report I read from CDV had factual data in it. Those results, if made up, were extremely lucky. To the point of," Luke laughed and using his forefinger, pushed his glasses back up his nose. "Well, that kind of luck just doesn't exist."

"Impressive," Danny said, nodding his head.

"I'm just getting started."

Luke waved his right hand, and the display shot forth another image – this time streaming story feeds from around the world and the scientific studies conducted thereof. He began explaining what they were looking at.

"You see this? This is from the war in Asia when people suddenly started going mad and attacking the Embassy. I believe the media reported it to be a terrorist attack, but look closer. These movements are detached – they are called 'Synchronized Actions.' At least, that's what SEH Morphers would call it," Luke referenced the renowned truth verification team.

"Synchronized? Like hypnotized?"

Danny's question was asked in all sincerity, he was inquisitive about what Luke was saying. The scientist noticed this, and slightly shook his head.

"No, there's a difference, although that's not a bad guess. This type of controlled behavior is typically going to be found in either biotech or implanted chips. Now, unless you believe people are randomly having controller chips installed in their arms or necks without their knowledge, I would be inclined to think this was a planned demonstration with biotech."

He turned and looked at Danny as he spoke. The words came out in a knowledgeable, confident manner. He wished all his talks sounded so learned and portrayed this confidence. Perhaps then Melinda Gore, or any of his associates from the Research Team, would treat him differently. But no, in that regard, just like always, he had caved to pressure and insecurity. Even as he thought about it, beads of sweat formed on his brow, his knees started to shake, and he struggled to keep his tone calm and steady.

"Why are you telling me this?" asked Danny.

"Because," Luke turned again and watched the streaming studies flashing before them. Cloud data immersion was one hell of a ride. He sighed, and looked away. "Because you're a fake and maybe this entire organization. I don't know."

He walked to the center of the room once more, and pushed his hands together. The sensors picked up the motion, and the light dimmed. Luke bent down, and picked up the device from the ground. Turning the knob, he shut it off. He stood up and straightened his drooping shoulders. He had been hoping, praying the CDV was more than a hack outfit. It was not.

"I just don't understand," he said. "That report was factual – groundbreaking, real," Luke looked back at Danny to finish his sentence, but never did. Instead, his mouth dropped, and his heart began beating fast. "Wh-aa-ttt are you doing here?"

Tessa Morgan stood next to the chair Danny sat in. Her face, though unsmiling, was friendly. She motioned Danny to move away. The big man got up and walked to the side, near the rear door. Tessa's eyes went back to Luke, and a smile broke across her face.

"Hello, Luke."

It was quiet for a minute as Luke tried to process what was happening. What was Tessa doing here? What was this place?

"I'm sure you have a lot of questions."

"You bet I do," said Luke, no longer silent. The words quickly and angrily spilled out of him. "What the hell, Tess? What's going on here? Who is this guy," he pointed his finger at Danny. "What is this place? Who is *she*?" He jerked a thumb towards Kelly, who had dropped a hand to her side, placing it on the holstered sidearm.

"I said there was no need for that," Tessa sharply rebuked Kelly, who reluctantly pulled her hand back up, and folded her arms across her chest. "This is the CDV. Some call us conspirators."

Conspirators. The word cut through Luke like a knife on warm butter. The name was ascribed loosely to any group that was ostracized and operated without permission. Luke felt blind rage that he had been so easily fooled by the files on his server.

"You aren't scientists!" he screamed. "You are peddlers – dissenters – haters!"

Danny held up his hand. "We are not dissenters. A conspirator works to reveal the real facts, not just dispute and rebel." He paused, blinking his eyes. "Tessa was right about you, though. You are smart."

"What do you mean, Tessa was right about me?" Luke's eyes widened as it dawned on him. "Are you playing me? Was this just a sham – an act – to get me here?" His eyes were on fire, and he glared at Tessa.

It was silent for a moment.

"It's not that simple, Luke."

"Really? It sure seems simple to me, Ms. Morgan." He started to move towards her, then noticed Kelly, who had the gun, began to move as well. He stopped. His anger had to be checked. "I just want to leave. I'm not going to hurt her."

"Oh, I know. I just wanted to intimidate you." Revers vulgarly snorted.

Tessa had enough. "You know, this is the problem when a group becomes more paramilitary than counteractive. Enough with the tough talk, Kelly. Please, Luke," Tessa's voice became imploring. "At least listen to what we have to say? If you then choose to go your own separate way, so be it."

"So be it?" his voice was flat. This woman he loved was telling him, 'so be it'?

"I know you think you hate me right now. But even more than any feelings you might have about me, you have a stronger feeling – a burning desire – for science and to find a cure. That report you saw, it was legit. As you noticed, we gathered information from one of the best truth verification teams out there. We also secured files from Tachi Yin. Haven't you often said you wished everyone would work together? Now you can!"

"With illegal information!" he cried. "Gathered, secured – these are substituted words for stolen and hacked."

Tessa ignored his comment. "We think the answers we're searching for might be here. We haven't been able to crack it yet, but we didn't have the right person. Now we do."

"Right person for what?" Luke growled.

"For this," Danny said, picking up a remote "Our tech isn't as fancy. Be patient."

He pressed a button, and a white screen began to unroll from the ceiling. Luke recognized it as a projector screen from back in the day when LEDs illuminated the world through peripheral lenses instead of 3D holograph.

It seemed to take forever, but the screen finally extended, and the projector began to display.

"Beware," a narrator said as the screen flashed black. "What you are about to see will change your life *forever*."

EIGHTEEN

The window drape fluttered slightly as Josh peeked from behind the drawn curtains and peered down the street. It was quiet. Street lamps were coming on. The activity would soon pick up as it always did in the evening around the neighborhood. It was the reverse of yesteryear when people would be out enjoying the beautiful Minnesota weather, and playing with their kids, gardening, mowing the lawn, fishing, or laying on a hammock reading a good book. Now the activity was more destructive. Burning large piles of materials...the brazier had become the thing to do.

He turned away from the window and ran both hands through his hair.

"Stressed much?" he mockingly asked himself. "Why would you be? Not like this whole thing is going to blow up in your face."

Scarcely four hours had passed since his conversation with Mark Jacobi and John Stevens. While the idea of traveling to Pittsburgh and San Francisco seemed inviting, the dreary reality of why was starting to set in.

He needs me to stay alert – to be a presence. He had decoded the words spoken by Jacobi. If the CEO wanted him to keep his eyes open – something must be amiss. Days like today, he wished he could talk to Amanda.

Flopping into the futon, Josh pulled out his handheld. His mind was a whirlwind. He could not focus. Dark loneliness surrounded him. At times like these, he could not decide if he felt a stronger desire for physical intimacy or simply friendship. He perused the listings that offered virtual reality sex. It had become the trend once virtual reality porn became common. After a minute, he realized it was not sex he wanted.

He was returning to Pittsburgh, his old alma mater – a place he associated with community. This was dredging up feelings of loneliness.

"Feelings felt more keenly," he said to himself in a 'professor-like' voice. "You must get in touch with your inner self, Josh. *Feel* the energy. *Embrace* your destiny."

Throwing back his head, he laughed out loud. He kept laughing. He could not stop laughing. He did not even know *why* he was laughing. Then as suddenly as he started, he stopped.

It took a moment to refocus, and when he did, he found himself visiting an old social media account. It had been unused for ages.

"Josh Cunningham avoids social media like the plague," he could hear Sam Walter's voice in his head. "Has to be the only morphing agent who does."

Josh smiled at the memory. He went to the notifications, and browsed the recommended connections.

"Hmm," he read the first one. "Jessica Lynn – I remember her. Sat behind me in class all sophomore year for social studies in high school; never liked her. Moving on...Luke Baer...oh wow. It's been a while too. Back in college, we shared science classes. He was super geeky and smart. Real whiz. I haven't talked to him since..." the self-monologue faded as Josh decided to click on the prompt. A message box opened.

■   ■   ■   ■   ■

An old train whistled sounded from Luke's tablet. He glanced at it as he finished typing up some notes on another device. Four hours had passed since his return from the meeting with CDV. The shocking bombshell from discovering Tessa had been using him was not going to wear off anytime soon. He did not know what to make of the initial offer CDV proposed. His heart was broken, and his mumbled response was along the lines of, "I'll let you know."

He felt like a chick used by some dude she had met at a bar. He felt stupid and ashamed. Confused and embarrassed. Maybe the tablet would distract him. He whisked the chair over to the table where the tablet was propped.

"Hello, what's this? Josh Cunningham! It's been forever."

■   ■   ■   ■   ■

Josh's notification center blurted out an alert, and a small red '1' popped up in the upper right corner. Smiling, he clicked the icon showing that Luke Baer had sent a message in response.

BEEN FOREVER, MAN. HOW'VE YOU BEEN?

Josh tapped a reply using the digital keyboard.

BEEN ON A CRAZY RIDE. WHAT'S NEW WITH YOU? STILL IN PITTSBURGH?

YES. WORK AT THE UNIVERSITY, AS A MATTER OF FACT.

NO WAY! SO HAPPENS I'M COMING THERE TOMORROW.

SHUT UP! WE'LL HAVE TO HANG.

ABSOLUTELY. I'LL SHOOT YOU AN IM ONCE THERE.

COOL BEANS.

WHAT ARE YOU DOING?

Startled, Josh jumped as the text popped onto his screen. It was not a message from Luke, but rather the unknown sender again.

YOU KNOW I CAN SEE YOU.

What in the world? Josh was furious. *Who is this unknown sender?* He quickly shot a goodbye message to his old classmate and signed off. He ignored the mysterious texts.

Pocketing the handheld, he picked up the i-Beam. He turned it on and out of spite for the unknown and unwanted texts, he navigated over to the folder from Sam. *There's more to this video file than it lets on.*

He double-tapped, and the folder expanded – filling his living room. The other files began opening automatically, tossing data content across the room in bright holographic rays. Suddenly, he saw something.

Opening the attachment, he stepped back, putting a hand to his mouth. After a moment, he began rubbing his jaw, studying the information in front of him in disbelief. He pulled his handheld out, and holding it up, spoke into the microphone.

"Sam, call me."

"The FDA, CBER, CDER, CDC, WHO, heck even NOAA and the EPA – have all been lying," said Sam matter-of-fact. "Look, I know it sounds crazy, but if you truly think the file is in any way, shape, or form accurate – than that's the only alternative."

"I mean," Josh scratched his head, though truthfully he felt like pulling out his hair. "Look at this money! This is some serious dough – going to where?"

"The financial backers. At least any entrepreneur would it call that," stated Sam.

"But there hasn't been anything that would suggest a viable product. No new drug has..." Josh's voice trailed off.

Your presence is appreciated...keep your eyes open...work hard...was Jacobi trying to warn me about something going on in San Francisco? Does it involve Pharma Group?

He broke off his thoughts and spoke out loud. "According to this, everyone quarantined in areas of outbreak, have basically been inoculated with medicine *already available* to protect against the Disease."

"Inoculated by what medicine? Who knew the Disease was going to hit? And it has spread so quickly – wreaking mayhem and carnage. How could someone have known that?"

The high-definition holograph pixels did no favors for Sam who looked sleep deprived and quite haggard. Yet, the field coordinator showed no sign of slowing down as he hammered away on a keyboard. It was a traditional one. The clicking sound gave it away.

"Okay, hypothetical situation," The typing stopped as Sam leaned towards the camera. He was facing Josh, and waved the forefinger from his other hand. "Tell me, how exactly does global warming fit into this picture? The freak snowstorms over the past decade should answer any questions there. Global temperatures have dropped dramatically over the past five years. I realize it's called 'climate change,'" Sam held his right hand up, preventing Josh from interrupting. "But if they could so easily predict the phenomenon of global warming, how did they 'miss' this whole unearthly cooling?"

"Hypothetical question – whatever does climate change have to do with this?"

"I am not sure," Sam answered, shaking his head as he shuffled a few things on the desk. "But there is a digital thread here referencing both

NOAA and the EPA and certain environmental and geological studies. I do not know if they're connected. I'm just trying to see what else might have been used politically or culturally these last several years that was directly profiting someone else."

"Haha," Josh laughed. "You sound just like a dissenter these days. 'The government is always making a buck,' 'good people don't exist; only mercenaries.'" Josh spoke in an overly dramatic, mocking tone. "Not everything is about someone making money."

Sam gave a short laugh. "Exactly, which is the very reason why this concerns me. You see, Josh, when the world starts going to hell people are going to ask who's responsible. There is going to be payback when you screw the world over. Whether from the universe, God, or Mother Nature!"

"This is exactly why I called," said Josh as he rubbed his hands together. "So who is responsible? Based on these figures, nearly two or three dozen groups affiliated with or operated by various world governments are making a fortune with the emergency response to these incidents."

"I told you. If it's true, then all these departments, and agencies, and organizations are hiding something. And why? Say," Sam suddenly changed topics. "What about all those construction expenses? The costs are astronomical and have to be funneling into something massive."

Building a massive city. Josh clapped his hand to his forehead as he suddenly remembered the Savannah shopkeeper, and the words he spoke regarding construction activity – the rumors of a massive city, perhaps multiple ones. He shook his head. *It can't all be connected. That's too simple.*

Sam's persistence of a cover-up, the echoing words of Lieut. Rhianna Adams, the tabloids, the files in front of him – it all irritated him. He was a truthseeker, not a fear-mongering conspirator.

"Whatever. I will find out the truth, and I don't care who I have to cross to find it."

"Even if it means doubling back on SEH?"

"How so?"

"You know as well as I, SEH could be part of this."

It's true then – my premonition of Jacobi's words.

Josh took a breath. "What do you know about Pharma Group?"

"That's an odd question."

The truthseeker confided in his coworker the conversation he had with Mark Jacobi and John Stevens.

Sam gave a low whistle.

"Knowing that – this doesn't make them look good. The profits, the lack of following regulations by the very groups that form the regulations, the shortcuts…this is not looking good," he repeated himself.

"It doesn't. We agree on that. I've been doing some digging on my end."

"I'm listening."

"I found some research by a group called CDV on the darknet. It's based in Pennsylvania. As you know, I'm going to Pittsburgh tomorrow."

"Right."

"I will look them up and let you know what I find."

"So it starts." Sam sighed.

"What's that?"

"The end of all we've known. You're a truthseeker, Josh. We shut down morphing. What if it turns out what we thought was truth, is actually nothing more than an image of truth."

"A distorted reflection?"

"Yes. As seen in a mirror – dimly."

"So be it. If all we see is the mirror image, one day…"

Josh's mind wandered. He could not remember the last time he felt free and clear, happy, at peace. He sighed. Sam contemplated him with understanding eyes.

"Safe journey, man. I'll send your travel pack over. I'm here if you need me."

■   ■   ■   ■   ■

The black paved parking lot basked in the sun. Heat simmered up, scorching the rubber tires of the automobiles parked in the spacious area of blacktop. The warmth caused the asphalt to smell; as if it was poured and rolled that day.

Walking briskly over to the rental, Josh whipped open the rear driver's side door. He tossed his briefcase in. His sports jacket followed in a disorderly fashion.

Who do they think we are? He started the car by forcefully jabbing the ignition button, and rammed the seatbelt into its lock. *Guinea pigs? Play dolls for their pleasure? We have a right to know!*

He whipped the car into reverse, and when he had backed up a distance that would be considered anything but appropriate, he cranked the wheel hard left, and jammed his foot onto the accelerator. The car responded with a jump, and he sped through the parking lot.

I will find out what's going on. I wonder if anyone at Pittsburgh knows about this CDV group. Thinking of CDV reminded Josh of the data from Sam. It made him seethe. It was bad enough to realize the horrific scope of plundering from Earth's natural resources for greedy profits. Throw in a manufactured deadly disease with pretentious offers of faux help – the world was screwed.

The ringing of his handheld jarred his angry thoughts. Swearing as he glanced at it, a look of consternation crossed his face. *It's the day of reckoning; when I find out what is going on.*

"Hello?"

At that moment, all was eerily quiet. The only ambient sound was the quiet hum of the tires on the hot pavement as Josh listened for the caller's voice. It finally came sounding robotic, yet fully human. An Asian accent was also distinctly present.

"Hello, Josh. Drive safe to Pittsburgh."

"What do you want?" he demanded.

"You are searching for the truth."

"Yeah, it's my job," he sarcastically barked.

"Are you expecting to find answers in San Francisco?"

"I expect to find answers regardless of where it takes me."

Josh had no patience for this ongoing game with the unknown caller. He was beyond ready for it to cease, yet made pretense with an overly polite tone.

"Very good. Do you know who we are?"

"Do I want to?" He was frustrated, yet strangely unsure. At this point, after months of cursing the unknown sender, he suddenly did not know what he wanted.

"We will talk again. Keep your eyes open – your presence is needed in San Francisco."

The line went dead.

The same thing Jacobi said? He isn't the one behind this, is he? He dismissed the thought. *What am I supposed to find in San Francisco?*

The handheld chimed with an incoming text.

WHEN YOU ARE READY.

There was an icon in the message, and he touched it. A watermark appeared, the acronym GSA in the background.

"Global Securities of Asia," Josh muttered out loud. "The security firm we worked alongside in China years ago. What was that incident about? We called it..." He shrugged, unable to remember. Just why were they spying on him now?

Confused, he tossed the handheld onto the passenger seat. He glanced around. There had been scarcely a dozen cars on the highway. He had enough of the pedestrian driving. The car bolted.

■　　■　　■　　■　　■

"Welcome back to Pittsburgh University!"

Melinda Gore held out her hand, and Josh shook it as he stepped to the front of the room. The applause of those assembled, embarrassed him.

"SEH is well-known for its groundbreaking, daring ventures into the biomedical world. I speak for all scientists when I say we're better off for that. To have one of our own proudly represented not just at SEH, but more specifically, as the lead field agent for the Morphing Division – my goodness, that's impressive!"

Melinda's words made him feel uncomfortable. He held up his hand as polite clapping broke out once again.

"I'm just glad to come and represent our new alliance. I'm eager to work with the University, and hope we can achieve good things together."

Melinda took Josh's arm, and steered him out of the room as the group broke up. Daily activities would resume. Once outside, she led him to a compact space that served as her office, and shut the door.

"You made it."

"Obvious, but yes."

"Here's our itinerary for tomorrow, both flight plan and the San Francisco schedule."

"Are you looking forward to it?" he asked.

Melinda thought about it for a second. Her traveling companion was quite handsome, and she had been secretly hoping SEH would send him when news of the accepted alliance broke. Josh Cunningham was an achievement hero at the University. The only graduate to work for a big-player like SEH, and that meant something.

"Yes," she responded. "I'm not fully aware of what is going to be presented yet, but if we can get a leg-up on TYM, we'll sweep the deck of competition for the cure."

"Pardon me, but I know little of Pharma Group. You speak of sweeping the competition – is it currently a crowded deck?"

"Yes," Melinda laughed as she threw a few items from her desk into a handbag. She looked at him, amusement dancing in her eyes. "TYM is one of our biggest competitors, and they have some very aggressive people. But," she stepped closer, and lowered her voice. "Between you and me, they don't stand a chance."

"Why? Will they be at the summit?"

"Oh, I'm sure they were invited," she replied, brazenly tugging on his shirt. "But they don't have you and me."

"Ha, very true," Josh pulled back, and Melinda released her grip. This could be a fun trip. "I'll look over this, but I do have a meeting set with an old classmate."

"See you tomorrow, Josh." Melinda flashed a smile.

. . . . .

The coffee shop was known intimately by any student from the University. Some called it the birthright of passage for an undergrad. The rich, dark smells of organic, fair-trade coffee beans permeated the air. A hint of the buttery croissant rolls wafted and amalgamated with the twisted caramel breading that was so popular with the frequent customers of the shop.

Josh had his own favorite drink. It was actually the same drink of choice for Amanda. It had been their first connection at school before they dated. Out of spite for its memory, Josh ordered a shot of espresso.

He was early, Luke was late.

"How long as it been? Six years, no seven?" Luke spoke as he approached Josh. The latter turned to greet his former classmate and friend.

"How are you, Luke?" he shook the other's hand as the two embraced in greeting.

"Oh, you know, some days are good, some days not as much."

"And today, is it a good day?"

Luke did not want to answer this. Truthfully, today was a crappy day. During college, he had always considered Josh a good friend, though.

"No. It's not." He replied in a flat, monotone voice.

"Oh, no. And why is that?" Josh was genuinely concerned about his former classmate.

"Long story, but it involves a woman, dishonesty, and utter betrayal."

"Harsh!" Josh tossed his head back, and downed the espresso shot. He immediately regretted choosing the drink. He swallowed hard, and slightly turned his head as he did so. "That isn't good."

"The drink?"

Josh laughed. "Well, that, but also the chick. It's something to love someone and…"

"Whoa, whoa, slow down!" Luke remonstrated, holding up his hands. "Who said anything about love? I knew this girl for like three months."

The truthseeker studied Luke's earnest face and pondered his friend's plight. He kept the incredulous out of his voice.

"It's probably my job talking or that crappy espresso shot, but how exactly does a woman betray you in 90 days?"

Luke sighed. "It's a long story. Suffice it to say, I've been working on the Disease outbreak and thought I was close to something. Turns out, it was nothing more than a data mine plant, and I was the bait."

"Let me guess," Josh chimed in. "She was the lure."

"I forgot you now live in the 'Land of 10,000 Lakes', fisherman."

"Hey!" Josh laughed. "We have 11,842 of them to be precise."

"Always ready with the facts," Luke smiled. "So, how are you? You got married, right? Amanda?"

A shadow passed over Josh's face. Luke saw it and figured this was an appropriate time to take a small sip of coffee.

"Past tense. We were married. She was killed two years ago. A truck driver fell asleep. Ran a red light. Plowed into her…I miss her."

Josh could not remember the last time he talked publicly about Amanda. Let alone admit his feelings. Somehow, the long-lost kinship he had with Luke made him feel safe and at ease.

"I am so sorry," Luke brushed Josh's arm with his hand, more to reiterate his sympathy than anything else. "That is tragic, man. I had no idea."

"Most don't. You know, I never was one for social media. Heck, the fact I was on it the other night was a first in months." Josh looked at Luke, and slowly shook his head. "I'm not even sure why I was on there. But here we are."

There was a pause between the two, but around them, the coffeehouse cackled. Beans in grinders, hot water sifting, mugs clanging into each other, fingers typing on keyboards, and even the faint rustle of a traditional book as its paper pages were turned. The nostalgia wore off.

"Dang," Josh sighed. "Enough talk of women. Obviously, not our lucky suit."

The two men laughed, and resumed their conversation. It was a good chat, and time quickly passed. So much, it was only when they were wrapping their visit that Josh suddenly remembered something he had meant to ask.

"Before I forget, I too am working on the stories surrounding the Disease. I've been following a lead. It's an organization called CDV, and they are based here in Pennsylvania. You haven't heard of them by chance, have you?"

Josh's question caught the scientist unawares. The latter stared at his empty coffee cup for a few seconds as mad thoughts chased about in his mind.

How in the world does he know about CDV? The very place Tessa works. Why is he asking? Is this why he wanted to catch up? Maybe I should go ahead and tell him. That witch used me anyway. Oh, why do I pretend to hate her? I love her, even if she hurt me. If I ever want it to work between the two of us, I can't backstab her the first chance I get.

This all ran concurrently through his head in a matter of seconds. He looked up from the mug, his decision made. His shook his head.

"No. I haven't."

Josh observed Luke's hesitation. Nevertheless, he replied carefree.

"That's a shame. I think they might know something about all these events."

"Could be," Luke sounded unsure.

The two stood up, and shook hands in farewell. Josh tossed his cup into the trash container a few feet away, then looked at Luke with a smile.

"Tell you what, if I learn anything, I'll let you know. Maybe it will help you as well."

"Sounds like a plan," Luke said. Inwardly, he cursed. Should he warn Tessa? Waving goodbye to Josh, he opened the coffee shop's door, and strode out.

Josh watched him leave. He could sense Luke knew something about CDV, but for some reason held back. Why?

"What to do," he quietly muttered. "Sam's not here. Maybe it's time I pull a few punches myself."

So he did.

NINETEEN

"Can you meet in an hour?"

The words echoed in Josh's mind as he recalled them. He was standing, staring out over the dark waters of the Allegheny. A chill ran up his spine as he heard a splash. Peering closer, he saw nothing. Attempting to soothe his nerves, he started to slowly pace back and forth, several yards or so, while rubbing his chin.

Despite being a person entirely use to thrusting his way into situations to find out the truth, this occasion was slightly different. Josh thought back to the conversation which led him here. His desire to 'pull a few punches' had taken his research to a darknet site. He attempted to contact anyone who would talk regarding CDV. A private message arrived from someone requesting a brief phone call. He accepted.

When he answered, the voice on the other side was heavily muffled by a modulator and had an ominous tone to it. The caller asked for a clandestine meeting at Point State Park. Josh did not feel great about this, but had no choice. If someone could provide him with information, it would be worth anything.

He asked when.

"Can you meet in an hour?"

He said he could.

"Come alone."

The call ended.

How cliché. Come alone! Like some spy movie. Josh laughed out loud, but he was the only person who heard it. The state park, a well known and popular tourist site, was nearly abandoned at this time of night.

"Besides," he spoke quietly to himself. "It's after hours. I shouldn't even be here."

He glanced at his 3D holograph watch. Sensing his face, a blue hue shot forth and displayed the time in front of him. He looked away, and the light died back down. The mysterious caller was running late.

Rubbing his hands across his arms, Josh tried to warm himself. It was chilly. Even with his childhood spent in Colorado, and now living in Minnesota, sifting chilly winds and temperatures were something he disliked. He was one person not unhappy with the changing climate, yet tonight was an anomaly for July. Abnormality had become more prevalent since what was called – Phase II of global warming – had begun a few years ago.

The wind bit through his thin sports jacket. Josh pulled it closer to his body, hugging himself. He kept up his brisk pace as he ventured further into Point Park.

I shouldn't be doing this! This is why I have Sam – to deepdive classified information. But Sam isn't here, I have to do this and find out what I can. Something about CDV doesn't add up.

The realization that finding the truth outweighed the risks won the argument. What was the Disease? How long had it been around? If he were to believe the tabloids, it had been spreading for the last several months – maybe even years. Cover-ups were happening daily, and only being leaked when best for business. What business, though? And where did the Disease come from? What would it evolve into?

Life itself was continually evolving. Ever since trans-life had been legalized three years previously, much had happened in the face of public opinion. The very questions about man's existence had been questioned. Radical religious followers – such as the Christians as well as the more conservative sects including the Mormons – bristled at the very idea that life was transient.

Back when Josh was younger, the rage from these groups was on men using women's bathrooms. That "outrage" was nothing compared to the fury when the Trans-Life Act passed. There were no biological or sexual identities. All was one, yet all was separate.

The biological entities of gender; psychological theories on adolescents; were now replaced by one's feelings. Age of consent was no longer a thing. As long as one had medical clearance, a person could pretty much do anything they wanted.

The debate raged long and furious. 'If nothing else mattered anymore, why have any boundaries?' Right-wing activists cried out. More reasonable voices responded and argued that the human race was evolving.

Throughout all of this, Josh stayed intrigued. Notwithstanding his own belief that there was no god or supreme deity, could nature start to corrode itself? It was here his research coalesced, and then abruptly imploded, and became confused. How could he accept the growth of humanity while questioning its stages? How could he claim to know the truth, when in reality, he was searching for the answers to why things were changing.

He could not speak out or question it beyond what his professional role allowed. It would not be tolerated. Dissenters – haters – were the most reviled of all. Besides, who cared? Life would continue to go on, he was sure of it. No one really knew what was next. At least, he thought so until last night. Now, he was unsure.

He swore. The caller was quite late. His nerves were wracked. He leaned against an old light pole – the LED bulb had been shot out long ago. The park had been a scene of a mass shooting several years earlier. It seemed to be a way to honor the dead to leave the socket empty. The memory of this violence reminded him of the chaotic world of yesteryear.

Religious people had seemingly become zealots overnight. Holding pray vigils to "cast" pansexual tendencies out of people; preaching messages of salvation to the transgender "demons." Muslims – especially in foreign countries – reacted to the sweeping change by performing several "cleansing" rituals. Americans called them terrorist attacks.

Meanwhile, alt groups called out religious entities as being hateful and workers of discourse among mankind. Churches were burned. Mega Trans-Life Conferences were bombed. Children from all walks of life were being killed. It was ugly.

The War in Asia followed, the eruption in South America, the reports of Phantom sightings…Josh's mind continued replaying the histories and atrocities that preceded the Disease. Had it been a chapter of life? Or rather a prelude of what was yet to come?

"You came alone."

The heavy voice was free of modulation. It startled Josh. He spun around, and saw the mysterious caller had arrived. A shabby overcoat hung from the shoulders, and the arms leaned heavily upon a cane as the feet limped forward. Josh could not make out the distinctive facial features, but could tell there was a week-old shave, and the eyes were hollow – they lacked sleep.

"So you're looking into the Disease?" the voice said.

Josh nodded in reply, still trying to ascertain what he thought of the stranger.

"You work for SEH?"

His mouth dropped slightly. "I, uh, how would you know that?"

"Come, come," the stranger coughed and sniffed while fidgeting. "You don't think I would meet a complete stranger alone at night, here at this abandoned park, right across the street from the site of a mass shooting, do you? What sort of idiot would do that?"

"I suppose I'm that idiot then," Josh replied. "I know *nothing* about you."

"And there's no reason to," the caller coughed again.

"What are you? An addict?" Josh was suddenly suspicious.

"What does it matter?" More sniffles. "You came looking for truth, and I can give you that."

"Fair enough."

The stranger cocked its head and looked at Josh. Then reaching a hand up, it scratched the heavy whiskers.

"So you know about photogenic properties and entities?"

"Entities? Photogenic? If you mean the systematic ideology that relates to the biological science that humans require light for their skin and…"

He meant to go on, but the stranger was impatiently waving a hand back and forth. The gesture annoyed Josh, but he got the point and stopped talking. He acquiesced to the stranger with an inclination of his own hand.

"No, I'm talking about light *versus* dark."

Josh cocked an eyebrow, and stared in disbelief at the caller.

"Light versus dark? Old Norse mythology?"

"Ha!" The stranger spat, a stream of liquid followed. Josh noticed some teeth were missing. "It's not mythology. It's reality. Listen to me, boy, if you want to know what's really going on, you need to start looking in the right places."

The caller's hands suddenly leapt forward, and seized the corners of Josh's jacket. Apparently, the cane was not needed at the moment. Feeling threatened, Josh struggled to break free, his eyes big with surprise. His struggle was in vain.

"I know what you are looking for, you smart ass. You work for SEH," the stranger dropped a hand into the overcoat's pocket, and dug around for a moment. The hand reappeared holding a small chip. "I have here the leading research on a cure from TYM. It was hacked last week, and this is the copy."

The truthseeker was incredulous. In one moment, the stranger was talking light versus dark. The next, it was propositioning him with a stolen research chip from the University's leading competitor which, with the new alliance, was now SEH's competitor. Josh gulped as he tried to take in the situation.

The stranger coughed again, and the hand came off Josh's shoulder, and pawed about for the cane. Gripping it tightly, the caller steadied as the cough subsided.

"Well?"

"You're an addict, looking for money. I'm sorry. I can't help."

"You already stated that obvious fact. You came looking for the truth. Everything you are looking for is right here!" The caller shook the chip. "This microchip not only contains all of TYM's research on the outbreak from the last several months, but it also contains information on other events happening."

"Like a fulcrum?" Josh's eyes opened wide in astonishment as he referenced a fictional telltale device.

"Is it? You know so little. Light versus dark is *everything* in this world. You heard of the Canadian biochemist, Jordan MacDonald? You heard about the helicopter shot down in New York? You know the president has the Disease? Yes, I said the president. And yet, you are so focused on what a small, unknowing organization called CDV might know. You were right. You are an idiot."

"Slow down." Josh was trying to process everything the stranger was saying. "How in the world do you know about Jordan McDonald? Or that the president might have the Disease? Where did you get that information?"

He was nervous, and held his breath. He hoped the stranger would answer instead of holding back. Somehow, this mysterious caller seemed to know everything that was going on.

"Everything is related to something – evolution 101."

Josh was unsure how to respond, or if he was supposed to. The stranger stared blankly at him for a minute.

"Alright. Listen to me, Mr. Cunningham, of course, I know your name. You may think you understand what you're dealing with, but you don't have a clue. If you want to proceed with your research – beware! Many have tried, none have succeeded."

Josh opened his mouth to protest, but the stranger merely turned up the collar on the overcoat. Pressing the chip into Josh's hand, it turned and walked to the edge of the Allegheny.

"I am an addict, but I'd rather be an addict today than tomorrow." The words were spoken cryptically. "Just wait until they start, you won't even know, that's how well they've planned it. All of this culminates in a grand finale. Earth only had so much to give. Look at what it's become, but my god, the finish is gonna be something else. The finish of all finishes!"

"Ha! Beautiful, ain't it? Just like these three rivers..." the caller waved the tightly clutched cane across the Monongahela, Ohio, and Allegheny rivers. "Three strands of life connecting here. Almost as if it was known that one day, you'd be standing here, holding the connection of *everything* in your hands. Be careful with that," the stranger nodded towards Josh's palm which held the chip. "That's all the power in the world. Don't trust just anyone, but do not fail to trust anyone."

Without warning or any hesitation, the caller calmly pulled a handgun from the coat pocket and raised it to the whiskered chin. Before Josh could even blink, it pulled the trigger and fell backward.

"What the!" Josh cursed and rushed to the edge of the planked walkway. He saw the stranger's lifeless body sink into the water.

Five seconds passed, maybe five minutes. Josh lost sense of time. *They just shot their brains out in front of me.* Breathing heavily, sweat pouring from his forehead, he closed his eyes.

"Think, Josh, think," he muttered to himself.

He looked up. He had to leave. Even though it was an ungodly hour, the gunshot would be picked up by ScatterShot. The police would be arriving any minute.

Turning, he began running down the trail. He felt sick, and needed to vomit. He choked it down, and pressed on.

Light versus dark, TYM, all the events that have happened were planned, and all the answers are contained on this chip. The finish of all finishes!

Josh's feet rhythmically hit the pavement as he ran. Turning slightly, he continued up a grassy slope to the location where he had entered the park.

What in the world have I gotten myself into?

TWENTY

The whine of the jet engine was both constant and aggravating. Josh leaned back in the seat, and peered out the small window. He gradually became aware someone was watching.

He glimpsed to his left, and saw his beautiful traveling companion, Melinda Gore. A smile spread across her face, unashamed she had been staring.

"You know," he said as he looked away from Melinda's face, and back out the window. "They *did* promise I would travel a lot in this gig. And they were right."

She giggled, vivacious and free. He smiled as he looked back at her again.

"Let's be honest, I'd love to sit at home and catch up on the four different shows I have yet to make out of season one, but…on the other hand, I do love what I do."

Melinda nodded, and took a sip of her coffee. She set the Styrofoam mug back onto the extended tray table, and carefully wiped her mouth with a napkin.

"You are practically a legend around Pittsburgh."

"Oh hush," Josh broke in, fiercely embarrassed.

"No, I mean that!" Melinda put a hand on his arm. It felt soft and gentle.

Some garble came over the plane's speakers. Based on how the engines slowed, and the loud brrrrr of the landing gear being lowered, Josh figured they were preparing to land.

"Few people have made it to a high-level research team. And you know the University's dire wish to be publicly recognized. You were a creampuff. And," she sidled over closer to him. "For the next two days, you are *my* creampuff."

Josh was slightly taken back by Melinda's shameless flirting. But, it had been a long time since a female was warmed by his presence, so he let her. He enjoyed it.

The plane landed with ever so slight a jostle.

"It's the 21st century," he cracked. "Can we not figure out how to land planes without such a bump?"

Melinda laughed loudly at this. He did not even think it funny, but he enjoyed the attention.

"What time do things kick-off?"

"Tomorrow, at eight o'clock."

"Weird, it's being held in-person. Can't remember the last time I heard of an in-person research conference."

"Well," Melinda informed him. "This mega-conference is bringing in some of the world's brightest doctors, physicists, biologists, scientists – all different fields. Pharma is planning something big, and promised a major breakthrough this weekend."

"How? From Pharma Group directly; or collectively as a conference?"

Melinda paused, preparing to give a lecture. She glanced at Josh, and remembered this was a man she thought handsome, and that she needed to refrain from giving him the "Luke Baer" treatment – something she was quite fond of doing. She took a different route.

"I would assume collectively. The belief is if all our forces are in the same place, the energy is going to cumulate and equally disperse – we'll become stronger together."

For a second, Josh thought she was kidding. Then he realized she was quite earnest.

"Really? You think that positive energy and mind over matter is going to cause some sort of cosmic reaction which will reveal the cure or truth behind the strange happenings?"

She shook her head. "No, I meant with all these brilliant minds present, the odds are in our favor of finding a cure. Honestly, more than anything, I think Pharma Group wants to show off. They just partnered with Pittsburgh University." She shot him a proud smile.

He returned the smile. While Pittsburgh University was a major player in the biomedicine research field, he scarcely thought a big outfit such as Pharma Group would feel compelled to boast of a partnership with them.

An announcement notifying the passengers they could start disembarking ceased any further dialogue on the matter. The two of them made their way off the plane and towards the ride-share area. Josh hoped the conference would provide a better scientific argument than Melinda gave. It did not.

.   .   .   .   .

"Complete waste of time," Josh spoke into the micro-recorder as he angrily paced the atrium floor outside the main conference hall.

The event had started off on a grand note. Big banners, people waving flags from many nations, a call of Unity and celebration of the Trans-Life participants. The mayor of San Francisco made a special appearance, as did the Governor of California. She received a warm welcome – the first transgender person to hold such a high political office. Josh applauded her achievements. He knew it was far from easy, navigating the waters of "social governance." Though, to be honest, ever since dissension had been made a state crime, it was easier. The Bible-thumping hypocrites had been publicly silenced.

Then came the first of many speeches. It was rousing, used a smattering of science phrases, even bordered on patriotic, and spoke of a better world tomorrow due to the results of the convention. After that, the speeches varied from inspirational to tedious. It was after the second straight boring speech that Josh went out, and sent a message to Sam. He was starting to doubt the sincerity of the convention.

"HANG IN THERE." The message came back. "THINGS COULD ALWAYS BE WORSE." Sam sent a trending gif from the last hurricane which struck Florida. It was an overweight woman holding onto her Chihuahua and a lawn chair. The gif text read: ONLY A WHITE PERSON WOULD BE WORRIED ABOUT LAWN FURNITURE AND OVERGROWN RODENTS.

Josh chuckled. *She's probably from Wisconsin. Those cheeseheads do love their lawn furniture and little yippy dogs.*

The rest of the day improved – at least there were no speakers. However, by the start of the second day, Josh had yet to see a shred of evidence that anything *good* would come of the convention. Questioning the sincerity of the event, turned to doubting the intent of the presenters and organizers. If a breakthrough was going to occur, would it not happen by actual discussion? The workshops being hosted that morning, allowed for some mingling and interaction, but one could scarcely call the professional pleasantries earth-shattering or scientific in nature. He struggled to believe that someone like he – not a scientist – could see this while the more learned attendees of the conference eagerly continued on.

"If I have one more dead-end assignment, I'll quit," he spoke back into the micro-recorder again.

It was his way of doing therapy. Research agents had long discarded the use of audio recording on an actual device. But the ancient practice helped keep his mind sharp, especially when he felt he was being lulled to sleep.

Bored, Josh flopped into a plushy chair on one side of the atrium. He pulled out his i-Beam, and snapped his fingers. A blue light came forth, and a holographic screen appeared. Absentmindedly, he pulled a microchip from the thin sports jacket's pocket, and set it on the i-Beam pad. It was the chip given to him by the stranger in Point Park.

Even without the horrific visual memory of seeing the mysterious caller blow its brains out, Josh had an eerie feeling after the meeting. Who was the strange addict? What drug was it taking? They were too focused and controlled for a meth user. The stranger foretold of impending doom – greater widespread catastrophe than the Disease. Josh did not know what to think. What was truth anymore? Did the chip really hold all the answers? Even any of them?

His forefinger hesitated, and he was just about to press "Analyze" when the handheld started to vibrate, and an icon indicating an incoming call appeared on the i-Beam display. It was the unknown number. Josh was exasperated.

"Yes?" he quietly, but tersely answered.

"Hello, Mr. Cunningham," the voice replied. It was civil, but no less cryptic. "At the convention, are you?"

"You can track my GPS all day long," he shot back. "I'm not scared."

"Come now, Josh. We are not trying to intimidate you. Remember," the voice suddenly took a normal tone. "We need your presence there."

"Why?" he questioned. It was that word again. *Is Jacobi behind this?*

The more he thought about it, the more puzzled he became. Global Securities of Asia had long worn an assumed reputation for rapid data grabs. They would never hesitate to use quantity over quality. There were other foreign powers and surveillance organizations better suited for precision.

"You doubt this conference, no?" The voice was back to a cryptic sounding machine. "No need to lie, we can tell you do."

"Sure, sure." Josh answered.

He surveyed the room, looking to see if anyone was watching. A custodian was pushing a vacuum over on the other side of the atrium; a couple ladies rolled cleaning carts. No one was paying him any attention.

"The real question is, do these people have any actual data? Or will the rest of the weekend continue as is? The charm that lulls; the truth that binds."

"Sounds like a Chinese proverb," said Josh.

"Perhaps."

"You warned me before about San Francisco. Why?"

"So did your boss. It's irrelevant."

"Maybe to you," Josh interjected, "But to me, it's quite relevant, and I'm really curious how you know about Jacobi's conversation with me."

An audible sound, like a sigh, escaped from the other end of the line.

"We told you before, Josh, we are always two steps ahead of you. But now, we need your help."

"How?"

"For a 'by-invitation-only, must attend in-person event,' the convention has a server encrypted beyond your government's *highest* levels. That is *highly* irregular." The Asian voice accented the words as he spoke.

Josh found the information not to be overly strange.

"True. But then this *is* being presented by Pharma Group. Of course, there'd be a lot of encryption – they hold a government contract." He mulled it over. "That's a lot of security though, and Pharma is being pretty closed vested. Perhaps they are hiding something?" he asked the last part as an afterthought.

"We are in agreement then."

Josh was sitting still, thinking about the encrypted server, he suddenly realized what the GSA agent had said.

"Whoa, whoa! Slow down. In agreement on what?"

"You must hack the server in person," the voice answered, clearly exasperated. "It is located right there at the conference center. We can't access it remotely, and you are the best chance we have at finding out what's really going on here."

"I…uh." Josh was unsure of how to answer. Besides, the request was something Sam would be good at. He was a truthseeker, not a cyber whiz.

"We'll walk you through the process. We'll send you blueprints to where the server is housed. We'll use your secure access. Being a field agent for SEH's truth verification team already gives you the needed clearance. Obviously, discretion is needed. We won't tell anyone, Josh, if you don't betray us."

The seconds seemed to pass as slowly as the minute hand on a clock. Closing his eyes, Josh clicked his tongue. He wiped a hand across his forehead – a surprised look came upon his face. He had thought he felt perspiration, but there was no moisture.

He weighed the request. He felt no contractual reason why he could not help GSA. While SEH was his employer, they had no stipulations that he could never freelance. But still, this was GSA – they had been tracking him for weeks, spying on his every move – could he simply ignore that?

To do something so secretive, illegal – hacking a server! The masked request of Mark Jacobi asking him to be a presence rang in his mind. *Did Jacobi suspect this? Was he asking me to pry deeper? As if giving his permission?*

"Dry sweat."

"What?"

"You feel like your sweating bullets, but there's nothing. It's common. Your mind is warning you *not* to do this; but in your heart, you know you were made for this."

"Oh, cut the crap," Josh snapped. "Enough melodrama." His mind was made up. He was tired of half-truths. It was time he found out some answers. "Send it over, I'll do my best."

"Let's hope so. If you get caught…tut-tut," the voice admonished. "This conversation never happened."

A small click was heard, and the line went silent.

Josh set the handheld down and picked up the i-Beam. He flipped off the holograph option; he was going to use the secure screen. He could not trust anyone or anything. Thirty seconds went by, his pulse raced. He squeezed his hand shut. Ever since he was a kid, Josh knew if he closed his right hand into a fist, tightly bending down his fingers, he could feel his own heartbeat.

. . . .

"Mommy, is it real?" Josh looked up at his mother, who stood next to him, holding his hand.

"Yes," Ellen answered impatiently, vainly trying to tug her young son away. "Stand up. Let's go."

"No," the little boy replied, continuing to lean forward, staring at the small plant in front of him. "It doesn't look real."

"Joshua Robert Cunningham, you know what a cactus looks like! You've lived here your entire life. You've *touched* one before."

"No," he remonstrated, visibly upset his momma disagreed. He shook his head. "I don't remember. I – I wonder what it feels like?"

He did not wait for his mom to answer, if he ever intended to. His small, four-year-old arm shot out, and shoved itself into the cactus. The sharp prickles instantly stung him. He tried pulling his hand back out, but it was stuck on one of the needles. Loud shrieks filled the air.

Ellen quickly bent over, and skillfully pulled the small hand out of the bush. With one motion, she swung Josh onto her shoulder, and carefully cuddled him as she began running towards their car.

There was blood, more than there should be. Josh felt woozy and sleepy as his mom ran, holding him tight. He felt safe; in lots of pain, but comforted. He tried smothering his cries without much success.

"There there, Bear," Ellen said, using a pet name for him. "It's okay. Momma's going to make it all better."

Tears streamed down Josh's face as he sat on the edge of their car. Ellen quickly pulled off the sweater she was wearing over her top, she undressed the pink top as well. Grabbing Josh's hand, she wrapped the shirt over it.

"There, Bear love," she whispered, pulling him close and kissing his head. She ran her hands through his soft hair. "Hold tight, and don't let go."

He squeezed tight. He closed his eyes. His little chest heaved less, the tears slowed. A smile came over his face. He could feel *something* inside his hand. Something that wanted to get out; kicking every so often as it tried to escape. On the trip that followed to Dr. Pepper's office, the good doctor told him the kicking he felt was called a "heartbeat."

•　　　■　　　■　　　■　　　■

Josh's hand felt moist. He opened it, and inspected the palm. Once more, there was no perspiration. *Dry sweat.*

Glancing at the screen in front of him, he saw a notification displayed. The blueprints had arrived. The decision had been made, but executing it seemed rather tricky at the moment. His index finger hovered ever so briefly.

What are you doing? You're not an IT geek! You're not someone who breaks into highly classified locations, and steals information! But I'm not stealing, I'm merely looking. Besides, I need to know what's really going on. 'Your presence is needed...keep your eyes open' said Jacobi...why am I really here? What does GSA know?

Whatever argument one side of his mind offered, the other perspective countered. And then, of course, there was always the part of him that attempted to provide a third or fourth opinion. None of this mattered right now. His finger descended, and softly touched the screen.

Game time.

TWENTY-ONE

It was eerily quiet in the long, white concrete corridor. After entering it, Josh stood still. Standing off to one side, he peered down the wide hallway.

For hosting a mega-conference that was pulling in some the brightest and best minds around the world, along with a military-grade server housing dark secrets, the security was minimal. He thought he would have seen at least a guard or two by now.

He glanced at his handheld. Based on the prints provided by GSA, he was moving in the right direction. Stepping out from his side perch, he strode forward. It was so quiet that even though his shoes were a soft-soled casual, the echo from the heel hitting the floor still reverberated the length of the corridor. Josh winced as he heard the sound.

Freaking spy movie. I'm Bond, James Bond.

A chuckle nearly escaped as he thought this. It struck him funny. The fact he was an analytical field agent sent to a conference with his old alma mater; where he was supposed to be listening to stodgy speeches in the auditorium. Instead, he was prowling unknown hallways working in cahoots with a foreign security firm.

Probably illegal in the eyes of our government, then again, who cares? Obviously, not getting the answers from them.

The handheld flashed brightly.

"What?" Josh did not intend to speak audibly. "This can't be right."

With a final turn to the left, the device told him he had arrived at the server room. Yet there was no room – just a blank white wall. It could not be right.

A memory triggered inside Josh's mind of an old video game where one might push on the wall, and it would open. That was not a bad idea, except, this was not a video game. It seemed an eternity as he stared at the wall, pressing his hands all around it, hoping it would budge. Suddenly, another thought triggered. He studied the blueprint on the device. A smile crept over his face. The answer was not in front, but *beneath*.

Josh took a step back and then another. That should be enough, his engineering background kicked in. Dropping to one knee, he felt along the floor. It was smoothly laid ceramic tile. A material not used in the last ten years; it had been deemed energy inefficient.

"Ah," he whispered as his forefinger ran into an edge that was slightly raised above the rest.

Shifting his weight to both knees, he set the device down. His fingers moved along the rough edge, slowly working their way in. In lifting the tile, the adhesive that held it in place cracked, causing a loud noise.

Instinctively, he dropped the tile and rocked back from his knees, so he was sitting on his ankles. He quickly glanced up and down the hallway. It was still empty. He waited for another ten seconds. No one appeared.

Reaching down, Josh became conscious of the dry sweat again. But it was real. A bead of moisture dropped onto the tile. He ran a hand over his balmy forehead. He was surprised at how fast his heart was beating. It felt as though it might punch a hole straight through him.

Fingers clutching the tile, he began lifting again. It only came up a half-inch and stopped. He was puzzled. It should not be stuck, and then he realized what was wrong. He was pulling it against whatever the tile was supposed to operate.

He shifted over to his right, so he was off the spot he had previously occupied. Immediately, a four by four area lifted a quarter-inch off the floor. He smiled. *Use that engineering degree, dude.*

With one smooth motion, Josh lifted the secret hatch to the underground staircase. He took a quick breath and scurried down the hatch, carefully making sure it did not fully latch behind him. He had no idea how to open it from the inside – if he even could.

A quick chirp sounded from his device.

OUTSTANDING, MR. CUNNINGHAM. YOU HAVE 90 SECONDS.

Ninety seconds? Then what?

Once underneath the hatch, the staircase – which turned out to be more sliders than anything else – weaved into the server room. It was large to be sure, but Josh was slightly disappointed. Too many TV shows had left him thinking he would stumble into a room with a couple hundred machines. There were roughly two dozen terminal banks. From the security vault diagrams sent over by GSA, he knew which one he needed.

Sprinting forward, he toggled the i-Beam on. The laser ray of the device leapt forward, and connected with the cyber wall security on the terminal. His brow furrowed, but only for a second.

"Of course, Josh," he referred to himself in the third person. "You have to enter the passcode key."

His fingers flew over the digital keypad as he entered the code. The laser flickered for a second, and then the red light turned a bright blue. His furrow disappeared.

Toggling the i-Beam, Josh changed to holograph display. Pinching his middle finger to his thumb, he flicked them apart. The image in front of him, expanded to full size, filling the space he was in.

Files and documents flashed before him. While he was no computer whiz, he knew how to dig through research – and quickly. His fingers flew back and forth, tossing this file, pinning that one. In a matter of seconds, the furrow reappeared, and a look of exasperation emerged on his countenance.

"What in the world?" he muttered in disbelief.

Fifteen seconds.

Josh closed the terminal access and flipped the i-Beam off. Turning around, he ran towards the staircase.

Ten seconds.

Scrambling up the sliders, his feet kicked awkwardly at the smooth, slippery surface. Reaching with his hand for the top of the hatch, his fingers clutched wildly for anything. He felt a hard, solid object and grabbed on for dear life.

Using all his strength, he hoisted himself up, pushing the hatch open. His upper body reappeared over the top, and he flipped himself onto the hallway's floor. With his left foot, Josh kicked the hatch cover back down. Spinning around, he quickly pushed the access tile as hard as he could. The hatch fully sunk into the floor. Everything looked just as it had before.

"Hey, what are you doing here!" someone shouted, and he heard footsteps coming up the hallway.

Do something, you nincompoop!

Covering the device with his right hand, Josh lifted his left hand to his mouth – purposefully shaking it. He started coughing as he fell to his side, sliding the handheld into his jacket pocket as he did so.

"Stay right there!"

The guard came running up, and shoved a 9mm into Josh's face. Another guard came running from the opposite end of the corridor

The coughing continued.

. . . . .

"For the last time, what were you doing in that hallway?"

Josh lifted his head from his hands, and looked at the well-dressed man interrogating him. Looking behind the man, he could see the two guards talking rather animatedly to someone else out in the hall, on the other side of the room's security door.

He knew it was only a matter of time. Turning his gaze back towards the man questioning him, Josh coughed, then sighed.

"I told you already. I was looking for the media room when I had an asthma attack."

"Why would you be looking for a media room when the conference for *all* attendees is being held on the other side of the building?"

"Look," he remonstrated, holding his hands up. "I was invited to this event. I am an employee of SEH, and I haven't been to this building before. I got lost, and then I couldn't breathe."

"So you said," the man sneered, bending in closer, and getting in Josh's face.

Josh pulled back slightly, but was unable to avoid being hit with the man's spittle as he talked.

"We will know soon enough."

The door swung open and someone walked in. It was the person with whom the two guards had been conversing. This man was dressed casually, wearing loose-fitting jeans and a pullover. He nodded at the interrogator who leaned back from his menacing position, but not before shaking a finger in Josh's face. The interrogator wheeled and walked back to the man in jeans. The two shared a brief conversation.

The interrogator was clearly perturbed. Josh overheard him say, "But something isn't right!" Obviously, whatever the man in jeans said upset the interrogator. The latter finally threw his hands up in the air, and turned once more to stare at Josh.

"Fortunate, my friend. Next time be more careful where you get lost." Then he stormed out of the room.

The man in jeans smiled as he took a seat. "I apologize for my colleague's rude manners. Your security clearance checks out on all systems, even with the top dog – Blair Leshief. You know him?"

"I met him…once," Josh started carefully, and then added. "I work in the Morphing Division."

"Well, rest assured there's no 'morphing' to be found here. And you undoubtedly understand we have to be careful. An event of this kind has never been held; people haven't even come to this convention center for almost four years."

Josh nodded. "Of course, sir. I understand."

The man in jeans smiled again. "I hope you can enjoy the rest of your day, and put this little misunderstanding behind you."

"Thank you," Josh pushed his chair back from the table, the legs scraping noisily upon the concrete floor. He tilted his head. "May I ask, why now?"

"Beg pardon?"

"You said it's almost been four years since people were here. Why now?"

The man in jeans contemplated Josh with a cool air.

"I'm not privy to those details. I just head up security." His steel-gray eyes darkened. "Good day."

Josh knew it would be pointless to press the man, perhaps even counterproductive. So he nodded in farewell, walked around the table, and strolled out of the room. One of the security guards, not the one who had shoved a pistol in his face, escorted him out of the holding area, and back to the main convention floor.

After the guard left, Josh's adrenaline dropped. Feeling weak, he leaned heavily against the wall of the atrium, deeply breathing as he closed his eyes. The doors to the convention hall were opening, and the attendees started to exit. Perspiration gathered on his brow. His hands were cold and sticky. He felt a drop of moisture fall to his right hand.

Wiping it on his shirt, he used his palm to vigorously rub both eyes. He straightened himself. That was that, except he knew it was not that simple.

"Well, you look like crap," said Melinda, looking at him with a smile. She batted her lovely eyes, and touched Josh's arm. "Kidding, obviously."

He gave a short laugh. "I didn't sleep well."

"Oh? Sorry to hear. I don't ever sleep well when I travel. To…restless."

The way her mouth formed words captivated him; her tongue gently caressing her lips. His mouth was dry.

"So, what did you think?" If Melinda knew how he was reacting to her appearance, she played dumb.

Shoot. I don't even know what the last workshop was on. He had to think of something to say. A sheepish grin came over his face.

"I gotta be honest. I was so tired, I came out here and dozed in those chairs," Josh flicked his wrist towards an arranged half-circle of plush red chairs off to the left side.

"Good choice," she nodded, and leaned in close. "Besides, now that you're not tired anymore, maybe..." She lingered momentarily, the meaning of her words sinking in. She then pulled back. "Anyway, we're done here. We're heading downtown for a special event. Well, everyone but non-science personnel."

"Oh goody," Josh quipped. "I hope it's special."

"Aww," Melinda smiled. "Look who's pouting! You know, I could sneak you over."

"That's sweet," he could feel desire rising. "I prefer to spend the evening in."

"Of course," she smiled. "*In* can be nice."

Her innuendo was not lost on him. Delectable tension filled the air, teasing, tempting, and beckoning. Josh locked eyes with Melinda. He knew what she was thinking. She had hinted at it on multiple occasions. He was at a loss for words. What did he want?

"Damn it, Josh. Do you wanna come back with me?"

The woman stood with her right foot carefully propped on its heel, her left crossing slightly in front of it. Her hand on hip accentuated her curves; her soft hair gently touched her shoulders. The offer was tempting.

The world may be going to hell in a handbasket; I have a beautiful woman offering me a reprieve. Actual pleasure. Why do I hesitate? He thought of Amanda.

"You are a beautiful, intelligent woman, Melinda. Honestly, I would love to..."

"Except?" she observed his hesitation; she was not used to rejection. Something of importance must be keeping him back. "You can't still be a virgin."

"Haha," Josh's laughter rang loud and clear. Despite the atrium being filled with hundreds of people, it reverberated with a faint echo. "No, no, but I was hoping to visit Sausalito. Alone," he added, when Melinda looked as if she might offer to accompany him. "It's a personal thing, but truly, I'm honored."

Her face wore a look of surprise. It faded into amusement. Then she gave a cold laugh.

"Don't flatter yourself, Josh. I like sex. The interest was nothing more than that."

She turned and started towards a mingling group of scientists. Glancing back at him, she puckered her lips and blew a kiss.

"Whatever your reasons, I hope it's what you want."

He watched her join in the conversations with other brilliant minds. Other people like her. The buses would soon leave to transport the attendees of the convention back over to San Francisco for the special event downtown. Standing there in the room, away from the others – scientists, doctors, biophysicists, people of higher education and scientific achievement – he never felt more an outsider. Watching the beautiful Melinda Gore walk away – he never felt more alone. At that moment, he half wished he had never married Amanda. He felt cursed.

I need some fresh air.

।   ।   ।   ।   ।

The shopping cart had once been used for groceries. Now years, maybe even decades after it had been assembled, the cart resembled little more than a trash can. That suited Jim, who was pushing it, just fine. He was self-professed to never be one for "fancy doohickeys or duds." If someone pointed out that "duds" usually referred to clothes, Jim would wave them off with a wink and a nod.

It was late afternoon and would soon be dusk. A few years ago, the sun would hang in the sky much longer than it did now. The effects of global warming, scientists had said.

"Bah, humbug," is what Jim said. "Natural phenomenon is all it is." And as much as sunlight bothered some people, Jim hated darkness worse. "You can't see in it," he would say.

The cart rattled on. One of its front wheels was misaligned, causing it to turn this way and that – making Jim's task of guiding the moving vehicle rather arduous. He stayed with it though, and was successful in missing people, and avoiding the large cracks in the cement sidewalk.

"Dang thing. Nobody's probably maintained this street for years," he said to no one in particular. "I don't know why people even bother living here anymore. I don't know why I'm still here."

That was false. He knew his reasons for not going. It had been a couple days since he and Patrick had watched the video claiming to show African countries being overwhelmed with the Disease, and masses of people running and screaming like a crazed herd of animals. Africa was many miles away, though, and he could not leave. His family had a stake in Savannah – traced back to when they had first arrived from Mexico.

"Why it's so bad, a man can't even take a walk without tripping over this thing or that." Jim swore in frustration as the cart jarred in a large crack on the walk and haphazardly jerked to the right. He arms flailed out to catch it as the wheels bumped off the modern pavement onto the old cobblestones. He tightened his grip on the handlebar, and maneuvered the cart back onto its original path.

There was nothing of value inside of it. A few empty beer cans, an old discarded radio, a large piece of aluminum, and some rolled metal. It looked like tin, but was instead the newer composite metal that was supposed to replace all metals. "Just like every other wacky invention," Jim would say while chortling – his fat belly bouncing with each guffaw.

He rolled up to the back entrance of the building, and pulled a set of keys from his overstuffed front pocket. His fat hands fumbled with the ring as he tried to fish the correct key from the bunch. Patrick had told him long ago to change it to the keyless cell lock. "Call me old-fashioned," Jim had replied. "I don't trust some electronic device that can be located anywhere in the world for my lock protection." So the physical key remained.

He finally had the right one and pushing it into the lock, turned it. It was somewhat of a tussle to get the cart in while holding open the door, but he managed. Once inside, he exhaled, and looked around. It was a sight to behold.

There were wooden crates filled with old electronics of yesteryear, several television sets were haphazardly propped against a wall. Chicken wire was neatly bundled and stored in the far right corner of the room. A small table with two chairs had been placed directly in the middle.

Jim pushed the cart in, tugging the door shut behind. The wheel of the cart swung back and forth, rarely making contact with the floor as he moved further into the room. It was a converted warehouse, originally built during the gentrification period, as taxpayer-funded discounted living quarters – if one qualified.

Being the man of principle that he was, and always refusing a handout – a characteristic he had learned from his father – Jim was quite happy to purchase an old portion of the warehouse when the public housing market fell through. "Shows you just why capitalism is God and socialism the Devil," he had sneered. Many in the public eye would have turned on Jim for being a hater, but of course, he was just talking to Patrick. So he was quite safe.

He shoved the cart up against the back wall, and carefully unloaded its contents onto the floor. A few other sheets of aluminum were lying against the wall already. It was not much, but apparently made the bald, fat man quiver with excitement.

"Makes a nice collection," he said, rubbing his chubby hands together.

Pushing the cart back towards the entrance, Jim paused as he reached it. A nip of cold air brushed his neck, and he instinctively shuddered. It was time to go home. While Africa was far away, one never knew when the Unknowns would be seen.

.   ■   ■   ■   ■

"It's all a lie. This entire thing is a sham. They have nothing. I've studied research files for my entire career. What I saw in there was nothing more than hyperbole, concocted squares, and triangles to resemble truth – if we even know what that is anymore. The level of detail was poor, almost amateur. The theories and ideas simply rehashed fables from 1980s sci-fi. I thought this was Pharma Group's drives?"

A bird chirped. Josh looked up to see a cardinal twisting its head, staring, as if observing him. It was strange seeing one in San Francisco, well outside of its typical habitat. Then again, nothing was inconceivable these days. Josh looked away from the bird, his eyes floating back towards the Bay to the south. A world that knew little of what it was about to face, yet entrusted its brightest minds to attend a convention of nothingness.

"It's as we thought," the Asian voice said from the other side. "We knew it to be a nothingburger."

"But why? Again, this is Pharma. Why would they assembled so many scientists and doctors and physicists together?"

"If you wanted to eliminate competition, what better way than to feed them red herrings under the guise of partnership."

"Wait – you're saying Pharma is deliberately lying?"

"What alternative do you offer?"

Josh thought for a minute.

"I don't know. There's some things that don't make any sense. For instance, this really isn't Pharma's headquarters – that's actually located south of downtown. Also, they are sectioning off parts of the city."

"What do you mean, like a quarantine?" The GSA agent's interest was piqued.

"I don't know. Take Tenderloin. They've completely shut down any transportation to or from there. Remember the bus tours? Use to run smack dab through there. Now? Don't go within six blocks."

The voice on the other end was disappointed.

"It's a bad neighborhood. Always has been, maybe it got worse."

"Maybe." Suddenly, Josh felt an impulse to rub his right eye. He did so. It felt better.

"Is everything okay, Mr. Cunningham?"

"Yes," he answered quickly. He felt sleepy, yet filled with exhilaration, all in the same moment.

"Well then, we appreciate your assistance. We will be in touch."

"I'm sure you will," he knowingly shot back.

He pocketed the handheld and reaching up, ran his fingers through his black hair. A small groan emitted from his mouth. In front of him, a railing overlooked a little pond. The spot aptly matched his current state of emotions. Any wildlife had ceased to exist in the pond long ago. Algae covered most of its surface.

What should I do? What is next? If Pharma's behind this, what did Jacobi know? He warned me about it, but why? And if Pharma was planning this all along, why the alliance with Pittsburgh University? It makes no sense. There were too many questions and no answers.

"What is truth anyway," Josh muttered, unaware he spoke out loud.

"If you are seeking the truth, you will find it."

"Huh?"

Josh jerked his head to the left, and saw a grizzled, older man standing on the sidewalk. He realized he had spoken out loud, obviously, the stranger had overheard him.

"Is that what they say?"

"Of course," the other answered as if surprised by the question.

The older man walked towards Josh. He was dressed in a plaid shirt, untucked from his pants – a faint grey-khaki color. It was hard to tell how old the stranger was, not terribly old, but old enough to be boring and philosophical. At least that was Josh's first reaction.

"Nothing is truer than that. You *will* find it."

"Ha," he replied. "If that's the case, why have I have come all the way to San Francisco and found nothing?"

"You came far?"

"Minnesota."

"Some travel across the world."

"To come here? Sure," he replied, already bored.

"No," the older man said patiently. "To find truth."

"Of course," Josh was slightly annoyed. "Then again, my job is literally to find the truth."

"And thus far you're striking out?" the man asked.

Josh sighed. How could he explain to a complete stranger what his job entailed and what the last year – what the last several years had resulted in? It was impossible. So instead, he merely nodded.

"If it's a matter of seeing, I must be blind, because I have been striking out – pretty much my whole life." He gave a short laugh. The irony sinking in that these last few months summed up his entire existence.

"Blind will be blind. Not seeing is another matter."

The words struck a chord. Josh could see his mom. It was her *exact* phrase.

"What's that?"

The older man did not repeat himself. He merely smiled.

"Eventually, all will be known."

To hell with this. I could've had a piece of hot ass; instead, I'm talking idiotic rhetoric with an old man.

"You don't believe me?"

Josh shook his head. "I don't know."

"Press on, Josh."

KAABOOMMM!

A deafening explosion was heard. The ground shook. Dark clouds billowed skyward. The air instantly filled with blowing pieces of debris, some of the particles as fine as dust.

Startled by the noise, Josh stumbled to his knees, and ducked his head in conjunction with the vociferous eruption. After a minute, he cautiously looked around. The older man was gone. Scores of shoppers and tourists were also crouched on the ground as they too had instinctively ducked.

Screaming broke out from the previously still crowd. Shouts filled the air.

Josh was not sure what compelled him, but he started racing forward. Near the edge of the shops' entrance was a walking bridge out into the Bay. He had to see it.

He shoved through the milling people. A little girl tumbled over as he ran on. He did not stop. Something was pushing – pulling him to see what had happened. He ran wildly, his right eye itching like fury. He was the first to arrive at the walking bridge.

Racing out, his feet made quick thuds on the wooden planks. At the end, he stopped – staring, not believing what he saw. He blinked once, then twice, and gave a firm pinch to his skin. He had to feel a sensation to make sure it was real.

Ahead of him, smoldering in some places, leaping fires in others, was the gigantic remnants of the Golden Gate Bridge. It had been blown to pieces. Large chunks of concrete were piled here and there. Cars were falling into the deep water, sending shrieking passengers to their graves below. The impact with the Bay's water would finish any survivors after the initial explosion.

"My god," Josh whispered.

He closed his eyes. He could see it all so clearly. The bridge packed full of vehicles transporting hundreds, even thousands of unsuspecting people. A bright flash, a terrible sound that would haunt forever, and then cars flying into the air – minivans, sportsters, SUVs, trucks, and buses – concrete breaking into rubble underneath them.

Those closest had died with the explosion, he was sure of it. The rest screamed, cursed, pleaded – begged God for help – if there was a god. Their fate sealed as the great bridge slowly collapsed, destroying any hope of survival.

Sobs choked at his throat. A knot rose in his stomach. He leaned over and retched. Nothing came out. Josh dropped to his knees as tears streamed down his face.

Ash and debris filled the air like so many balloons at a birthday party. Only they were not held in place, attached to a string. These just kept rising, more coming behind them, until the entire sky was brushed in foreboding hues of red, orange, and black. A pall was cast over the area.

Through his tears, he saw them: the entourage of buses from the conference. What was left of them, at least. It appeared they had been near the middle when the blast went off. Only one bus remained on the bridge – it had been flipped up onto its roof, fire raging from the spilled fuel. Pieces of the other coaches floated in the Bay.

The devastation was horrific. The scene was terrifying. Josh knew the death toll would be staggering. He struggled to his feet. His right eye itched furiously; it started to twitch on its own. Such a burning sensation — as if his eyes were dead tired yet fully awake all in the same moment. Shutting them brought a refreshing relief, and he could think.

It was then he thought of Melinda.

TWENTY-TWO

Nobody was summoned in the early evening to the Tower unless something terrible was going to happen. The Tower was a place where students would be expelled, teachers suspended, and interns dismissed. It was nicknamed the Tower simply because it was a rounded building with an old bell tower at the top of it. Any current student had never heard the old bell sound. One would be hard-pressed to find a staff member who could remember it. In fact, only one member of the faculty – a professor of history – could attest to ever having heard the bell toll under normal circumstances. For a while, after daily use of the bell ceased, it would still be rung on holidays like Christmas, but as that holiday became too politically charged, the University had decided that, rather than offend a few, they would simply stop ringing the old bell altogether.

So that was that, and nobody knew why or how but the building became known as the Tower. Some radical Christians claimed that the building was cursed for punishment due to the ceased recognition of Christ's birth. That was hogwash according to most people, though. It was by chance that only bad things would happen there. It was the place where the University's Council Committee would meet, and nothing good ever came from those meetings.

Knowing this, Luke was mortified to be summoned to the Tower.

"Why me?" he muttered to himself, hurrying along the sidewalk. "Though I shouldn't be surprised, ever since Melinda Gore usurped control I've been receding into the shadows. I mean…hey, watch it!" He yelled at the student who ran into him. Obviously, she was not watching where she was going.

"Shut up!" she retorted, spinning around to shout back at him. It was then he noticed the tears streaming down her face. She spun around, and continued running.

"What the heck?"

He began to notice other students near him sobbing, falling over, and hugging one another. He saw a couple of the University's emotional stability counselors emerge from one end of the courtyard. Whipping out his handheld, he swiped his thumb. His eyes enlarged, and he swore as he stared at the feed. Details of a massive explosion in San Francisco, photos of a crumbling Golden Gate bridge, burning cars and buses – they all streamed in front of him.

Is this for real? Does the Committee know about it? His feet kept moving. *Aetatis progressu, always forward.*

■　　　■　　　■　　　■　　　■

"Mr. President."

If William heard the voice, he gave no heed. He gingerly held his head in his hands as he methodically whispered ancient prayers to himself over and over again.

"Mr. President, your coffee."

One of the secret service agents stepped forward and lightly touched his shoulder. They had seen him in this reverie enough to know they would have to physically break the trance.

Without a word, William reached out, and took hold of the mug. He lifted it to his lips, and sniffed.

"It doesn't smell like coffee."

"Sir?"

"I said it doesn't smell like coffee."

The aide glanced towards the agent on the president's right and shook her head while shrugging her shoulders hopelessly.

"I guess I could go see..."

"Damn you!" Pres. Turouning's patience was worn thin. "Fire the man or the woman who made this. This isn't coffee! This is rat urine."

With that, the president flung the cup against the wall, splattering its contents over the interior decor of the oval office. The china shattered into tiny fragments.

The aide put a hand to her mouth. The agent took a half-step back, and spread both of his hands out and to the side. He motioned for the doors of the office to be shut as the buzz of people outside the room clamored louder, vainly trying to see what was going on.

"Mr. President, I am not sure what was wrong with the coffee, but I will look into it."

"You better," the president rasped as he nervously wrung his hands; his eyes looked off to one direction on the floor.

"Mr. President, they are waiting," said Charley Conners, Secretary of State.

William blearily looked at her. He dreaded stepping outside the room. He did not want to face them. Yet, another tragedy had happened on his watch. It was like a record repeating itself, refusing to stop. A long sigh escaped his lips. With great pain, he stood up, and straightened his shoulders.

With a curt twitch of his neck, the security detail sprung into action, and moved him to the door and out of the room. Lights flashed as cameras went off. Despite all the technological advances, a good picture still required a light bulb.

One of the photographers stood casually near the back of the congregated press. He did not come for the statement on San Francisco, but rather something else. Adjusting the focus on his camera, he carefully pressed the button. He glimpsed at the screen, and with a quick flip of his right thumb, zoomed in on the photo. There it was; he had seen enough.

Before the secret service shut the doors to the briefing room, the photographer slipped through the exit. Once outside, he used his prosthetic hand to pull out his handheld. His real thumb flew across the screen. Taking a deep breath, he looked around. No one noticed him.

Danny Graves pressed send. He needed no further proof. The photo snapped was confirmation enough. The president had the Disease.

· · · · ·

"Josh, Josh? Are you there? Are you okay?"

Sam's panic-stricken voice loudly reverberated in Josh's ear. The latter pulled the earpiece out, and turned his head sideways as if ridding himself of a neck crick.

"I'm here," Josh tried to maintain the pretense of being calm.

"What just happened, man? Things are blowing up over here! Sorry," Sam immediately cursed himself. "Awful choice of words."

It came as no surprise to Josh that he was getting a call so soon after the Golden Gate explosion. Modern technology spread news faster than ice cream on a hot day. People around him were streaming, messaging, or snapping media bites for their family, friends, or followers. The horror of the moment fading into oblivion, eluding their consciousness as they held up their devices to share the bleakness via an impersonal social media presence, instead of ingesting it into the fabric of their actual reality.

"Yeah, well, things did blow up over here," Josh responded, ignoring Sam's apology.

His tone was dry and sour. How he hated social media. He could already see the stories morphing about whom or what caused the bridge to collapse. He doubted there would be a shred of truth in any of it. The humanity – the absolute tragedy – was being eviscerated as quickly as the lives of those who had been on the Golden Gate Bridge.

"Well, there's another story too. Remember that outbreak in Africa? Turns out, they've found a link in chromosomes to the guy in Canada and," Sam's voice lowered. "They are now saying the president has it. Can you believe it? Our freaking president has the Disease!"

The mysterious caller at Point Park told me that, Josh's eyes narrowed. *How did it know? How does Sam know?*

"What proof do you have?"

"CDV," enunciated Sam. "The group you told me about."

"I knew there was more to that group!"

Josh's eyes darted back and forth, observing the throes of people around him. A strange feeling befell him. What was happening in the world was too uncanny. It was as if they were actors in a play with an unknown ending, or a script that was being written as it unfolded – holding everyone in suspense. *A pawn. I feel like a pawn.*

"Well, at least I'm glad the buses made it over," Sam remarked.

Josh's eyes grew big, and he lifted his head as if hit by a sudden realization. He pushed a button on the device, switching off Bluetooth, and pressed the phone up to his ear.

"Wait, what do you mean?"

"I, uh," the field coordinator stammered. "I figured you knew. This has to be about the conference. I mean, why else would they target San Francisco?"

"Target? Who would target?"

"That's beside the point," Sam was impatient. "Did some of them *not* make it?"

Josh felt sick again. He was fatigued and beaten down. Doubling over, he stumbled to an unoccupied bench, and slumped onto it. Saliva swirled in his mouth. Leaning over the bench's side, he spit it out. Above him, so much debris floated in the sky it blocked the bright sunlight, and made the day appear overcast.

"Nope," his voice sounded empty and lifeless. "None of them. They were all in the middle."

"Wait, what? You weren't on them? Wow," Sam gasped. "That's luck – surviving a targeted attack on the convention attendees. Why weren't you on one?"

This seemed a good time for Josh to share what he had discovered at the convention center, his excursion with GSA, and finding the useless terminal banks. There was not a person he trusted more than Sam. He needed to talk anyway. His nerves were all jangled and needed to loosen up.

"This whole thing was a bloody setup. It was all a ruse," he ended.

"No joke."

"I can't believe someone would be trying to kill me."

"Don't take it personally, only a few thousand others have been killed."

"Don't be crass," he retorted.

"Get your head out of your crack," Sam shot back. "People are dead man, and *why*? You literally just told me they had nothing! The GSA – a highly secretive intelligence agency – was investigating due to global ramifications. The conference had *nothing*, yet assembles the world's leading scientists, doctors, bioengineers, chemists – anyone with a brilliant mind? Are you kidding me? I don't like this," Sam's tone changed from angry to worried. "This isn't right. It's all screwed up."

Josh sighed. It was a long, hard sigh. At this point, he was almost willing to believe the conspiracies. Everything over the last three months seemed connected. Yet, how could he prove anything? Each time he felt he was getting close to something real, it would change and morph in front of his eyes.

The Bay's water tossed and splashed about. An overturned car floated by, no doubt its former passengers deceased. Laggardly standing up, Josh faced the once magnificent Bridge. Its old double arches had been reduced to a lone span and a crumbling pile of concrete, steel, and twisted iron melting from the hot fumes of raging fires. Screams of people still reverberated in the air, sirens wailed – a nightmarish scene he wished was unreal.

Meticulously licking his lips, he absorbed the flavor around him. His brow furrowed, and his eyes narrowed. The flavor was familiar. It was the taste of death.

.   .   .   .   .

"Melinda is dead?" Luke could not believe his ears.

"Presumed to be, and in light of the news, we need you to take responsibility for her work and lead the Research Team. Especially given our new alliance with SEH, we need to keep things moving forward on our research for the cure." Chairman Simmons paced the floor of the Tower as he spoke.

The building seemed less intimidating once seated inside on the plush red cushions of the hand-hewn cheery wood furniture. A cocktail sat in front of Luke. It was a curious thing, the last two meetings he had – the one with CDV, this one in the Tower – both served hard liquor. He approved.

Aside from Chairman Simmons, the Vice Chancellor of Research Operations, the Vice Chair of IID, and the Chief Financial Officer were present. It was large enough space for several others, but this small contingency of the University's leadership was all that was needed.

The large table in the middle had etched designs on the sides. Luke gazed closer and realized they were scenes from the Bible. He recognized Daniel in the Lion's Den, an old fable for sure; the famous Jonah and the Whale. But then the others, perhaps the Plagues of Pharaoh? Or the Desolation of Times? A smile crept over his face. He was proud he knew so much of the great Book. The Ten Plagues, the Seven Bowls, the Ten Heads of the Beast, Luke cocked his head slightly as he studied the designs. They all seemed connected like part of a pattern more significant than it first appeared.

"So what do you say?"

The room was quiet for a moment; the Vice Chancellor cleared his throat. Luke's eyes blinked, and he looked back at the Chairman who stood at the opposite end of the room, his hands resting on the sill of a window overlooking the courtyard outside. The pleasant afternoon had turned to evening. The dusky hues of fading sunlight filtered through the window's glass and gently struck the Chairman's face, illuminating it with a soft glow on one side, while shadowing the other.

"I believe we need to change directions. Chart a new course," answered Luke honestly. "Nothing major, but it is something I would like to try."

The four heads of leadership looked at one another. He knew they were well aware of Chem-Lab. He also knew they had little choice.

"Do as you see fit, Mr. Baer. But," the Chairman enunciated clearly, punctuating his words. "Our alliance with SEH is critical. Don't muck that up. We're counting on you, sir!"

The other three stood up, and walked with the Chairman over to the door. They motioned for Luke to leave. Rising from the chair, he brushed his pants flat, and walked steadily out of the room, stopping to shake each of their hands on the way. The sturdy door clanked shut behind him.

He stared at the descending brick staircase. Was this really happening? Had he just been put in charge of Pittsburgh's Research Team? His lifelong dream was coming true? Luke gleefully rubbed his hands together. Then he remembered Melinda, and his mood dampened.

■　　■　　■　　■　　■

"Those poor people," Jim murmured out loud, running a hand over his bald scalp.

Having arrived safely home, the fear of the Unknowns had been replaced by another emotion. Whimpering, he leaned forward in the rocker, trying to catch his breath, unbelieving what he was seeing. Large tears rolled down his chubby face, and he wiped them away with an equally chubby hand.

"Two bad things at once; what else is new?" said a dour Patrick. The pub owner had stopped by when the news broke a short time ago. "First, the Golden Gate Bridge is blown to smithereens. Next, the blimey president has the Disease."

"They warned us!" Jim's voice rose as emotion seized him. "They said something was going to happen there."

"They warned of a cure. Is this the cure? Blowing people up? Infecting the president?" Patrick's voice was tinged with scorn.

Jim slowly leaned back in the rocking chair, and stared dumbfounded at his friend.

"The broadcast said what happens in San Francisco wouldn't *stay* there!" his voice shook. "It's already made its way to the White House. What if this is the beginning of the end?"

The two men watched as the news provided all of the horrific details surrounding the San Francisco tragedy as well as the leaked story of the President's secret. Each lost in their own opinions of what it meant.

"Well, if this is only the beginning," Jim said, head bobbing as he voiced his opinion. "I, for one, don't want to see what the end will be."

TWENTY-THREE

The dull hues of a setting sun cast a dim light across Luke's office. The blinders were raised; there was no reason to have them closed. Pressing a button on the wall, he watched as the old projector lowered. Biting down on his lip, he turned his head, not wanting to watch but not being able to resist watching as the machine descended. He was unable to remember the last time it was used. But he had to prepare, he had to lead the team. There was no doubt in his mind that all those anomalies he had spotted before held the medical code they needed for the cure. He remembered the Tower and the table in the middle. Something about those designs spoke to him, taunted him, begged him to find the pattern – the hidden sequence – the solution.

There must be a cure, he was convinced. While overly cautious, Melinda did pursue the alliance with SEH and their Pharma Group. Why would she do that, unless she too believed they could find the cure for the Disease? He nodded to himself. *I will find it!*

"Luke!"

His head shot up from his work as Brenda's voice cut through his reverie.

"Wow. You must be concentrating on something pretty special. I called you three times."

"Sorry," he mumbled, lowering his head again as he stared at the study in front of him.

"Someone's here for you," Brenda leaned against the side of the door, and winked.

His head came back up again. "Who…" the question died as Tessa Morgan entered the room.

"Hello, Luke."

Her presence both shocked and cut him. Anger flooded his body. Rage froze his movement. Words tried to escape. He wanted to lash out and say many vile things. He took a short breath, compressing his emotions.

"What are *you* doing here?" the words were innocent enough, but his resentment and betrayal threatened to spill over. Abysmal bitterness coated each word. He tried to check it, though, and keep a level disposition. "Haven't you done enough already?"

"Have I?" Tessa's voice was equally cool. "If I'm not mistaken, until like five seconds ago, you were nothing. You had played all of your cards and practically extinguished all of the good grace you earned while Grafton was Chair. You were going to lose *all* of your funding, and only *one* intern would even work with you."

Tessa tossed her head towards Brenda, who still stood in the room. The intern opened her mouth to protest, but caught Luke's fierce glance. She glowered at Tessa, and stomped out of the room.

Luke closed his fists. The anger still present. Walking a few steps, he glanced around his office. It was true. Until the recently completed meeting at the Tower, things had been going rather poorly, and the overall lookout quite bleak.

A handful of aged LED monitors were scattered about, streaming all sorts of information. The old projector, which had finally finished its creaky descent, was a relic of yesteryear. His 3D holograph was so small it looked like a button on the desk. Forget about funding, he did not possess the necessary tech to perform his job well.

"Chem-Lab was nasty business, nobody wants a repeat."

That was it. He snapped.

"How dare you!" he shouted, jabbing a finger in Tessa's face as he came storming over, stopping within inches of her. "You have no right to talk of Chem-Lab, my status at the University, or even Brenda! You used me. Played me. Tricked me. You win, okay? I don't know what you want, or why you did it, but you win. Now please, just stop and go away. I have a job to do."

Luke put his hands on his head and slowly rubbed back and forth, trying to soothe the pounding in his brain. Slumping back, he leaned heavily upon the corner of the desk. His shoulders sagged.

My gosh, she played right into my reckless, ambitious nature. Dr. Grafton warned that I should curb it.

"That's right. You do have a job to do," said Tessa.

Luke shook his head. "Do I even want to know how you know about the promotion?"

"Really?" Tessa cocked her head sideways and glared at him. "You think I would pick someone without a prominent position to help us?"

"I literally just got this position…" A sudden thought popped into Luke's mind. It caused him to stagger as he considered the awful ramifications. "You didn't have anything to do with Melinda's disappearance, did you?"

Tessa ignored his question, and merely rolled her eyes while shrugging her shoulders.

"We both want to make our world better. You *are* our best option for the next stage."

Why won't she just shut up and go away?

Luke lifted his head as he tried to read Tessa. She was an actress – a chameleon. And her professed feelings towards him, merely made her a charlatan.

"How so?" he scornfully asked.

He did not wait for her answer. Instead, he walked to the other side of the room, ignoring her. He contemplated some reports on one of the screens, and clicked his tongue. It was interesting; then he remembered Tessa was still in the room.

"So how do you propose to make our world better? I have been researching for months and have no definite answers. And while we suspect it's all connected, we don't know. Besides, I saw CDV's actual research – shoddy, conspiracy-filled, complete dribble. A stark contrast to the illegal folder you installed on my computer." Luke was getting worked up as he started pacing in front of Tessa. "Even my friend Josh Cunningham was asking questions about you."

"What?" Tessa's voice was short. "What did you say to him?"

"Ha!" Luke's laugh was hollow. "Nothing, my love. Nothing. I couldn't betray someone who had *betrayed* me because of those *feelings* of mine. And now…Melinda Gore is presumably dead. While we didn't get along very well, she was good at what she did, and from all I know, we still have very little in the way of the cure. How do we even know a cure is to be had? Hmm?" He sneered at Tessa.

The woman stood calmly, arms folded; her eyes never left his movement. Taking a deep breath, she licked her lips and unfolded her arms.

The quiet hum from the fans on the electronics was the only sound for a few seconds. They were at a stalemate. In that moment, many feelings rushed through Luke's mind. Primary among them, love and lust. He did not know what he wanted more from Tessa. To have her disappear and be gone from his life? Or to rip off her clothes and throw her onto the desk? He felt ashamed, used, but conflicted because he was genuinely enthralled by her presence.

"You keep talking about a cure, Luke, but that isn't our main concern. The new partnership with SEH is going to do more harm than good. We want you to terminate that."

"Pardon?" He choked, taken back by her words.

"C'mon," the woman was impatient. "It is an alliance formed but a short time ago. A deal made with the devil. SEH only cares about money, and they are being plowed by the US government. What makes you think they won't do the same to you?"

"Are you crazy?"

"Quite the opposite. Look, Luke," Tessa stepped closer, her heels stacking behind one another as she leaned in close. "You are pure, and care about the truth. This much I know: SEH will use you like a cheap whore, and when there is nothing left from the University to give, they'll drop you like one too."

The hum of the fans was noticed again as Tessa stopped speaking. Luke was shocked speechless. He knew the theories of CDV were not only conspiracy-based, but borderline crazy. The University was counting on him to come through, to deliver. Enduring another Chem-Lab was not an option.

"You do realize keeping the alliance intact with SEH is literally the only charge the Committee gave me when handing over the reins."

He rubbed his hands together. The palms were cold and clammy. His mouth was dry. He tried swallowing, but it got stuck halfway. His throat tightened. The grim memory of Chem-Lab reared its ugly face.

It was the first year after Luke's internship had finished. A successful meeting concluded with one of the largest biomed technology groups in the country. An accomplishment made no less significant when it was revealed that Luke had waded through 14,000 pages of research to ascertain the group was onto something with their tech.

Two days before the partnership was formally announced, he had been approached by the Chairman of the Committee who questioned some of his research on the matter. It was then Luke found out he had a detractor of his projected models and data analytics. Melinda Gore.

She questioned the stability and design stages outlined by Luke. He countered that the anomalies were all backed by concrete data and statistics. Presentations, booklets, 3D models, even a cheesy colorful banner helped Luke win the committee's approval. To the eleventh hour, Melinda protested the move claiming Luke was relying too much on his spike model and disregarding the factors of historical trends.

Less than six months after the meeting with the Committee, the tech group with whom the deal had been signed, went bankrupt due to failed results. The University had been co-signor on the terms, and the financial hit as well as the black mark on the University's reputation, was unrecoverable. Melinda had been right. Chem-Lab's history would forever be sealed as an unmitigated disaster.

"So will you do it?" Tessa's words brought Luke back to the similarly drear present.

His mind flitted back and forth. Research and studying atoms; breakthroughs in medical science; cures for the uncommon illnesses – these were all he cared about. Quick thinking on his feet had always been his Achilles heel; the reason Melinda Gore had won.

"I think I'll pass."

"Ha," Tessa's laugh was short. She tossed her hair and cocked her head, a mocking smile on her lips. "Will you now? I don't think that's an option. You remember the folder on your computer?"

"What of it?" Luke was defiant.

"Well," Tessa said matter-of-fact. "That isn't the only thing I put on your computer."

Rage boiled inside the scientist. "What did you do, Tessa?"

"You're aware of massive data hack at Tachi Yin Merger. Sure, the folder you've seen had some *obtained* information from TYM, but none of it was from the hack. That event was far more reaching than a few files. Years of confidential research and information. Biometrics, scanned chips, secret formulas…"

"What else, Tessa?" Luke interrupted.

"One single device in the whole world holds the hacked info, and it's here…stored on your server. Which technically," Tessa was evilly enjoying herself. "Is the property of the University. What do you think would happen when the press finds out *you* have the entire hacked TYM database stored here in your office?

"Why – why," he stammered, her words befuddled him. "Why would you do this? TYM was working on a cure, and they were working with FDA-licensed pharmaceutical companies to find a vaccine for use across the world! You would jeopardize that by stealing the information and then storing it here just to manipulate me? How could you have even known this was going to happen? Did you *plan* this?"

Luke sunk into a chair and grabbed his curly, chestnut hair with both hands. He could not take anymore.

"CDV did not execute the hack, we merely obtained it. And TYM had no interest in releasing a cure. Think about it. Every year they tell us to get a flu shot, well, at least it started as the flu shot. Then they wanted us to start receiving annual doses of medicinal weed – to prevent violent outbursts like we saw in Las Vegas, Seattle, and Chicago. There was no choice given, but to simply accept. Then the mandatory 'supplements' became monthly, weekly, daily; this entire time, we were ignorant. We had our senses dulled. We were lulled to sleep by a vicious enemy."

"What enemy?" Luke muttered. He was too tired to articulate his seething anger regarding the wide-ranging conspiracy theories of CDV.

"TYM, SEH, FDA, WHO, CDC, the US government, the UN – you name it! My god, how can you be so blind?"

Luke had nothing to lose. It was strange, but he suddenly felt resolved, even calm amidst Tessa's violent outburst. He watched the woman hug herself as she paced his office floor. Perspiration caused soft ringlets to form in her hair around her ears. Her body was tense. She was obviously under tremendous stress; overwrought with irrationality and fear. She stopped at the far side of the room, closest to the window, and turned to face Luke.

Nothing was said for a moment, yet at that moment, incommunicable words passed between them. Something about the situation, something about their destiny that seemed so intertwined neither could quite let go.

Fleeting thoughts passed through Luke's mind. For the first time in a while, he could look at Tessa with the same old warmth and affection of old. Yet, something still held him back. Deceit. Betrayal. And now, blackmail.

"Why are you so full of mistrust? Do you really believe all of these organizations, governments – people – you are accusing of lying and abusing, yes abusing humanity – are really all that?" Luke was surprised at his calm tone. He pushed the feelings of anger, love, and annoyance, burying them far beneath. Later he would digest them, not now.

"I have to go," Tessa ignored his words. "Remember, you're to cut ties with SEH."

"Did it cross your mind that I just might be done with this little game you're playing? That maybe I won't, and you can do your worst?"

Silence returned. A dark, foreboding silence. Luke looked around his office, and instead of monitors displaying streams of information and reports of every kind, he saw hollowness. A deep, dark hole of emptiness.

Tessa had taken a step towards the door, but she turned, her eyes narrowed.

"Seen the news lately? Nasty stuff. I'd hate for it to get worse."

She was gone.

Luke's eyes widened. Rage filled him. He walked over to the 3D holograph projector and swiped. A menu came up, and he touched the icon he wanted. A simple monograph – CDV. The folder opened. It contained all the files on the Disease he had previously seen. Even his own research file – or rather the late Dr. Grafton's – had been uploaded. One file was new though. He tapped it.

Streams of information from medical panels, labs, samples, and tested hypotheses flashed across his monitors. The data began to stack; it was going to overrun his system. He quickly clapped his hands and yelled, "stop!"

The A.I. on the server recognized his voice, and immediately stopped spewing the data. His eyes scanned the displays. At a moment's glance, he could tell. The hacked TYM information was stashed away on his server.

The threats to his own future meant nothing. He had lived through too much disappointment and failure to care at this point. But something else Tessa said bothered him, "I'd hate for it to get worse." She mentioned San Francisco. Was CDV behind the horrific, deadly attack? He knew not, yet the very possibility chilled him.

A cold shudder ran down his spine. Slumping against the wall, he tried to breathe. A soft footstep was heard. A gentle hand touched his shoulder.

It was Brenda. There were no words spoken. None needed to be. He knew she had heard the conversation. He knew she had his back. He knew he had a choice to make. Just which one?

Perge movere.

TWENTY-FOUR

Less than twenty-four hours had passed, and smoke continued to lazily rise to the heavens. Detritus fragments filled the air. While the morning haze had lessened the smog, the atmosphere nevertheless felt quite heavy. The horizon wore a strange blackish orange appearance – like burning blood.

Josh coughed. Due to the exterior conditions, the air inside the car was also less than desirable. He commanded the window of the vehicle down. That, of course, was worse. Another cough escaped him as he quickly reversed the command. What complicated matters more was the congestion of vehicles. Cars were barely moving, lined up one after another.

"Looks like a parking lot for one of the President's rallies," he said out loud.

He drummed his fingers on the steering wheel. Automated driving was quite ordinary, but he preferred to steer himself. "Always have," he would say when asked. "Why would I trust myself to a machine?"

The silence inside the cabin did nothing to calm his nerves. Most of the traffic was probably headed over to I-580, and then back down to Oakland and the Bay. Josh, however, had no reason to return to the Bay. He needed to catch a flight back home, and the Bay area airports would be jammed.

Bzzz, bzzz.

The vibrating handheld shook his pants pocket. He reached in and pulled the device out. The motion activated the call.

"Josh? Where are you? We need you back in Pittsburgh ASAP!" John Stevens' voice came through. "It appears some knucklehead is now running the Research Team, and decided to terminate our relationship with them!"

If a near-death experience brought no change to Josh's reaction at his boss' voice, nothing would. It annoyed him. He half-heartedly punched the steering wheel. The vehicle's intelligence system thought he wanted it to retract and engage auto-driving. Quickly, he grabbed the retreating wheel and yelled, "Stop!"

"Hello? Josh, are you there?"

No questions if I'm all right. How did I survive when everyone else died. Maybe Sam filled him in. Ah, who cares.

Taking a quick breath, he closed his eyes. It seemed forever, but was actually only a second or two.

"Yes, I'm here, and confused. What's going on?"

"The University. Some nincompoop named Luke Baer decided to pull all University panels from SEH's labs less than an hour ago. What happened in San Francisco? Why would they do that?"

"Well, maybe it had something to do with the fact their director was killed at the conference. News you're aware of, I'm sure."

"Of course," John Stevens angrily shot back. "I can read, you know."

"Hmm," Josh feigned surprise. "I wasn't aware anyone read anymore."

"Enough of this," the Morphing chief was overly annoyed. "You need to catch a flight back to Pittsburgh as quickly as you can and meet with this Mr. Baer to see what gives."

Great, not even getting a respite after nearly being blown up. Josh took another deep breath.

"Will do. So happens I know *Dr.* Baer. We were undergrads there once upon a time."

"Wonderful! The flight is set up for you. Sam checked traffic, and we have you going out of Sonoma County. Can you get there in two hours?"

Josh chuckled. "John, I'm sitting in a parking lot of morons. We haven't budged this entire conversation. I'll get there as soon as I can."

"Well, haul ass," John rudely interjected. "We haven't got all day. Something isn't right! Pharma Group has gone off the grid and with the University pulling its panels – something fishy is going on."

"Maybe it's a walleye."

"Okay der, minnow. Ya sure, you betcha." John did not find the joke humorous, and mocked Josh. Then his tone changed and became quite dry. "Keep us informed."

■　　　■　　　　■　　　　■　　　　■

Normally, the sight of students running across the Park, which separated the administration building and the Applied Sciences & Biotech Center, would make Luke wistfully smile. He would remember the days of his youth, when he was an energetic student, eager to impress and learn. Those days seemed far behind now.

He slowly surveyed his office. He meticulously rubbed his hands together, more for stimulation than anything else. The last day had been a whirlwind. First, the promotion to head of the research team, then the clandestine meeting with Tessa, followed by termination of the SEH alliance.

The decision to withdraw from the alliance with SEH was going to be met with tremendous backlash from a board already shell-shocked with Melinda Gore's death. And that was most shocking – the day had passed with complete silence from the Committee.

A soft step was heard at the door. Bleary-eyed, Luke turned and saw Brenda. She was standing there, looking quite neat and proper. Her hair was done in a bun. The plain blue dress ran down just past her knees. She smiled at Luke.

"You look terrible," he teased.

She snorted and said, "Someone's here to see you."

Instinctively, he grabbed the back of the chair in front of him. Brenda watched, a sympathetic look coming over her face.

"It's not *Tessa*," she said scornfully.

A sigh escaped Luke. Relief swept over his face.

"He says he's an old acquaintance – a classmate."

Luke merely waved his hand in acknowledgment and resumed staring at the floor.

"What is going on, Luke?" With a puzzled look on his face, Josh strode into the room. "The campus is buzzing with talk of dismantling the Pittsburgh Research Team for retaliation to pulling out of the alliance with SEH. The whole purpose of this was to *help* people. I don't understand why you decided to leave? And you of all people? The Luke Baer I remember wouldn't have done this."

"Oh, really?" Luke was offended. "I haven't seen you in what six – seven – years? You have the audacity to come here, to my office, and yell at me? Enough people are lining up to do that already."

Josh watched Luke speak and immediately regretted his words. His old classmate was clearly under duress, and his eyes were troubled. Spreading his arms, Josh shook his head.

"Hey look, I'm sorry. I don't know what got into me. Maybe almost dying…"

"Yeah, what are you doing here?" Luke interrupted, his eyes widening. "I mean, dang, you should be dead! How is it you survived? How did you get out of there?"

"Working for SEH has its advantages."

Luke gave no response. Instead, he looked towards the fountain in the middle of the courtyard. He watched as streams of water shot skyward, hung in glory for a split second, and fell dashing down into the pool below. It felt like his life. One moment, he was at the top – named director of the Research Team. Then he was embroiled in a conspirator organization against his will. Next, he was plummeting face first to the cesspool below – waiting to crash upon its abhorrent currents.

"I'm not reversing my decision, Josh. I might as well tell you."

"I wouldn't expect you too."

"No?" Luke was surprised. "Isn't that why you're here? To demand the reinstatement of our panels to SEH's labs for further research?"

"Well, at least my boss thinks so. But that isn't why I came."

"Pray tell then, why?"

"CDV."

The word caused Luke's heart to stop beating for a moment. He drew a sharp breath, and watched the fountain again. The water was rising and crashing down, ever constant with no delay. He partially turned to face Josh.

"You mentioned them last time." Luke carefully chose his words, maintaining his composure.

"Yes, I did," the truthseeker said quietly. "And I know you know more than you're letting on, but that's beside the point. I got to thinking. There was only one major player not present at the conference. One organization failed to send a representative, despite the fact they have information related to the Disease. CDV. Now I wonder, how come?"

Luke knew his old classmate was onto something. While it was already too late for him, he resolved to not let Josh walk into the clutches of CDV.

They would use someone like Josh, trapping and squeezing any use they could drain.

"Frankly, I doubt they know anything." Luke pondered for a minute, thinking of a plan. "I *know* they don't know anything."

"Really?" Josh was interested. "How so?"

"You were right. I do know more than I let on before."

An idea seized Luke. He stepped away from the glass window, and walked over to the large desk in the middle. He turned the 3D holograph on. A blue hue brilliantly flashed. Luke navigated through the screens and clicked on the CDV-monograph icon. Josh's eyebrows rose.

"You see," Luke calmly explained. "I've been gathering data panels from CDV. It's intriguing, but turned out to be nothing."

Luke noticed Brenda slip into the room, her mouth open in surprise. She was shocked he was revealing the stolen files to Josh. Giving a small nod at her, Luke sent reassurance he had the situation under control.

"Most of the information had some relevance, but when we looked deeper – it was garbage. In fact, this was part of the reason I decided to terminate the relationship with SEH." Luke did not further explain any correlation between the CDV data and the termination of the University's alliance with SEH.

Josh was only half listening. He stared, transfixed by something. His left hand lifted, and he pointed at the screen.

"What is that?"

"Hmm?" Luke acted surprised; worried Josh had seen the stolen TYM ghost folder.

"*Diabolus.*"

"Ah." Luke was relieved. "That was work by the late Dr. Grafton."

"Where did that research take place?"

"China," Brenda volunteered.

Josh pivoted and saw the intern standing in the room. He studied her expression.

"How old is it?"

"It was from two years ago," Brenda would fiercely protect Luke at all costs. "We thought there was some resemblance to what CDV was showing. There was not."

"Ah, maybe not to CDV's data – but there is to the Disease!" Josh was breathless. "Look, Luke," he turned, and put both hands on his friend's shoulders. "I must meet with CDV. If they are influential enough to sway

Pittsburgh to end their alliance with SEH – they are the big player we'll need to spread the truth."

"The truth? You know what's going on here?"

Josh wet his lower lip and sucked his teeth. He gave a slight shake of his head.

"No, not all of it yet, but that's my job. To be a truthseeker. I too worked in China. This file was lost to us. But I believe it holds the answer key. *Diabolus* – this changes everything."

TWENTY-FIVE

"Sam, I just sent you the file. Deep dive your drives for *anything* else you have on this."

A low whistle sounded in Josh's ear. He pulled his handheld away and bent his neck sideways, trying to flush the ringing noise from his eardrums. He opened his mouth wide and rubbed his jaw. Moving the device back to his ear, he was now greeted by the unpleasant sound of Sam chewing gum.

"I'll go as deep as I can."

The chewing became obnoxious. Josh tried to ignore it.

"I found a few things already that I've saved to an offline location."

"Oh yeah?"

"Yeah, but..." suddenly, Sam was terse. "I gotta go now." He hung up.

It was an abrupt ending. Josh had no time to think for his device chirped again. It was another inbound call.

"What happened in Pittsburgh?"

The sharp voice grated Josh's nerves. He took a quick breath.

"I don't know, John. I tried. It appears Luke is convinced the University's best path forward is without SEH."

"You didn't try hard enough!" John snapped viciously.

There was some commotion on the other end, Stevens cursed – obviously talking to someone else.

"I don't know what you want me to say," Josh was frustrated. "I was not involved in the alliance, nor am I responsible for the dissolving of it. I'm a truth verification analytical field agent, John. That's why Jacobi hired me, and that's what I'm good at."

"So you say – get out of my way!" John was again speaking to someone else. "I tell you what, Cunningham. If I could…"

A tirade followed of all the things John would do if not fettered by the "bureaucracy" Pharma Group confined SEH to operate in. Josh knew John could probably let him go anytime he pleased, but Josh also knew his own intrinsic value – and enormous talent. John would never be such an idiot to assume responsibility for firing the Morphing Division's best field agent.

"Look, John," Josh calmly interjected. "I just got out of a meeting, came back from hell, was almost killed…"

"And why weren't you?" John shot back, his voice dripping with facetious ferocity.

That did it.

"I gotta go," Josh snapped. "There's a lead I'm going to pursue. I'll be in touch."

▪   ▪   ▪   ▪   ▪

"What in the…"

Jim's voice died mid-sentence as he entered *Savannah Souvenirs*. Pulling the door shut behind him, he fixed his eyes on his niece who sat upon the shop counter. A syringe was laying next to her, along with an empty packet.

Anna caught the disapproving glance of her uncle. She tried to speak, but her voice was raspy. Her dyed blonde hair hung in tiny ringlets formed by the sweat pouring off her brow. Her brown eyes were glazed over.

"What have you been doing, girl?" Jim tried to keep his voice calm and flat, yet it shook with emotion.

"Nothing," the girl impudently laughed.

She reached down and nearly fell off the counter as she clumsily pawed at the shopping cart which Jim was pushing. Hovering over it, she abstractly pushed around the few pieces procured during his daily collection.

"What's this for?" she scorned, while snorting and sucking mucus.

Her attitude and the way she said the words, jarred Jim's insides like a javelin hitting a target. His face pained, and Anna rolled her eyes as she saw his shoulders sag.

The initial sight of the needle and the poor state of his niece angered him. But now, resolve beckoned to his inner strength. It stirred old feelings of courage. Mustering up every ounce, Jim replied, "Aluminum brings good money these days."

"Oh yeah? How much money? Arndt will ask."

The mention of Arndt, the young ruffian Anna chose to spend her time with, stopped him for a moment. But then the courage he felt moments before returned, and ignoring her last part, he began answering her question on how much money it would bring.

Jim soon realized he was blabbering to no one though. His niece had walked back to the far side of the counter.

"Whatever, who cares," she picked up her handheld, and ignored him altogether.

Jim stood for a moment, and then shrugged his shoulders. He shuffled towards the back of the shop. The hazy, faraway look in Anna's eyes had not escaped his notice. She was thin, *too* thin. And the ruffian she hung out with – Arndt – was far from the aspirations Jim had for his niece's future husband. Of course, nobody believed in getting married anymore – aside from the gay community – but he failed to see any future whatsoever in the "useless hobo."

Hearing padded footsteps behind him, he turned, and observed Anna pluckily walking behind.

"Seriously, how much is it worth?" She repeated her earlier question.

Though he had already answered it, Jim patiently repeated himself.

Anna swore. "Wow."

"Does Arndt buy aluminum?"

"No," she retorted.

"Oh," he said meekly. "I thought maybe that's why you asked."

"Stop it," she snapped. Her head was down as she thumbed away on her handheld.

Jim's eyebrows cocked, and he curiously glanced at his niece. At the moment, he was unsure what to make of her – whether she was high and off her rocker, or if she was just having one of those mood swings. Whatever it was, she was off.

"Three beer cans and a sheet don't equal lots of money," Anna interjected as she surveyed the contents of the rattling cart again.

"No, but it helps, and besides…"

Jim paused as he stopped the cart in front of a medium-sized container located in the back of his shop's storage area. He dug his right hand into his pocket, and started fishing around.

"Now where did I put them?"

"I know," said his niece sympathetically. "The fat gets in the way, doesn't it."

The musical melody of her mocking laughter made Jim both want to hug her, and fall sobbing to the floor. Anna gave an exaggerated sigh, expressing her exasperation and disgust at her uncle's weight and slowness of action.

Choking back tears, he finally located the correct one for the large padlock on the door of the container. With the right key in place, the lock gave way, and the metal door swung open.

"And," Jim continued his sentence as if he had never stopped. "It only adds to this pile."

He proudly stepped back and let Anna peek inside. Her hand went to her mouth, and she swore as she stared at the generous pile of cans, scrap pieces, and random cutouts of aluminum sheets. It was an impressive collection that would fetch good money.

"*That's* a pile of metal!"

They were the first genuine, non-belittling words he had heard from her in a long time. A smile crept across his face, and delight filled his heart. He articulately rubbed his hands together while his eyes danced in excitement.

"I know. It'll come in handy as prices continue to rise. Why, a gallon of milk costs $6!"

"I always wondered what was in this container," she playfully kicked the side of it with her heel. The metallic storage unit clanged as her foot collided with it. Her tone changed simultaneously with the harsh noise resonating through the small room. "But still, how much do you really think is here? Enough for when the world ends? You fool."

The girl spat onto a crumpled beer can, and strutted cockily away to the front of the store. Jim watched her depart, wanting to shout after her. He wanted to tell her about his secret warehouse just a mile away, which housed far more metal and precious items, but the words died in his throat.

Shoulders slumped, he tossed the cans and dented sheet in with the rest of the items in the container. He carefully relocked the crate, and pushed the cart over to a dark corner of the room, where he parked it.

Plopping into the rocking chair, he ran his chubby fingers over his sweaty bald scalp. A sigh escaped him. Absentmindedly, he turned on the small TV. He sat watching, but his mind was not on the images and stories flashing in front of him.

Instead, he was thinking about something he and Patrick had seen regarding aluminum. It was a far-fetched idea, but sometimes, those kinds of ideas were the solution. Who was he to question a potential find when it came to combating the Disease?

There was a bell jingle as the shop's door opened. A male voice came from the front of the store. He immediately recognized it as Arndt's.

No love was lost for the boy. For one, Arndt was the ripe old age of 19. For another, he was homeless. He always wore a baseball cap jauntily off to one side, and rumor had it, he was involved in drug distribution. From what scarce facts Jim had scoured around the neighborhood, Arndt either worked at the hospital or lived at the adjoining safe house on Lincoln Drive. He had been unable to confirm which, but that little mattered. He had a strong distaste for both places. "Any hospital or safe house that offers hard drugs should be damned to hell," Jim had said more than once.

The federally-funded hospitals and recovery houses offered drugs to users in a safe environment. The reasoning for them was that professional care would preside over the patients while they used, and thus would have the equipment and supplies available in the event one required medical attention.

The last thing Jim wanted to think about was Anna's boyfriend. Yet he could not seem to focus on anything else. He thought of the ruffian's arms: tattooed from wrist to shoulder. That was never a good thing, or at least Jim thought so. He gave a heavy sigh. The day's physical exertion tired him. He was exhausted. Slowly, his eyelids drooped shut.

■　　　■　　　■　　　■　　　■

Rain gently struck the large windowpanes. Outside the great house, a massive crowd of people assembled. Reporters scurried to their assigned spaces waiting for what was to come next. For so long, the house had stood a constant as the world around it changed. For centuries, it had been a symbol of hope, endurance, and fortitude.

Inside, scattered about the house were monitors and screens. News coming from around the world – London, Tokyo, Beijing, Moscow, Istanbul, Cairo, and others – all displaying messages of solidarity and sympathy for those lost in San Francisco. The convention had been billed as a beacon of hope, and possibly even the birthplace for the development on the cure to the growing pandemic. But then the explosion, and shortly thereafter, a video leak stating the president of the United States had the Disease. It claimed he was being manipulated and controlled by an unknown force and power. That he no longer had the presence of mind to run the country. The San Francisco attack shocked the world. The accusations towards the president shattered it.

Within a matter of hours, the World Council and G9 summit leaders urged Pres. Turouning to address the rumors. The message was clear and straightforward.

"Given the San Francisco attack, our plans must proceed – with renewed courage and strengthened resolve. Panic must not be allowed to fester."

Generally, the Capitol would be used as a public setting when addressing the nation. When Pres. Turouning acknowledged the World Council and G9 leaders' request though, he said it would be done from the White House. With the accusatory video trending, spreading "fake news" as he succinctly put it, he dare not risk going all the way to the Capitol. The Truman balcony would have to do.

Inside one of the many restrooms of the great house, William leaned over a clean, white porcelain sink. The restoration of the bathrooms to an earlier era had been performed under the previous administration. It was their attempt to a return of yesteryear in hopes of erasing the crazed phenomenon they inherited.

William slowly turned off the white knob for the cold water. The gushing flow slowed to a trickle, and then to a few lingering drops. He was hypnotized by it. He looked up at the mirror.

"We've come a long way, William," he muttered, watching his mouth move and the syllables form. "We have a little more ways to go."

Standing tall, he straightened his shoulders. His tall Native American frame still true to the body he had displayed in his youth while being an All-American Division II athlete. The abundant black hair was combed back, a slight ripple at the top. His brow furrowed as he studied his own face.

The etches in his forehead a constant reminder of who he was, where he had come from – the history he had made when elected President of the United States.

A violent coughing fit overtook him. He bent over the sink, and spat into the bowl. Bright red blood spilled out. Grabbing some paper towels, he moistened them with cold water, and dabbed his mouth. The cloth turned pink as blood collided with the water.

"Be strong, my son," he whispered. "You must have courage. You must provide hope to these people."

There was a rap on the door. It was time.

■   ■   ■   ■   ■

"My fellow Americans, today, I address you regarding the recent events in our nation. You have seen the video that accuses me of having the Disease. You are well aware of the videos from Georgia, Canada, and other episodes from around the world – including London, Bangkok, and Nairobi. These are dark times. We must stand as one. The attack in San Francisco only proves to us that someone or something is capitalizing on our fear. They are spreading terror by lies, and are killing our brightest minds and best people. Today I stand here to assure you I am not being manipulated by a foreign power. I have not succumbed to some genetic modification by an alien force," William gave a dry chuckle. "What I am going to say is that we must pull together. I have been reduced to a single useful eye through infection, but even with one eye, I can see that there are many strong people. It is this that gives me hope that we can work together to provide a better tomorrow for our kids …"

A sudden, coughing fit interrupted his speech. William stumbled, and grabbed the podium in front of him. Millions of eyes watched as he raised his hands heavenward. They watched as the once-dignified president began shrieking in agony. Secret service agents started moving towards him. Reporters craned their necks. Mounted cameras pivoted to capture the best angle.

Suddenly, a man stepped forward from the secret service detail. Even though it was cloudy and rainy, his dark glasses glinted in the day's gray light. He looked at Pres. Turouning.

William turned and was facing the man. Weakly lowering his hands from his face, the president opened his right fist. An eye was cupped in his palm, blood dripping from his fingers. The ravaged socket spewed blood as the artery leaked its life source. There was no recognition from William as the agent approached.

The dark glasses wearer raised his arm. He was holding a pistol, a silencer attached. Without hesitation, his finger squeezed back. William slumped, and fell down to his knees, then fell sideways onto the floor, an unspoken prayer upon his lips. The detail rushed in. The assassin was not to be found.

TWENTY-SIX

Clairton, Pennsylvania. Once upon a time, the small community had been home to the steel mill industry. Before that, it boasted a booming mining operation. Treacherous roads, far from modern with all their twisting and turning, would bring travelers down from Jefferson Hills to Clairton.

Disaster struck, first with the tales of legend. The stories told of a creature – perhaps more than one – that prowled at night. The creature would howl into the dark, night air, and scratch at doorways. Domestic pets were said to go missing – only to come back wholly mutilated a day later. Terror was struck in the hearts of the local inhabitants. Perhaps legends could be endured, but when amalgamated with sudden collapses of soil and buildings, mysterious flash fires, along with a flailing economy – it made for a rapid exodus.

That was years ago. One might think after decades, the past could be forgotten, and life could forge ahead. In the case of this small community, that was not so. Years of political strife, corruption, and the terrors of the creatures, fires, and sinkholes took their toll. The town was all but abandoned.

A lime green SUV made its way down the slithering road towards Hwy 837. Josh attentively manned the wheel, navigating around tight corners that were missing guardrails. It was one of the old mining roads. Faded signage warned travelers to be careful when making the turns. He mused they were from the 1960s, maybe older.

On an impulse, he laughed out loud. He was quite familiar with the stories of the old borough. His truth-seeking curiosity was stoked. He told himself one day when he had the time and was no longer chasing one crisis after the next – when the Disease had been eradicated – he would come back to the old town and study its tales. Dissect it for what it was worth; find the morph, and uncover the truth.

"Eerily similar to the Phantom sightings in Kentucky," he mused out loud, remembering his last assignment.

The sightings had caused mass terror and panic. Though nothing was ever found, the area drained of its occupants faster than one could say Christopher Columbus: Murderer of the Indians. Then again…

"In Kentucky, it was white flashes of light; here in PA, a monster with fires and pits. A duel of the mythological heaven and hell," he suddenly threw back his head and laughed. Amidst the cacophony of the turbulent world, the thought stuck him hilarious.

Josh fell silent again. His mind chided him for disregarding the wise words of his former professor. Once more he had spoken out loud to himself, showing his need to be heard. *Screw that,* he was proud of himself for stating his feelings.

The meeting he was driving towards had been set almost immediately after finding the *Diabolus* folder on Luke's computer. The research from Dr. Grafton correlated with the SEH research conducted by the Morphing Division. At the time, *Diabolus* had been discarded and filed away. It seemed in the aftermath of the War in Asia, people demanded news from the Far East be brushed under the proverbial rug and forgotten.

Just seeing the file brought back flashes of long, cold nights in the rain. Digging through graves of those lost; analyzing past behavior along with the reported statements from neighbors and friends. The outbreak was considered contained, and to be of no further consequence. That was the difference between then and now, though. In China, there had been survivors: family and friends. Now…the answer must lay in the balance.

The Disease spreading today was only different in symptom. It held a similarity to *Diabolus* in what it affected – the brain – and the rabid behavioral changes in people who seemingly had no other accompanying symptoms. It was an illness *inside* an illness.

The old mining road ended up at an intersection. It appeared to have once been a bustling intersection. Long wires looped from one end of the crossing to another. Dangling from them were stoplights to control all four patterns of traffic. There was no traffic now, and a single, broken stoplight was the only indication of its predecessors. It swung dangerously close to the road as most of its supporting wire had fallen down. Josh carefully avoided it, and accelerating, turned sharply to the right.

It would make sense for CDV to be hiding out here, he decided. Any organization that was hiding something, better stay hidden. Besides, where better to stay out of the public's peering eye than in the middle of a town that fit post-apocalyptic descriptors.

Mentally, he checked off the questions he needed to ask. Why weren't they in San Francisco? Why did most of their "research" appear on the darknet? Who were their primary backers? Top-level scientists? He wanted credentials.

Suddenly, Josh hit the brakes. He had arrived. A concrete barrier blocked the entrance to the once charming street of a little neighborhood. Stepping from the vehicle, he made his way around the SUV to the front of the road, and peered down the avenue. He shook his head. The street was no longer inviting.

Silence permeated the entire area. Not a pleasant silence, the kind he grew up with in Colorado – where one could hear the birds, trees, air, and nature – the sounds of life. This was the kind of silence that made one's skin crawl and stomach tighten.

Ivy crawled up the sides of many homes. Moss covered the roofs. Overgrown shrubbery and plants partially hid smashed windows. Some of which had exposed jagged glass, while others had been boarded up with plywood. The street itself was cracked and growing nature – wild grass, weeds, and even a small oak tree. Further down the road, Josh could see an old iconic pickup truck. One entire side had rusted off entirely.

"Wow. Can't believe someone hasn't cleaned this up by now," he muttered.

The irony was too obvious to be missed. An abandoned neighborhood possibly holding the answers to desperate questions; a place forgotten might bear the fledging hope the world needed

"Josh Cunningham?" A female voice cut across the unnerving silence.

"And who are you?" he responded firmly.

"Kelly Revers and this is my associate, Danny Graves, who heads up our intel – er – research division."

Kelly stepped from the shadows near one of the broken-down homes. Danny was right behind her. Josh uncrossed his arms and walked up to them. He shook hands and eyed the surrounding area.

"A bit desolate out here, huh?"

The two CDV representatives chuckled.

"You could say that," Kelly said.

"We like the quiet," added Danny. "Helps us think."

"Oh sure," said Josh puzzled.

The comment struck him odd. *What sort of research facility has ex-Military muscle heading it up? This Danny Graves is clearly former special ops; medaled seeing he has a prosthetic,* he calculated. The man looked more killer than a scientist.

Together, Revers and Graves led Josh behind the broken-down home and into the backyard. A command trailer was parked there. A satellite mounted at the far side of the yard, pointed up at the cloudy sky.

Josh began feeling skeptical of the meeting, and started to wonder why he did not pause to consider the fact their research was only on the darknet. Danny Graves read his mind.

"I suppose you wonder why the darknet?"

"And I suppose you have questions about our – setup here," Kelly chimed in.

Josh merely nodded. He was seated on a slightly uncomfortable folding chair, on a floor that was a mishmash of laminate and vinyl roll. From what he could tell, Revers and Graves were the only two people there. And while there were a few workstations with flashing monitors and some analysis panels, nothing suggested serious research. Essential lab equipment was not even present.

"This is our mobile transport site, so the only equipment here is to send and receive information," said Kelly.

"And the reason we're on the darknet is that we're censored," Danny shared. "Very little interference occurs out here though, as you probably figured out."

"Ah," Josh answered. "This place makes more sense then." He paused, and looked at both of them. His eyebrows rose along with his skepticism. "Who is censoring you?"

"The government, the New World Order, or whomever you want to say runs things in this country and the world."

"CDV is a network of people from around the world," Danny interjected, putting a hand on Kelly's shoulder. "We have varying backgrounds. Kelly and I are ex-military, as you can probably tell. We've been targeted on many levels by cyber terrorists and others claiming to be rogue information bots, but we do have credible intel that it originates from the government and World Council."

"Why would your information need to be hacked? What have you found?"

Danny sighed. "It's not so much the research we've found, but rather the discovery that this entire thing is nothing more than a giant hoax! What better way to convince people they need a massive, powerful force telling them what to do than with fear-driven propaganda. It's not just about governing us, but controlling us."

And that's why you're censored. You are conspirators. Why didn't I see this coming?

Josh's skepticism had reached its limit, and his blood pressure was not far behind. In a world threatened by catastrophic calamity, it never ceased to amaze him that alternative facts were embraced as truth.

"Do you really think the President's death in front of the whole world was an accident?" Revers said. "Do you think he just 'happened' to turn at that moment? It was planned. All of it. Word on the street: it's all part of a mass-effort to control people. Do you know what's next? Chemical dependency on a drug of their choosing. We don't know what it's called yet, but it will be required on anyone exhibiting 'dangerous' behavior. And who makes the call on what is dangerous behavior? Do you think it's us, the common people?"

Rever's brow was sweating with perspiration; her spirit agitated. She delivered her words in a concise, short manner; as if briefing a mission. Her military background clearly visible.

"It certainly wasn't the president's fault. We believe Turouning was being manipulated and was merely a prop." Danny cut his eyes at Kelly. "We also have it from a credible source that the actual number of people infected is more in the hundreds of thousands, not even close to the millions that are being broadcast on the news feeds."

Josh had heard enough. Leaning forward in his chair, he interrupted the CDV operatives. His voice was low, but firm.

"Well you know what they say about 'credible sources' or 'word on the street' – they are assumptions, half-truths that redirect from the actual truth. What you might *think* you know, I've experienced. Do you think it's just a game? San Francisco killed many people, I was nearly among them. A lady in Georgia, a guy in Canada, the President – it would be easy to deduce it all as a mass conspiracy if it weren't for the masses of Africa or the outbreaks in Europe. And this isn't something new. I encountered it before – two years ago in China."

Josh was surprised at his cool. Their manner was so imposing, he half expected one of them to take a swipe at him. Neither Kelly nor Danny moved, however. They were listening, but doubting his words.

"Crisis actors, we saw this before in the mass shootings or the measles hoax a few years ago," Danny remonstrated. The man was clearly set in his beliefs.

"Look, guys," Josh stood up. "I've heard the theory – it's false. My job, my entire career, has been spent studying morphing – whether that'd be a story, a trend, or a disease. My team is never wrong. I *will* find the truth. And what I can tell you is the current broadcast stories don't tell half of it. The Disease is global and huge and spreading. If you – the CDV – really believe it's a conspiracy cover-up, you are wrong. Dead wrong."

Josh gravely considered his two interviewers, letting his solemn words sink in.

"Now, I have discovered synchronized actions in some of the videos, so maybe there is someone or something manipulating all of this, but regardless – at this point, it's time to start focusing on the origin and cure, not fighting a system. Because while you can rail on about the manipulators or causers of an incident…The victims? They are not crisis actors. The victims are always real."

Kelly opened her mouth to argue, but Danny shot her look that caused her to clamp it shut.

"I'm sorry you disagree, Mr. Cunningham," Danny spoke with great restraint, holding out his hand in farewell. "I wish you well on your quest for truth."

Josh shook the outstretched hand, and left through the shabby door on the trailer. It banged shut as he strode off. The fury he felt! The absolute disgust – yet another dead-end just like the rest of them. And worse, this sham organization was presenting a false narrative to any who would listen.

He walked around the concrete barrier, and leaned heavily against the SUV. He swore, and smashed his left palm into the side of the vehicle. It was a stupid action. He cursed himself.

Hand throbbing in pain, he opened the door, and slid into the driver's seat. He aimlessly moved his eyes over the decaying area surrounding him. No one lived nearby – or if they did, they showed no signs of it.

The irony came back. Just minutes ago Josh was hopeful this obscure place in Pennsylvania would hold the answers for everyone. Now it was on display for what the world had become – something that presented hope, but in reality, gave nothing. A place forgotten; abandoned; a place where even the dead ceased to exist.

Josh pulled out his handheld. John Stevens had messaged him to communicate if the lead panned out.

THE MEETING WAS A DEAD-END.

The reply came a moment later. It caused Josh to curse and strike the steering wheel with his left palm. *Idiot!* His hand really smarted now. He rolled down the window, half tempted to chuck the device when suddenly it rang. The number was unknown.

Last time this happened, it was GSA. And if anyone knows more about Diablous, it would be the Global Securities of Asia.

Josh's hand started to tremble with excitement. GSA had been two steps ahead of him the entire time. Was it because they knew what was going on? Maybe now the truth would be revealed.

"Hello? Josh?"

He was suddenly aware he had accidentally answered the call. The voice was not the robotic Asian GSA operative. It was Sam.

"Yeah."

"Man, where you've been?" Sam's voice was distraught.

"Um, I've been chasing a lead in PA. The CDV…"

"Yeah, yeah," Sam interrupted. "That doesn't matter. We just got fired."

The words shocked Josh. He stammered, struggling to respond.

"Wh—why? I mean, what? What are you saying?"

"The entire division has been scuttled. Everyone is out. Our entire team! I don't know if you've been reassigned, but – I'm out."

"No way," Josh was in shock. "I just texted John and he didn't…"

"I doubt it was John," Sam interrupted, his voice strange. "He's dead."

Josh fell back against the soft leather seat. It could have been made of bricks, for all he cared. He stared dumbly at his handheld – rereading the message which caused the sudden flash of anger just moments before.

WRONG ANSWER!

John Stevens' phone, but…who is it from then? Do they know what I'm working on?

On the other end, Sam was breathing heavily. "Josh, something big is going down. We need to meet."

"Okay," Josh took slow, deep breaths; letting his emotions settle. "Where?"

"Clarence's on Chesapeake?"

"In Maryland? Sure, I can catch a flight out of…"

"No, you can't. Unless you're paying for it."

"Right!" Josh sucked his teeth, and exhaled. "I don't have a job anymore, so I'm stuck driving then. It's going to take me at least three hours."

"Fine," Sam said. "Watch the broadcast in thirty minutes."

"What broadcast?"

"Any," Sam's tone was haunting. "See you in a bit. Drive safe."

.   .   .   .   .

The lime green SUV was making progress. That was not too surprising considering the roads were mostly empty. Josh sped along, watching his speedometer hit 95 MPH. Gone were the days of 70 MPH. With most cars having automated drivers, the chances of a wreck were slim to none. Josh preferred to steer; the SUV was in manual operator mode.

While the vehicle was moving fast, time crawled. Josh half-wished it had been GSA who called. He knew they had answers. Thirty minutes had nearly passed. He voice-activated the beam display on the vehicle's front screen. He toggled the stations. It was as Sam predicted. The broadcast was the same on each one.

> "TODAY, SEH ABSORBED THE PRIMARY COMPANIES OF TACHI YIN MERGER OR TYM. THE NEW ORGANIZATION WILL BE KNOWN AS SEHTYM …"

The voice droned on. Josh could not believe his ears! SEH was absorbing TYM? Pharma Group's staunch competitor and corporate enemy was Tachi Yin. Spinning the steering wheel, he slammed the vehicle against the highway's side guardrail. The broadcast had his full attention.

> "SEHTYM HAS OFFICIALLY ANNOUNCED THE RELEASE OF THE FIRST DRUG ON THE MARKET TO FIGHT THE DISEASE. THE HEALTH PATCH WILL BE ADMINISTERED THROUGH A TWO-PART PROCESS: INJECTION THEN MAINTAINED BY ACCOMPANYING DOSES OF ORAL MEDICATION TO BOOST IMMUNITY AGAINST THE DISEASE. THIS BREAKTHROUGH CAME FROM THE FORMER PHARMA GROUP, DEVELOPED SHORTLY BEFORE THE HORRIFIC DISASTER IN SAN FRANCISCO. IN LIGHT OF THIS NEWS, WE'LL REISSUE THE BULLETIN

RELEASED A WEEK AGO FROM THE MORPHING DIVISION – THE FORMER SEH TRUTH VERIFICATION TEAM. REMEMBER, THIS REPORT WAS INITIALLY CREATED AFTER THE GEORGIA INCIDENT IN APRIL. UNTIL RECENTLY, IT WAS CLASSIFIED. THE BULLETIN SAYS: REPORT THOSE WHO DON'T WEAR. COMPLAINTS OF LIGHT OR SUSPECT BEHAVIOR SHOULD BE TAKEN SERIOUSLY. TELL SOMEONE… AND NOW, WE URGE THE FOLLOWING: GO GET YOUR HEALTH PATCH. IN OTHER NEWS RELATED TO SEHTYM, A FORMER EXECUTIVE OF SEH, JOHN STEVENS, WAS FOUND DEAD, APPARENTLY SUICIDE BY GUNSHOT."

Josh scoffed to himself. Disbelief written all over his countenance. None of what he was seeing could he fathom.

There's no way Pharma had a cure before San Francisco. And if they did, was it their plan to destroy all those other people?

His newfound confidence – on display when he addressed Kelly Revers and Danny Graves at the mobile CDV site – was starting to morph to doubt amid the rush of renewed questions. John Stevens dead? His boss' low moral character aside, if he had been driven to commit suicide, then Sam was right. Something big was about to happen.

The broadcast continued, but Josh shut it off. He enabled the connection for his handheld via the SUV's dash. Mark Jacobi's face flashed onto the display. The call rang and rang, there was no answer. Without skipping a beat, Josh dialed called Sam. It went to voicemail.

Drumming his fingers on the steering wheel, Josh's mind whirled with what he had just seen. Swiftly putting the vehicle into gear, he stomped on the accelerator. A roar came from the engine as it responded, and the automobile flew down the freeway.

Josh became aware of an acute calmness coming over him. *That's weird. I shouldn't feel calm at all.*

"Breathe, Josh," he spoke softly, addressing himself in the third-person. The calm oozing into his veins; he embraced it. "We've got a date with Sam to catch. Time for the truth to come to light."

TWENTY-SEVEN

The brick building was located just outside Chinatown, Washington, D.C. Its reddish color from the blocks of fused clay and shale had faded over the years. The glass windows that ran in horizontal lines around the building, unwashed for ages and several were broken.

The neighborhood around the building did not improve the overall impression. A respectable park once existed kitty-corner to the red building. Now it was a conglomeration of overgrown shrubs and trees. Tall weeds had taken over the walkways. The green space looked unattended to for years.

The area did not show it, but it had once been a place of prominence. The sacred middle: a perfect triangle with Downtown to the west, Chinatown to the northeast, and the magnificent White House to the southeast. However, when the cleanup process by the Washington Metropolitan Area Transit Authority began, the subway station was one of the first to be abandoned. One of the board members – a resident of Virginia – had said there was no need for a "middle station" when they had miles of track to update and other more modern facilities to improve.

When the Virginia committeeman took his idea to Congress, a representative from Maryland seized upon it. She cited security measures as reasons to abandon the station. "It is too close to the nation's greatest home" and "the cost of maintaining security protocols would be more expensive than practical in keeping the station operational."

After that, condemning the once-popular hub to its fate was merely a formality. It was buried in an obscure section of a bailout bill for the health insurance industry. Nobody even noticed it. At one time, language had been written in the proposal for the station to be demolished. By the time the President signed it, that had been replaced with a clause that "a project research team would be organized to best determine what the next steps are for the station." That too never happened.

Years passed. When a drunk driver took out one of the Metro signs indicating the station was there, it seemed to be the final seal of fate for the once-bustling station. A common passerby would not even know the place existed.

. . . . .

The truck hit a bump in the road. Luke jostled as he tried to keep his balance. Ever since they had picked him up, he had only the foggiest idea where he was. Riding in the back of a vehicle, a heavy black scarf wrapped around his head as a blindfold, was scarcely what he imagined hours before. In fact, the last twelve hours were anything but expected.

The morning started innocent enough. The usual morning brief with the Pittsburgh Research Team, at least with the small handful who continued to show up. A quick shot of espresso. A swift run over to the lab to grab the latest results. The 24/7 feed he had established in the last week to identify any markers on the Disease, yielded constant results.

Brenda had come up with the idea of having an intern sift through the many bogus findings to establish a pattern of "regularity in the anomalies," as she put it. It really was quite genius. As tech evolved, so did the disdain for spikes and anomalies. They were frequently discarded as "irrelevant," rather than notated where and when they occurred.

The results that morning were routine enough, but then the normal routine of the morning activities changed. The Vice-Chair of IID popped into the lab, and gestured at Luke.

"Mr. Baer, would you come with me please?"

Luke rushed across the campus, keeping up with the long-legged Vice Chair. His heart sank when they started to ascend the stairs to the Tower. This could not be good.

"Mr. Baer, it is the opinion of the University's committee that your idiotic decision to sever ties with SEH has cost us *millions* in funding. Let alone the ability to take the lead on a cure for the disease."

"Anytime someone is offering a cure to millions without any proven results, a true scientist should be worried. I believe Dr. Grafton would agree with me." Luke protested meekly. His words sounded childish.

"Well, he isn't here now is he?" said Chairman Simmons.

Just days ago, the chairman had handed the cloak of leadership to the young scientist. Today Luke felt the man's dark eyes penetrating right through his shirt – blasting his heart into a million pieces.

"Why are you now so damned conservative with your words and actions? You've always been ambitious, reckless, even impulsive! Chem-Lab is a lasting testament to that. Why the hesitation and lame excuses for further tests? With the University out of the picture, SEH wasted no time in merging with TYM. A complete organizational unification, the two companies are now one. A prudent move that cannot be easily dissolved by a fop parading as a research scientist!"

"The decision to change research methods is supposed to be cleared by our department, or the Vice Chair of IID," the Vice-Chancellor of Research Operations nodded to her counterpart in Immunology and Infectious Diseases. "Not a substitute on Pittsburgh's Research Team."

There were several others assembled in the room, and they nodded approval at the Vice Chancellor's words. They watched in agreement as the short and stout chairman shook a stubby finger at Luke.

"You literally had one charge. We were willing to let you change course as long as our alliance with SEH remained intact. Yet, the first thing you do?" the Chairman was shaking from rage. "Sever ties with them! It blows my mind, sir. It absolutely dumbfounds me. And still," the chairman's voice escalated, and Luke feared he'd blow a gasket. "We were almost ready to overlook that, but...that isn't even the worst, is it? Hmm? Why don't you tell us who Tessa Morgan is? Tell us why the Vice Chancellor was asked about countless documents in our server, specifically coming from your office, that have a mysterious monogram – CDV – all over them?"

Chairman Simmons' was shouting by the end, and spittle flew from his mouth. His fist descended and pounded the table. Luke watched it, and kept staring at the wooden surface. Once again, he examined the Biblical sketches. They had come to life. This was his ten plagues; his time of desolation.

"Our IT Department contacted me wondering if these files were authorized to be released," the Vice Chancellor of Research Operations added on to the accusations. "Tessa Morgan was the digital signature used. I confirmed with the VC of IID, and neither of us had any knowledge these documents existed. The documents leaked confidential information from the University's findings to an unknown address!"

"Isn't CDV the group who spread paranoia on Pres. Turouning before his assassination? They are nothing more than a rogue conspiracy group, and now they have countless, confidential, and highly-classified research studies on an unlimited number of projects!"

Luke's insides felt numb. His heart sank to the floor. He felt sick. Tessa had used him once again. She had been stealing information from the University! Words escaped him. The silence did not aid his plea.

"Look at the imbecile," the long-legged Vice Chair who fetched Luke now mocked him. "He can't even answer. It's all true then. You are a disgrace to our department, to this fine University, and a dishonor to the man who mentored you."

Quiet murmurs approving the Vice Chair's words wafted through the air; a much louder clamor was heard outside. One of the board members – an accomplished transwoman who had defied traditional norms by being the first transsexual scientist to win a Nobel Prize – tiptoed to the window and looked out.

"Look at this, Mr. Baer," she said. "Look what you have done."

He dragged his feet to the window, his mind a million miles away, vainly trying to figure out why he had betrayed the University he so loved. He knew his fate was deserved.

Hundreds of students were assembled outside. Some were marching around; others were shouting and waving posters.

"Go to hell, Luke Baer!" one student yelled as they waved a red-dyed American flag. "Haters aren't welcomed!" chanted one small section of students. Luke recognized some of the protestors as members of the Research Team.

"You see," the board woman spoke again. "The consequences of one person's actions have shattered this school."

"We would've had a deeper medical bench." "Don't forget about the funding!" "Scientific breakthroughs, medical advancements – the things a true scientist dreams of!" "The coveted first-finder privileges for the cure to the Disease." The voices raged on.

Chairman Simmons held his hand up, and the clamor gradually quieted. Luke turned, his lip trembling, tears building in the corner of his eyes as the stout Chairman pronounced his sentence of doom.

"Mr. Baer, pack up your personal effects. You are hereby banned from entering Pittsburgh University's grounds, facilities, buildings, or otherwise properties henceforth."

Even in death, Melinda Gore was right. He was incapable of leading.

．　　．　　．　　．　　．

Brenda was ablaze with fury when Luke entered his office. She heard the gossip circulating the school that the Board was terminating his role. She was beside herself; furious for allowing "that slut" – as she called Tessa Morgan – to enter his life.

Luke listened as Brenda vented her feelings of wrath; ever appreciative of her friendship and care. Taking her hands in his own, he looked into her eyes.

"Brenda, I can't thank you enough for your support. Through all of this, you've remained at my side. I didn't deserve to work with someone like you. All of this is my fault. I was reckless and foolish. My entire purpose was to preserve Dr. Grafton's work. I have, in essence, tarnished it. The school is many steps back from where it was last week, and a hundred steps back from when he passed."

Brenda opened her mouth to speak, but stopped as Luke held up a hand and shook his head. She closed her mouth and licked her lips.

"Promise me one thing then," she demanded.

"What's that?"

"Promise me you'll never talk to her again."

A chirp went off on Luke's phone. He glanced down. It was a text from Tessa. Brenda's eyes narrowed, and she looked at him, anger seeping from her every fiber. He glumly stared back, his face crestfallen. This was what he had chosen. It was now his future. Who could he blame but himself?

"I need to see why she did this, Brenda. There has to be a purpose in all of this."

"You are too good; too pure for this world, Luke Baer. I love you, and I'm sure gonna miss you."

Brenda threw her arms around the man she considered a brother. He hugged her tight. It brought one last moment of comfort and familiarity. It beckoned farewell to everything he had known.

．　　．　　．　　．　　．

Tessa's text asked to meet him. Of course, Luke had accepted. At this point, he was going through the motions.

She requested to meet at seven o'clock that evening. Time dragged during the day. He felt sick and weary. He wandered through downtown Pittsburgh. The smells of the city that usually comforted him, made him feel nauseous.

With nothing better to do, he silently rode the tram car up the cliff to the streets above. He stopped at a pizza joint, and downed a beer while slogging through an entire pie along with a side of Buffalo wings. His life felt worthless.

The sun was beginning to descend in the west when he rode the car back down and headed home. He had no idea what Tessa would want. Anxiously, he paced his living floor. He thought of the nasty words he would say, how he would curse at her, and throw things. He realized he was thinking like a petulant child. That only made him feel worse.

Tessa was prompt. The rap on the door came thirty seconds past seven. He did not even have a chance to say hello, before she grabbed his arm, and whisked him off to a waiting car. She slid into the backseat with him. Before he could say – "Pittsburgh" – they were out of the city and gunning towards the airport.

"Come on, Tessa," he complained to her. "Where are we going?"

A curt look from the redhead silenced further questions. So he slumped back in the seat, and stared moodily out of the window. His life was ruined because of the woman. His entire existence changed. He was sick of the game she was playing, yet he felt compelled to play along.

At the airport, they boarded a small twin-engine plane and hurriedly took off. Where they were headed, Luke knew not. CDV's only location, known to him, was the one downtown in Heinz Tower. They were obviously headed somewhere else.

Heavy shades were drawn over the windows of the plane. He was unable to see out. The flight was quick, though, so they did not go very far. He guessed maybe Philadelphia or New York. That seemed logical for a group like CDV – maybe upstate New York?

Once they landed, he was whisked into the back of what he guessed was some old box truck retrofitted with a hard bench. The way he moved up and down, with every bump they encountered along the road, further convinced him of this.

The recollection of the day's events passed, and the truck hit another bump. Luke was unable to keep his balance, and tumbled onto the hard truck bed.

"Ow!" he yelped, crashing down on his left shoulder.

"Really?" a man's voice said.

"He's okay," Tessa replied.

Luke crawled back, feeling with his hands; the blindfold was still on. Finding the bench, he pulled himself back onto it.

Fifteen minutes later, the truck lurched to an abrupt stop. Luke was roughly grabbed by the arms and whisked off the vehicle. With someone holding his arm and steering him, they walked for maybe a couple hundred yards. Then they stopped again.

The blindfold was pulled off. He blinked as a streetlight shined brightly upon him. His eyes adjusted, and he saw he was in an urban area.

"Quickly, come now."

Tessa started forward, not looking back. Luke paused for a moment, realizing that whoever had been pushing him was no longer there – unless it had been Tessa.

After a minute, he realized they were walking down an alley. It was uninviting. Dark and dank; water seeped at the sides of the shabby curb. It reeked of sewer and mildew. The windows on either side were barred or enclosed with shutters. Once they had left the lit area by the streetlamp, there was not a single light of any kind along the passageway. A cat shrieked as Tessa half-kicked it out of her way.

Luke thought back to the day he first met Tessa – in April – before the world was changed. She was a flirtatious redhead, beaming her captivating eyes alluringly at him, offering her phone number like it was a precious gift. His life course altered when he decided to call. Ever since she had revealed her role at CDV and her real purpose in pursuing him – a recruitment assignment – he had not stopped wondering who she was or what she was capable of.

Tessa's pace slowed, and he saw they were standing at the back of a reddish-building. It had not been maintained for years. Horizontal rows of once-glistening windows ran around the exterior, several of the panes were broken. The neighborhood appeared to be all but abandoned.

"We've arrived."

Reaching into her coat pocket, there was a jingle as she withdrew her fingers, holding a small ring of keys. Finding the right one, she inserted into the lock.

"You've got to be kidding me," Luke said unbelievingly. "You use a physical key?"

Her eyebrows raised, and she quizzically glanced at him.

"You're a smart man, Luke Baer, but tell me, what's easier for a person to hack nowadays? An electronic keypad? A chip? Maybe a fingerprint? Or a key with an electric pulse in the middle that is nearly impossible to duplicate or replicate?

"Fair enough," Luke held his hands up in mock surrender. "I get there's a lot I'm going to have to get used to."

"You can say that again," said the recruiter, not unkindly.

A loud grating noise echoed in the alley as she pushed open the door. It reminded him of old movies set in past times, when there were dungeon doors with rusted locks. It was ironic because he felt compelled to see what was behind the door, rather than forced.

Tessa stepped aside as the door swung open, and motioned with her arm for Luke to enter. He took a deep breath, muttered "here goes nothing," and stepped across the threshold.

TWENTY-EIGHT

Josh slammed on the brakes as he pulled the SUV to the curb. The vehicle jerked to an abrupt stop. Opening the door, he jumped out. Straightening his shoulders, he adjusted his shirt and tugged on the sleeves. A deep sigh escaped while he glanced both ways down the street before swiftly crossing.

Clarence's on Chesapeake – the brightly illuminated sign hung above the entrance. Josh stopped short of the front doors though, and entered a side court. This is what made *Clarence's* so popular – a large outdoor bar area with high-top and sit-down tables scattered on the patio for guests. The area extended with a grassy knoll down to a large walkway alongside the Chesapeake Bay.

Soft music glistened through the night sky as Josh made his way among the swarms of people. He stopped at one of the bars, and ordered a drink. Lifting the glass to his lips, he took a sip as his eyes searched among the crowd. Finally, like waves parted by the wind, he caught a glimpse of Sam standing by the water. Josh made his way down to where his friend stood.

"Sam."

The former field coordinator turned and Josh stopped his hurried advance. He peered closer. Sam's face was haggard; eyes bloodshot. Sleep had evaded him for weeks, shaving discarded for days. It brought back memories of the meeting with the mysterious stranger at Point Park. A sense of déjà vu came over Josh.

"You saw the broadcast, didn't you," Sam winced.

Josh nodded, and leaned against the wooden guardrails on the walkway. He looked out over the water. It was so calm, quiet, and steady. A paradox to the happenings in the world. The glass in his hand tipped back, and another swallow of the smooth, hard liquid flowed down his throat.

"This whole time," said Josh. "You were right. Our research was being destroyed, altered to fit another agenda. They were just waiting for the right moment. San Francisco provided the moment."

"We've been duped," Sam cut in. "They've changed the truth of our reality. You know, I've been cheated on before, man. But this isn't like a woman cheating on you. You know, when you feel like your heart is going to explode? This is worse because instead of just cheating on you, they've taken everything you've ever had, anything you've ever done, and twisted it into some alternative truth that fits their narrative. It makes you sick. Makes you angry. Makes you want to smash someone's skull against the rocks."

Josh listened to Sam's vehement words. Uncomfortable to hear or confront, he knew truth rang in them. The ice in the drink clinked as he twirled the glass, staring moodily out into the night.

"How do they know this health patch is actually going to work? I mean, who found it? I thought Pharma had nothing? I mean, I saw the drives – there was nothing!"

"C'mon, man," replied Sam. "You're smarter than that. Everything has been coordinated from the get-go. I bet Pharma was lying to Jacobi on their progress; safely stashing it somewhere else. What better way to hide the truth from your own team that to send them on a massive scavenger hunt – the whole time holding the trump card."

Your presence is needed…you are a truthseeker…keep your eyes open. Dammit! Jacobi was asking me to find out what Pharma was hiding! I failed…miserably. Josh downed the last of the drink.

"But seriously, dude," he turned from the railing, and looked at Sam. "We found things. We know this is all connected."

"Sure, it makes sense – now." Sam seethed. "They couldn't hide it from us forever. But even as messed up as San Francisco and this new Sehtym merger – which by the way puts a complete hold on the market for any cure – there's something bigger at play." Sam looked wildly around as he spoke. Moving closer to Josh, he pulled his i-Beam out. "Look at this. I found it right on the server before I left."

"You found something?"

The look of doubt in Josh's eyes ebbed Sam's eagerness.

"Okay, well, when I heard about the merger, I knew something wasn't right. I browsed the main server, and roamed around for a bit. I only had a little bit of time, but what I found suggests something much more than a drug. Something so big it involves several governments and the World Council."

"Look, dude, I just wrapped a meeting with a quack organization," Josh was skeptical.

"CDV?"

"Yeah."

"The mystery organization. What do they know?"

"Nothing. They are conspirators."

"You say that like it's a bad thing."

"Sam," Josh lifted a finger in warning.

"Look, I'm just asking you to take a quick look. This isn't from a conspirator site, just some raw data stashed away on the server."

Josh twirled the empty glass, and stared contemplatively into it. If it were any brighter out, he was sure he would see his reflection. He was glad it was dark, though. When one sees their reflection, they see themselves as others do. They see themselves for what they are. Right then, he did not want that. Because all he felt was hopelessness and anger. The last flicker of hope to find the light of truth had deteriorated.

"I will, just not right now. I need some time to think."

"Of course," Sam nodded, pushing his glasses back up his nose. "Gonna hold you to it, though."

"Fair enough."

"Come here, man," said Sam brusquely as he reached out and pulled Josh towards him.

The two men hugged – the feeling of needing something familiar, never keener. Josh pulled away.

"We'll talk soon. Take care, Sam."

"Watch out for yourself too, man."

Sam managed a parting smile as he walked away down the boardwalk, and ambled up the grassy banks to the exit above. Josh turned, and looked out over the Chesapeake. A long sigh escaped him. His spirit was heavy. Setting the glass down, he rubbed his palms across his eyes. He felt drained.

Bzzz, bzzz. Ding-dong.

Reaching into his pocket, Josh pulled out the handheld. It was a live conference i-Beam request.

Curious, he turned his back to the water and flipped the toggle, accepting the request. A faint blue hue rose from the i-Beam. He quickly minimized the picture so that the outline of the screen hovering over his device was roughly the size of an old paperback book.

"Mr. Cunningham," a man in glasses emerged onto the screen. He was Asian, though Josh was unable to tell from which part, the rendering quality was poor. "We meet face to face."

"First time for everything," said Josh dryly.

"We were wrong."

"How so?"

"We failed to discover Pharma Group's plans before it was too late."

"Jacobi knew." Josh uttered his long believed thought: Mark Jacobi knew something was amiss in San Francisco. Jacobi had tried to warn him on the conference call before Pittsburgh.

"Mark Jacobi was a good man. He had his suspicions, but his hands were tied. It's why he picked you to be the liaison to the conference with Melinda Gore from Pittsburgh."

Josh felt no relief in the confirmation of his opinion, only sadness. Then he realized something. It hit him like a ton of bricks.

"What do you mean, Jacobi *was* a good man?"

There was silence as the GSA agent looked away. Josh watched him intently, trying to figure out what was going on. The agent slowly turned back towards Josh, and when he spoke, it was measured and solemn.

"Jacobi's gone missing. We are assuming the worst."

Josh felt his heart drop, and he staggered to stay on his feet.

My god, is the world coming to an end? People dying, disappearing; everyone I knew at SEH is no longer part of the picture. The bizarre merge with TYM. When will the madness end?

"Be careful, Josh. Do not be bold like your former co-worker Sam."

"What do mean 'like Sam'?" The cryptic statement irritated him.

The GSA agent ignored the question. "The altered reality must be accepted as truth until proven otherwise. It's time to adapt to this new world. If you try to fight the systematic change before the time is right, you will be discovered, and the consequences will be ugly."

A new world? What ugly consequences? Suddenly, Josh was worried about Sam. He scrutinized the GSA agent.

"What do you mean by that?"

"Eventually, more will be revealed to us all. For now, be vigilant. Be watchful. Above all, be careful. Change is coming, but nobody knows when it is coming."

Josh closed his eyes, his mind racing like an endless spinning top. The conversations with Sam, the stranger at Point Park, the secret files, *Diabolus*, even the tabloids from the shopkeeper in Savannah – all hinted something was coming. Now GSA warned of it as well. What sort of doomsday would it be? Was the progression of the Disease worsening? Would mayhem break loose? A biological war? Josh ran a sweaty hand over his hair.

Fake news spoke of aliens and zombies; religious fanatics said the Second Coming of Jesus Christ; the alt-groups claimed mind control. Josh did not know what to think. Whatever lay ahead, there could be no way to prepare for it. His last shred of hope had died away, and now all he felt was isolated loneliness.

"Mr. Cunningham?" The GSA agent spoke, bringing Josh back to his present reality.

"Yeah. Sorry."

"We will continue our efforts to find out what's going on. Right now though, we're going to cease all external communication."

"You know, I'm going to miss these cryptic calls and messages," quipped Josh sarcastically.

"Ha!" the Asian man in glasses gave a weird, short, little laugh. "Goodbye."

■　　■　　■　　■　　■

A sweet smelling aroma wafted through Luke's nostrils as he entered the brick building in Washington, D.C. Inside the hovel, dozens of people were sitting at small tables, desks, or curled up on pod couches. All of them were busily typing away on their holograph keyboards or tablets. Some were talking on the phone, speaking so rapidly an auctioneer would have a tough time competing against them. Most were speaking in English, but Luke caught snatches of Spanish, German, and Russian as well.

A woman stood in the middle of the room. She was clad in a fit khaki uniform. Two silver bars glinted on the side of her collar. Her shirt top had golden buttons down the middle. Several medals ran across the right side, signifying moments during her time of service. Her black hair was done up nicely, rolled together in the back. Her long lashes snapping as she barked out commands.

Luke was transfixed and followed her body with his eyes. The khaki skirt traveled just below her knees; her legs continued on. Such legs! They were shapely, and a beautiful brown. The woman was gorgeous.

"Quite the looker, eh?"

"What? Oh," Luke pulled his gaze from the woman in the middle. "She's pretty."

"Yes, she is," Tessa gave a short laugh. "She's our Chief, and she's a bitch."

"Really?" he was incredulous. How could someone who looked so lovely be a bitch?

"But what does it matter," Tessa continued, exasperated with Luke's obvious interest with the woman in the middle. "Wherever there are boobs, a guy is gawking."

Embarrassed, he looked away. He *had* been staring at the woman. He glanced about the room, and continued to take in his surroundings.

Aside from the dozens of typists and phone talkers, there was a conglomeration of panels, computers, screens, and holographic programming in the middle by the beautiful woman. Holograph projectors were scattered about the room, displaying screens and models that any designated person might swipe or toss onto another's workstation.

Several people were near the middle station, and Luke watched as the screens flashed information back and forth. It was quite a feat any of them could read the data that fast. He marveled over their perceptive readiness and began to wonder why he was here. While he had a few tech skills, and could certainly skim a report, his specialty was medical research not whatever *this* was. He asked Tessa.

"You don't smell it?" she queried.

"I noticed it when we first entered," he said defensively. "What is it?"

"A serum being developed in the back, where the lab is."

"You have a lab? In this place?"

"We're not trying to get the serum FDA-approved, and it's not like the CDC is going to come knocking on our doors. The serum will combat the so-called 'Disease health patch.'"

Luke stared at her with a confused expression.

"Wait. Why would you want to counter the health patch? Isn't that the *opposite* of saving people?"

"The patch is a gimmick," Tessa was exasperated. "Well, for the Disease that is." Her hands made air-quotes as she said, 'the Disease.'

Luke was crestfallen. He had secretly hoped he could still help fight the Disease even though he was no longer with the University. He hoped Tessa was doing something about it. Fighting the health patch was the opposite of what he had intended.

"Where are we?" he asked, setting aside his disappointment.

"CDV headquarters. The Heinz Tower office was just a shell," she said in reply to his perplexed expression.

"And who is this?" they were interrupted by the beautiful woman from the middle – Chief – as Tessa called her.

The woman's dark eyes looked Luke over, sizing him up. He felt intimidated by the woman, and yet, strangely, not afraid. She had a different aurora than Tessa. Her confidence based not on her ability to charm, but rather to lead.

"Chief, meet Luke Baer," said Tessa. "Former student of Grafton, former head – for however short – of Pittsburgh's Research Team." She winked at Luke.

"Oh! Your special recruit."

"The same."

"Welcome, Luke. People here call me Chief," the woman spoke. "I'm sure you have questions, but I don't have answers for you right now. I don't know you, and I don't know how good you are. But I will tell you this, if you stick, you will find the answers to the questions you have. All of this – all of these people," Chief swept her arm around the room as she swiveled to her right and left. "They are all here because they are searching for those very same answers."

It was an intriguing offer. It hinted at secrecy and investigation into something so close to Luke's heart. Yet, this organization had used him, *ruined* him. Could he look past that?

"I know you have reason to hesitate," Chief paused as she sternly looked at Tessa. "Some of the recruiting methods used have been…somewhat obtuse."

Luke was dumbfounded. "Obtuse? How about seriously screwing over a person's life? Playing with their emotions like a cat to a mouse!"

"I was starting to tell Luke of the serum," Tessa interrupted his rant. "We believe the health patch is a gimmick and more. We believe it'll be used for chemically-altering purposes."

"Really?" Luke had his misgivings.

At times, CDV seemed well organized, even informed. Then he would hear statements like this. Such grand theories, he doubted they believed it themselves. He felt a sudden rush of adrenaline. He had nothing left to lose; even the various firearms and guns strapped to the people running around the room did not bother him. If one of them were to be upset with his words and pull a trigger – what would he really be losing?

"So you now believe in mind control?" Luke started. "You know, I knew the CDV had very little in the way of actual – or rather factual – truth. Conspiracies have always been your strong suit. A former classmate of mine – he's a truthseeker – said the same thing."

"Oh, really?" Tessa was mad. She disliked this new, brave Luke. "You still don't see the whole picture. Luke, you can be part of something great here, just like Chief said." She put a soft hand on his shoulder, her eyes turned to pleading. "Just give it a chance?"

"Ha!" he laughed. "That's what Josh would say too."

"Josh?" Chief spoke, turning her head sideways at Luke. "Who's this Josh?"

"Josh Cunningham, the former classmate I mentioned. The truthseeker."

"Ah!" The woman from the middle turned, and leaned close to Tessa. She whispered something in the latter's ear, and then straightened herself. She smiled at Luke. "Tessa will get you started on your new responsibilities. That is, of course, assuming you're in?"

Luke inhaled slowly, feeling the air intake flow down his throat. He closed his eyes for a second and thought. There was nothing else left for him in the world, and if there was *some* good he could do here – even if the *how* escaped him at the moment – why not?

He shrugged. "What the hell."

TWENTY-NINE

It had scarcely been a few hours since he had met with Sam. Ahead of him on the road, Josh could make out the faint, but familiar outline of SEH's concourse. He was unsure what else to do after the rendezvous, and decided to return to headquarters, and play dumb. Besides, nobody knew Sam had told him the Morphing Division had been dissolved. It would be business as usual.

Josh carefully steered the light sport-utility vehicle along the long drive. *Eventually, I'll have to return this thing.* He glanced at the digital clock. *How am I not tired?*

Pulling out his security pass, he prepared to show it to the guard as he neared the entrance. The post was empty though, certainly not uncommon for after hours. For a fleeting second, Josh wondered if the pass was still active or if he should even attempt to swipe it.

Of course, it still is, he told himself. *Nothing's been officially communicated to me yet.* He swiped the badge, and the barrier lifted. Pocketing the pass, he pulled through the entrance, and into the parking lot.

The main building was mostly deserted. He kept a rapid pace as he climbed up a flight of stairs. He only wanted to refresh his data and power packs, and to see if anyone had heard from Jacobi. GSA believed him dead, but Josh refused to believe both John Stevens and Mark Jacobi died the same day.

"Josh Cunningham?"

A voice called out as Josh exited from the stairs onto a landing. Josh recognized the person speaking as one of Sam's former assistants. He was a member of the morphing team, but one he did not know personally.

"That's me." Josh shook the outstretched hand of the speaker.

"What are you doing here?"

"Oh," Josh pursed his lips. "Not much. Just dropping off some stuff; quick check-in."

"Have you seen Sam at all?"

"No," he lied. He did not know why; it happened instinctively.

"Oh, well if you do, can you please let us know right away?"

"Why?" Josh was puzzled. If Sam was just fired, why would they be looking for him?

"Because," the assistant was irritated. "Someone is looking for him."

"Who?" Josh checked his apprehension. This did not compute.

The assistant rolled his eyes, while shrugging his shoulders, and walked away.

Confused by the exchange, Josh looked around, and noticed he was by the entrance of one of the conference meeting rooms on the primary level. A large crowd was assembled. He ventured into the room, and recognized few faces of the many seated. The men and women standing at the front were equally unfamiliar except for one. The man standing in the middle he had met once before. It was Blair Leshief of Pharma Group.

"Josh Cunningham?" one of the unfamiliar faces spoke. The wearer sported a black coat with a suit to match.

"Yes?" he answered, his voice hesitating. His heart pounded. Something was off; nothing was quite right.

"Just in time for the meeting. Please, take a seat. Oh, feel free to grab a doughnut."

Josh slid into a chair near the back of the room. Pulling his handheld out, he flicked his wrist. A digital clock emerged.

3:40 AM

. . . .

"Come on, Sam, pick up!" Josh muttered under his breath. The line rang and rang, finally hitting voicemail.

Four attempts in the last twenty minutes. Something was wrong. Sam would not tell him to be in touch and then go radio silent. Josh had worked with the man long enough to know he wouldn't spend ten minutes without responding – unless something was wrong.

"We hope you enjoy your new role!" A voice came from behind Josh, and a firm hand grabbed his shoulder.

Josh turned to face the speaker. Graying hair, smooth-shaven face, pleasant enough looking – yet, Josh noticed something he missed the first time he'd met the Pharma Group Director. The man gave off a robust political smell.

"I'm sure I will." Josh answered numbly.

He tried concentrating, but his mind was spinning from the bizarre early morning meeting just completed. News had been shared regarding the Morphing Division dissolution. Remaining team members such as himself were scattered across several new projects as part of the merger with TYM. Josh's role would change from morphing research to engineering – a throwback to his college days. The entire presentation he simply sat, listless on the chair in the back. Not quite believing what he was hearing; doubting any of it was real.

"Please let me know if you ever need anything," Blair Leshief pulled Josh from his reverie.

The former truthseeker nodded in response.

"I believe our paths crossed before. You were part of Sam Walter's team?"

Another nod.

"Something bothering you, Mr. Cunningham?"

"I do not understand why Jacobi isn't here?"

"Ah, yes," answered Leshief. "But Walter's team, right?"

"Um, yeah," Josh was unsure how this related to Jacobi.

"The truth verification team…you see, TYM already had their own data analysis department. It made no sense to duplicate."

"Sure." Josh was confused.

"Reassignment makes even more sense in your case. You're going to be working in your hometown. And an engineering project too – that's what you majored in, right?"

"Yes."

"Perfect. I know you'll do well."

Leshief finished speaking and nodded in farewell. Pirouetting on his right foot, he walked away before another word could be said.

Josh watched the new Sehtym executive depart. Something was wrong. His question on Jacobi had gone unanswered. Leshief knew Jacobi well.

The man had worked directly under SEH's former CEO for several years. And how was it that Blair Leshief was the new executive director of Sehtym? That was perhaps, the most perplexing thing of all.

Why would he ignore the question? It practically confirms GSA's fears. Who holds a meeting at 3:40 am? Brushing a single strand of hair back from his face, Josh began walking towards the exit. *Where are you, Sam? Why aren't you calling me back?*

. . . . .

The sun was starting to rise in the east as Josh parked the lime green SUV at the hotel parking lot where he stayed when working out of SEH headquarters in northern Virginia. Nothing sounded better to him than a night of good sleep. He would catch a flight back to Minneapolis later in the day. It had been nearly twenty-four hours since he had last slept. Exhaustion clung to him like a damp cloth.

There was a suite always on hold for him at the hotel. He did not consider the room might not be available given the termination of the Morphing Division. Swiping the keycard, he unlocked the door. Turning the handle, he opened it, walked inside, and pushed the door shut with his foot. Reaching for the light switch, he flipped it. Nothing happened. Puzzled, Josh stood there, and let his eyes adjust to the faint light in the room. It was dim, coming only from the flickers of sunlight dancing at the corners of the drawn shades.

"What in the..." his voice faded.

Papers were scattered across the room. A mounted 3D TV had been ripped from its spot on the wall and thrown to the ground. Dishes had been pulled from cupboards, the office chair tipped over.

He took one cautious step forward, and suddenly heard a sound. A tremendous blow hit the back of his head. Staggering, he fell to the ground. He had enough sense to flip over. Kicking his legs, he scrambled back to his feet.

Another blow hit his face, causing him to stumble backward. He stopped as he collided with a side table. Blood pooled in his mouth.

Josh's hands felt along the hard surface – fingers searching for something, anything to use against the assailant. In the darkness of the room, he could scarcely make out the shadowy figure. Then his fingers touched something sharp. It was a piece from the broken TV screen.

The silent attacker moved forward, and Josh cocked his arm back. Loosely holding the glass, instinct took over. A motion familiar from years of playing youth baseball, he expertly snapped his elbow forward and released the shard. It clocked the intruder, who stumbled back as the projectile hit him squarely.

Cradling his head, Josh's eyes closed. Blood flowed down his forehead, and leaning forward, he spit more blood onto the floor. It was then he realized he was all alone. The attacker had fled.

Pawing about, his hand frantically found the hotel phone. His fingers clumsily punched the keypad. His eyes closed again.

.   .   .   .   .

"They are called 'shelters.' They'd be better named pits of hell," Jim nearly spat into his drink as he complained to his good friend and bartender, Patrick Flannigan.

The latter leaned over the bar, resting both hands on it, one clutching a towel.

"I hear they are setting up a couple more in the outer neighborhoods. The first few have done wonders in Savannah."

"Bah!" Jim snarled again. "I remember back when we use to tell kids 'drugs are bad. Say no.' Seems like a hundred years ago."

"Well," Patrick reasoned. "It was a different world then. We didn't have people going berserk with the Disease. There was no worldwide pandemic. A dead president. We didn't have sightings of the Unknowns."

Jim mumbled something that sounded like a "yes" and continued to sip his drink. The ice cubes rattled as he set the glass back down on the counter. He stared at the TV above the bar. The news anchor was reading off their teleprompter, spewing propaganda left and right – at least according to Jim.

"Can't trust anyone anymore," he said, more an afterthought than anything else.

"You're worried about her, aren't ya?" Patrick said softly, brushing his friend's arm. "I've seen this look before, Jimmy. Back when she was eight and first came to live with ya. Back when she had the scare at eleven. Back when she first began noticing blokes."

"Okay," Jim held up a fat hand. "I hear you. But I'm also worried about the new health patch. It came too quickly. We're supposed to believe there's a cure for the Disease already? We've had cancer for centuries, and aside from a few types, there's still no cure."

"Easy. One is fear-driven, the other is science-driven."

"People are afraid of dying, Patrick, whether it's from cancer or something else like the Disease."

"True," the bartender nodded his head as he dried off a mug. Finished, he set it on a shelf above the back bar. "But fear sells easy. If ya think ya *could* get the Disease, you're going to take the health patch. I mean what person in their right mind wouldn't?"

"Haha." Jim started to laugh. "Then I guess you and me both are plumb crazy!"

"Blimey mate," Flannigan said, picking up another mug. "We already knew that."

.   .   .   .

"You need to stay in bed, Josh."

"No, I don't!" ten-year-old Josh sat up, and defiantly pointed to the window. "I want to go outside."

"You can't go outside. You are sick," his ever-patient mother responded, gently caressing his forehead. In that touch, he could feel the warmth of her fingers, and the love in her heart.

"I'm not sick," Josh tried to hold back a cough – the force of which caused him to double over and clutch his small chest. "I just have a cough."

Ellen laughed. The soft, gentle laugh which made Josh feel bigger than the whole world, and better than any well person could ever feel.

"You must rest, my little man."

"But I'm supposed to pitch today?"

"No," she remonstrated. "You must rest and get well. Then you can play again."

"But why," the young lad lamented, crying into the bedsheets. "Why today? I've been looking forward to pitching against the Lions all year."

"I don't know why, Josh," Ellen smoothed his hair again, and kissed his forehead. "But I do know one day all the unknowns will be revealed. And then we will not wonder *why* anymore."

.   .   .   .

Josh's eyes opened. He was lying in a bed, but he was not a child. He tried sitting up.

"Whoa, there, cowboy! Not so fast," a woman spoke.

While not his mother, the person was familiar.

"Amanda!" he yelled. "Amanda, my love."

Tears formed and began streaming down his cheeks. A bright light suddenly flashed and grew stronger. He closed his eyes as he held up his hands, trying to block the powerful rays.

"Based on your medical history and this examination, we're prescribing medication for you. It will help with muscle and mind relaxation – help you sleep – which is the best thing given your current condition."

The words came from somewhere in the haze of bright light. Though he tried peering and squinting ahead, Josh could see no one.

"Your body has suffered an emotional and mental breakdown. You are overworked, and the stress level readings in your blood samples are significantly high."

Josh's face twisted in puzzlement. What medical history? He had not been to a doctor since he was a little boy. An emotional and mental breakdown?

"I was beaten up! Someone broke into my hotel room," he shouted, but somehow the words died in his mouth.

The light dissipated and the clouds cleared. Josh became aware he was leaving some sort of medical clinic. He walked through the doors, turned around, and looked at it. He knew this place. It was an Urgent Care facility located near the hotel.

What was that? He shook his head. *Was it a dream?*

■   ■   ■   ■   ■

The cab's windshield wipers rapidly flapped back and forth. Rain poured onto its glass and also made a heavy clatter on the roof of the newer taxi sedan.

"It's been like this all day?"

The cab driver glanced into the rearview mirror, and nodded while scratching his grizzled face.

"Been raining buckets for two days straight now. Where've ya been?"

"It's complicated," Josh answered.

For a moment, the gentle *swoosh* of the wipers hurriedly clearing the drops of water was the only sound. Traffic was at a standstill – typical for an afternoon in the DC metro.

Josh glanced at his watch.

"Will we make the airport soon?"

"Depends," the driver replied, his air too casual to suit Josh. "Traffic gets bad this time of day, add the rain in…" he spread his palms emphatically. "Anyone's guess."

"You don't say." Josh tried to sound matter-of-fact. It came out sounding quite smug. The driver looked in the mirror again, pulling his face into a scowl.

Josh ignored him, and leaned back in the seat. Staring out of the window, he looked around as best as he could with the cascading rain streaming down the glass pane. Crowds of people were moving through the streets. A few had umbrellas, some wore hats, most just tried to avoid the dripping gutters and spots where water would tumble from a gathering spot above them.

The cab nudged forward and stopped for a red light at an intersection. A solitary boy sitting on the curb caught Josh's attention. He curiously regarded the boy – something about the young lad intrigued him.

The boy was doing nothing. His feet were immersed in a gathering pool of water running down the street's side and into the gutters. The lad's clothes were tattered, his face smeared with dirt and grime. The disheveled hair had streaks of blonde in it – probably the original color. A faded red scarf was wound about his neck in disorganized fashion.

Suddenly, the boy looked up, and stared intently at Josh, who returned the stare. The boy's eyes were dark, but a reddish sort of light seemed to emanate from them. It was an intoxicating, enchanting set of eyes.

The boy abruptly smiled, and raised his hand as if to wave at Josh. All of a sudden, his hand dropped, and simultaneously, so did his head.

Josh was engrossed by the rapid, unusual movement and did not notice the jolt of the cab as the driver peeled rubber through the intersection. He was unaware of the screaming in the streets, until the driver swiftly rounded a corner and hit the horn.

"Move out of the way!" the man screamed, profanity freely falling from his tongue.

Putting his hands on the headrest in front of him, Josh pulled himself closer to the driver.

"What in the world, dude?"

"It's *Them!*"

"*Them?*"

The driver turned around and stared, dumbfounded by Josh's words. "Where have you been? It's the infected ones – the Unknowns – *Them!*"

"Infected ones? Like sick?"

The driver slickly maneuvered the car through a throng of running people – all trying to move in the same direction as the cab. He quickly glanced back at Josh again.

"It's the freaking Disease."

Josh slumped back into his seat.

If I haven't been dreaming, how long was I in that clinic? What has happened since then? Heck, do I even have a plane to catch?

He became aware of his hand wrapped around an object. Looking down, he saw a capsule of pills clutched tightly in his right hand. Josh felt the driver watching, and looked up to see the cabbie staring at him in the mirror.

"I'm fine," Josh answered in reply to the fierce, questioning look of the cab driver. "Just get me to the airport."

Suddenly, he thought of something. *Where's Sam been? Why isn't he reaching out?*

■   ■   ■   ■   ■

The small TV screen flickered; horizontal lines ran parallel to each other, stacked in black and white. They chased themselves up and down the picture. A fat, chubby hand smacked the side of the tube, and the picture flickered once more. But this time, the lines chased themselves away, and a relatively clear picture emerged.

Jim leaned against the shop's wall, and watched the feed. He was streaming from a satellite that was no longer operating with a valid license. The FCC had shut down any "dissenter" networks during the last administration. And now with conspirators spreading their propaganda on the Disease, the FCC was further restricting the airwaves. He scoffed at this. He did not trust the mainstream media. The illicit source made suitable proof that *something* he should be aware of was happening in the world.

The shop was vacant, save Jim. Tourism had been tanking, it started before the lady went berserk on the wharf – but that event certainly contributed. Now as the Disease became a pandemic, it slowed the primary livelihood of the charming riverfront city to a screeching halt.

There was a sudden commotion outside in the street. Jim nonchalantly picked up the TV remote and turned off the set. Walking to the front door, he looked out. Suddenly, his eyes widened. Moving quickly, he opened the door, and grabbed the exterior gate. Great bars of iron ran its length. Swinging it shut, he stepped back into the safety of the shop, locking it tight.

The shop's main door followed. He locked that one too – twice locked. Then as quickly as his short fat legs would let him, he waddled over to the windows, and pulled on the locks just to be safe.

Loud, muffled cries were heard, and then a sharp scream. Suddenly, a bloody face, mouth open, eyes drooling, smashed into the shop's window!

Jim jumped back in shock and horror. The face was hideous. It closer resembled a demon than a human.

Rattling began at the door. His heart beat fast, and he began to mutter the Lord's Prayer. Backing up to the front counter, he reached for the loaded shotgun stored underneath. If he needed to die, he was not going down without a fight.

The face at the window watched him, sneering, gnashing its teeth. Its eyes appeared to be empty, devoid of any living thing. But then, as quickly as the face appeared, it was gone.

"The back door!" Jim shrieked, but then realized the noise had moved further down the street.

At the same moment, he became aware that a profuse amount of sweat had formed on his brow. It came running off him in streams of liquid. Immediately, his shirt dampened. The hand he wiped across his face became wet and slobbery.

He tried to slow his breathing and calm himself. It was to no avail.

"The TV was right," he moaned. "The Unknowns are real. *They* have arrived."

THIRTY

"Tray tables and seat backs up," the flight attendant said as she passed Josh's reclined chair.

Josh watched as the attendant continued her way forward through the rest of the cabin. He slowly raised the chair back to its normal position and sighed. He had sorted out a flight back home to Minneapolis. With the termination of the Morphing Division, there would no longer be chartered flights, and his original commercial flight to Minnesota had long departed.

Everything had been a whirlwind, and his mind hurt thinking about it. The secretive meeting with CDV in Clairton; the clandestine meeting with Sam at *Clarence's on Chesapeake*; then the bizarre 3:40 am gathering at the former SEH headquarters. All three were oddly connected, he just did not know how yet. Then came the assault at the hotel and spending days at the medical clinic – it all seemed like it happened yesterday, but yet, a lifetime ago.

The exhilarating and terrifying cab ride had blown his mind. He had little knowledge of what was really going on anymore. Nor could he comprehend the rapid deterioration of the world he knew. His heart was racing, and he opened the medicine capsule. He downed a couple of the relaxation pills.

Exiting the aircraft's gangway, Josh glanced around for directions to the rideshare base. He had enough of traditional cab rides. Preoccupied with reading the signs above, he did not see the two men in black coats until they forcefully grabbed his arms.

"Mr. Cunningham, please come with us."

. . . . .

"No, this is not right."

Luke ran his fingers through his chestnut brown hair and sighed. He pulled the dark-rimmed glasses off, and absent-mindedly chewed on one of the ends. Tossing them onto a table, he stood up and stretched.

The door opened, and Tessa Morgan walked in, followed by Kelly Revers. Tessa smiled, tossing her red hair flirtatiously as she greeted Luke. His face reddened. No matter how much the woman had destroyed his life, he was helplessly attracted to her.

Like electrons in an atom. Damn science.

The smile faded from Tessa's face as she observed Luke's frustration. She opened her mouth to speak, but Revers beat her to it.

"What's wrong, doc?"

"This is not right. Something's amiss."

"How can you tell in this mess," Kelly muttered under her breath, but still loud enough for Luke to hear.

Papers were scattered all around the table, and the two holograph projectors were both displaying eight screens. Luke did not expect a layperson like Kelly Revers to understand. He looked at Tessa; hopeful she would help him out. She did.

"The man is looking at sixteen points of data simultaneously, plus doing calculations on actual paper, Kelly. Lay off him. He's our best shot to crack the new patch."

"This shouldn't be here…" Luke tapped a spot on the paper as he spoke.

"What should?"

"I don't know. Our tests on the patch have all proven to be inconclusive. Without the exact ingredients and formulas, we're just guessing."

"Better get working then," Kelly persisted.

Luke glared at her. Tessa intervened.

"We just wanted a status report for Chief. We have one. Thanks, Luke."

. . . . .

"Where is he? We know you talked to him."

The light shone brightly into Josh's eyes, blinding him. It was as if someone had taken one of the can lights used at baseball stadiums and mounted it directly in front of him. He was unable to see much of anything, let alone the person asking the questions from behind the light.

Based on the footsteps he heard, he surmised there must be at least two or three people in the room. So far, though, only one person had addressed him. And the voice – male, baritone in range, and middle-aged – was growing more agitated as time passed.

"Listen," the man spoke again, his fist crashing into the table. "We know you talked to Sam Walters. He told you something. What was it?"

The line of questioning had not detoured. It was all about Sam. *Same as that assistant from SEH and Blair Leshief after that,* Josh recalled. *Why is everybody obsessed with my colleague? And why haven't I heard from him since Clarence's!* He was worried. The interrogation did not help.

It was quiet for a moment, a longer pause than previous. Josh strained his ears, hoping to catch a glimmer of the conversation being held by the other people in the room. Suddenly, a new voice spoke – also male, though older and tenor in sound.

"What can you tell us about Lieut. Rhianna Adams?"

Josh looked up, straight into the light, and blinked his eyes. *Rhianna Adams? What the heck does she have to do with this?*

"Um," he stammered, showing obvious surprise. "She was a Homeland Security liaison for a project I did with SEH involving the Public Health Agency of Canada. She was arrested for treason, though."

"That's all?" the voice asked.

"Yes. I wouldn't lie to you. I haven't lied about anything I've said," Josh remonstrated.

His eyes moved, investigating what he could make out; vainly trying to catch a glimpse of the two men behind the bright light.

"You didn't know she was dead?"

"No? When did she die?" Despite his lingering questions from their mission to upstate New York, hearing news of Rhianna Adams' death saddened Josh.

"She died months ago, during transport to a hospital. Unknown medical condition, which was surprising," the voice grew closer, and Josh was suddenly aware of the light being pushed back, away from his face. "Because she had a high-level security clearance which is only issued after passing an exhaustive medical examination."

"Oh," he whispered. "I didn't know."

Everybody I know, everything I interact with, is turning to dust. Death surrounds me.

"More than surprising," the voice's body took final form, and a fiftyish, lightly gray-haired gentleman sat down on the edge of the table. "It's doubtful. We believe she's still alive."

"And that's bad news?"

The man laughed, and switched the light off. Three other people were in the room, two men and one woman. All of them were sporting dark glasses over their eyes, and wore gloves on their hands.

"Well, ironic, I suppose. Why is it that all your former colleagues from SEH, and your former associate Rhianna Adams are all mysteriously missing?"

"I admit, it's strange," Josh agreed hurriedly. "Though I'd hardly call Lieut. Adams an associate of mine."

"Enough," the man shouted as he stood up, pounding his own fist on the table. "You are lying. You know more about this than you are telling us, Mr. Cunningham. So let me tell you this," the man leaned in close; so close his breath enveloped Josh's face. "We are watching you. Always watching."

The gentleman then stood up, straightened himself, and walked towards a wall. A door was there apparently, for as he approached, the wall gave way and opened. The man passed through.

The woman in the room and another one of the dark-glasses-wearing men came over to Josh, and roughly grabbed his arms. They dragged him to his feet and quickly exited, shoving him ahead of their swift strides. He struggled to stay on his feet, but he resolved to remain upright, and not show any weakness.

Another hallway, and then a door opened. The man and woman threw him out into the street. Josh stumbled and grabbed a post to keep from falling. The bright, violent sunlight seared his eyes. He put a hand up, shading them as best as he could.

He had no idea where he was. A powerful *zoom* from an airplane taking off was heard, so he figured he must be near the airport. His head ached tremendously, his eyes burned like crazy. He wished he had a pair of those heavy glasses the interrogators were sporting.

"Blasted sunlight," Josh muttered as he started down the street. "It hurts. Who were those people? Why am I being targeted?"

A fit of shakes suddenly overtook him, and sweat poured down his forehead. Stumbling a few more steps, he then stopped. Pulling out the capsule, he shook it. A couple pills emptied into his palm. Josh tilted his head, and tossed the pills back into his mouth, swallowing the dose. He shook his head and closed his eyes, trying to clear the cobwebs.

His eyes opened, and ahead, he saw a sign for public transportation. He would take that.

. . . . .

Josh had no recollection of the bus ride or how he ultimately got home. He would have had at least one or two transfers during the process and yet, here he was propped up in his bed. His delirious, blurred eyes stared out of the window, and into the side yard. Was it his yard?

He was back in the hospital. His vision was hazy, it gradually cleared, and he saw her again. The love of his life: Amanda.

"Stay with me!" he pleaded. He tried to snatch her hand, preventing her from leaving.

Amanda laughed. It was light and airy. "You need to stop fighting, Josh. You need to accept this and embrace it."

"Embrace what?" he coughed, and fell back onto the pillows.

His eyes cleared again, and he saw a bubbling brook. Dark green and red leaves generously filled out the robust branches of the majestic, soaring trees. Robins and cardinals alike were sitting on the tree branches, singing a merry song. The sun shone brightly, yet its rays not as bright as he remembered. Come to think of it, he could not remember the brook either – but the feeling was so lovely and peaceful.

"Embrace. You are stronger than the Disease. Stop fighting; join the survivalists."

"Survivalists?" Josh propped himself up. His elbow was supported on nothing though – it was just dangling in midair.

Amanda was walking around, wearing a nurse's smock. Her back was to him, but he could still hear her voice as she addressed him in low, soothing tones.

"Yes, do not become like them. Stay strong, be well…" she turned to face him; as she turned, so did Josh. He saw the capsule sitting on a nightstand next to him. "You need to sleep, my love. You need to rest."

"Sleep and rest," Josh repeated. His vision hazy again, his eyes groggy. They felt heavy, like a soggy shirt just out of washing. "Survivalists. Don't be like them. I must survive."

He swallowed another dose and leaned back. His eyelids shut. He felt himself being picked up, carried forward, and placed in a sort of pillowed bed. It was warm, inviting, and soothing. There was nothing else he would rather be doing.

Sleep was coming. Peace from the terrible nightmare he had been living. The answers might be out there, who knew? But why pursue any longer? The chase was over. What good had come from it? Sam Walters was gone. Mark Jacobi too. John Stevens was dead. Melinda Gore was dead. His old classmate Luke Baer had been outcast by the University. Even his career was over. He was a truthseeker no more, assigned to be an engineer on some obscure project – if that was even real.

Josh felt himself smiling. He had no reason to, except he had just remembered a person – the Mexican shopkeeper from Savannah, Georgia. Jim was the man's name. Josh then remembered someone else; the person who first mentioned Jim. A woman he had met only once. She had been at SEH. He could see her smile, and the memory of it comforted him.

It doesn't matter who that person was, she is gone too. Just like everything else. Why bother to think anyway? Much good that's done. Much good will it ever do.

.   .   .   .   .

"Ambassador Omach, what a pleasure to finally meet you."

The congresswoman stretched out her hand, and the tall Ugandan reached out and clasped it tightly. She slightly winced from the pressure, and quickly pulled her hand back as Derrick Omach released his grip.

"Did you have a pleasant journey?"

"I did," the ambassador spoke evenly. His perfect English gave away his college and doctoral education in the United States. "I am sorry about the recent tragedies. My condolences on the passing of Pres. Turouning. I worked with him a little, and even though it was brief, I found him to be a man of courage and great fortitude. Perhaps that is why his death perplexes me so."

"I'm sure," said Congresswoman Elisha Atkins, not trying to be condescending.

"How is it that you were picked for the Council?"

"Well, as you know, once Pres. Turouning died, the Vice President was impeached. You can't have a VP running the country who knew full well what the President had and did nothing about it."

"I heard the proof was inconclusive."

Atkins smiled at the ambassador. While not unpleasant, her countenance shared little warmth.

"It was proof enough for our Congress to hold an emergency meeting and vote unanimously to approve the World Council to serve as the supreme leadership in our country while keeping Congress and the judicial systems for the day-to-day affairs."

"Ah yes, unanimous," said Derrick, thoughtfully stroking his chin. "Wasn't there many votes abstaining or absent?"

A curt nod of her head was the reply from the congresswoman.

"I'm a little surprised a sovereign nation like the United States would allow the World Council to sit as supreme leader. Obviously, as a delegate for the Council, I'm always happy to help sort of these world crises – it's my job. But the fact your country has a document in place outlying who and what should assume leadership in times like this, I'm surprised Congress saw differently."

"It's an ancient document, Ambassador," Elisha Atkins tried to keep her smile. "Perhaps leave the governance of our country to its citizens, and let *us* focus on what the Council can do for not only our country but the world."

"Of course," Derrick leaned forward, spreading his hands in apology as he discerned her meaning. "I meant no disrespect."

The congresswoman poured herself a cup of tea and lifted it in the air. She offered it to the ambassador. He shook his head and settled back into the large, oversized chair. Elisha lifted the teacup to her lips and took a small sip. She then put the cup back onto the saucer and set it down on the ornate side table next to her.

"Now as to why we are all here. There is a cure coming out."

"I thought a cure had already been released?"

"Ah," Elisha said. "A common misunderstanding."

"One that your country has been purporting."

"Look, Ambassador," the congresswoman's polite tone took a substantial turn and tinged with anger. "If we don't present a cure, panic ensues. We have more deaths, more riots, more fear-mongering. Dissension is already at a higher rate than ever before."

Derrick had started to open his mouth to say something, but thought better and closed it. He would merely listen to what the congresswoman had to say and keep his opinions to himself.

"The drug being used right now is temporary, but Sehtym has been working around the clock for the next version. It *will* be the cure. We are sure of it."

"Great! Then what do you need me for?"

"Ah." The Congresswoman's smile returned again. She picked up the saucer and took another dainty sip of her tea. There was a slight clink of china as she set it back down. "I can see why William liked you. You have a certain *assertion* about you."

"I have a job to do, and I like making sure I am best at it."

"Well, we are depending on you to be at your very best, for it's the nature of your job that we meet. Mr. Ambassador, how is everything going with Operation Laja?"

Derrick carefully studied Congresswoman Atkins as he contemplated his answer. Depending on who was asking him that question – they would get a different answer. The ambassador was not looking to play chameleon, there simply wasn't a suitable alternative.

The World Council had demanded progress continue without delay. The rapid spread of the Disease only heightened anxiety, and raised the slimming stakes of survival to a new level. Finding suitable locations was one thing, creating sustainable living environments another, and still preserving humanity by keeping all in check raised the stakes. Naturally, he would give different answers.

He cleared his throat. "I suspect as best as one could expect."

Elisha laughed, it sounded unkind. "Well, that's reassuring."

Derrick decided to elaborate. "One of the primary problems we are encountering is ventilation. But, we have made some strides and recently procured some new personnel who will greatly assist in engineering a practical and life-giving design."

"Let's hope so," Elisha took another sip of her tea. "All of humanity depends on it. Our hopes and dreams rest in Laja."

THIRTY-ONE

The holograph lights flickered as if being controlled by a knob that was turning back and forth. The effect created weird, glowing orange and blue streams across the room. Quiet but distinct "zoom" and "whoosh" noises could be heard as people in the room expanded and contracted their hands and fingers. The sound was coming from the notification libraries installed on the holograph projectors. Its purpose was to notify the engineer of an action just completed.

For instance, when expanding the picture, a slight "pop" noise was heard. If an image was shrunk or minimized, a "kish" noise was heard. Discarded files and windows would generate a "swoosh" noise, not unlike a basketball passing through the hoop on nothing but net.

The amalgamated noises generated a hypnotic ambient buzz. Overhead streaming videos from around the world showed the latest field and lab reports. In one corner of the room, several holographic people were standing in a circle as they were debriefed by the mysterious woman called Chief.

The room had become a home of sorts to Luke. The past weeks had blown his mind. Just months ago, the very suggestion of participating with conspirators would have been discarded without a second thought. Too much had happened and unraveled though, he had seen too much.

Pres. Turouning's assassination, coupled with the announcement that the World Council had been assigned the senior authority in the United States was one thing. Another was the strangely unified approach in the Middle East towards eradicating new outbreaks of the disease. It was abnormal; something that should not have happened given what transpired a few years earlier when a previous administration boldly sided with one country over the other. Times were changing.

"Hey, dreamy boy, can I get some help here?"

Luke shook his head, clearing the daydreams, and saw the smiling face of Tessa. Her red hair was pulled back into a ponytail, and her bright hazel eyes showed slight irritation.

"I'm taking a break," he grumbled.

"Taking a break? What's that?"

"You know what I mean," he mildly argued. "I'm not at the lab."

"Come with me," Tessa commanded.

They walked down a dark corridor, and passed through an old Metro check-in station. The stanchions once used to keep the thronging crowds in line as they swiped passes were long broken apart. Tessa strutted to the edge of an old, dilapidated escalator, put one foot on it, and cast a longing look at Luke.

Man, she's sexy, he gawked.

"Come on, we're going topside."

.   .   .   .   .

"You want to break into the University?"

Luke was incredulous. His eyes bulged as he spoke. Much love had been lost when the University had terminated his position and publicly shamed him, but still, the thought of breaking into the place that had been his home for most of his life – it hit a nerve.

"That was our *old* plan," Tessa said, cutting her eyes at Danny Graves who impatiently paced the floor with his arms folded. "I have a better one."

"Hold on a second," Luke felt emboldened by the fact it was something familiar to him. "Why do we need them in the first place?

Tessa smiled. Luke realized he had said 'them.' Without thinking, he had included himself as one of the conspirators. It was a first for him.

"We've tried hacking the server," Kelly Revers explained, slight irritation showing in her voice. "But we've been unable to do that."

"And if we can't hack it," Danny interrupted, "that means we need to hit it."

"Nobody has answered my question: why?"

"You said previously we need the actual formula and ingredients to create the counter drug," Tessa explained.

"Yes, I did."

She held out her hands, palms open. He grasped her meaning.

"What makes you think they have the formula at the University? Sehtym is the one who released it, and I cut ties with SEH before that happened."

"True," the recruiter nodded. "But remember, I installed all of TYM's secret documents on your computer."

"Yeah, but Tachi Yin didn't know anything. Pharma Group is behind the patch."

"Oh, come off it!" Kelly angrily snapped, walking over to Luke and jabbing a finger in his face. "Do you have a better idea?"

He thought for a moment, and then acknowledged he did not. It *was* worth a try at least, he conceded. "But weren't all those files discovered when I got fired?"

Danny snorted and smirked at Luke, who ignored him.

"I lied to you," Tessa began.

"Shocker."

"I also put the TYM dump on the mainframe. I did not anticipate they would change the encryption across the entire University when you were ousted."

It was peculiar, but the confession, an error on Tessa Morgan's part, made Luke feel strangely satisfied. His greatest weakness had a flaw of her own.

"We need the information, but we aren't going to break in – so what's the plan?" Danny was tired of this detour from the plan of action.

"In all honesty," said Tessa, her face colored slightly. "We'll still be taking the files, but with inside help."

Graves stopped pacing, and stared at Tessa, amazed at her words.

"Now that's an idea. Who do you have in mind?"

"Brenda Myers – Luke's old intern assistant." Tessa's hands were on her hips, nostrils expanding as she spoke, prepared for a blowback from Luke. It was delayed.

His eyes widened, and he stammered for a minute. Then he ran both hands through his hair while shaking his head. The words came out in a torrent.

"You can't be serious! She's the only friend I have left there. Heck, the *only* person I have left in my life."

"Which is exactly why we can use her," Kelly jumped in. She perceived the gist of Tessa's plan. "She trusts you."

"More than trusts," Tessa interjected. "She *adores* you, Luke. To her, you are the echelon of moral purity, a victim of my own manipulation. Why ever since you were cast out, she's been ostracized for having worked with you. She's in danger of losing her position, and with the stigma of your association, she might not even get another job."

"We'd see to it that she was provided for," chimed in Danny.

These guys are *smooth operators. They're always thinking ahead.* Luke wondered how someone could live like that. Always looking for the angle, a way forward; plotting who could next be used to get the job done.

His eyes closed. His mind sifted through memories of the University. Brenda had practically been there since his post-graduate work. She was family to him. Could he do this? Could he involve her? There was only one choice. *Aetatis progressu.*

"I'll call her."

·　　·　　·　　·　　·

"I'm only helping because I care about you, Luke. It certainly isn't for *her*," Brenda glared at Tessa, who sat ahead of her in the vehicle.

Dark clouds hung low in the sky, blocking the large, oversized moon. The omission of light bode well for the clandestine operation which the small party was about to initiate. The black vehicle rumbled along the street, its engine noise muffled by the heavy night air.

"I know," said Luke as he reached over and squeezed Brenda's hand. "And I'm grateful. You've always been there for me."

"Blah blah," Kelly said. "To review: Brenda's going to enter through the side entrance into the tech center. Based on our surveillance, that's the only place where the proD security is streaming. Once inside, go to the server room, and insert this into the mainframe," Kelly held up a small, thumb-sized drive. "Once inserted, our system will automatically do everything else. You just leave then."

Brenda nodded.

"Tessa and Luke will remain here with Jackson," Kelly referenced the IT hacker in the sting vehicle. "The rest of us will handle any foot traffic," Kelly flipped her short hair towards the other four armed operatives in the truck.

"No killing," Tessa warned. "Chief wouldn't like that."

"She's not here, is she?" Danny growled.

He pulled his handheld from its holster, and simultaneously racked the slide. A round propelled into the firing chamber as he released it. The gun was ready for use.

"I'm serious. We aren't here to start a war. We're here to snatch and grab."

"We know," Revers rolled her eyes as she grabbed a rifle from the swinging side pocket. "But if anything happens, we'll be ready. Silencers a go?"

The other armed agents nodded.

Luke peered out the window. A bitter feeling of nostalgia came over him as he recognized the area – a park-like glen located just north of the tech center at the University. Many lunches had been spent in the green space as he racked his brain, trying to solve the latest problem assigned to the Pittsburgh Research Team. The glen was also located just south of the fateful Tower. His brow furrowed as he remembered the last time there.

He became conscious of someone watching him, and lifting his eyes, saw Brenda. Her countenance was perturbed. He tilted his head as if to ask what was wrong.

"I'm angry," she said. "I won't ever forgive them for what they did to you. I'm doing this for you, Luke, and Dr. Grafton."

The black vehicle stopped abruptly, and without a moment's hesitation, Brenda swung open the door, and dropped to the ground. Danny, Kelly and the other CDV militia followed. The dark night enveloped them.

Luke remained sitting as he watched the group leave. Brenda's words were kind, but he knew it was his own fault he had been banned from the University. It was his choice to join the Conspirators. He did not deserve a loyal friend. He did not deserve any friends.

Tessa and Jackson, the IT guy, were still in the truck. The latter fired up his tracking gear, and even though the dark night obscured the team from physical view, the tracking technology began to follow Brenda as she moved forward.

"Exciting, isn't it?"

There was too much enthusiasm in Tessa's voice for Luke to agree. He knew she enjoyed it, the thrilling rush of adrenaline. The idea she was doing something illegal, illicit, taboo. *A shrink would have a field day with her.*

"I guess that depends on your point of view," Luke simply replied as he leaned forward to observe Jackson's apparatus. The IT hacker sat toggling between the different cameras. "What are you seeing?" he asked.

"This is your girlfriend's feed…"

"She's *not* my girlfriend," Luke forcefully interrupted.

It was so adamant, Tessa's lower lip curled into a smile. The IT hacker glanced back at Luke and Tessa.

"Oh, sorry, I thought…then Tessa is?"

Luke sighed. "It's complicated."

"Huh, well, anyway, what we're watching is the live feed of Brenda's cam. We're using a night vision LED to brighten the picture. This way, we can see what she is seeing."

"Sounds pretty 2000s to me," Luke was not impressed.

"Hey, don't knock the old tech! We use far more of it as a society than we care to admit. Most of the new stuff is just flimflam; gimmicks to distract. If you want to do real work, real power – you use the old stuff."

"If I ever open a TV & appliance repair shop, I'll remember that when I lose the business."

Tessa laughed. Jackson smirked, and shook his head.

Brenda slowed and then stopped at the exterior of a building. Luke squinted and despite the dim computer image, recognized the side entrance of the Tech Center. Brenda entered a code on the keypad, and the door unlocked. Once she entered the building, the image grew considerably worse. Jackson sighed.

"The downside of the old tech is reception can be spotty. I was hoping this wouldn't happen." He switched channels on the headset. "Danny, Kelly, can one of you hear me?"

"Both," Danny growled back.

There was almost zero static.

"I've lost visuals on Brenda."

Danny swore and consulted with Kelly for a moment. His voice was muffled as he talked to her; it became coherent again.

"Kelly's going to keep eyes on the security outposts – I'll move in. Can you recall the code she entered?"

"Like you have to even ask," Jackson guffawed, and rattled back the code.

"How did you do that?" Luke was amazed. "I mean, that's incredible."

"Not really," Jackson looked back at Luke, his brown eyes dancing. "I had my logic programmer enabled on Brenda's camera, so even though we couldn't see her physically key in the code, the programmer tracked the electronic pulses on the pad to extract it."

Suddenly, a noise was heard over the broadcast. Tessa's eyes narrowed at the familiar sound.

"Was that a gunshot?"

"Yes." Jackson snapped. He grabbed the boom on his headset and yelled into it. "Hey! What's going on?"

"I've got two bogies," Kelly replied evenly over the radio. "Well now just one, but he's making a break for it. I'll handle him."

Her voice cut off as she started to chase the guard. Luke put his hands on his head, and leaned back in the seat, his face white. This was not supposed to happen.

The three anxiously waited in radio silence. The suspense was more than Luke could bear. He rubbed his hands across his face, then his legs. He was stressed out by the situation. A hand touched his shoulder. Looking over, he saw Tessa with a warm smile on her face.

"It'll be okay, Luke. Brenda's going to be fine."

He nodded. Her words sounded reassuring, but he was still anxious.

Danny's voice broke the stillness. "I got her, we're coming back out!"

"Second bogie down, coming back as well," a triumphant Revers crowed over the radio.

The three watchers smiled, and shook each other in celebration. Then suddenly, a loud gunshot echoed through the night air! An audible scream came from outside the truck.

Tessa pushed open the door, and stood up on the foot railing as she peered out into the night. Luke scurried after her, completely emptying from the vehicle as he squinted, trying to help his eyes focus in the darkness.

It was then he saw it. Four guards were running down from the Commerce Building towards the Tech Center with another four bearing down from the Museum's courtyard. The operation was blown. The agents spotted.

"Kelly, you almost back?" Jackson screamed into the radio.

"We got hit!" Revers yelled. "We're coming back as fast as we can."

More gunfire erupted as cries filled the night air.

No, no, no! This wasn't supposed to happen. Luke felt sick to his stomach.

Kelly and two of the CDV militia emerged from the dark. Tessa's eyes widened.

"Where's Jase?"

"Down," cried one of the younger operatives. Luke suddenly realized this particular agent was a young girl, not more than twenty.

Kelly pushed the girl back into the truck. The other agent scampered aboard as well. Jackson pushed the ignition, and the vehicle roared to life.

"Wait, where are we going? What about Brenda and Danny?" Luke was alarmed.

"We're going to leave the moment they arrive," said Tessa, her voice terse.

Luke strained his eyes, searching the dark night for any sign of Brenda. Suddenly, she and Danny appeared, running for their lives. Behind them, scarcely a hundred yards away, two of the University's police officers were madly chasing after them.

They were going to make it. Luke's face began to relax. He smiled at Brenda, and in a glimmer of light, he caught a glimpse of her face. It was composed, but resolved. Then she fell.

Danny hit the side of the truck, his full weight crashing into it. Recovering, he jumped into the vehicle. Sticking his head outside the open door, he screamed at Luke.

"Come on! Let's go!"

"Wait," Luke was still outside, his hand outstretched. "Brenda tripped."

"Get in," Tessa grasped Luke's shoulders and pulled hard. "Get in before you get killed."

Another hand latched onto him, and Luke felt himself being lifted into the vehicle. He shouted and fought back, tears streaming down his face.

"We can't leave her. She needs our help!"

"She's dead," Tessa said softly, almost tenderly into his ear as she held him close. "She did not trip, Luke. They shot her."

The flash of light, the brief moment he glimpsed Brenda's face – the moment her life had been taken. He cursed and punched the vehicle's roof. Falling back, he sobbed and clutched at his throat – trying to ease the pang he felt welling upside him.

Jackson engaged auto turbo, and the sting vehicle roared forward, tires spinning wildly. The campus police fired their guns towards the retreating truck. The shots were inaccurate.

What else do I have to lose? Why did I ask her to help? Poor, sweet Brenda. All she cared about was science and using it to better mankind. She cared so much for me, and I killed her. I killed her!

Luke's heart felt like it had been smashed into a million pieces. He felt dead inside. The sobs came unfettered and unabated.

THIRTY-TWO

A faint blue light glowed from the laptop as Jackson's fingers flew over the keyboard. The CDV militia agents were gone, presumably to the trailer parked beside the stopped truck.

The area was abandoned entirely, at least as much as one could tell in the darkness that covered the area. The moon was still hidden by heavy clouds, the scent of rain hung in the air. Not a sweet smell, but rather a heavy, somewhat putrid smell that rain brought these days. It was almost as if vinegar would fall instead of water. A swinging road sign a few hundred yards away identified the street as the Forgotten Avenue in Clairton, Pennsylvania.

Luke clutched his arms, tightly hugging himself. He stared straight ahead, oblivious to the fact Tessa was stroking his arm, trying to calm him. There was no calming down from what had just happened.

What could calm me anyways? Why should I be calm? My dearest friend was just shot and killed in front of my eyes! And while doing what? A rendezvous for a secret organization – its cause she knew nothing about.

"It's here," Jackson said, his fingers slowing their rapid movement. "All of it." The IT hacker looked away from the screen and directly at Luke. "We owe it to Brenda."

Luke mumbled, his words incoherent.

"We need to get this to Chief," Tessa said. She scooted over and looked at the laptop's screen. "Yeah, it's all on the health patch."

"Here, Luke," Jackson said as he tapped the monitor. "You should verify it though. You're the scientist."

It's not something I want to do, though. Is anything worth doing anymore? What am I, a minion? A bot that merely performs duties as assigned, regardless of the consequences to others? I'm worthless.

"Luke."

Pushing his dark-rimmed glasses back up his nose, Luke straightened himself and held out his hand. Jackson handed over the computer.

His eyes darted back and forth as he began browsing the chemical properties and lab test results. It surprised him how easily and naturally it came to him, even though his heart had been wrenched out and trampled to pieces.

The moments passed, the screen flickered. Red, blue, yellow – the primary colors swirled and amalgamated together as the images changed, then again reversing itself when Luke sorted the information as he saw fit.

Suddenly, he bit down on his lip, and ran a nervous tongue over his dry lips.

"Um, guys, forget about the patch."

"Why? What do you see?"

"Here," he pointed. "It's a new drug – for relaxation and stress management. But the chemical properties are way out and the substances used – heck, this would be far more consequential than anything I've seen on the health patch."

"It is mind control, isn't it."

Luke lifted his head, and contemplated the earnest countenance of Tessa. *What is it with CDV and mind control?*

"More like mind-numbing."

"Like opioids?"

"Worse."

Luke moved the cursor and double-tapped an icon named 'Compile.' The files and information on the screen fused together. A single lab document remained. He tapped the screen with his forefinger.

"This is it. It's called xY0b5."

■　　　■　　　■　　　■　　　■

The soft, burning sensation of brandy washed over Jim's throat. He closed his eyes as the recently acquired taste of warmth encircled him. Setting the glass on the bar counter, he became aware Patrick was watching him.

"Rough day, my friend?" The bartender asked.

Jim preferred to not think about it, so he changed the subject. "Going to watch the broadcast?"

"Shh," Patrick leaned in close. "Keep your voice down. There are strangers here tonight."

Jim waved his hand. Patrick was always cautious.

"Well, I'll be heading out anyway. Goodnight."

Patrick nodded in farewell, and Jim rose clumsily from the barstool. Raising his chubby arms, he stretched them out, before walking towards the entrance to the tavern. When he reached the door, he opened it, and stepped out into the nippy evening air.

He surveyed the street as he walked along. A loud belch escaped him. Irritated, he waved a hand in front of his mouth, brushing the stinky fumes away.

What have I become? What is my life now?

The avenue seemed to stretch on forever when in reality it was only a short distance, and a couple turns from *Flannigan's* to *Savannah Souvenirs*. He covered it as fast as the short, fat legs would let him.

The broadcast is going to begin soon, and I don't want to miss it.

At last, Jim reached the rear entrance to his shop. Grabbing the key, he thrust it into the lock, and turned the deadbolt. Bustling inside, he hung his jacket on a crusty metal peg that stuck out from the wall. It was not designed to be a coat hook. The original purpose forgotten as the building aged, but he found it suited his jacket just fine. His scarf followed, and then his flat ivy cap.

In the corner of the rear storage room was the old TV set. Situated in the front of the TV was the old rocking chair, as well as a reclining chair with plush arms. It was into this chair that Jim plopped and pulled the wooden handle on its side. The footrest came up, and the chair reclined.

"That's better," he mumbled out loud, fishing for the remote.

Having space at the back of his shop was quite the luxury. Extra room in the heart of Savannah's tourist locale was hard to come by. The existing shops had been renovated during the millennial phase when all the old, classic looks were "refurbished" to a more contemporary setting.

The redesigned movement had been complete hogwash, and Jim doubted he would ever be able to forgive the mayor of Savannah who allowed such a travesty to occur. The promise that the tourist market would skyrocket proved to be underwhelming. Tourism had increased for those located near Wharf ONE, but for the rest, they experienced shrinking profits. This forced several of the small business owners to sell off their prime real estate for ridiculous prices, well-below market value.

Of course, the downturn prompted Jim to believe this had all been part of the plan the entire time. He would ask, "What better way to get the common man out than to force him to lose the very thing that makes him valuable?"

"And what is that?" he answered himself in response.

"A man's identity," he replied, not caring it was inane to hold such a conversation with oneself.

Jim thoughtfully stroked his chin as he reenacted the private conversation once again. The broadcast would begin quite soon, but the idea stuck with him. Comfortably resting in the old recliner, he pondered: *A man's identity. What exactly is my identity?*

Of course, he had an identity as a shopkeeper, a citizen of good standing in the community. But after events from earlier in the day, he wondered if it would be his utter failure in raising his niece that chiseled his true identity.

.   .   .   .   .

The front doorbell jingled. Jim was hard at work in the backroom organizing boxes, so he paid no heed. Anna was operating the sales counter; she could handle it. Soon, however, loud angry voices broke upon his ears, and he stopped what he was doing. Concerned with the escalating noises, he began plodding towards the front of the store.

"I'm not your whore!" Anna's voice shouted.

"Knock it off," a young man shot back. "I didn't call you a whore. But this stuff isn't cheap! If you want to keep getting it, you have to give some."

"Please, Arndt! I used up the last of it today."

"I know," a third person joined in. He was also male, and he was laughing. "Just before we came, right?"

"C'mon, please? Pretty please?"

Jim lurched to the side, stopping his forward progress. His hands shook as he struggled to stay on his feet. His heart beat fast, and he could feel his throat tightening. His worst fears had been confirmed. Anna was an addict, and worse, she was selling her soul for it.

"I have five kilos coming in. Buyers lining up fast and heavy already."

Upon hearing this, Jim pursed his lips, and came bursting around the corner. He was out of breath as he reached the front of the shop, and leaned against a display rack to catch it.

"Who's this fatso?" the third person asked.

"My uncle," Anna answered as she faced Jim. "Go away. This isn't about you."

"Yes, it is!" The shopkeeper's voice was loud and authoritative. "Anything regarding my family *is* my business!"

"Good. Maybe you have the $500 your niece needs for her next fix?"

Jim looked sideways at Anna. Her eyelids were vibrating. He failed to notice it before, but he could see she had recently used; perhaps even within the last hour. The telltale signs: the shaking frame, eyes out of focus, flushed skin – a look of saturated drowsiness. Shocked by the realization, he was ashamed it was happening right under his own roof.

"I don't have $500," he addressed Ardnt, looking back at Anna's boyfriend. Sudden courage flowed through his veins. "Business has been terrible, but please, take a look around. You can have anything you want. Just leave her alone."

"Haha," both of the boys laughed.

Arndt stepped closer to Jim. "I don't want your stuff. This babe's mine already; I can't just give her a high for nuthin! You know, Blubber, head is cheap, getting booty fine; what I ain't got is money."

The boy rubbed his fingers together and cruelly laughed. Jim's glare of hatred brazened the youth.

"Don't believe me, Blubber?"

Arndt stepped to Anna's side, and slapped her backside. Her face winced at the unwarranted sexual aggression from her boyfriend. Glaring at Jim, Arndt slowly moved his hand up, past Anna's waist, and underneath the pale brown hoodie. The teenager began to grope Anna's breasts. Jim's wrathful eyes narrowed. It was an act of defiance – a power struggle to demonstrate who was really in control. Jim perceived this, and he knew he had lost already.

After a moment, Arndt snickered, and pulled his hand from Anna's shirt. He turned away in disgust.

"Whatever. I need the money, girl. End of story."

Jim noticed Anna's eyes were beginning to dilate. He could hear her increased difficulty in breathing. It was the aftershock of using Zetox. The street drug had become prevalent the last couple of years and only seemed to accelerate with the advent of the Disease. Once addicted, the drug-ravaged a body.

Far too many lives had already been claimed by Zetox. It had become a silent killer. Ever since the legalization of cannabis, people had turned to more ingenious ways to deal with everyday life. A mad dash by society in an attempt to create a pseudo-reality rather than embracing the actual world in which one dwelled. Zetox was the pinnacle of that crazy race – an all-arounder that gave the rush of an opiate. The devil's drug if there ever was one.

Jim's shoulders slumped as he watched Arndt assault his niece. Despair seized him. With all that had been happening, he failed to notice the changes in Anna. He watched as her eyes caved, the focus all but gone. His spirit dropped. He disliked Arndt. Hated him maybe.

But what am I to do about it? He's young and has friends. I am old and alone.

An idea came to the good-hearted shopkeeper. He was unsure if it was a good idea, but he was desperate.

"Tell me…Arndt," Jim struggled to say teenager's name, so filled with rage towards the young man. "You work at the Lincoln safe house, right?"

"What's it to you, Blubber?"

"A failed idea, but that is what will save her."

Arndt looked at Jim as if the shopkeeper was crazy. "What are you talking about?"

There was no stopping now. The man knew he had to do this. Patrick Flannigan had said something back when the Unknowns first appeared. *"Leave the dead to bury their own dead."*

"I want you to take her there. Please take my niece to Lincoln Safe House."

Anna laughed. It was a sad laugh – devoid of any mirth and hollow as an old log in the woods.

"I'm not going to some dinky safe house, Blubber!"

Jim blinked his eyes twice, fighting back the tears. It was one thing for Ardnt to call him that, but for his niece to insult him as well – and in front of others… He struggled to maintain composure. The new, strange courage returned, flowing through his veins. He continued on, ignoring Anna's words.

"Take her, Arndt. I will cover all expenses."

"Really? How's that? You just told me you ain't got $500." Arndt laughed and waggled a finger in Jim's face. "It ain't cheap living at the safe house – even if they do free fixes – room and board ain't."

Without hesitation, Jim pulled his keys from his pocket. He singled one out, and started to remove it from the ring.

"Here, take this. It's for a container in the back of the store. It is filled with whatever cash I have on hand, and hundreds, perhaps thousands of dollars in materials – you can sell it off. Go look for yourself."

He stepped to the side, holding out a hand, offering Arndt to go take a look.

"It's true," Anna croaked, her eyes heavy with subdued drowsiness. "I saw it myself a couple weeks ago."

"Why are you doing this?" Arndt asked. He was genuinely confused by Jim's behavior.

"Anna has made her choice. I have made mine. She needs to be somewhere safe."

An awkward silence fell over the room. The second boy, who had remained silent during the exchange, moved to Arndt's side and whispered in his ear.

Arndt nodded his head as he listened. The necklaces around his neck danced a dim reflection of the hanging lights above.

"Fine. We've got a deal, Blubber."

Jim demurely nodded.

"C'mon, babe." Arndt grabbed Anna's rear, and steered her to the door.

"Anna!" said Jim suddenly. One last time, his voice was loud and strong.

She turned and looked at him. There was no visible cognition left in her eyes. The aftershock had a stranglehold on her.

"I love you."

The two boys burst out into rude laughter, and pushed Anna out into the street.

"Let's get out of this dump," the second boy spoke. "Besides, you said she could ride me."

The voices faded as the shop's front door swung shut with a loud bang. Jim stood still in the middle of the shop floor. A sudden heaviness overcame him.

"Goodbye, Anna," he whispered.

The realization of what had just transpired started to set in. He slumped against the counter, and slowly sank to the ground. The years flashed before his eyes. He saw Anna as a young, scared child. A trembling adolescent – a young girl blooming into womanhood.

He had endeavored to care for the girl as best as he knew how. He had tried to protect her. But yet, she was now gone – the same way as her mother – selling herself in return for a cheap escape from reality. Who knew, perhaps with the Disease, it was the best alternative anyway?

Did I do the right thing? To what hell did I just send my niece? It's my worst nightmare come true!

Jim wrapped his overly large arms around his chest and hugged himself. The adrenaline from the rush of courage he had felt before vanished. Reality set in. He was crestfallen and overweight; he was alone. Slowly, he began to rock back and forth. It was a soothing, rhythmic movement.

. . . . .

Jim's chubby hand wiped the falling tears away as he remembered he events from earlier in the day. The sting of the loss, and monumental failure on his part, remained unabated. He doubted it ever would.

Just how am I going to get past knowing my entire identity is nothing but a failure? Failure to protect, to admonish, and to hold?

The man was being overly hard on himself, he knew it too. But it did not matter. It was all in the past now. Anna was gone. He had to focus on the future. He stuffed the feelings down, concealing them for later. The broadcast was beginning.

He pressed the ON button, and the TV flickered. The screen came to life.

"xY0b5 is the real name behind the newest drug from Sehtym, and while said to be a relaxation drug for lowering stress levels, we've discovered otherwise. With all the fear and stress caused by the 'Disease,' a drug to assist in calming the mind was in need – *obviously*. There is much to be concerned about with this drug though – reports say it actually dampens the consciousness of its users!" The announcer spoke in rapid-fire, using suggestive narrative tones as he delivered the script. "Even of more concern is that xY0b5 is the first drug in a series of new drugs to be released by the CDC. A hybrid drug is being developed right now – it will take the dampening a step further, according to our sources, and will create complete dependence on the doses to maintain normal bodily functions. Your life, as you know it, will not exist."

The voice droned on. Jim paid attention. All the talk of drugs made him think of Anna. The greatest job he ever had was when he became the guardian of his niece. And he had failed at it. He had failed *her*. To put her care into the hands of Arndt and a safe house that would only strengthen her use? She would not get better. Her fate was sealed. Her life no longer existed. A look of panic spread over his face.

"My God," he whispered. "What have I done?"

THIRTY-THREE

October

Stepping from the car, Josh straightened himself. He instinctively shivered as the cold Minnesota wind whipped about. Tugging at the jacket sleeves, making sure they were not bunched up, he looked both ways before crossing the street.

Nobody was out. Behind him was the Stone Arch Bridge – the murky waters of the stagnant Mississippi river underneath. The stream could hardly be called a river. Its movement of water – slow swishing back and forth – scarcely what one would describe as flowing. Decades ago, the fear had been the earth's water resources would be used up. People thought it was a globalist conspiracy. Something Leftists concocted while they plotted gay rights and killing babies.

A tight smile appeared on Josh's face. They were right after all. Water was a precious commodity these days. Sure some rivers had seen an increase in their water supply – the nearby St. Croix was a good example. Three times already, the banks of that river had flooded over. But the abundance was more anomaly than precedent. Far too many lakes and rivers in the 'Land of 10,000 Lakes' had seen significant water reduction.

Of course, the displacement theory had been discussed. Water evaporated by the environment, and then disbursed to another body. Perhaps this is how the St. Croix flourished just twenty miles away while the Mississippi floundered. Who knew?

Josh swung open a large door at the entrance of a tall building – a skyscraper – one of the many recently constructed in downtown Minneapolis.

Ever since the re-assignment, he had worn a scowl. The medicine he was taking, while good at inducing sleep and lowering feelings of stress, did little to change his rancor. He felt if he actually had a soul – which he did not – but if so, his soul was outraged.

"Please, sir, may I *have* your ID?"

Josh became acutely aware someone had been trying to get his attention.

Of course, Cunningham, you dunce! Every day is the same routine. How could you forget? Check-in right after entering.

The security guard scanned the ID he handed over, while studying him with her eyes. She handed the ID back to Josh.

"Thank you."

He re-clipped it to his pocket, and walked into the main concourse. The skyscraper had been designed as an upcoming condominium palace. When the housing offset occurred a few years back, though, the more expensive apartment and condos downtown were abandoned for cheaper housing outside the busy confines of Minneapolis.

Opportunistic entrepreneurs snapped up the former housing sites as soon as they hit the market. They knew one day the buildings would have immense value. That day was now.

With the Disease progressing rapidly across the country, people were forced to live near health clinics and treatment centers. Less travel was better. The advert went, "You never know when you might encounter *Them*. Stay close, be vigilant, get your patch! Report suspect behavior."

The commonality they all bore with the widespread Disease reminded Josh of an old video game. *Everybody dies of dysentery at some point.* A grim smile crept over his face.

"Josh?"

Again his reverie was broken as someone addressed him. This time, the voice arrested his attention, though. It sounded familiar. He lifted his eyes, and observed the woman.

"Carrie. Carrie Haselow from SEH headquarters in Virginia. Remember?"

"Oh, wow. Yes, I mean, wow!" Josh could not believe it. He had not seen anyone from the past since he was reassigned, and that was months ago.

"I have a bone to pick with you," Carrie's eyes danced. "I never got my tea!"

"Tea?" Josh thoughtfully scratched his chin. "Wait, Chamomile Cinnamon, right? I could've sworn I... Shoot, I did pick some up, but when I got back, things were crazy. I must have forgotten. I'm sorry!" He apologized, his tone sincere.

"Oh my gosh," Carrie's left hand went to her open mouth. Her soft lips parted as a look of compassion swept over her sweet countenance. "Now, I feel bad! I was just teasing."

Visible relief showed on Josh's face.

"Ah, I feel better." He paused. "I'm sorry, but isn't cold, sweet tea more befitting a beautiful Georgian than hot, herbal tea?"

Carrie threw back her head and laughed. It was an infectious laugh, and he smiled broadly at her merriment.

She nodded. "You are bold, but I suppose you're right. I would love to keep chatting, but I've got to be running. I'm late for a meeting. It was nice to see you again though, Josh. I did not realize you were working here. Catch up soon?" Carrie waved a delicate hand at him. "Bye."

He watched her go. For some odd reason, it felt refreshing to have seen her. He was not sure why. He scarcely knew the woman. Yet his spirit's temperament had changed; his entire disposition seemed lighter. Why?

Brushing off the thought, he started up the stairs. He too had a meeting. The project he was working on, as an outsourced engineer from Sehtym, was presenting its latest work on air filtration and sediment saturation to a couple of visitors from Congress, as well as an Ambassador Omach from the World Council. Just why the World Council would be interested in air filtration and sediment saturation was beyond Josh. Only months ago it would have prodded his interest. But now...

He stopped outside the conference room, and opened his capsule. His hand tossed back a couple pills.

These days I just need to take it easy.

■   ■   ■   ■   ■

House hearings. Senate subpoenas. While they had different functions and operated under different parties, the same dreary process was employed each time. And for some reason, the room where the juicy details hashed out always had no windows, drab lighting, and flat red chair backs.

"Ms. Atkins, are you saying that after your meeting with Sehtym's biomedical division you believe the health patch is *not* a cure for the Disease?"

"This is correct," a scratchy voice responded to the question.

The speaker addressing the congresswoman continued to peer intently at the notes scattered in front of him. He turned a page, and without looking up asked, "Ms. Atkins, are you saying that despite the billions of dollars invested into corporations and organizations such as Sehtym, the Centers for Disease Control, the World Health Organization, or Global Medical Alliance – despite all this, they have *not* found a cure?"

"This is correct," the scratchy voice responded again.

The audience in the room was clearly agitated. The speaker asking the questions looked up, and his face showed grave concern. The news cameras started to pan around, and faces of other Congressmen and women, aides, journalists, and civilians – all bore looks wrought with consternation, distress, and worry. The camera continued to pan, and the face of the congresswoman being asked the questions came into focus...

"What the heck are you doing?"

A light switched on, and the dark room lit up brightly. The House Committee faded and disappeared into a holograph projector. Danny Graves stood at the entrance to the room, and his glowering look caused the young CDV operative, sitting by the projector, to cower back.

"Working on my newest assignment."

"What's that?"

The operative merely held up his right hand and motioned, the projector fired up again. Danny obliged and shut off the room's light.

"This is the senatorial hearings last night on what Congresswoman Elisha Atkins found with her meetings at Sehtym, the CDC, and WHO."

"This should be good," Danny growled.

"It is. The report is filled with inaccuracies and general propaganda. They are saying the Disease could *kill* someone merely by airborne contact with an infected person. They are announcing a Code Orange alert across the country." The young operative was eager to show off. "Orange is used to identify hazardous materials."

"They think infected people are hazardous?"

"Right?" the operative slid back the chair and stood up. He started to walk around the room and point at different displays. "I began thinking what would be the easiest way to cull a crowd? It wouldn't be by mass infection. It would be by mass hysteria. This is how they're going to do it."

"Do what?" Danny was confused.

The door opened, and Tessa Morgan walked in, closely followed by Luke.

"Ah, here you are, Bryan."

"Hey now," Bryan, the young video artist, held up his hands. "I'm doing an assignment."

Tessa nodded her head, and shrugged as if to say, "so what?"

"I think the kid's on to something," Danny interjected.

"Okay."

Tessa motioned to the young operative, and Bryan began repeating what he had discovered while watching the House Hearings the night before. Luke listened carefully, his eyes narrowing when Bryan callously raised suspicions on the accuracy of the official report.

"Be careful, sir," he remonstrated. "We're talking about some brilliant scientists and medical people. Sehtym is not some hack organization; the CDC and WHO are a far cry from it as well."

Bryan sat back down in the chair, and idly swung about in a half-circle. His lips pursed, and his eyes blinked as he considered Luke's words.

"Naw," he finally said. "You're wrong. What we're doing is stopping fear-mongering and propaganda from spreading. That's really our job, isn't it?"

Luke opened his mouth to protest, but Tessa started to nod in agreement with Bryan, so he clamped his jaw shut.

"I mean, science guy, they've stuck you in our lab," Bryan held up his hands, and made air quotes on 'lab' as the spinning chair continued its constant motion. "But the reality is our job is to disrupt the fake news as much as possible. We might be the only voice of reason left. I mean there's a couple conspiracy satellites, but nobody has the amount of resources CDV does." Bryan's chair stopped twirling, and once more, he was in front of the projector's controls. "Watch."

The video began to play, the speaker questioning the congresswoman. Luke's mouth opened slightly as he heard the responses to the questions.

"Did she really say that?" he was shocked.

"Of course, not. That's a digital sound bite you're hearing," Bryan tapped an old audio mixer lying on the desk in front of him. "The mouthpiece said whatever they paid her to say. People are dying; this disease is highly contagious; any quarantine measure should be considered, regardless of how drastic it may be. Even threw in a 'God help us!' for the religious folks."

"Good work!"

Tessa beamed at Bryan. He meekly nodded. Praise from Tessa Morgan was high praise indeed. Danny was also excited about the work performed. Luke stood scowling, and Bryan noted it.

"Aw, c'mon, science guy. Why the long face?"

"I don't like it," he simply said. "I thought we were trying to find answers here, not disrupt official hearings that might be quite accurate."

"Bah humbug. You don't believe that?"

Luke shrugged. Tessa wrapped an arm around him, and hugged him close.

"We'll find the truth here," she said softly. "But we have to keep the fake news and fear-mongering to a minimum. Right now they are literally hunting down those infected and shooting them. Danny showed me a video the other day of this happening. They are killing people."

Danny nodded, confirming Tessa's words.

"I mean, don't you want to stop all this?" she looked into Luke's eyes.

He tried to look away, but her manner and beauty captivated him. His head dropped, and he bit his lower lip.

"I wish this was as easy as curing Zika or Ebola. Compared to this, those were a cakewalk."

"If you say so!" Tessa moved her arm away. "Carry on, Bryan. I'll let Chief know you're close to uploading."

Luke and the two CDV lieutenants turned to leave the room, but Bryan stopped them.

"Wait, there's more!" his voice earnest. "Culling the crowd, like I was telling you before they came in," Bryan motioned to Danny. "I was saying it's going to happen through mass hysteria."

"Culling a crowd?" Tessa asked, slightly shaking her head. "What do you mean?"

"It was on the files you brought back from Pittsburgh. There wasn't much, as you know, but there were fragments of a file that I managed to piece together. Well, *I didn't*, Jackson did."

"That makes more sense," said Luke. "Jackson, that is."

The video artist sent the scientist a miffed expression.

"Anyway, on this document, there were references to a 'New Day,' something about resetting the scientific and medical communities by cleansing it. You can't cure a disease if you don't have one."

"Wait a minute," Luke was skeptical. "Are you saying that the Disease is completely fabricated?"

Bryan nonchalantly shrugged his shoulders.

"No way, dude. You're crazy!" Luke's eyebrows rose as he vehemently spoke, his nostrils flaring.

"Think about it," Bryan persisted. "What better way to reset medical findings than by hosting a global convention – an *in-person* one too – and then bombing it?"

Luke was stunned. This accusation hit close to home. Despite his lifelong conflict with Melinda Gore, she *was* a colleague, and the very suggestion that her demise had been strategically planned, shook him to his core.

The CDV technician solemnly nodded, confident in his work. His arms folded across his chest as he stood by the projector desk. Tessa and Danny both remained calm and resolute. Bryan's words of discovery merely enforced their beliefs. For Luke, though, it was an entirely different reaction. His hand shook as he raised it to his forehead and wiped perspiration.

"Why would you have to reset and cleanse the medical communities if it was all smoke and mirrors anyway?"

"Because you were right before. The people killed in San Francisco were the brightest and best bioscience and medical minds in the world. You really think someone could fabricate a disease with global ramifications and *not* have one of those people realize it? Think about it. Before San Francisco, you had someone getting pushed out of a window, a lady getting shot on a dock, a missile hitting a chopper..."

"Wait a minute," Luke held up a hand. His face was red; blood boiling. "What do you mean, someone getting pushed out of a window? A woman getting shot?"

"Canada – the guy didn't jump, he was pushed. Georgia – the woman didn't shoot herself, she was murdered. And the missile? Do you really think it was some random attack as Prispuss tried to pass off? He wanted to know answers too. Why do you think they ended up silencing him as well?"

Luke slowly sunk to the floor, overwhelmed by Bryan's revelations. Everything had been planned and staged. They had been nothing more than pawns, and Brenda was dead because of it. He pulled his legs close, and buried his face into them.

■   ■   ■   ■   ■

The room had no windows. The white lighting illuminating the space did not help its appearance, but instead caused it to have a rather cold, sanitized look. The red-backed chairs with black trim were neatly arranged, and a large audience was seated in them. Ahead of the chairs was a sectioned off area where a lady sat facing a panel of Senators and World Council members alike.

"Ms. Atkins, are you saying that after your meeting with Sehtym's biomedical division you believe the health patch is *not* a cure for the Disease?"

"Not entirely. While the health patch is a much-needed booster to help prevent the Disease, that in and of itself will not save us."

The speaker addressing the ambassador continued to peer intently at the notes scattered in front of him. He turned a page, and without looking up, asked, "Ms. Atkins, are you saying that despite the billions of dollars invested into corporations and organizations such as Sehtym, the Centers for Disease Control, the World Health Organization, or Global Medical Alliance – despite all this, they have *not* found a cure?"

"Not at all. What I'm saying is all the research is on treating the symptoms. We still have no idea what has *caused* this pandemic. We don't know the origin. And the truth is, the situation is much worse than we thought before."

The room was clearly agitated. The speaker asking the questions looked up, and his face showed grave concern. The news cameras started to pan around, and faces of other Congressmen and woman, aides, journalists, and civilians – all bore looks wrought with consternation, distress, and worry. The camera continued to pan, and the face of the congresswoman started to come into focus.

She was middle-aged, her ancestry from the great tribes of North Dakota. Her face had been beautiful once. It was now ravaged by a vicious scar running from her forehead to the lower part of her right cheek. She pointed to the injury.

"I, more than most, know what havoc is ravaged by the disease. There are *few* survivors. My husband became infected and…well," she shrugged her shoulders. "With the help of fellow Council members, I was lucky to escape before he turned. I'm saying that without any unforeseen breakthroughs or unexpected developments, we have a limited time remaining before the Disease all but dominates our world. It's highly contagious and creates violent behavioral changes in the victims. Even if the slightest majority of a given area contracts the Disease, it doesn't matter who has the health patch. Their very lives will be in danger. *All* our lives are in danger. God help us, quarantine measures – drastic as they may be – must be taken. I urge you, Senators and Council members to move forward as quickly as possible with the launch of Operation Laja."

THIRTY-FOUR

The Hub, as CDV operatives called the mainframe room in DC, was quiet. Most had gone home for the day. Despite the progressive and cultural shifts ever changing normal precedents, Sunday was still the day to rest and catch up on sleep. Daily protests were in full swing, and the physical exertion required to maintain and propel the conspirators' movement drained energy from the team.

New recruits were added daily to the Hub, but most were immediately dispatched to other Hubs across the US. So the number of actual people in the DC station stayed the same. All the activity kept Tessa busy in her line of work.

Even with all this talent acquisition, she harbors a soft spot for me, Luke reasoned. *Or maybe I'm just delusional. I don't know anymore.*

Luke's own task required complete dedication and constant attention. The files they had found in Pittsburgh's Tech Center proved earth-shattering. xY0b5 was not a deadly drug. But it created both a physical and psychological dependency. The idea that a government, or a body of people, would want to control the masses was an evil motive in the eyes of CDV. Luke was skeptical at first, and he said so to Chief shortly after the raid in Pittsburgh.

"You guys argue that mind control is evil, which I do not disagree on. However, I doubt the existence of it. Mind control defies science itself. It is the manipulation of a species and falls outside normal medical practices – *if* it could even be done."

"Isn't that what you do, though?" Chief's dark eyes searched Luke's countenance. When she looked deep into his eyes, he always felt uncomfortable. It was as if she was reading his very thoughts. "Is not true science merely a manipulation of things as we know them?"

"We can define definitions all day if you'd like, but the only reason I'm here is because you guys picked me. So let me do my job, okay?"

Chief's eyebrows lifted, but she refrained from further comment.

After that, nobody really talked to Luke. He preferred it that way. The lab had a few, well-qualified people to conduct tests and experiments. It left Luke to pour over the results, cross-analyze, and evaluate – to do the actual research, which is what he was good at. During this time, Luke discovered he preferred solitude. He had always enjoyed another's company, but he liked working by himself. He found it to be self-invigorating.

It had been different when he worked with Brenda. And the thought of Brenda made him sad. It made him hate CDV with a passion. He focused though, and funneled his rage into discovering what mysteries xY0b5 was hiding. The paradox was such that he wasted no time disseminating and studying the origins or supporting elements. He simply ran with it. It felt like the old days, back when he shot from the hip, and went with the anomalous spikes. Back before everything in his life fell apart. Before Tessa, the Disease, Dr. Grafton's death – before Brenda had been killed.

On this particular Sunday, Luke was observing Tessa and Danny working on their newest list of potential recruits. He watched as the two of them poured over academic scores and studies, professional achievements, even family trees, and pedigrees. He wondered if they put the same amount of thoroughness into their investigation of him.

While watching, he also kept an eye on the data in front of him. It was streaming the latest test results from CDV's lab – as well as several others from around the world that the team had hacked. Suddenly, something grabbed his attention.

"Hello, what's this?" He did not mean to speak out loud, but the feed captivated him.

"What's up?" Danny asked from the other side of the room. The burly man's concentration unyielding as both he and Tessa continued to sort through recruit bios.

"Just something interesting. One of the primary components of xY is benzodiazepines; there are a couple of major active ingredients here, but one of them is temazepam."

"Wait, isn't that the sleeping pill?" Tessa lifted her head, curious at what Luke was saying.

"Yes, but this is a modified primary of that drug. And when you take temazepam outside the limits regulated by the FDA, scientific studies have found a tremendous increase in behavior. Namely – short-term memory loss and extended drowsiness. This we all knew, early on, but," Luke stepped from behind the desk, and pointed to a video feed on one of the holograph projectors. "I started checking for reports *of these* symptoms. I mean if someone is reporting them, it clearly falls outside the scope of normal behavior. I then cross-referenced the reports to prescribed medications for xY0b5. Here's what I found."

He moved his hand right and flicked his fingers. The video expanded. Tessa and Danny's attention shifted from the recruit bios to what Luke was saying. They watched as the screen flickered momentarily, trying to buffer the high definition image.

The feed finalized and began streaming. On a couch, laid a woman fast asleep. Another woman, younger than the first, was speaking into the camera. It was in Chinese with English subtitles appearing at the bottom.

SHE'S BEEN ASLEEP FOR 38 HOURS. IT'S AS IF SHE'S IN A COMA. SHE HAS DONE THIS BEFORE. WHEN SHE AWAKES, SHE JUST GETS UP, AND CONTINUES AS IF NOTHING HAS HAPPENED.

The senior CDV operatives exchanged looks as they stepped closer to Luke. The latter calmly swiped his hand to the right, fingers trailing palm. The next video loaded.

It was in Russian. Again it had English subtitles. A man was standing, perfectly still, at a street corner. Cars were passing on each side of him. Some pedestrians walked by, casting a curious glance at the man statute.

HE HAS BEEN ASLEEP FOR 14 HOURS. HE FELL ASLEEP LIKE THIS. HIS SON TRIED WAKING HIM, BUT HE WILL NOT RESPOND. VITAL SIGNS CHECK OUT. WE SAW SOMETHING SIMILAR TO THIS DURING THE OUTBREAK IN SIBERIA YEARS AGO.

"He's referencing the time when two villages in Kazakhstan – Kalachi and Krasnogorsk – both experienced its citizens randomly falling asleep for *days* without warning," Luke informed the other two.

"What?" Danny was intrigued.

A firm nod from Luke. "At first they thought it was counterfeit vodka."

Tessa gave a short laugh. "You're kidding."

"No," Luke shook his head as adamantly as he had nodded it moments before. "They really did. Eventually, they settled on the fact the uranium mines were causing it, but no medical diagnosis ever emerged. Well, now, it appears the phenomenon is back, and this time affecting only those who have been prescribed xY0b5."

"That is freaky," Danny said; his voice chilly.

Luke loaded another video showing yet another person sleeping. This time the person was seated in a chair at a table, with food on their plate, and a glass filled with wine. The plate was half empty; a fork clutched tightly in the person's hand. It was as if sudden paralysis struck while digesting a bite of beef.

"And you've only found reports of this by users of xY?" questioned Tessa.

Luke held up his hand. "I did not say that. I only found cross-referenced reports of non-explainable drowsiness with xY prescriptions. I didn't search for all reports of sleeping or memory loss."

"And who knows how many of those exist," Tessa pursed her lips. "Why would someone do something so evil?"

"Mind control," said Danny matter-of-fact.

"Sure, but why? And how are people falling asleep the same as mind control?"

"The devil is in the details," Luke muttered.

"What's that?" Tessa looked back at Luke.

"It's not the sleep, but rather the ability to manipulate people's memories and knowledge of what happens *when* they are in that deep state of sleep. Think about it. If you really wanted to screw up someone's reality, you need to do it without their knowing anything has actually happened. On every report of these incidents, the person has zero recollection of falling asleep or any idea of how much time has actually lapsed by the time they awake."

"Ah! Now, this is something I can truly revile," Danny said, angrily rubbing his hands together. "Chief will be interested to know what we found. How soon can you verify some of these reports?"

"Ha," Luke gave a short laugh. "Do you think I have superpowers? It's going take days, maybe weeks, to prove these people have had their reality altered. You need someone really good at research and really good at digging deeper than you could imagine...like a truthseeker," his voice trailed off.

Could this be why I'm here? Why Josh Cunningham came back into my life? The Universe does work in mysterious ways. The feeling of a grand scheme of destiny swept over him. *First New Day, now this alarming discovery of xY0b5's true nature – something evil is happening. What if someone is behind it – manipulating everything we know?*

"What are you waiting for?" Tessa asked. "You've got work to do."

. . . . .

A buzzing noise from Josh's handheld woke him from his slumber. He looked at the face being displayed and slowly sat up, holding the device in front of him.

Luke Baer.

The sun was starting to dip for the late afternoon hour, and he knew that soon, large braziers would be burning in the neighborhood. Kids would be out playing. Loudspeakers would be set up. The area's activity would increase. He just wanted to sleep, but the buzzing had interrupted his nap.

Thumb swipe.

"Josh?" Luke's breathless voice came through the traditional speaker as Josh held the handheld to his ear.

"Luke," Josh replied.

"I need to meet with you. Remember when you told me, earlier this year, about the questions you had on Canada and Georgia?"

"What of it," Josh's mind was groggy; he struggled to shake the sleepiness.

"I found something. You're gonna wanna see it."

Josh pulled the device away from his ear, and stretched his arm. If he had a dollar every time someone had told him 'he wanted to see this' in his career…well, he would be sipping Pina Coladas in Cancun and letting some tanned-beauty rub her chest all over him. The arm slowly lowered, and he put the phone against his ear again.

"Josh? Are you still there?"

"I'm here," he replied gruffly.

"So can we meet?"

"Where and when?"

There was a pause on the other end. Luke was obviously conferring with someone else. Just who, he could care less. Perhaps there was a day and time when he would have, but today, it was just another phone call.

"I'll come out there. Tomorrow afternoon?"

"See you then." Josh set the handheld on the nightstand, and fell back on the pillow with a sigh. He rolled over, his eyes drearily looking out of the window. He wondered why Luke wanted to meet.

It can't be anything too exciting. I couldn't handle that. Life's already too exciting with all this research and design on underground ventilation and sediment layers.

The sarcastic thoughts failed to bring a smile to his face. He felt empty and sleepy – not tired or stressed – just mundane; as if life were passing by in a fog. His eyes moved to the capsule container next to the handheld. It was time for another dose.

■　　　■　　　■　　　■　　　■

Jim sighed and pushed the cash register drawer shut. Another day was over. Another day without a single customer. There had been far too many of those lately. Business had worsened each day since that fateful day in April. He often wondered how different life would be had that not happened. Then he remembered Anna, and figured nothing much would have changed. She would still be gone.

Moving sluggishly from behind the counter to the oversized show window, he took one last long look down the nearly abandoned street. Giant lights mounted on tall beams around the area were beginning to turn on, and soon the activity would increase. Every night he could hear the ruckus and mayhem caused by the Unknowns as the streets were ravaged. Yet by morning, everything looked normal, and one would be hard-pressed to show where the beings from Hell had wreaked havoc the night before.

"It's good I'm ready to give this up," Jim muttered out loud, talking to himself. "I can't stay open without any customers."

Moving away from the window, he examined his small shop. For the last couple of decades, aside from Anna, it had been his sole focus. It was all he could remember.

"Close up and move out," he muttered again.

He did not know why, but something was telling him to leave Savannah. The idea intrigued him. He entertained traveling south to Florida, to the coast, perhaps. Or maybe go west – Tennessee and the Smoky Mountains with their vibrant trees. He was keeping an open mind.

Walking past the shop's counter, he reached and picked up a large Styrofoam cup that was sitting on it. It was his evening pick-me-up. He slowly plodded along the aisles towards the rear of his shop. When he was almost to the backroom, he reached a small alcove and a doorway that led to a small winding staircase.

One foot in front of the other, he climbed the wooden stairs to the living quarters located above *Savannah Souvenirs*. A long sigh escaped as he padded over to a rocking chair in the corner of his living room. He tumbled into it. Reaching for the TV remote, he pushed the power button. The screen on the old set flickered, and then a sharp *pop* was heard, and a reasonably clear image emerged.

With his other hand, Jim picked up the enormous Styrofoam cup with its lid and straw. Without looking from the TV, his tongue lashed out trying to find the straw. Finally, it did, and his open mouth encircled the thin plastic and clamped tight.

Sugary liquid streamed down his throat. His eyes bulged as he savored the taste. Aside from his recent tradition of a daily glass of brandy, his favorite drink had always been the sugary, caffeinated blends refined by Mr. John Pemberton. He enjoyed it flavored. Thankfully, the 21st century had caught up with the times, and he had a vast assortment of over two hundred flavors of tasty deliciousness to choose for his soda.

Jim's eyes narrowed as he watched the streaming news. It was terrible. People falling asleep for days. Forgetting who they were, or where they were. All because of some stupid drug being pushed by the government – the TV screamed. Yet, in all of this, the eye infection was the worst. Some people, the broadcast claimed, had lost both eyes – pulled from the sockets by their very own hands.

Ghastly images floated in front of him and Jim half-turned away, holding a chubby hand in front of his face. His fingers spread wide so he could still see through; too scared to see; more afraid *not* to. Blood dried faces wearing patches met his gaze. Then the picture changed and he saw howling humans, standing at the top of a hill, overlooking a city – like a pack of wolves. The dramatic narrative continued.

The sound of a gunshot rippled throughout the room. Jim leaned back, his eyes wide, but this time not from the sugary contents of the beverage. The horrific shock as an unseen killer on the TV gunned down the howling humans, one by one!

Hunted by friends and family, the poor souls were victims of the latest round of mind control being enforced by governments from around the globe. Be vigilant. Be watchful. Be aware of what is consumed. The TV commentary droned on and on.

Jim's eyelids were heavy. He could only watch so much bad news before pure exhaustion overtook him.

THIRTY-FIVE

The Stone Arch Bridge was a place where memories were created. Many a
happy family gathered there for photographs – graduation, engagement,
family snapshots, wedding parties. A famous trans couple had used the
spot for their birth announcement, and the photo went viral. There were
very few people in the Twin Cities metropolitan area who were unaware
of the Stone Arch Bridge or what it represented. Love. Life. Limitlessness.

Josh scuffed his shoe along the railing of the bridge. He was standing
out, roughly halfway across the Mississippi. He was unsure why he
wandered onto the bridge instead of just waiting for Luke.

*Maybe I wanted to connect with a perfect median – a reflection of my life
quest,* he gave a small smile as he thought of his old philosophy professor.
Maybe it was true, maybe it wasn't. He did not know, nor did he care.

Instead, he leaned back and slowly exhaled. The stress in his life had
evaporated. The questions remained, but he felt nothing towards them. It
perplexed him. It made no sense that life should be less complicated, the
burning thirst of truth-seeking quelled, and yet he felt nothing but
hollowness. He had no answers, but no desire to find them either.

Looking down, he watched the water as it dripped over the cutoff and
down another outlet before streaming back into the larger body of water.
The mighty Mississippi, he scoffed. It was far from mighty these days. *A
disappointment as is all of life.*

It had been a life goal of his, since he was a small child, to see a real
river. He closed his eyes. The past flashed before him.

"Momma, why don't we have rivers?"

"What do you mean?" Ellen eyed her young son. "We have plenty of rivers."

"I mean real ones. Like those Lewis & Clark paddled with Sacagawea."

The memory of his mom's merry laughter at the way he pronounced Sacagawea's name jarred Josh's insides. He leaned over the Stone Arch Bridge's side, and spit into the Mississippi below. His eyes turned away, towards the north shore, remembering his mother's kind face.

"My little boy sure loves water. Would you like to take an adventure?"

"Yes!" The little boy's brown eyes danced as he excitedly replied to his mom.

"Good. Because you are in an adventure, my little man. Your life is just that. And you are in your own little canoe, and sometimes you paddle with the current, and sometimes you have to paddle against it. But always, wherever you go, adventure is sure to find you."

"Josh!"

The memory faded at the sound of hearing his name called. He turned to the south and saw Luke hurriedly walking towards him, waving a hand. Lifting his own in return, Josh forced a smile. The vividness of his mother's words stayed.

'An adventure, your life is that. Sometimes you paddle with the current, and sometimes you have to paddle against it.'

"I was looking for you in the park," Luke began.

"Sorry," Josh muttered disinterestedly.

"Hey," Luke sensed a change in his old classmate's behavior. "Are you okay?"

"Yeah," Josh sniffed, and rubbed his nose. "I'm fine. What do you have?"

"Do you remember *Diabolus*?"

"Ha. Of course, I do. The dead end. Just like the rest of them."

"Right," Luke started, surprised at Josh's reaction. "It did seem that way. But now, we found something."

"Who's we?"

"Some people I'm working with — now," Luke replied. "I'm sure you heard about my dismissal from Pittsburgh."

"Yeah, whatever," Josh brusquely replied, letting curiosity die. His glance fell again towards the river below, and he stared into their murky depths, however shallow.

The bespectacled scientist was puzzled by his former classmate's actions. Josh's behavior was out of character compared to the old Cunningham he remembered.

"Well," Luke began again. "I found something that reminded me of *Diabolus*, and I remembered how you had some insight into the event. I thought you might want to see this."

"A likely assumption."

"Hey man, are you sure you're okay?" Luke peered into Josh's eyes. Something was troubling the truthseeker, Luke was sure of it.

Josh looked away. His eye hurt and itched like crazy. *Enough of this old Diabolus*, he was bored by the meeting with Luke already. The scientist was not to be deterred, though.

"As you probably know, there have been some new drugs put on the market. One is supposed to be a relaxation drug, not directly related to the health patch – though it would appear to contain some of the same ingredients so it could help inoculate a person against the Disease…"

Josh looked wearily at Luke. The latter clapped his hands and shook them in reply, reminding himself to not get stuck in the weeds of science.

"Anyway, this drug has some massive side effects. I'm talking comas – people randomly falling asleep for hours. And the scary thing? The formulas being used to create this drug can be altered enough to induce mind-apnea – a psychosis that would allow someone to essentially create or delete things as they see fit."

Josh gave a lazy stare. "You're talking about mind control?"

"Exactly."

"Bah humbug," Josh spat into the Mississippi. "That's bull, man. Nobody is programming anybody's minds."

"Look, I know it seems far-fetched, but there's something else I found. Tied in with this new drug, at least from the same sources, is something called *New Day*. It talks of purging humanity, a culling of the crowd," Luke thought of Bryan, the propaganda video artist. *Maybe he was right to produce the film! CDV is doing its part to warn others.* He continued. "The sources point to an Eastern awakening that, if I remember, *Diabolus* did as well."

"Like the second coming of God," Josh laughed hoarsely. He turned and saw the serious expression on his friend's face. "Look, Luke, *Diabolus* went nowhere, and this *New Day* probably will too."

"*New Day* proves San Francisco was planned," said Luke firmly.

This caught Josh's attention. He had long-held suspicions that the Golden Gate Bridge attack was deliberately targeting the convention and its attendees, as Sam Walters had suggested.

"What do you mean?"

"The very theories behind *New Day* prove the Bay bombing was orchestrated by a rogue organization that is seeking to cleanse humanity by eradicating the very people who could heal them."

"Doctors and scientists," breathed Josh.

"Yes. And there is no one better than a truthseeker to find out the morph on this one." Luke cracked a small smile as Josh quizzically lifted his eyebrows. "I need your help, man."

"I am no longer a truthseeker," Josh replied curtly. "Now, I research and design ventilation systems." It was his turn to smile as he saw Luke's puzzled expression. "I know. It's as boring as it sounds."

"But, Josh, I mean, I don't care who employs you. I don't want Sehtym's help. I want yours!"

All of a sudden, as if in synchronization with Luke's repeated plea for help, Josh felt tired. He was terrified by the very idea that there was still another thread of nothingness clamoring for his attention. Exhausted that one even existed. He spoke, more irritable than he meant to.

"Just leave me alone, man. Seriously."

Luke stepped back, bewildered by Josh's reaction. He had worked too hard, convincing Tessa and the CDV team to let Josh know of their inner circles, to ask for Josh's assistance. He refused to give up that easily.

"Look, man. Ever since I first heard of *New Day* and saw the theory presented, I've learned more. And as I learned more, I found out that TYM and maybe even Pharma Group were involved in San Francisco."

If Luke thought this would flabbergast Josh or cause him to get angry – that it would create any sort of reaction and drive him to help CDV – he was wrong. Josh merely lifted his head, and calmly nodded.

"That's not entirely implausible, but highly improbable. There are too many half-truths in the world, Luke. Some group or organization – something – has gone to extreme odds to make sure any credible piece of research and accurate analysis gets destroyed. It began years ago with the eradication of the press. No one knew who they could trust anymore."

"There were the 'national' brands of news, which were more or less entertainment fops. Then you had the 'state' news, which was nothing more than propaganda for the administration. Any person seeking to find the truth has been subjected to nothing more than facades and red herrings to keep you always sniffing and never finding. If SEH, Pharma, or TYM were part of this process – the very company I worked for as a truthseeker – then everything I have ever known is a lie. And while the probability of that exists, I do not want to accept it just now. For when I do…"

Josh paused his lengthy speech to straighten himself and deeply exhale. His shoulders drooped as the air left his body. The hot breath forming wisps of clouds as they collided with the cool stiff breeze.

"For when I do," he repeated. "Everything I've ever believed in or known will cease to exist. I will be undone. I will be nothing."

Luke nodded thoughtfully as Josh delivered the soliloquy. He may have always been the smarter of the two as far as science was concerned, but there was no doubting Josh's insight or ability to articulate just what he was thinking.

"I hear you, Josh, but you must know there is more to all of this…"

"How could you?" Josh suddenly turned, and sneered at Luke. "Didn't the University fire you from your post for failing to protect your data against a cyber threat? You know nothing, Luke. You've always been two steps behind."

The criticism hit Luke like a ton of bricks. His mouth agape, he struggled to regain his composure. This new Josh was definitely not like the old Josh. Maybe he had been wrong to come. It was then he saw a small plastic capsule container stashed atop the right pocket of Josh's thin sports jacket. The label was familiar. It all made sense now. He missed it before. The thin frame, worn expression, a body racked with evident signs of elongated duress and sleep deprivation.

Here I've come to him – begging him to look at all the evidence pointing to a cover-up, to New Day, to the dangers of a drug and…he's an addict of the very drug. What to do?

"How long have you been taking xY0b5?" the words blurted out of Luke's mouth, surprising not only Josh but himself as well.

The former truthseeker turned away from Luke, and stepped back from the bridge's side. He even took a half-step away from the scientist, but then stopped.

"What of it?" he spoke, his back to Luke.

"It's the drug I've been telling you about. It's a counterfeit. A fake. And it's dangerous!"

Josh threw back his head and laughed. It was not a rude laugh, neither was it pleasant. He cocked an eyebrow.

"How so, dear professor?"

Luke's face flushed.

"Haven't you been listening to me? They *will* alter your mind. It's a dreamcatcher – without the dream. You'll believe in a pseudo-reality that only works by distorting the actual reality – the world around you. It's extremely addictive and causes your body to think it's sleeping without ever falling into a REM cycle. Let alone the ability they now have to control…"

"Oh, stop it," Josh held up a hand. "Did you think I was serious? Of course, I heard you. But what you are speaking is common dissension. Sure, it's relaxation medication. It's also an antidote against the disease, as you admitted. What's the harm in taking it? A few years ago, people were popping edibles like no one's business."

"Yeah," Luke shot back. The flush that remained was from indignation, not embarrassment. "And we all saw what good that did."

"You want me to stop?" Josh chuckled again.

"It wouldn't matter if you wanted to," Luke shook his head, the chestnut curled hair shaking slightly. "The chemical ingredients have already been altering your brain activity."

"Ha! You're speaking like a true conspirator."

"Conspirator!" Luke was now defiant. "I'm telling you the truth."

"Never mind, my good man," Josh waved a hand. "If it's altered me already, so be it. With all that's going on, does it really matter? What is our existence anyways?"

They were at an abyss. They both knew it. Luke had tried and failed. CDV would receive no help from the former truthseeker. The task was Luke's alone to handle. The puzzle of xY0b5, his alone to solve. He had one thing left to say.

"Well, just so my trip over here was not a complete waste…here," he pulled a small chip from his pocket. "This is a microchip embedded with military-grade security, coated with stealth protection. It's undetectable and provides a secure, direct line of communication to myself."

Jackson had repeatedly explained it to Luke, who struggled to grasp how it worked. Now though, it sounded smooth – rolling off his tongue. He felt like a geek.

"If you ever change your mind, please let me know. I would love to have your help." Luke nodded at Josh, more in farewell than anything else. "Take care of yourself."

"Good luck."

The two parted as if leaving a eulogy. Not a further word was spoken, both walked their separate ways in silence. The sun, which had been shining brightly overhead, was suddenly hidden by a large cloud that had come in from the south. Darkness descended.

THIRTY-SIX

Her name was Kaci. That was not her birth name, but at this point, she hardly knew herself by any other. The name was bestowed one night at the club. Perhaps it was the way she would shake her ass, or maybe the way she would flaunt her breasts, winking as she played to her audience. Whatever it was, the name stuck, and Kaci quickly became a favorite among the men and women who would lecherously leer at her nude body.

Kaci was far from fashionable. Perhaps because of the stereotype that ran in tandem with her occupation. That was not to say she was trailer trash. Outside of the club, aside from having the bodily profile of a dancer, one would not be able to possibly guess what she did for a living. She dressed respectably, even borderline trendy. Her appearance mattered. She made do without being wealthy.

Beautiful is not the word one would use to describe Kaci. To be sure, her body was aesthetically pleasing. Her curves pronounced; her face without blemish. Her fine resemblance, coupled with the frequent performances at the club, attracted the attention of the son of a rather prominent member of the Senate.

The dancer was unaware of the man's background, but she thoroughly enjoyed the attention and financial dividends from the son, whose name was Jack. He immensely enjoyed frequenting the club, and took a fancy to her. Jack swore Kaci's main stage performances were the best on the west side of the Atlantic. And the VIP experience? Mind-blowing. But more than all of that, he claimed, she was a genuinely good listener.

Regardless of all the reasons, the two of them hit it off. While still oblivious of Jack's background, Kaci knew he had a well-to-do upbringing. She was flattered someone of his prestige was interested in more of her than just the front and back.

After a while, it became apparent to Kaci that Jack actually, truly *liked* her. Many had fawned over her body, stuffing dollar bills in between her cheeks, swearing they loved her. Telling her all the ways they could have sex; the trips they could take; admiring her body. The thrills they might experience; the naughty games they might play; the pleasures of waking up to her performing on them. And if they were not paying those compliments, they were saying terrible, degrading things. Being rough and treating her of no more worth than the few paltry dollars they flung at her. Jack did neither.

Kaci knew he was different. Sure the man liked having a good time, and immensely enjoyed watching the other girls perform, even sharing VIP experiences with them. But he was kind to her. He was interested in her and what she liked – her dreams and hopes for what the future might hold.

He asked her out on a date. And for the first time in a long time, Kaci felt the tingle of romance. She enjoyed the pleasure received from the kicks at the club, but this was different. This was passionate, tender, and loving. So began their relationship.

After they had been seeing each other for some time, Jack told Kaci of his prestigious family. She was surprised, but not shocked. If anything, the country's citizens had become quite accustomed to members of its government having less than noble hobbies. More than one politician had been found to have paid off women and men for sexual favors or secret pregnancies. And of course, the "harem" president blew all scandals out of the water.

Notwithstanding her knowledge of his family, Kaci's own identity remained a secret, most specifically to the Senator. For in his case, it would have been treacherous. The senator touted reform, especially in the civil liberties areas, and swore by his white Southern roots which said all men (aside from black men) were created equal with women just a step below. Since she was a woman and her skin brown, Kaci would lose on both counts.

The Senator also pushed forcefully for the trans-life movement members to be condemned and imprisoned. When that proved fruitless, he pivoted his attention to other vices: virtual sex, robotic slaves, cinematic orgies, and the place where the stench of vice originated – the good old-fashioned gentlemen's clubs.

With these damning characteristics of the Senator, Kaci was kept from his knowledge. Also hidden was the fact she became pregnant with the Senator's grandchild. The Senator, for all his 'virtues' and 'profound righteousness,' would have demanded an abortion, and Kaci wanted none of that. At Jack's urging, she determined it would be best for the boy to be kept a secret.

Consequently, Dylan Knudson was born into the world, taking his mother's maiden name (the one name she did remember). His father was a tall, mysterious man who would pay visits to his sweet, caring mother, and as far as relatives…there were none.

Unbeknownst to Dylan, when the disease first broke out, his grandfather was quite involved with less than trustworthy news sources claiming that there was a government cover-up going on. However, as the dire reality began to sink in, and the pandemic spread, survival of the fittest became obvious. The Senator changed his stumping platform, and began pushing the World Council to keep the "chosen" classes from extinction. Due to his efforts, he was recognized and chosen to sit on the Committee for Public Health & Safety.

Before these events would happen, though, the Senator's son began to change. Jack chose to spend more time with Kaci and Dylan, less time in DC with his father. The old patriarchal-minded Senator was angry at his son's absences, and began to investigate the long, ambiguous, unaccounted for disappearances. Through his meddling, he discovered Jack's secrets: Kaci and Dylan.

The backlash was swift and severe. Jack was utterly cut off from his family's amassed fortune, left out as heir. The grandson disavowed of birthright and lineage. Kaci was not even mentioned in the disposition.

Then something strange happened. Only months after being cut off from his family, Jack fell ill and passed away the very same night. Kaci had no money to care for him, let alone bury him. Stricken, she watched as public health enforcers came, and carried away her beloved dead one.

Dylan, who was by now six, watched the unfolding events with his eyes wide open. The dark, threatening world little scared him, but he gathered no great comfort in it either. Now, even these events were but ghosts of the past, an ever-constant reminder of the pain and suffering young Dylan endured.

The eviction notice arrived less than two weeks after his father's passing.

THIRTY-SEVEN

The creaky wooden sign swung lightly back and forth in the unseasonably bitter cold breeze. The simple, yet distinguished board stood out in sharp contrast to the broken neon signs of the neighboring buildings. A relic of the past standing alone in the future.

Flannigan's was painted in broad, red strokes on the wooden board. It hung by two rusty hooks looped around an old pole that looked as if it would snap in two any moment. There was a broken LED rainbow light that ran next to the sign, and one could tell it had once been a very inviting entrance, welcoming guests in for a bite to eat, and a pint to drink.

Those days were gone, and now the pub merely looked its age. It sat on the corner of an intersection in an abandoned part of historic Savannah, Georgia. The only people left in this part of town were either too poor or too stubborn to move.

The street was empty, save a few parked vehicles scattered on each side. Nobody was traversing the sidewalks – if they could be called that; broken pieces of concrete with jagged potholes and cracks running across its path. One could not even roll a cart or bicycle over them without a jarring ride.

The neighborhood was no longer a pleasant part of town – the part inhabited by wealthy folks. Nor was it the business park area – which once had teeming corporations and upcoming billionaires – that too was a shadow of the past. Even nightlife activity was absent in the crumbling neighborhood. The strip clubs, sex shops, and grooving dance clubs – they stayed away. All of these, mere symptoms representing the dismal fate of a city struck by the Disease.

Inside the pub over which the sign *Flannigan's* hung, a few men sat about in the smoky hues of the room. The ban on public smoking long discarded as the e-cigarette world had collapsed. If the end was near, people preferred to enjoy their final moments with the real thing. 1990s classic rock streamed from the overhead speakers, and snatches of conversations wafted through the air.

At one end of the bar sat a bald, fat man slowly twirling a shot glass in front of him. A moment earlier, he had emptied its liquid content with a single swig. It had been some time since his hair had been washed; nor had he shaved in God knows how long. A putrid stench came from him. Gutter man would be an apt description.

The bartender leaned over the bar counter, and stared at the disheveled figure of the downtrodden patron.

"That's what they say, Jimmy. If ya encase a room with composite and don't allow more than fifteen minutes of sunlight a day, ya won't get the Disease."

"That iss stuupid," Jim's speech was slurred – the alcohol from five downed shots affecting him. "There's noo way a piece of aluminum iss gonna to fix anything."

"Not aluminum, but the new composite metal that came out a few years ago. Some scientists are saying it has a protective element against the sun."

"The sun ain't our problem," Jim's bloodshot eyes lit up with passion. "It's the dark. Don't you remember as a kid being terrified of it?"

It was alarming what a short time of unkept hygiene did to a man's general appearance. Ever since he had sent his niece to the Lincoln Safe House, Jim's life deteriorated. The lack of any sustainable traffic to his knickknack shop contributed as well. His daily tumbler of brandy turned to two, then three. The old shadow – a disease so prevalent in his family, long before *the* Disease – beckoned to him.

The pub owner waved a hand as he dismissed Jim's statement.

"That was then, this is now. Things have changed. We've changed with it. Sunlight is eroding our planet. Look at it! Used to be a time when this pub would be packed with customers. We had DJs and karaoke. Dancing and even some strippers," he winked at Jim.

Jim snorted vulgarly. "I thought you a good Catholic, Patrick Flannigan."

"Oh come on, Jimmy, things are going to get better!"

"You can't be serious," Jim gave his friend a stern look. "Look at it. There isn't a decent soul left. And where has everyone gone? And what has become of those left behind? My niece is an addict, selling sex for the drugs…but that's just normal today. We've created drugs to help us cope with reality. Drugs to help us function. Drugs to ease our pain. Our bodies weren't made for this crap. It's just a cruddy attempt at a fake world so we can escape who we are. We're hell-bent on destroying ourselves."

"Shhh!" Patrick leaned over the bar, and earnestly looked Jim in the eyes. "I've warned ya before, Jim. I can't afford to have folks get the wrong impression about this place. I've got a living to make – as meager as it might be – and blasted hard to do right now!"

Jim nodded apologetically and burped. He was not so drunk to realize he was being a bix obnoxious. Patrick put both hands on the counter.

"Look. I know this year's been rough. Anna splitting, the lack of business at the shop, the Disease… I have no problem with ya hanging out here, but *this*!" he grabbed Jim's tattered jacket sleeve. "*This* isn't my mate, Jimmy. Ya hate boozers, and that's what you're becoming."

"Conspirator!"

Jim unsteadily righted himself on the stool, and then clumsily slid off. He stood his full height, however short, next to the bar. Maybe it was stupor befalling him, or perhaps somewhere, deep inside, guilt from his conscience pricked him.

"You're conspiring against me, Patrick. But mark my words, I'm not giving up. I may be down and out of luck, but I'm not going to stay walled up in my house. I may be fat and useless, and maybe I should be dead as Anna told me every day, but by St. Christopher, I'm not just going to let *Them* win."

"There's a good bloke," Patrick laughed uneasily. "Ya talk as if it's a real thing."

"Tell me," said Jim. "When is the last time you could step outside without glasses? Without fear of falling to your knees, and ripping your eye out? Or fear of running into *Them*?"

Patrick was silent. He picked up a nearby towel, and wiped down an already dry bar. He had no answer.

Jim sighed. He felt bad. Pushing his glass forward, he beckoned to Patrick.

"One for the road."

The bartender shook his head, yet poured one last shot of brandy for his longtime friend. He watched motionless as Jim took one gulp, and downed its contents.

The shopkeeper burped again, and patted his stomach.

"Good stuff. Might as well enjoy it while we can," he turned and headed towards the door; he stopped. "I heard that theory on the sheet," he referenced Patrick's earlier comment. "It was on the…" Jim suddenly remembered the others in the room and put an unstable finger to his lips. He continued. "Anyway, I heard a theory. Actually found a piece that would work perfectly for the top. I thought I'd use it, but…" he paused. "I changed my mind – I'm leaving town for good. I'll give it to you."

Patrick came around from behind the bar counter. He gave a big friendly smile to a couple guests seated at one of the high-tops, and then hurriedly grabbed Jim's arm. Quickly ushering him over to a booth, Patrick pushed his friend into it. Then he slid down onto the bench himself.

"You're leaving? Are ya serious, Jimmy?"

"Yes, I am." Jim was surprised at how sure he sounded. It reminded him of when he had faced Arndt the day Anna left. "With my niece gone and the shop all but closed up, nothing is keeping me here."

The pub owner nodded as he listened. There was no arguing with Jim's reasons.

"Do ya have enough money?"

"I have a secret warehouse. It's filled with valuable items – perhaps thousands of dollars. Scrap metal, electronics, jewelry, knickknacks."

"Ya'd have to sell it though. It's not worth anything just sitting thar."

"True," Jim tugged at his chin.

The two old friends sat side by side, quiet next to each other. The thoughts of each man varied. Patrick was thinking about the past; how far he'd come since first opening *Flannigan's* many years ago. Jim was thinking neither of his old shop, *Savannah Souvenirs,* or his niece. His mind had been made up. His only thought was getting out and moving elsewhere.

Somewhere up north, he decided. Just why north, he knew not. And why he had decided on this particular day, he also did not know. The alcohol was not affecting his decision, he was sure of it. He had pondered the move for some time. *But I do have to sell my belongings first.*

"Well," Patrick broke the silence. "It's going to take time to sell off a whole warehouse. So tell ya what: I'll do it for ya. I'll advance ya what's needed."

"You'd do that for me?" Jim's eyes misted over at the kind and generous offer from his old friend.

"Aye," Patrick said nonchalantly. "That's what friends are for."

With that, the bartender stood up, and motioned for Jim to follow him. They walked to the back of the tavern, through a door with a sign that read 'Employees Only.' In the backroom, Patrick walked over to one of the furthest back shelves and stopped. Putting both hands on the shelf, he pushed down. A false wall moved, and a large safe appeared.

Jim's eyes widened as Patrick entered the combination and turned the giant knob. The big door opened. His half-drunken state aside, Jim was thoroughly impressed.

"How much gold do you have?" he gasped.

"Enough for me and ya both," the bartender reached in, and pulled a large knapsack off one of the safe's walls. He began filling it with cash and a few pieces of assorted jewelry. "Trinkets lost by my patrons over the years," Patrick chuckled, tying the bag shut. He pivoted and reached out, handing it to Jim.

The fat man stood, tears in his eyes. Wiping them away, he smiled.

"You are a good man, Patrick Flannigan."

"Aye, I know."

Patrick returned the smile and pulled the safe door shut. Moving away, the false wall slid back into place.

Jim took the knapsack. He reached into his pocket and circled the warehouse key off the ring. Stretching his hand out, he dropped the key into Patrick's outstretched palm.

"I wish you well."

The two embraced in farewell. The bald, fat shopkeeper broke away, and opened his mouth to say something, but suddenly, the door to the backroom flew open.

"Hurry! We need to lock up! The Unknowns are coming."

. . . . .

Sirens blared. Red, blue, and white lights chaotically flashed. Cars rammed into each other on the streets. The narrow passageways were made even smaller. The emergency lights danced off the neglected old, beautiful Savannah houses, casting eerie shadows. The tall trees with their foreboding barren branches towered over the entire borough, making it seem a scene from a horror movie instead of the once peaceful and friendly neighborhood where *Flannigan's* was located.

Patrick and Jim hurriedly emerged from the backroom with the well-meaning patron. Jim was panting, trying to catch his breath. Patrick continued on to the tavern's front doors, and flung them open.

"What are you doing?" Jim cried out, wrapping his fat arms around himself as the frosty air rushed in.

In spite of his present state, it did *not* seem a good idea to have the pub's doors wide open given the warning of the Unknowns.

"We need to close the shutters and fasten the gates! Help me, Jimmy. Quickly."

Struggling to get to catch his breath, and pulling on a heavy jacket, Jim started forward, waddling to the tavern entrance. He stepped outside into the cacophony. The Savannah neighborhood's transformation stunned him.

Shrieks of terror filled the air. Horns blasted as cars and trucks tried to maneuver around each other on the street. Peopled yelled as they pushed through the crowds of people. There were scores of them. All trying to leave.

It shocked Jim to see so many people. He thought the neighborhood mostly abandoned by now. Yet, people flooded the street, which was now littered with smashed cars, abandoned vehicles, cardboard boxes, and piles of debris. The people were all coming from the riverfront area – near *Savannah Souvenirs*. Based on the number of people, and the rapid pace they were moving, he figured there must be many more behind them as well.

"Hurry!"

Patrick interrupted his thoughts, and nearly pushed him over as the burly bartender closed one of the giant iron gates. It grated and squealed as it shut. Jim rushed over to the windows and started to close the shutters. He rapped on each one as he did so, hoping someone on the inside would latch them tight.

A loud noise that sounded like a roaring animal came up the street. It seized Jim and Patrick's attention, and they both stopped and turned to look up the dimly lit cobbled-block avenue.

People – men, women, children – were scrambling over each other, over the stalled vehicles – running as fast as they could. Behind them, shadows emerged. A bright red light seemed to emanate from each of their heads. Jim swallowed hard, his mouth dry. His legs were numb. He tried running as he heard Patrick screaming his name.

But he could not. He stood, his legs as jelly, staring transfixed at the sight in front of him. People passed by – clamoring as they ran, shouting at him to run. A small child bumped into Jim. He looked at the little girl, and she threw her head back, teeth bared, and screamed.

She moved on as quickly as she stopped. Lifting his head, he was mesmerized by the shapes and figures coming towards him. Perhaps even for him.

Suddenly, he felt himself being ripped from where he was standing. Patrick and one of the pub's patrons had reached out and clutched his heavy jacket. They grabbed him, and pulled back with all their might. Their strength, along with Jim's momentum once he started to move, threw them all tumbling backward into the safe confines of *Flannigan's*.

Patrick reached out and grasped the edge of the iron gate. It started to swing slowly, catching on the bricks below. He tugged harder, and it suddenly gave free, and swung shut with a loud bang. The pub owner slammed down the bolt securing the door, and not a moment too soon.

The noise outside was deafening. A dull red light inched its way underneath the door as one of *Them* stopped outside. Maybe it was more than one. Jim knew not. His only thought of survival. The *Unknowns* had come for them. Was it their time? He closed his eyes, breathing heavily, sobbing freely, praying God to save them.

Then it was over.

THIRTY-EIGHT

It was cold. There was no denying that; even for early winter in Minnesota, it was cold. Regardless of the sun projecting bright rays of light, no warmth was to be felt. It seemed the intensely hot weather that permeated the nation during much of the year, even autumn, had all but evaporated. A bitter cold had been brewing for the last several weeks, and now descended vociferously. Today it was keener than ever.

It was on this bleak morning, on a quiet residential street in the outskirts of St. Paul, a still shiny but now less than new, blue sedan convertible was parked alongside a curb bordering a small yard. A small, white and brick two-story house sat in the middle of the landscape.

The front lawn had weathered the bizarre climate of spring and summer. Now instead of thick, lush green grass – dull, grayish patches were clumped here and there on the ill-maintained lot.

Down the street, a once gurgling brook lay stagnant, icy patches coating its surface. Train tracks from yesteryear passed over a culvert nearby, and on either side of the tracks, sad trees hung their bare, gloomy branches – the leaves long departed.

It was late morning on a Saturday, and in pastimes, most of the neighborhood residents would be engaged in general busyness typical of a sprawling suburban community in this season – hosting family and friends, throwing a football, or sharpening ice skates. Now it was irrelevant what day of the week it was, or the time of day – the typical busyness one would find was gone and had been for awhile.

Propped up on his futon, Josh sat idly watching the 3D TV streaming a movie. His eyes watched the images flashing before him, but his disinterest had already waxed strong. His left hand reached to his side and grabbed a beer. Putting the bottle to his lips, he tipped it back. The amber liquid poured down his throat. He belched.

His gaze turned towards the window. The bright sunshine was barely visible behind the drawn shades. Even in the darkened room though, his eyes still hurt from the light.

What time is it?

Josh slowly looked at the old clock sitting on the fireplace mantel. He had set it there long ago – when he and Amanda had first purchased the home. *Amanda*. He blinked his eyes, refusing to indulge in memories of the past.

11:11 am. Tempus est somnium – the time of dreams.

His eyes slowly moved back towards the illuminated TV screen, displaying the latest headlines from around the world. He could hear the talking and see the graphics, but it all seemed incoherent.

Frustrated at his lack of understanding, Josh abruptly jumped to his feet, and began pacing the floor. He wrapped an arm around each side of his head, cradling it as he walked.

"It's all gone to hell in a handbasket. It's all hidden. Nothing makes sense anymore." He turned when he reached the opposite wall, and started back in the direction he came. "What matters, anyway? This conundrum I live in – consistent, but gradual confusion – a moving pendulum on a giant clock…I know there is more than what I see."

He reached the wall and turned on a heel. His left foot moved forward.

"In order for the light to shine so brightly, the darkness must be present," he quoted Francis Bacon. "Well, it's pretty dark right now." He gave a hollow laugh.

He was a truthseeker. It hardly seemed plausible. Once employed by one of the most respected analytical research groups in morphing – and now, stuck on the outside, a victim of a bad joke. All was hidden as if blanketed by a darkness so thick and deep, even the brightest ray of light was unable to penetrate the ominous, unknown presence.

"If you are seeking the truth, you will find it."

"Huh?" Josh said out loud as he heard the words plain as day.

Twisting to his left, he saw a grizzled older man sitting on his futon. He blinked again. Nobody was seated there. Shaking his head, he looked to the right. The older man was standing, carving a wooden handle from a stick. The man looked at him. Josh closed his eyes.

You're hallucinating..

He opened his eyes. The man was gone. The person, though, was familiar; Josh knew him. Where had he seen him before?

"Some travel across the world…to find truth."

The words floated across the room – more a part of his subconscious memories than anything real. Next came a phrase that riveted his mind.

"Blind will be blind. Not seeing is another matter."

"What's that?"

Josh was no longer in his living room. He was standing outside a small shop in Sausalito, California. His sharp gaze stared skeptically into the older man's unassuming face. The same words Josh's own mother had oft repeated to him during her waning years.

The man, the crisp green leaves on the handsome trees, the lush grass, the smell of sea air – it all began to fade into oblivion. Only the man's echoing voice remained: "Eventually, all will be known."

Josh wiped a hand across his trembling brow. Sweat pooled around his fingers. His head felt hot, like it would explode. Shaking, he slowly lowered himself back onto the futon, and leaned against the wall.

What is reality anymore? Aren't we just victims of our own mind's creation?

His head hurt thinking about it. Closing his eyes, he allowed his mind to float away. He was outside near water again, but this time, it was a river.

"I'm talking about light *versus* dark."

The speaker was clothed in a long, dark coat, five-day shave covering its face. Josh's mind played tricks – taking him on a psychedelic journey. He watched the scene unfold from high in the air, spinning 360-degrees. He saw himself standing in Point Park, listening to the unknown caller.

"It's not mythology. It's reality…"

The mysterious stranger's hand was in the coat pocket; its mouth continued to move, but Josh heard no words. Just like the older man, this stranger too faded, and Josh was left alone, sitting in his own warm sweat on the futon, in his darkened living room.

"I need to go to bed," he muttered, and then he swore. "I can't take this anymore."

Standing up, he padded towards the master bedroom, his left hand rubbing his aching forehead. Tightly clutched in his right was the small cylindrical capsule container.

Truth and reality don't matter. Maybe they never mattered. Neither does the fairytale world of light and dark. Even if there is such a thing, darkness is kicking butt. This fog of my mind – is it being caused by darkness? Inside this darkness, is there light to be seen? Who are these strangers from long ago? Why do I now see them again?

Josh considered it might mean something, but he was too tired to care. His head hit the pillow. He pulled the container closer, holding it helped calm him. Too many questions, too few answers.

Story of my life.

.   .   .   .   .

"What have you found, Luke?" Chief's authoritative voice spoke as she entered the room.

"A breakthrough," Luke breathlessly replied, his face alit with burning passion. He thought he might finally have an answer. "Here's what we know about the drug xY0b5. It distorts your vision – not physical vision, but mental vision. It allows you to 'cope' without your mental and emotional faculties actually engaging the subject matter."

"Sounds like pot," Chief was not impressed.

Tessa Morgan glared at her. She knew how hard Luke had been working on the xY0b5 drug – ever since the fateful night at Pittsburgh University that past summer. She was responsible for bringing him here, and she was desperate for him to succeed.

"Yeah, maybe, but the genetic properties of the drug are vastly different. When I recreate the drug, and run it through the simulators, I find the drug works by physically *dulling* one's senses. In essence, your mind is lulled to sleep."

"It's a relaxation drug, Luke. How is this a breakthrough?"

The scientist took a breath. "Because it confirms your worst fears."

"You mean mind control?" Chief was intrigued. "How so?"

"Through the memory bank."

"To the non-scientists gathered here, could you please clarify that?" Tessa interjected, sensing the frustration of others gathered in the room.

Luke nodded in agreement and collected himself.

"We think of the brain through traditional science and medicine, consisting of three parts – cerebrum, cerebellum, and the brain stem. They fire with the help of a hundred billion neurons in the human brain. However, with all the advances made the last decade on dementia and

Alzheimer's diseases, we've discovered our brains are also wired with a memory bank – a vault that stores old random bits of information – they could be memories, bodily functions, even how our nervous system last defeated a virus or illness. Immunology is obviously a component of that, but the memory of *how* it was done is from the bank. While the core three components are actively engaged daily, it is the memory bank that allows us the magical resilient repetitiveness with which our brain operates. It's not only integral to our brain activity and memory functions, but also the maintenance of the central nervous system in the body."

"So we remember things because of the memory bank?" Tessa questioned; her face showed genuine interest.

"No. That's the core three. But say you learn swimming as a toddler, and then never go in the water again. Yet, fifteen years later, you're drowning in a river, and *suddenly* without explanation, you start to swim. That's the memory bank – not the core three."

"Okay, I get that," Tessa nodded. "But what does that have to do with xY0b5?"

Luke saw her point. He was going to have to break it down further.

"There's a vault of information, and we've tried breaking into the vault before without any success. There was a theory, it was a wild one, but I do love wild theories. The theory was on a master set and how with it, one could essentially *unlock* the memory bank – as if you had a key."

"Master set as in some medical code or scientific theorem?" Chief asked.

"A formula. A chemical concoction," he replied, pointing towards the displayed holograph of information.

Chief leaned in close, her brown eyes earnestly searching his face.

"What did you find, Dr. Baer?"

"The master set."

He let his words sink in. The faces in the room were more puzzled than excited. Again, he realized he needed to elaborate. This was not the Pittsburgh Research Team.

"xY0b5 has produced the right formula to open the memory bank. The drug taps itself into a person's memory bank and can manipulate by both eradicating the memory or even," Luke shook his head, astonished at what he was going to say next. "They can *even* create new ones!"

"So," Chief clasped her hands behind her back, and stared into the holographic pixels. "xY has found a way into a person's memory bank, that can drain them of conscious thought, and even create new ones. Hence the reason for the mysterious comas we discovered occurring around the world."

"Yes, but no," Luke swiped through another set of holographic data. "If that were true, people wouldn't be waking up from these long slumbers – comas – and they wouldn't have *any* memories. They wouldn't have a pulse – it would be purely robotic. No," he tapped the physical display to his right that showed the chemical breakdown of xY0b5. "It's more subtle than that. This *is* mind control. Pure chemical manipulation to ply a person's conscious enough, so that you can basically reprogram them."

Loud laughter was heard from the back of the group. Turning, Luke saw Danny Graves standing there, hands on hips, a cocky smile on his face.

"So it's what we suspected was happening all along." Danny exclaimed, shaking his head. "Well then, why don't we do something about it now? Let's start doing some fighting for a change!"

"All muscle, no brain," Tessa snapped.

Her bright eyes flashed with anger as she stared Graves down. She was tired of putting up with the paramilitary stylized-missions that went south, and caused the death of innocent civilians like Brenda Myers.

"Let's see what Luke says we should do." Tessa said as she glanced at Chief for approval.

Chief concurred. "What is the gameplan?"

Rubbing his hands together, Luke bobbed his head up and down, as he thought.

"We need our own serum. Ha!" he laughed. "A truth serum to fight xY0b5."

"How do you propose doing that?" it was Kelly Revers who asked the question. She stood near the entrance to the room, next to Graves.

"Simple," he replied as he turned to look at her. "I mentioned we – scientists and doctors around the world – have tried breaking into the memory bank before. We know what does *not* work. I plan on using those formulas to create a counteractive drug that neutralizes the effects of xY. We probably all know of someone who's been using." Luke thought of Josh and wondered how his old classmate was doing. "I know it's risky and goes against *everything* I've ever been taught, but – we may need to skip traditional development and begin experimentation."

"That would be somewhat extreme," Chief contemplated Luke's suggestion. "Have you consulted with the others on the team about this?" She was referencing the other CDV lab scientists.

"Not yet, but I know I'm right." His eyes held steady. "And the longer we wait, the more victims fall prey to xY."

"True. We'll follow your advice, Luke. You can't afford to be wrong. We don't have time for that. The only question remaining is the one that matters most. Can you create this counteractive serum?"

A serious expression crossed over Luke's countenance. He slowly nodded, pondering the risky steps ahead. He was leading this battle. Chem-Lab and Pittsburgh University would have to be put behind him for good.

"You bet I will."

THIRTY-NINE

Jim's sweaty palms clasped the steering wheel. Perspiration poured from his every fiber. He felt as if he were going to be immersed in a pool of fluid within minutes. The cars were stopped up against one another – a parking lot in the middle of an interstate highway.

I-95 ran north, joining Hwy 278 from Hilton Head Island. Cars, trucks, buses – vehicles of all kinds – were jammed tight. These formed a long line from the state borders of Georgia and South Carolina, all the way through North Carolina to Virginia.

Where Jim sat, just south of Coosawhatchie, he was oblivious to this, though. He was simply thankful he had made it this far safely. Despite the distance being less than forty miles, he had already been on the road for four hours. *Could 've walked faster than this,* he laughed at himself. He knew his own girth, walking more than a mile was out of the question.

The cars moved sluggishly forward, inching a few miles per hour. Jim desperately fought off the urge to disengage auto and take over. His imagination saw the vehicle shoving the cars in front out of the way. But he also saw the quick burst, and then a massive pile up. So instead he patiently leaned back, and drummed his fingers over the dash.

The car was not his. If not for the overwhelming generosity of Patrick, he would have been forced to try for a ticket on the high-speed rail.

"Those will be sold out," the pub owner had cautioned. "I heard they are sold out for the next two weeks!" He pulled Jim close. "Take my car, querido amigo. You have more a need of it than I."

Jim shook his head. "I can't do that, mi hermano. What will you drive when you leave?"

There was silence as Patrick looked about the near-deserted tavern. Its better days were fast fading, in a way not unlike the demise of *Savannah Souvenirs*.

"I'm not leaving. Aye, I will stay, regardless of what happens. Go, Jimmy. Godspeed and may the Holy Mother watch over ya." Patrick kissed his hands, and held them up as a blessing.

Jim's reflections ceased as a sign for Hwy 17 caught his attention. He was nearing the intersection for the highway, and it presented a proposition. Looking ahead, for as far as he could see on I-95, cars were lined up, laggardly progressing forward – that is if the slight rotational movement of the tires could be called progress.

"Humph," he snorted, his mind made up.

Disengaging auto driver, Jim grabbed the extracting steering wheel. Turning it clockwise, he pressed down on the accelerator. The car gathered speed, and smoothly moved onto the off-ramp. No one else exited.

On the newly paved highway, his face broke into a broad smile. While he had been in dense, congested traffic the last four hours, Hwy 17 was practically devoid of traffic.

The peculiarity of this failed to strike him as odd. He scarcely gave it a second thought as he proceeded to motor on towards Charleston.

．　　　．　　　．　　　．　　　．

It was snowing heavily. In Charleston, South Carolina that was an anomaly – regardless if it was winter. Despite the constant weather changes over the last decade, life still stopped in the colonial city when snow descended. They were unprepared and unequipped to handle it.

To be fair to the native residents, this particular snowy day was beyond an average snowfall for the area. It was day two of a tremendous blizzard sweeping through the city. It had come down the coast, from the Outer Banks sweeping around Wilmington, and now sat stalled and hovering over Charleston doing its worst.

The snow was heavy and furious. At times, it would abate, and the snowflakes would just lightly float about. But the descent of the white powdery moisture was always constant. Some parked vehicles on the side streets, which remained unmoved since the storm began, boasted fifteen inches on top of their roofs.

With it being South Carolina, the temperatures were hovering just below freezing, so the warmer temperature caused the first snowflakes hitting the payment to melt. This, in turn, created a thin sheet of ice to coat the now snow-covered walkways. Pedestrian and vehicular traffic were equally hazardous, and if one could stay inside, out of the elements, that was the recommendation by the city's mayor.

Jim stood near the front of the shabby room at a rundown motel on the far side of the city. He had arrived in Charleston the day the storm hit, shortly before the snow started its descent. He found the city to be quite a different scene than he imagined as he drove along Hwy 17.

His giddiness at the vastly improved traffic dissipated and turned to consternation; the peculiarity in the absence of other traffic heading *into* Charleston finally dawned on him, and a growing, gnawing feeling set in. When he arrived, his fears were confirmed. Too late he realized the Disease had already hit the great city. Many of its inhabitants had already fled.

The clerk at a gas station told him most had left a week ago, when an outbreak claimed the lives of a few thousand. He advised Jim to get out as well, but while Jim was stopped at the station, snow began to descend. His first thought was to wait it out – the storm arrived in force. There was no leaving.

He found a cheap motel on the outskirts of the downtown area. It seemed a bargain, but then he noticed the other occupants, and regretted paying in advance. Drug dealers, call boys and girls, and some people whose appearance suggested they had just crept in from a cave.

The first day passed uneventfully. Jim merely hunkered down in the cheap motel room and ate a can of beans, a bowl of ramen, and drank a few bottles of water. On the second day, he was over the snowstorm already.

■   ■   ■   ■   ■

Kaci leaned forward in the chair as another coughing fit overtook her. The last few weeks had been rough. The sudden eviction from their home forced her to leave with only as much as she and Dylan could carry. They bounced around shelters and even lived outside for a few weeks, but due to the unseasonably cold temperatures, she was forced to find more permanent quarters.

She hastily found a rundown motel with a shabby room. Scarcely a week passed before bad weather descended – a fierce snowstorm – quite unlike anything she had ever seen. To compound matters, she had developed a sort of virus – coughing fits, random chills, and a constant pounding headache.

Notwithstanding her trials and troubles, Kaci was thankful for the little bit of protection, space, and personal comfort the shabby room offered. They had snagged free WiFi as part of their room payment to the motel, and Dylan spent much of the past two days watching movies on his tablet.

The rundown building scarcely fit the word: motel. An eyesore that mostly housed drug addicts, prostitutes, and a handful of seedy-looking characters who always were hanging outside and drinking cheap beer.

Relaxing her position, Kaci sat back in the chair. She was wrapped in a thin blanket keeping an eye on Dylan as he cradled his tablet, watching the latest episode of *Ultimate Heroes*. He was sitting against the bed on the floor and his most prized possession – a new pair of *Ultimate Hero* sneakers – were proudly worn on his feet.

A loud rap came on the door. Before Kaci could answer, the door was pushed open, and in the doorway stood the owner of the motel.

"You're out, lady."

It was quiet for a minute. Kaci was initially confused by what he meant. Then she grasped his meaning and jumped off the bed and started shouting. The owner shouted back. Dylan cowered against the bed.

"The digi-dollar key you gave me came back expired. Never should've taken that outdated currency in the first place." The motel proprietor swore.

"You're lying! It wasn't expired. And I paid two weeks advance."

"Yeah, with bad money."

"I even gave you the, you know, deposit?"

"Ha!" the owner glowered. "Get out. You thought a half-hearted effort would buy you something when the card bounced?"

Kaci tried covering Dylan's ears while the man continued to shout and curse at her. The reference to the deposit – sexual favors she had performed on the man – being mentioned in front of her son, shamed her. It made her angry and defiant. She turned and confronted the motel owner, her face a picture of wrath.

"I didn't know the key would bounce. I don't know why it did. It wasn't expired and should've had good funds on it. You can't throw us out now – not into this weather! My son can't be out in this."

"You should've thought of that before you tried stiffing me, you whore!"

Kaci and the proprietor continued to argue. Dylan turned away and stared at his tablet, large tears forming in his eyes. Even at his young age, he sensed what was going to happen. They were going to have to move again – and be out in the miserable weather.

In short order, Kaci assembled their items. They had few possessions, the previous eviction had seen to that. The owner stood at the entrance, roving Kaci's body with his eyes as she moved about. She was bent over picking a pair of socks off the floor, when she noticed his lecherous glances. Thrusting her right hip into the air, she stuck her butt out, and glared at him. He coarsely laughed, and took a step back.

If he's going to gloat, it's only because I invited him too, she glowered. It was something she had often repeated to herself ever since she first started dancing years ago.

"Where are we going, mom?" Dylan asked innocently, watching his mom gather their scant belongings.

Kaci dropped to a knee next to him. She tugged the strings of his hat, pulling it down, snugly over his ears.

"I have no idea, baby. But we'll find somewhere."

"Are we broke?"

"No!" she shouted back.

Dylan's eyes opened wide at her quick outburst of wrath.

"No," Kaci repeated, calmer this time. "We might not have any money, but we are not broke."

She stood up and reached for his little hand. He placed it confidently in hers. His mom would take good care of him, he was sure.

"Let's go, baby. Let's find somewhere worthy of our presence."

Kaci started forward and passed the motel proprietor who stood, arms crossed, just outside the door.

"Good luck with that, whore."

The man's hand reached out, and smacked one of Kaci's buttocks. It was hard enough to cause her to lose her balance. She slipped forward, letting go of Dylan's hand in the process.

Down the metal stairs, she slid; her little boy screaming in the background. She landed at the bottom and immediately started coughing, oozy from the tumble. Dylan's little feet scampered down the slippery staircase, and he landed next to her.

Lifting her bruised head in his little hands, he tried to cradle her.

"Are you okay, momma? Are you all right?"

A bag landed next to them, then another. The evil owner gave a coarse laugh as he walked away.

The coughing began to subside.

"Momma's okay, baby boy. Momma's okay."

.   .   .   .   .

A loud noise caused Jim to stick his head out of the room's door. The sharp cold wind instantly greeted him. He hurriedly tugged his heavy jacket closer.

When does it snow here? It's South Carolina, not Minnesota! He furiously rubbed his hands together in a vain attempt to stay warm. He looked about him. *Now, where did that noise come from?*

Through the whistling wind, he heard it again – a child crying, quite distinctly. The sound broke his heart. It brought back a flood of memories from when Anna was a child.

"Help! Please help!"

The voice of a little boy carried through the cacophony of the blizzard. Jim surmised it to be the same child who was also crying. The small voice cracked with emotion as the pleas for help were made. They did not fall on deaf ears.

Trudging out, Jim rounded the corner of the motel. He stopped in his tracks. Ahead of him was a metal staircase. At the bottom, a woman was crumpled over, blood dripping from her head, her body shaking violently. Scrunched down next to her, holding his little knees, was a small boy – maybe five or six, Jim guessed. He hurried forward.

"Oh, no! What happened here?" his voice was warm and comforting.

"She fell," the little boy cried. He looked up at the older, bald man standing above them and tried to sniff back his tears. "My name's Dylan."

"Nice to meet you, Dylan. Is this your momma?"

Dylan nodded. The tears came back.

"There, there," Jim soothed. He was surprised how naturally and easy it was to comfort a child again. "Are you guys staying upstairs?"

Dylan shook his head.

"Is your room down here?"

Again, the small head shook, causing the ruffled black curls to dance and frolic about.

Such a small child to be out here in the cold, all alone with his momma. Jim buried his concerns and gave a warm, friendly smile.

"Well, I have a room right around the corner. Let's go there for now."

Bending down, he picked up Kaci. She was very light, which caused him to think about Anna again. *These days, girls are always trying to be as thin as possible.*

Stretching down, he picked up one of the two bags. He looked at the other one, and then back at Dylan. The little boy understood, and scrambled to his feet. Extending his hands, Dylan clasped the large handles of the other bag.

Nodding in approval, Jim turned and started to trudge back towards his own room, Dylan in tow. The snow had given no reprieve during this time, continuing to rapidly accumulate. So even though he had only been out for a few minutes, his previous footsteps were already being covered up.

He staggered ahead, carrying both Kaci and one of the bags. His feet pressed down the snow once more, allowing the boy to carefully follow, setting his smaller feet inside the much bigger footsteps of the man ahead.

Jim's mind was a whirl. *Who is this young woman? Why is she and the child out in this weather? Why am I here?*

FORTY

"What is the point of all this analysis?" Josh's brow furrowed as he studied the latest reports displayed in front of him.

"Maybe you should ask a different question. What could this analysis be used for?"

Josh turned and saw Carrie Haselow standing in the doorway.

"What are you doing here?"

"So happens, my job is being on the review committee for ongoing projects. *Inner Earth Ventilation* is up next!"

Josh was unaware of the review committee, but he was part of the *Inner Earth Ventilation* team, so he nodded and said dryly, "How exciting."

The usual empty feeling was creeping over him. Instinctively, his hand dropped to the pocket where the capsule container was stored. His fingers spread over the plastic, starting to encircle it. Then he pulled them back, and retracted his hand from the pocket. It was not yet time. He had to preserve them. He slightly shook his head.

"Are you okay?" Carrie's soft Georgian accent was tinted with concern.

He nodded and flicked his hand. A holograph projector started up. Leaning in closer, Carrie began examining the status of *Inner Earth Ventilation*. Josh scarcely knew who else was on the project team. He generally worked alone. That suited him fine.

While Carrie viewed the files, Josh's mind went back to a conversation he kept replaying in his mind. Though some time ago now, the Stone Arch Bridge meeting with Luke haunted him.

Fear-mongering and borderline falsehoods generally accompanied the anti-vaccination world, yet, something seemed different in this conversation, and it tugged at his heartstrings. Perhaps it was Luke's passion for science and humanity, or maybe it was the words themselves. After all, Luke was an educated scientist who worked in immunology and biomedicine research. If someone as smart and intelligent as he had concerns about what was being pushed as a health patch, a drug, maybe...

"Did it ever cross your mind that perhaps we are involved in something bigger?"

Carrie's voice cut into his thoughts. She raised her head and looked at him as she asked the question. After a moment, without hearing any response, she resumed scrutinizing his work.

"This?" Josh's surprised reaction was delayed. He jerked his head towards the designs she was reviewing. "No. This is nothing more than some busy dribble designed to waste away funds in order to qualify for government grants. I've seen it before. TYM was really good at it. Part of the reason I'm so puzzled Jacobi ever merged."

"Oh," Carrie began as she turned from the files, and made some quick notes on her tablet. She had seen enough. "I highly doubt Mark Jacobi had anything to do with the TYM merger."

"That's ridiculous," Josh snapped his fingers, and the holograph shut off. It had been a brief review. "He was the founder and CEO."

"When is the last time you actually saw him? Or talked to him?"

"I know he disappeared, but that doesn't mean," his voice trailed off.

"Before the merger, wasn't it," persisted Carrie. "And what about Sam Walters?"

"What about?" Josh retorted.

"Doesn't it strike you strange that both died around the same time?"

Her words cut through him. His face blanched, and his arms dropped numbly to the side.

"What do you mean Sam died?"

Carrie's hand went to her mouth in evident horror. "Oh my gosh! I had no idea you did not know! I'm so sorry. I once lost a friend to suicide. I would never have wanted to find out from a casual acquaintance! I am sorry."

Hurrying over, Carrie gently wrapped her arms around Josh in a light embrace. Then she stepped back, and quickly left the room.

Josh stood in silence. Suddenly, his shoulders sagged, his entire body began sinking. He crumpled into an office chair. Dark, empty feelings rushed over him. Tears began streaming down his face.

Behind him, the holograph display malfunctioned and flickered back on. The pixels floated about and then came together. An outline appeared. It was a blueprint for a city – a massive city. In the lower right, a single word appeared.

LAJA

■   ■   ■   ■   ■

Luke crossed the small lab, his footsteps falling noiselessly on the commercial-grade white tiled floors. A thoughtful expression was on his face as he perused the latest panels.

There were a few other people in the lab with him. They all boasted varying levels of experience and achievements. One of them, a young Asian man, was fresh out of undergraduate school with the education of a lab assistant. Another – a man from Michigan, Dr. Strong – held four doctorates in highly technical areas – including microbiology and immunizations. Two others were highly-accomplished scientists whose publications had appeared in *Scientific American*. These people made up CDV's bioscience team.

Luke could care less about their own individual backgrounds, if combined together, they could find the antidote to xY0b5. While the group had only been working together at CDV for a few months, they had already developed good rapport and working methods. The others were more comfortable and skilled in the lab. Luke preferred analyzing and writing theorems. He worked better with his mind than his hands.

And I need to be better, he chafed. *It's already been months since xY hit the market. Each day that passes means more victims. And the further the victims progress, the less a chance we have at saving them.*

For the first time since he had joined CDV, Luke felt purpose and excitement in his work. He was not participating in propaganda filmmaking; or accompanying a midnight raid of a college campus; or standing in a downpour of rain, one of many in a line of protestors, chanting for change – demanding Congress and the World Council tell the truth. He was *actually* doing something that could save a person. It was the entire reason he had become a scientist in the first place.

Maybe this is why everything has happened to me. I can now be part of something bigger; something of great significance.

A frustrated look came over his face. "If we can create the serum, that is. It's all for naught if we don't."

. . . . .

"They are ready for you, Mr. Ambassador." The aide addressed the tall Ugandan standing to her right. He acknowledged the words with a slight bend of his head.

The large red hickory doors stood guard over the entrance to the room. The ivory handles on the doors were etched with gold, and their round, knobbed ends glinted brightly. The red hickory and contrasting ivory gold echoed the irony of what was to soon happen. For on the other side of these doors, history was about to be made.

The two doors slowly swung open. They scarcely made a noise, yet as they opened, Derrick Omach felt as if they were jeering at him, taunting his presence – daring him to find a better recourse.

The room was airy, and well-lit with hanging LED lanterns. Tall windows took up much of the wall space with heavy drapes pulled in front of them. The pattern of the curtains formed a sort of mural as they ran around the three sides of the large and open room.

Ambassador Omach stepped forward, his black dress shoes sinking into the soft, plush red carpet. Ahead of him were a series of chairs, arranged in a half-circle. The chairs were as luxurious as the carpet, their high back metal frames arching above the cushions and forming a sort of crescent above the occupant's head.

Not a single chair was empty. Nearly every continent in the world was represented by the men and women who sat in them. At the head of the group was the Chair of the Council. His clean-shaven face showed little age, which contrasted with the rest of the Council members.

Derrick stopped as he reached the edge of the half-circle and slightly bowed. The gathered group returned the courtesy with inclinations of their own heads.

"You've reviewed the report regarding the ventilation?" Derrick spoke, his Ugandan accent noticeable, but his voice soft.

"We have," a woman answered; her ethnicity from Southeast Asia. "We find it to be complete, and it affirms our projections."

"I thought it would," Derrick responded.

"And not a moment too soon. Even today," added a gentleman who was from east Africa. He was sitting a few spaces down from the left of the Chair. "I've heard reports of the growing famine and unrest spreading across South America. The scores of thousands have now increased to millions of infected species. They are ravenous wolves!"

"Rabid," an American spoke up. His Queens accent gave away his New York roots. "You know what fear does to a person? It binds them. They feel no escape. And rabid is *good* for fear. If we don't get moving now, there's no telling how much we might end up losing."

"This is what we've been working towards these last two years," the Southeast Asian woman declared.

The ambassador shook his head. "We are talking about sending mankind into the depths of the earth. We were made to live above. We have 365 days to reset – *at most.*"

"Peoplekind have existed for millions of years and will continue to, topside or underneath," the Chair of the Council spoke for the first time, his bass voice booming out as he readjusted himself on the seat at the far right of the group. "Our evolution is yet beginning, Ambassador Omach."

The room was quiet as Derrick bowed his head. He took a step back.

"I meant no disrespect, Your Excellency, only concern for what lies ahead."

"We are all concerned and perhaps afraid," the Council member from east Africa spoke up, empathizing with his fellowman. "My country is overrun and ravaged by the Disease just as yours. If we don't do something now, *billions* will suffer."

"It's because of fear, some must die for the sake of many." The New Yorker spoke with a thoughtful air. "We cannot control fear, but people...we can control their future."

Ambassador Omach lowered his head again, and nodded to the Council.

"It's agreed then, I will notify our contacts the final piece has been finished."

The council members all murmured their agreement, and Derrick slowly turned and walked from the room. The large red hickory doors methodically swung shut behind him, and he overheard the Council members' voices clamor as they began to discuss the next stage.

His face clouded and his brow furrowed as he walked in deep distress.

I am to survive, yet why do I not feel happiness or joy but only sadness? What is my life worth or my family's that someone else should sacrifice?

Reaching the stairway, he descended the grand staircase to the foyer below. Sunlight peeked through the heavy drawn shades in the atrium. Instinctively, Derrick reached for the heavy shades residing in his jacket pocket, and slipped them on over his eyes.

I pray peace for what is to come.

The silent prayer would go unanswered.

FORTY-ONE

A rustling noise on the bed caused Jim to turn around. He watched the restless young woman sleep. She was beautiful – brown skin, black hair, brown eyes – her head resting on the propped up pillows. He continued to wonder who she was and what misfortune had befallen her that caused her and the child to be left all alone in the cold.

Perhaps the rest of her kin were inflicted by the Disease. They must be the only survivors. She definitely isn't one of Them. Neither is the boy.

Thinking of the young lad, he turned and gazed kindly on the tousled-haired kid sitting next to a knee-high coffee table. The boy sat with his back against it, one leg folded underneath with the other bent over. The ever-new *Ultimate Heroes* sneakers still adorned his feet, but were wet from the trudge through the heavy snow.

The rustling noise grew louder. Jim looked back at the bed as the young woman's eyes fluttered open. A startled look came over them.

"Where am I? Who are you? Where's Dylan?"

Kaci hurriedly sat up, her eyes quickly darting around the room as she tried to ascertain her surroundings. Jim stepped to her side, and put his hands on her arms, gently squeezing them in a comforting and non-threatening way.

"There, there," he soothed. "You're safe. Everything is okay. The boy is right here."

As if on cue, Dylan rose to his feet, and came prancing over to the bed.

"Momma," he said, "This nice old man said we could stay with him. Cool, isn't it?"

Kaci smiled at her energetic little boy, and the weary smile carried up toward Jim. He acknowledged it with a curt bob of his head, and placed a gentle hand on the boy's hair, ruffling the black curls.

"You have a polite little boy here, Miss…" he stopped, not knowing her name.

"Kaci. This is my boy, Dylan Knudson."

"Ah! Dylan told me his name. He is a very polite little boy. But you are quite ill, Miss Kaci." Jim smiled at Dylan as he spoke of the lad, but a concerned expression crossed his face as he looked at the young woman.

She blushed. She was unfamiliar with such genuine manners.

"You don't have to 'miss' me, sir."

"No sir, either. Just Jim – Jim Burillo," he shook her soft hand. It was quite small and by its feel, had endured much recent hardship.

"I'm not used to such politeness. Don't see that much these days."

"Well, my mother and pops weren't much in the way of teaching manners or respect, but somehow I learned them anyway. Least I can do is show it once in a while."

Jim smiled at Kaci and Dylan. The boy gave a grin in return and ran back to his tablet. Plopping his little frame down next to the small table again, he resumed watching his show.

"Can I get you anything?"

Kaci still struggled to believe the sincerity in Jim's voice.

"I'm quite fine, thank you."

"Begging pardon," Jim said. "But you look far from fine, Kaci. You're sick. I can tell it's not the Disease," he added as he saw a look of alarm flash across her face. "I've seen enough infected ones, but…you aren't well," he repeated.

Kaci looked away, tears forming in her eyes. She let them fall as she observed her little Dylan, sitting quietly, watching his show. Lifting her face, she gazed into Jim's sympathetic one, and bit her lower lip.

"I'm not well, I haven't been. I've been telling myself I am, but I know that isn't true. It's because," her voice broke. "I don't know what I'm going to do with my precious baby."

Jim quickly looked behind him to make sure Dylan was not overhearing their conversation. He carefully sat down on the bed next to Kaci. The weight of his body caused the mattress to sink tremendously, but the young woman was so small and light, she scarcely moved. He took one of her delicate hands in his much chubbier ones.

"Are you saying…do you mean…you're dying?"

She gave a small, hesitant nod.

This was an unexpected turn of events. *I just wanted to go North. Why am I being thrown into this trouble? It's almost like I'm a magnet for predicament. And I can't just leave them!* The moral dilemma challenged him. What was he to do?

Studying the friendly, older man's face, Kaci sensed he felt an obligation and a difficult choice to make. She felt terrible telling this helpful stranger such ominous news, but the stark reality was now driving her actions. She had tried thwarting it, but alas, she knew her days, maybe even hours were limited. Her strength was waning.

Reaching out, she gently touched the forearm of her new friend. Jim tried to smile.

"It's okay," she murmured. "I wasn't inviting you to join in my pain. I have to tell someone, though, and you seem a good man. Can I tell you more?"

■　　■　　■　　■　　■

Sitting on the edge of the bed, Jim's fat fingers entwined with each other. They propped up against his double chin as he listened with rapt attention to Kaci talk. It was a narrative he had seen one too many times before – played out on the old backroom TV which warned of the dangers provocative attire and flirtatious mannerisms attracted. Of the utter doom which followed when one forsook the advice of its seniors.

While his viewpoint may have been formed by antiquated and oppressive ideologies, his heart felt genuine care and warmth for the young woman. His only emotion was compassion as she told him the tale of the Senator's son, and the subsequent banishment from said Senator when it was discovered that Jack's lover was black.

"I thought those days were behind us," Kaci cried into a pillow. "I mean what sort of racist bigot still believes in that kind of hatred?"

"You just said why," Jim said. "He's a bigot."

"I don't care so much for myself," Kaci elaborated. "It's my little man. Who's going to take care of him? I am not well."

"How did you get sick?"

Kaci sighed. "I was prescribed antidepressants, but when things hit the fan with Jack dying, I didn't have enough money to refill the prescription. A doctor recommended I try a new subsidized drug. That seemed to work the same, but they didn't tell me one of the most potent side effects – blood poisoning. I've been slowly dying for weeks now."

Jim clucked his tongue, and leaned back. This too he had seen – played out on the broadcasts. Drug poisoning had been on the rise ever since the removal of FDA standards – or rather, since the indictment of the FDA's top deputy by the FBI when it was learned the health official had authorized fake results from several top pharmaceutical companies so their drugs could proceed. Naturally, he had been receiving a kickback on the soaring profits.

"Putting someone in jail doesn't fix what they did," Kaci said, tears flowing freely. "How am I supposed to explain to my son that he's going to grow up motherless just so someone could make a buck now instead of waiting a little while?"

Jim continued to listen. It was a hidden skill of his. A skill honed while Anna rambled on and on. He was surprised how attentive he could be, understanding what was being said. The words pouring from Kaci's mouth also were not insults or derogatory comments about his person. They *were* hurtful words, but from someone hurting and not looking to injure others.

"I think God placed you here," Kaci said suddenly, a feeling of euphoria sweeping over her. She wiped the remnants of tears from her beautiful face. "Why else would you have ended up here? Hardly anyone is staying in Charleston anymore, yet you're at the same hotel as us. I don't know if I believe in God, but someone is watching over us."

Jim nodded. "Perhaps we should take you to a doctor," he said while unfolding his arms and unclasping his hands.

"Haven't you been listening to my story? I'm *dying* because of what a doctor gave me. What good do you think they're going to do now?"

"It's just like I saw on TV," he muttered, his voice betraying him, emotions spilling over. "You can't trust anyone anymore. Doctors are supposed to help us, and instead, they poison us."

Kaci gave a wistful smile. She recognized the skeptic in Jim.

"Not all doctors are going to poison people. It wasn't intentional; they just can't help us."

Another coughing fit overtook her. This time blood came out in a little stream. Jim dabbed it away with his handkerchief. Kaci mumbled thanks. Then she turned and buried her head in the pillow. Her fingers squeezed, and clenched the coverlet.

Glancing around, Jim saw Dylan still sitting calmly on the floor, oblivious to his mother's pain. *The blissful ignorance of being six.* The young boy was thoroughly absorbed with the video streaming on his tablet. Jim, who usually thought modern technology a menace, put aside his personal feelings. Anything to keep the boy from the pain that would come with the realization that his mother was dying.

"What kind of person throws someone out of shelter into this crappy weather, in my condition, with a small child?" said Kaci indignantly. "I mean, I get it. It's happening all over, and it's what *they're* doing too. But doesn't anybody stop to think about humanity? Like why are they even doing it?"

"They? How do you mean?"

Kaci shook her head. "I shouldn't say anything. It's supposed to be top secret. But…" a wild look spread across her face. "What a fool I've been! Why would I keep it secret? What do I have to lose? My life? I'm already dying."

What was she talking about? Her words intrigued Jim, and he stepped back to the side of the bed and sat down. Propping Kaci back up, he handed her a small cup of water that was sitting on the nightstand next to the bed. She swallowed a small sip, her face twisting with pain, and handed it back.

"As I said, Jack was the son of Senator Daniels. The Senator heads the Committee for Public Health & Safety. The committee is not widely known; it was created after the dissolution of the Department of Health & Human Services. Anyway," Kaci swallowed hard. "He told me a secret and said I shouldn't tell anyone. I've been a good girl, but…" the wild look was back, her eyes worried. "Who's going to care for my little boy?"

"There there," Jim tried to soothe her, running a soft hand over her hair. "What in God's name are you talking about, Kaci? What secret?"

"The Cities. The Golden Cities."

The words were spoken simply enough, but they caused Jim to fallback, shoulders slumped as he put a hand to his forehead. He closed his eyes and saw the old TV. He was watching a broadcast with Patrick. It warned of increased building activity at "secure" locations where heavy machinery was being brought in.

"The same type of machinery that is used in demolition and construction," the broadcaster narrated in ominous tones. Of course, that was really quite vague then, but could it be that they were right all along? The broadcast had been months ago, even before the incident with the woman on the wharf.

"There are several cities, but the one Jack told me about is in Virginia. Only certain people can enter. 'A community of survivalists to be spared from the undesirables outside – a Garden of Eden' – that's what he said. Right before they killed him."

Jim ran a heavy hand over his chin, his mind churning as he contemplated Kaci's words. What if it was all true? For a man who absorbed much conspiracy news, he still thought for himself. No one owned him.

Suddenly, Kaci sat up and screamed, clutching her throat. At the sound, Dylan jumped to his feet, and ran over to the bed.

"Momma, momma!" he cried. "What's wrong?"

Jim stood up, his eyes quickly moving back and forth as he took in the situation. Kaci's scream turned to a coughing fit, and more blood began to come. A strong impulse seized him. He started to shake. The thought went against his core, but he knew he had no choice. He knew what must be done; he was surer of it than sending Anna to the safe house.

Leaning down, he scooped up the small frame of Kaci. Wrapping the bed sheet around her, he laid her head on his shoulder. His own strength surprised him, but the adrenaline of the situation propelled him.

"C'mon, Dylan, we have to take your mom to the clinic. And we have to hurry!"

FORTY-TWO

"We're sorry. The number entered is no longer valid. Please check your Secure ID and try again."

Josh gave up and threw the handheld across the room while screaming at the wall. Staring at his reflection in the 3D TV, he contemplated smashing the screen. Thinking better of it, he stepped to the front door, opened it, and walked outside.

The cold snap had given way to unseasonably warm temperatures. The area's residents took advantage of it. Happy noises floated down the street to where he stood. He watched as the neighborhood kids frolicked about. Down at the far end of the street, a DJ finished hooking up a massive speaker set. Soon loud music would be pulsating through the air, and people would dance.

The sight was one to behold. These days the neighborhood usually looked more a ghost town than an established suburban community. Actually seeing people out and about was in and of itself surprising. Dozens of people – maybe even a hundred – were milling on the streets. A handful of more adventurous ones made their way to Three Corners Grill & Bar, a half-mile back near the main road. Burning braziers were sending orange flames skyward, and the sweet smell of barbeque permeated the air. It was such a stark contrast – day to night – and it was night.

Josh stepped back into the safety of his home, and shut the front door. He slid down the metal frame, clutching his stomach. Was his mind imagining that it was squeezing and cramping, overcome with stress? Or was that the actual reality?

The empty capsule container that once held his ever-constant supply of xY0b5 tablets rolled on the floor by the futon. Josh blinked as turmoil raged within.

"Am I inoculated now? Immune to the world outside?"

He had tried repeatedly over the last two days to get the prescription refilled. The same error message played audibly while simultaneously displaying text. Each time, he was skeptical and disbelieving. He assumed the system must be experiencing an outage.

Why would the supply be cut off? Who would do that? He knew the whole purpose of the drug was to not only relax and calm the nervous system, but that it contained active ingredients to help inoculate against the Disease. He never took the health patch, as he was already prescribed xY0b5, so it was his only protection.

The inability to refill the prescription came with horrible timing. The urge to down the meds had never been higher. Ever since Carrie Haselow had told him what happened to Sam Walters, his world was shattered. The fact Jacobi also played chump and did the same thing? It devastated Josh.

Inoculated or not, the urge persisted. But with his prescription gone, and the system's inability to recognize his unique Secure ID, he was at a loss for what to do. He felt he was losing grip on reality. He remembered Luke's words of warning.

"xY05b *will* alter your mind. It's a dreamcatcher – without the dream. You believe a pseudo-reality that only works by distorting the actual reality – the world around you...Let alone the ability they have to control...mind control..."

Dang, he slowly breathed out. *Is Luke on the money after all*?

"But what of it?" he suddenly spoke out loud. "Am I programmed now? Is my mind being controlled by aliens or some other force – a freak of nature? Hmm? Are they listening? Can they hear me now? What does it matter? I have no real purpose anymore – no family, no friends, no job – one that matters anyway," he savagely added as an afterthought, thinking of the ever-pointless *Inner Earth Ventilation* project. "Basically, you could take me out back and..."

Josh's voice trailed off as the sudden thought entered his mind. It scared him.

Was this how the Unknowns felt? A hopeless, listless way knowing something is coming – something must *be coming, but there isn't a damn thing you can do about it?*

He closed his eyes and saw the man in Canada. The woman in Georgia. The countless feeds he had viewed from around the world. He saw a collapsing Golden Gate Bridge. A burning helicopter. Then he saw...Amanda. His lost love. His lost life.

"Everything changed after she was gone," he bitterly exclaimed.

And at that moment, if there was a God or a Supreme Being or multitude of Beings, Josh used every curse word in his vocabulary to call them out.

∎　　∎　　∎　　∎　　∎

The lab was quiet. All five scientists were present, hard at work. A strange feeling hovered in the air – like the early morning on a fall day when everything is still. The nocturnal animals have gone to bed; humans are not yet awake. The birds silently huddle in their nests. A leaf trembles ever so lightly in the soft breeze; hanging on for dear life, yet knowing that life is about to end. Slowly, the leaf is loosened from its branch.

The feeling dispels. The leaf breaks free.

"Guys, we've got something!" the young Asian scientist excitedly spoke while holding up a test tube. "It's changed colors."

A bright orange tube meant nothing to anyone else, but inside the lab at the CDV bunker underneath Washington, D.C., seeing orange in the tube instead of the ever-steady blue meant everything.

Happy cheers broke out. Feelings of joy swept over them. Luke thumped the young man on the back. The two scientists of published accolades congratulated the discoverer of the tube as well. It had been a team effort, but the one who noticed the different color – he was a hero of sorts.

The door to the lab opened, and in walked Tessa. Her face broke into a smile as she saw the happy faces.

"Good news, I presume?"

"We got orange!" the Asian said, still holding the test tube triumphantly aloft.

"And orange is good?"

"Yes," Luke nodded. "We've found a serum to combat the effects of xY!"

Smiles and high fives went around again, but then Luke noticed Dr. Strong refraining from the excitement and standing quietly to the side. The man who had earned four doctorates stood still during the celebration of the monumental breakthrough.

"Is this not cause to celebrate?" Luke asked, bewildered by the doctor's reaction.

"We've spent months trying to find a cure to xY. Since we started, another *seven* strains have been released to the open market. We're fighting a losing battle."

Dr. Strong's words cut into the joyous atmosphere. Tessa's smile faded, and the others also broke out of their happy trance. General glum set in. It made Luke angry.

"Why would you minimize today's success? Did you really think we would come up with a serum to combat all strains of the drug? It'd be like creating a super-flu shot, which has never worked and only caused the reverse effect when attempted."

Luke stood his full height of five-foot, nine inches, and instinctively pushed his glasses back up his nose with his right middle finger. He was unsure why his reaction to Dr. Strong was so vehement, but he felt insulted by the doctor's demeanor. He prepared for a counter-argument.

Dr. Strong's face displayed no emotion as he was scolded. When Luke finished, the doctor slowly nodded his head. Holding a tablet close, he looked around at the lab instruments strewn in front of him – beakers, test tubes, flasks, funnels, droppers, burners, balances – these were instruments he had spent far more time in his life interacting with than anything else. He knew he had exponentially more experience and education than Luke, but he remained humble.

"You worked with Dr. Charles Grafton at Pittsburgh University?"

Luke nodded in reply.

"A learned man. He and I collaborated on a couple papers once. You wouldn't happen to be the hotshot student who came back to work alongside him at the University, would you?"

Luke's face slightly blushed. "I wouldn't say hotshot."

"How to create something out of the nucleus of nothing – that is beautiful. Tell me," Dr. Strong scrutinized Luke. "Have you ever used xY05b?"

"No." Luke was indignant. "Why would you ask?"

Dr. Strong put down the tablet he had been pretending to examine, and walked closer to where Luke stood.

""Because I know, literally, every student or intern working at the University has been identified as a xY0b5 user."

Luke did not believe Dr. Strong. He laughed out loud.

"How do you know that? What proof do you have?"

"Proof? Practically every associate from the Department of IID, as well as Research Operations, at the University have either been admitted to mental confinement or have had their bodies discovered. As far as I know, you are the *only* non-infected, surviving member of Grafton's late team."

Luke ran his tongue over his dry lips. The news shocked him. He had not paid any attention to the University since starting work for CDV. At least, ever since the fateful night when Brenda was killed.

"That is impossible. I...I mean Melinda Gore was killed, most likely targeted in a direct attack at the conference in San Francisco...but..." he stammered and sputtered to a halt.

"Perhaps you can understand my skepticism, Dr. Baer. Why is it that the single person remaining from Grafton's crack team is working here, at CDV, for a serum that will *supposedly* combat the effects of xY when every colleague of yours is either dead or completely poisoned by the drug?"

Tension built in the room. The young lab assistant backed up against a table holding test tubes, while the two published scientists both acted busy while doing absolutely nothing. Tessa stood by Luke's side, arms folded. She broke the awkward silence.

"I vouch for Luke," her voice tinged with anger. "I personally recruited and vetted him. Chief herself signed off on it. Let's stop this nonsense. Any such concerns should be directed to one of the lieutenants in the future or me. This is completely unproductive."

Dr. Strong inclined his head downward, receiving Tessa's rebuke.

"I meant no offense, Ms. Morgan. I am perhaps surprised at the good fortune Dr. Baer's sustained in making it this far without disappearing or having his work compromised."

Tessa shook her head. She ignored his excuse and stepped forward, jabbing a finger into the doctor's chest.

"We are the CDV, Dr. Strong. Our assets *aren't* compromised. You would be wise to remember that."

"So I shall," he evenly answered.

The two locked eyes momentarily. Dr. Strong looked away first, turning toward Luke.

"As I said, I mean no offense, I hope I am completely wrong – both about you and the serum, Dr. Baer. I envy your confidence. Perhaps you are right, I *hope* you are right. Maybe this will work; we've had but a single test show improvement. Our hopes are pinned on blood work samples being uncontaminated and becoming orange. Remember when blood ran red?"

"It runs in the streets," Kelly Revers broke in, catching the last sentence of Dr. Strong. She had burst through the door with Danny Graves. "We are looking for you, Tessa. Something's about to break."

"What's going on?" Tessa faced the two CDV lieutenants.

"We knew something was coming. *New Day* wasn't just about San Francisco or the development of a mind-control drug. It hinted at an apocalyptic doomsday. A purge. The chatter on our mobile units have picked up a code word: *Laja*." Danny said, his muscular chest heaving as he caught his breath.

Kelly jumped in. "Our latest espionage reports have indicated an exorbitant amount of activity lately through the World Council secure lines. The last few weeks have shown a considerable spike."

"Well then, Dr. Strong, you may be right. The problem is we don't have time to wait and find out. Luke, what's next?" Tessa meant no disrespect to Dr. Strong's prodigious background, but she deferred to the brazen, daring research scientist she had personally recruited for the job.

"We need to wrap testing and begin the production phase as quickly as possible. If something else – a doomsday – is coming, we don't know how much time we have. And…" doubt crept into his mind. What if he was wrong? This was not the time for a Chem-Lab repeat. "Perhaps we should do more testing?"

Luke was unsure, and glanced at Dr. Strong. The doctor opened his mouth to say something, but Tessa interrupted.

"You sounded so confident before, Luke. We need that confidence now. If the apocalypse – *New Day* or *Laja* – is coming, we'll need every able-bodied person we can get. This serum may give us that."

Eyeing the five members of CDV's science team, she flashed an encouraging smile. All their hopes and dreams rode on the effectiveness of the drug they had just created.

"Godspeed."

Luke watched as Tessa left the lab with Kelly and Danny. He studied the four other scientists. Ashen faces greeted him, all sensing something terrible was about to happen. He looked last at Dr. Strong who alone, wore a look of quiet resolve.

"Well then, Dr. Baer," said Dr. Strong in a low, calm tone. "Here's hoping you are right and I am wrong. Shall we begin?"

▪   ▪   ▪   ▪   ▪

"What is one to do when you realize you've spent your whole life searching for answers – the truth – and at the end of it all, you're undone by the reality that *nothing* is as it seems? You discover everything you've ever believed is a lie. Everything you've ever known turns out to be nothing more than a mirage. Can such a person exist? *Does* such a person exist?"

Josh spoke into the recorder on his handheld. His tone devoid of any emotion – monotone by definition. His manner and demeanor held steady and perfectly flat. He paused the recording, and stared out the front window.

For someone who had been a truthseeker – an analyzer of information and procurer of research – he felt like a worm in a sea of fish.

Previously tasked to find the source of truth in events – the origin story – and dissuade the morph, he now found himself *as* the morphed subject. He had been the intellect behind published fact. Now, he was the beneficiary of random data sampling. If the world of metaphysics and the realm of the unknown, long-held at dubious arm's length, would collide in his world, it'd be a welcome break from his dreary existence.

A man who knew how to dissect the perfect architecture of a morph – was now forced to watch the greatest morph ever engineered without being able to intervene. The entire fruits of his career – strenuous labor and hard-pressed analytical work – had yielded what amounted to nothing. At the end of the day, people believed what was peddled as news – the common myth.

Take the sun. It was to be avoided as much as possible. The very process of rejuvenation that had existed for millions of years was suddenly discarded, and people rejected the natural light and avoided any direct contact with sunshine. The very idea caused Josh to laugh out loud. How ridiculous and yet, was the Disease a byproduct of climate change? He knew not.

It made sense, in a way, he rationalized. The ozone layer was corroded beyond recognition and had been spewing harmful rays and gases for decades. The released toxins into the hemisphere had to wreak havoc one way or another. It made the perfect scapegoat. Besides, it had been at the forefront of the political discussion for decades.

But he knew there was more. The median of the moral compass had swung widely in one direction. The evolutionary growth in *peoplekind* was the real juggernaut behind reason, thought, and moral code. Not bound to 'traditional' norms, gay marriage was only the start. Not just in America, but across the globe. Then the Trans-Life Act passed. That changed everything.

Thinking about this caused him to consider the dissenters and haters. They rejected the claims of science and biology, as now interpreted, and clung to old-fashioned ideologies. Supremacy, ignorance, and phobias reigned chief among them; the mold they were cast into – Nazis of society. Josh knew some dissenters were so alt, 'terrorist watches' had been slapped on their organizations and communication means. While previous traditional science and biology had taught something different, it did make sense people would evolve into the next stage of their existence.

"How else are we to survive this new, dark world?" he muttered to no one, his mind ravaged by the memories of the tumultuous past.

"So maybe," Josh continued to stare out of the window. "It really is the dissenters and haters fault for all this." He laughed suddenly. "No, if there's hell to pay, it would be a god or the Universe to pass judgment on mankind for rejecting its natural science and desecrating the world. Irregardless, any way you slice the pie, the Disease is here and has embedded its grimy fingerprints into the fabric of our past, present, and future."

Sighing, he slumped onto the futon. None of these thoughts were new. They had been chasing him round and round for weeks now. They were not even original! His mind merely supported the truth that everyone else knew. So why was he fighting it?

There is more than meets the eye. 'Blind may be blind, not seeing is another matter.'

He pondered his mother's expression. It was true. Humans may or may not have morally declined. The world may be experiencing extreme temperatures, either for the first time or as part of an ongoing cycle. Whatever it was though, the presence of a disastrous pandemic was well-founded and spreading. Close friends and colleagues were killing themselves. A world bent on mind over matter was, perhaps, letting the power of their minds be stripped away. They had already let their planet be eviscerated. And yet… at the end of everything…

Does it matter? Is it all due to the degradation of our world? The decay of humankind? Or rather, is this the next step in our evolutionary process as peoplekind?

Josh closed his eyes, and rubbed his hand across his forehead. He wished he could make it all stop.

FORTY-THREE

The line for the heart monitor took up about two or three inches near the middle of the screen. Several other machines had their information feeding into the display as well, but Jim could easily pick out the heart monitor as it was the only one that had significant spikes and drops as it tracked Kaci's erratically beating heart.

The young woman lay in a hospital bed, IVs in both arms, a tube going into her chest, another into her nose. Dylan sat next to the bed in a big chair, his brown eyes fraught with worry as he watched his momma.

When they had first arrived, the room bustled with activity – a doctor and a couple nurses connecting machines, prepping Kaci for tests, analyzing her symptoms. Now though, things were much quieter. One nurse was present, but she was simply doing routine checks of the monitors to make sure they were working correctly.

Kaci had gone into cardiac arrest as Jim ran holding her through the Charleston streets. They had attempted to take the automobile, and the car did push through the first half-mile, but then they were forced to abandon the car due to a road closure with the snowstorm.

Dylan had been a good trooper – soldiering on, holding back tears and questions as the three of them burst into the clinic. The strong smell of chemicals nearly knocked Jim over. He had forgotten what the inside of a health clinic looked like. He remembered the first time he had been in one of the new clinics. They were quite different from the hospitals he had grown up with – the 'clean and sterile feel' one would ascribe them.

The hospitals of old were certainly clean and sterile, yet also warm and inviting. Magnificent buildings that rivaled in ideology – more so than architecture – the splendid old cathedrals from centuries past. It seemed to be a contest – which health provider would have the most impressive atrium. Hospital after hospital seemed to build upon the last, until one day, they were no more. The new 'Health First' clinics started to pop up.

First, it was out of necessity for the opioids epidemic, then to handle the massive increase in people needing health treatment when the government took away funding for healthcare programs like Medicaid. Now the clinics resembled more a factory to let someone endure their life as a second-class person rather than an inviting place to quickly heal and leave.

The line on the screen started to become less erratic. There was a slight stirring on the bed. Jim looked over, and while Kaci was the one lying there, he thought of someone else.

His mind went back to an evening he had buried deep in his memories. It was a dreadful night. One that Patrick Flannigan alone knew of, and one the pub owner would only mention when speaking of Jim's resolve. Back before Anna had met Arndt, back before she was even a teenager. She was but a scared eleven-year-old girl. Jim rubbed his hands over his face as the memory overtook him.

■   ■   ■   ■   ■

It was a cold night, one early spring. The day had been a busy one, and Jim was quite thankful for Anna's help. Her cheerful smile and positive attitude made the day go by quickly and profitably. She helped tend the cash register, restocked floor items, and eagerly shared information to the passing tourists and their similar questions.

Once the store closed, Jim set about tidying things in preparation for the evening and to save some time in the morning before reopening. Anna offered to take out the trash, and he thought nothing of it. When she had been gone fifteen minutes, he became worried and decided to check on her. The trash bins were located right outside the back door. It should not take that long. Exiting *Savannah Souvenirs* into the back alley, he saw a scene he would never forget.

In the corner of the building's exterior, a man was on top of Anna, holding her tight. Jim recognized him – a customer from earlier that afternoon. Anna was trying to scream, but it was muffled. Her legs moved frantically as she vainly tried to escape the man's grasp.

Jim went after the assailant like a madman. Grabbing two glass bottles from the recycling bin, he rushed forward. Throwing one bottle through the air, it hit the stranger in the back. By the time the assaulter turned around, still stumbling from the blow of the first glass bottle, Jim had smashed the other over his skull. It shattered into pieces.

Anna was sobbing uncontrollably, her small frame shaking violently. Jim scooped her up and ran to the hospital. The attacker lay unconscious in the alley, never to be seen again.

The sole focus and attention of Jim was taking care of his niece. That meant getting her to professional medical care as quickly as possible, even if he hated hospitals and doctors. She would need to be examined. It would be scary.

"It's my duty to care for her; it's my great honor and privilege to protect her." He said it then to Patrick and many more times in the years that followed.

.   .   .   .   .

A dubious expression came over Jim's face as he ruminated on the horrific event. How life had changed.

You…remind me of a slug. Someone who merely exists to eat, sleep, and eat some more. How Anna had changed. *Did I actually do anything good for her?* He considered who she had grown up to be; her hurtful words; her spiteful conduct.

His mind brought him back to the present. Here he was, years later, finished with yet another mad sprint to a health facility carrying a woman with a young child in tow. He had failed the first time. Was this to be a second chance?

The nurse checked off a final box on the clipboard, patted the bed skirt, and left the room. Dylan sat, slumped forward in his chair, holding his momma's hand as he dozed off to sleep – exhausted by everything happening.

"Thank you, Jim," Kaci's voice was soft. "We were destined to meet."

"It was nothing," he said gruffly. "We need to get you well so you can take care of your little boy."

Her eyes fell, and her expression turned sorrowful. She slowly stroked the hand of her sleeping boy.

"It's too late," Kaci murmured. She earnestly looked up at Jim. "Promise me, you'll take care of my boy."

Her words cut to Jim's heart. His mind flashed, and he saw another woman dying from poisoning – by her own hand – her insides wracked by drug overdose. Forced to helplessly watch, hold, and pray for her on the bedroom floor while eight-year-old Anna cried outside the door.

Then he saw Anna, a little older, but the same little girl who was now scared and shaking as the SAECK exam finished. The result came back negative, yet what did it matter? She was scarred and changed for life. The memory morphed, the girl grew older; her countenance grew ugly and rebellious. It jeered at him, taunted him, mocked him. He saw sadness and pain. He saw the pleading face of Kaci.

If this is a second chance, do I want it? What if I fail again? Can I even do this?

He could not speak. Even if he wanted to, words would not come. He simply nodded.

"The city," Kaci's breathing started to become more difficult. "I have passes. Jack got them for me. Only the elite, the rich, and powerful were supposed to be chosen; but he had two passes from his father. A final slap in the face – he told his son to find a suitable woman and start living for the future. Jack gave them to me, said Dylan and I were his future. Then he fell ill. I doubt the Senator even knows his son is dead."

Jim nodded again, still unsure what to say.

Kaci glanced at her little boy, and a smile appeared on her countenance for a second. It was replaced with an amalgamated blend of concern and determination.

"You must go to the city. But *never* tell anyone who you truly are. People like *us* aren't supposed to be there. It sounded so dangerous I wasn't going to risk it, but now," she paused to take slow, painful breath. "I want Dylan to be safe. Please take care of him."

Jim gave another slow, deliberate nod.

"The coordinates to the City's location are uploaded onto Dylan's tablet along with the passes; ID numbers for you both."

"How can I use your ID, though?"

"My Jack was clever. He never trusted anyone. The passes given to him by the Senator were normalized – which meant it would be programmed to a person's DNA. He traded those – with all the first-class perks and benefits – to someone else for prototype passes. These are programmed generically, so one could create a customized identity. You can create your own identity, with Dylan as your son."

"I wouldn't!"

"You must."

"I can't do this. You just can't give him to me. He's your son! Why do you trust me so?" Jim protested; his voice cracking.

A curious expression came over Kaci's face. She thought for a moment.

"You showed me kindness. You didn't know me, yet you took us in, rushed me to this clinic…what sort of person does that? I can tell you – someone I trust. We live in a very dark world, Jim. An awful, ferocious world – I should know. I made a living wetting and appeasing the basest of desires. Nobody has ever shown me kindness like you did. Unprovoked, without recourse, or intention. You know what I think? I think it's only through kindness that we truly glimpse a person's soul."

Jim choked back his emotions. Kaci's words humbled him, challenged him to accept his destiny. He pushed back one last time.

"We'll be caught. If it's as risky and dangerous as you say, there will be consequences. I don't care about me, but the boy."

"It's for my son that I do this," Kaci's voice was starting to get raspy. "He must live to see another day – a *new* tomorrow, a kinder tomorrow. Darkness is coming, but light will follow. It never stays dark forever."

The room was quiet. The only sound audible was the soft breathing of Dylan as he peacefully slept, oblivious to what was happening around him. His curly hair rested on the bed next to his mother. Kaci wrapped her hand around both of her son's, her fingers entwining his.

She looked back at Jim. Tears trickled from her eyes, and rolled down her cheeks. He watched silently. Begging, pleading for courage for what was to come.

"Jim?"

"Yes."

"Promise me."

Can I do this again? He slowly breathed in and out. *Courage, man, live not for today, but for tomorrow – a kinder one.* A final pause.

"I promise."

It was quiet for another minute. The only sound that of the machines' fans – cooling their electronics as they worked. A sort of heaviness, the kind that hangs over the morning when a heavy mist hovers in the air, was present in the room. Jim was unsure what it meant, but he certainly felt it. A crushing weight, as if life itself was too big to fit into the room.

"Jim?"

"Yes."

"Remember the tablet."

"Of course."

Silence again. Suddenly, the lines started jumping. A coughing fit befell Kaci, but it stopped as quickly as it begun. She painfully moved her head downward, softly kissing Dylan's cheek. Her eyes brimmed with tears; her heart filled with love.

Kaci looked at Jim. Her lips parted. A whisper.

"Tell my boy, I loved him."

The lines leveled out.

FORTY-FOUR

Once upon a time, people feared the turbulent Islamic factions in the Middle East and the unstable dictatorship in North Korea. Now, however, a new fear had arisen and replaced it. It tenaciously gripped the entire planet, striking them comatose in their fear. It came not from one country or region, but rather smoldered and thrived amongst every tribe and nation.

Long past were the days of trust and friendship. Long past were the days when one's word was as good as their bond. It was not as if friendships ceased to exist nor that everyone was liars, but no one knew who their friends were or what was truth. So instead of fighting the delusional mediocrity of existence, it was embraced. The world had come to look much like an illustration from a "Where's Walter" book.

It was a dystopian world, and progressing forward each day. What is at the end of such a civilization? Does it just end? Or does it continually morph itself and evolve one season at a time?

Josh's weary eyes surveyed his neighborhood as the thoughts ran through his head. The digression of humanity went hand in hand with what was considered rational thinking, which had disappeared ages ago. Forget about friendship and community. Those had been replaced, slowly over time, by mere imitation which, as it became incorporated, convinced one that the replica they were clutching onto was a suitable sense of 'belonging.' So tricked was society they traded genuineness for a counterfeit – and now they basked in isolation, without any conscious reality of it.

Chewing his lower lip, he recalled one of his favorite hobbies – window watching. Evenings spent observing his neighbors' chandelier lights, flickering TV sets, dancing candle flames, lively dinner parties, running kids at play, a young couple in love – all visible through the glass. It provided him a glimpse into their daily routines. It made him feel part of a community. It had been a cheap counterfeit. Who was he really? Where did he truly belong?

The fickle thing about glass – depending on the angle, density, and clarity, what one sees could be a mere distortion. The glass creating a mirage, a misrepresentation of reality, perhaps true to its original form – heated sand turned liquid to present transparency. The ironic parallels were not lost on Josh.

The loneliness he had been feeling for years was real. He had substituted many things for it, and now, was unsure why he even cared that he felt lonely. Perhaps it was the use of xY0b5. Luke's words of warning rang in his ears: a dreamcatcher without the dream. Maybe he was now seeing his literal self. Dimly at first, as in a mirror, then face to face.

One way or the other, did it even matter?

There was a rap at the door. It caught him by surprise. Sluggishly rising up from the futon, Josh sauntered over to the door and opened it. A white package lay on the welcome mat.

"That's weird," he said out loud.

He bent over, and picked it up. The label was from an obscure sender somewhere on the West Coast. He stepped back into the house, and shut the door.

Padding across the floor, he walked into the kitchen to grab a knife. Setting the sharp edge against the tape, he sliced the package open. A small capsule was inside along with a piece of paper. He pulled them both out.

WE ARE SORRY FOR THE DELAY! OUR AUTOMATED REFILL SYSTEM WAS EXPERIENCING NETWORK DIFFICULTIES. ENCLOSED IS A NEW SUPPLY OF YOUR xY0b5 PRESCRIPTION. WE APOLOGIZE FOR ANY INCONVENIENCE OR SUFFERING THIS HAS CAUSED YOU.

Turning the new capsule over, Josh inspected it. The container was orange-brown as always, but it seemed different.

He did not know why or for what reason, but suddenly, a heaviness overtook him – a crushing weight. The fight was over. The questions that had been racking his brain for the last several months mysteriously eased. Why fight any longer?

Clutching the capsule container, he stumbled over to the futon, and flopped onto it. A cold sweat broke out over his forehead. He stared at the bottle. It was a means of escape. His nerves wracked too far – for too long. The long, stressful hours – even years – chasing down leads and dead-ends. What about all those years of terrible loss and pain?

I deserve to feel peace and calm.

As if in a trance, Josh stood up, and walked over to the kitchen counter. His key fob was there. Still holding the capsule, he opened the door to his garage and stepped out. He thumb pressed the opener, and the double-wide door ascended. Strong sunlight burst into the garage.

Squinting from the light, he opened the door to his car and slid inside. The door shut behind him. He stared ahead for what seemed several minutes before reaching down, and jabbing the ignition button. The car quietly started.

Putting the sedan in reverse, he backed out of the garage. The capsule container lay on the passenger's seat. He closed the garage door, and listlessly gazed at the house in front of him. So many dreams, hopes, plans – all smashed two years ago. Ever since that day, the fire had been slowly drained from him.

This was not home anymore; just an empty structure where he slept and stewed in. Nothing of value remained; certainly nothing worth living. The end of the world might be coming, but the end of his world had already happened. Everything he ever had was gone. Everything he had ever known – evaporated like water on a blistering hot day.

A tear trickled down his cheek. Josh wiped it away with the back of his hand. He knew of a spot. He had passed it many times. If there was a better spot, he doubt it existed.

He remembered her. Her smile. Her laugh. The way she made simple things feel like treasures. Silly things worth a belly laugh. Her zest for life. Passion and care for *people*. More tears came.

He slowly put the car into gear, and backed out of the driveway. Turning the wheel, he slid the car into 'drive', and looked out the window one last time. A sad smile crept over his face. He reached for the capsule.

"I love you, Amanda. I always will, until forever." His lips blew a kiss. His foot pressed down on the accelerator.

Opening the capsule container, Josh poured an amount far exceeding the daily dose into his hand. He tossed the pills back and swallowed.

Who needs water? It's not like we need it to live, we've found ways around that. No such thing as living water.

The idea struck him as funny.

The blue convertible rolled down the street. Gripping the wheel, he blinked away further tears, and checked the emotion within.

Conceal, don't feel; soon, very soon.

The release beckoned to him, drawing him closer. Somehow, amid the chaotic, horror-filled world, his inner peace seemed imminent.

Josh reached for the container again. His hand swished through the air. The plastic touched his lips. The capsule tipped up, still higher. Swallow. The car moved steadily along the road.

Suddenly, he felt a vibration in his pocket. It was his handheld. He had no calls to take. Time had run out for that.

Pressing the side button, he tried to silence it. It kept buzzing. Reaching into his pocket, he dug the device out and jabbed at the screen. The persistent *bzzz, bzzz* kept up despite his efforts.

The car veered dangerously as Josh stopped abruptly on the side of the road. Somewhere, somehow in the midst of the mental blackness, he found himself heeding an old lesson his mom taught him about cell phones and driving. For some reason, it had not crossed his mind to answer it wirelessly.

Breathing rapidly, shaking violently, he stared at the screen. There was no call. It was blank. Forthwith, a message flashed onto the screen. It was from an anonymous contact.

FLIGHT TO DC FROM MSP AT 10A TOMORROW. SEHTYM MEETING – SECRET! DON'T TALK. KEEP YOUR EYES OPEN, NEED YOUR PRESENCE THERE. PASSES WILL COME. EVENTUALLY, ALL WILL BE KNOWN.

"What in the world?"

He reread the message twice. The dark thoughts he had moments before evaporated. A cold sweat broke out. His palms felt clammy, and a chill ran down his spine. It was as if he was in the presence of something foreign and mysterious. The explanation for it evaded him, but for the first time in a long time, Josh felt something familiar surging; the truth-seeking emotions long checked, now loosened in his veins.

"Who is this from? Sehtym?" he continued talking out loud. "Why would they use an unknown sender? Is it the GSA again? The words 'need your presence there'…"

He remembered Mark Jacobi's masked comments before San Francisco. He sat back, dumbfounded. It couldn't be, could it? What if…he shook his head as another chill ran down his spine. The very idea was nerve-wracking.

Glancing down at the capsule container lying next to him, Josh saw the pills left inside. Too few remained. He swore, and hit the steering wheel. He started to cough and gag. Opening the car door, he leaned over and heaved – forcing himself to vomit. His body was weak and abused, but something had called out. Something had beckoned him. He would not ignore it.

The old rush of adrenaline returned. The thirst for truth-seeking wet his tongue. Instead of dismissing it, as he had been doing for months, he now embraced it. It was his only hope.

■　　　■　　　■　　　■　　　■

"Attention, please! Everyone, listen up."

Chief stood near the center console in the main CDV monitor room, and addressed the entire force of the Hub. Luke had come rushing up from the lab, moments before, with the other scientists as Tessa hurriedly summoned them.

"Danny just received a transmission from our contact at the Hill. A meeting is about to go down, and from the sounds of it, something big is about to happen."

A weird sensation, like a threatening hot breath, flashed over the room. Luke felt his spine crawling, and rubbed his arms to rid the sensation. His eyes clouded over.

"Is this it? *New Day*?" one of the CDV data analysts asked.

"We aren't sure."

It was Danny, and not Chief, who answered the question. Kelly was standing by his side, arms folded across her chest. They both looked quite fierce and prepared for whatever was coming. Their presence comforted Luke.

"It doesn't matter if it's *New Day* or doomsday – we have to be ready – for anything and everything. How goes the serum's production?"

"We are working in a small lab with limited resources, mass production is out of the question, but we are coming along as best as possible." Dr. Strong provided the update.

"Good. Finish the batch as quickly as you can. The rest of you help secure the facilities as outlined in our emergency protocols. Tessa, Danny, Kelly," Chief instructed the lieutenants. "Touch base with the other Hubs and make sure they are securing the outposts."

The huddle up was over. Chief watched them break. Her brown eyes were troubled. Traces of unknown fear rankled her countenance. Her uniform was pressed, though, it showed considerable wear. The two silver bars still shone proudly on the side of her collar. She was the formidable leader of CDV, yet she dreamed of simpler times. She wished she could go back to when she was known by another name.

Minneapolis-St. Paul International Airport was among the busiest airports in the country. It had seen a sizeable surge in flights after the repeated disasters in Chicago. Defying the public cry of classlessness, the then-governor of Minnesota did not waste a second in pulling favors from Congressional representatives to convince the FAA to route more flights over to MSP. Obviously, Chicago was inferior and unsafe.

Until recently, Josh had not flown out of the Minneapolis airport in years. All of his work for SEH involved chartered flights, usually out of Blaine. He forgot the drag that was security. Not that he had much luggage. All he bothered to bring today was a carryon bag. He had thought about packing a suitcase, but had no reason to. The enigmatic message from the anonymous sender provided few details. He figured if more had been needed, more would have been said. Recently the situation might have presented a conundrum, but he found it now, to be a delicious, refreshing change of pace.

Walking along towards the designated gate, he suddenly noticed Carrie Haselow walking a few feet in front of him! He was ready to call out her name when he remembered the instructions from the message: *"Don't talk...Sehtym meeting secret."* Seeing her here – was it a coincidence?

Carrie stopped at the same gate. For a second, Josh panicked. Then he remembered this was Carrie Haselow. While he would not consider her a close friend, he had come to know her better during the last several months working on the *Inner Earth Ventilation* project at the Assignment Building.

She was always pleasant and delightful. The soft Georgian drawl was not lost on him either. In fact, if he had cared worth a darn, he might have been interested in her. But he was not.

A flash of surprise crossed Carrie's face as she caught glimpse of him. A friendly smile appeared, and she half-waved at him from the other side of the waiting area. To Josh's chagrin and horror, she started walking over to him. Drawing closer, her mouth opened as if to speak. Thinking quickly, he hastily held up a hand, and curtly waved it. Her mouth closed, and she stopped her approach, a puzzled expression on her face.

Peeking around the waiting area, Josh alertly crossed over to where Carrie had stopped.

"Act like you don't know me," he whispered through clenched teeth as he reached her.

"What?"

"Where are you heading?" Josh casually asked, his voice a reasonable volume. He reached down and pulled a pen from his breast pocket.

"Washington, DC," Carrie replied as she glanced around the gate, perplexed by Josh's strange behavior.

She's going to DC too. Is she attending the same meeting? Did she get a cryptic message as well?

He merely smiled, though, and nodded.

"Cool! I hear it's a nice time of year, generally, not too hot and not too cold."

The pen finished writing, and Josh held his right hand up, facing Carrie but close to himself. He shielded the top of his right hand with his left so the security cameras could not distinguish what was written.

CAN'T TALK. YOU DON'T KNOW ME.

The woman gave a quick nod of her head, acknowledging the scribbled words, but also as if she agreed with Josh's statement on the District's weather.

"How about you?" Carrie responded pleasantly, but her eyes were clouded with concern.

"No idea," Josh answered, and then he laughed. "I mean, I'll see how it goes, and play it by ear. Doing a freestyle vacation."

The gate attendant came to the podium, and spoke into the intercom system. The flight was about to board. Josh flashed a parting smile to Carrie.

"Enjoy DC!"

He moved away and not a moment too soon. A man's voice called out, "Carrie?"

Walking away, Josh half-turned his head to observe a dapperly dressed man with pointy hair talking to Carrie with an air of informality. *Must be someone from her team here in Minnesota.* He did not recognize the man with pointy hair, but there were so many people at the Assignment

Building that in and of itself was no surprise. Also, aside from Carrie, who was a reviewer of projects, he had rarely worked with others.

The realization struck him odd. All the people working so close, but yet so separate. *But again*, he realized, *the sense of belonging has long eroded, and been replaced by isolation*. He had felt this isolation so keenly himself – for too long.

The gate attendant finished announcing the boarding group information, and people began lining up. Josh gave his baseball cap a tug and wiped his hand across his pants, smudging the pen's ink. He stuck the handheld's earbuds in, and turned on some music. His mind went back to the enigmatic message.

He was reasonably sure it was GSA. Who else would be so mysterious and use the words 'Your presence is needed?' Of course, Jacobi had first said them…the thought from the night before re-entered his mind. He shook it away. It couldn't be, it just couldn't.

FORTY-FIVE

At three o'clock in the afternoon, the meeting at Sehtym started. All who had been assembled were standing in the vast atrium of SEH's former headquarters in northern Virginia. After the merger with TYM, the campus had been reduced to a mere outpost for the huge pharma company. Knowing this, caused Josh to be exceedingly puzzled as to why they were gathered there.

The encrypted pass, sent by the anonymous contact, allowed him to quickly scan in. He followed the instructions and avoided talking to anyone. Thankfully, aside from the primary speaker, there was no one he recognized in the room (not counting Carrie). The principal speaker was Blair Leshief.

"You may ask yourself, why are you here? The answer is very simple. You have been chosen due to your background, your skillset – your value," Leshief added as an afterthought. "What you are about to learn has remained a secret for the last two years. It was started before any news of the disease ever appeared. It was formed by the early members of the World Council. A safeguard should catastrophic calamity ever strike. That day is approaching, and it is time to implement the safeguard."

Blair lifted his right hand, and motioned to one of the people sitting on the temporary stage. It had been hastily constructed at the front of the standing crowd. A man rose, and the familiar faces in the room went from two to three. Josh had once delivered a presentation to the man now standing. A Ugandan and delegate of the World Council: Ambassador Derrick Omach.

"We at the World Council are interested in preserving humanity, regardless of the cost," the Ambassador took a breath, and cut his eyes towards the rest of those seated on the platform. His eyes traveled back over the atrium, and he cleared his throat.

"Each of you has been involved in some capacity for Sehtym on the creation of our safeguard – *Operation Laja*. In Arabic, the words mean 'refuge'. The idea came from one of the first members of the Council, who was also president of Syria. Their government initiated the building of the first *Laja* city."

"From the beginning, the safeguard cities would be buried deep in the Earth's crust. The intent was to protect us when catastrophic calamity would strike. Each person was given their own responsibilities, and from the first keystroke to the first shovel of dirt, the cities' development was engineered in such a way that it would be virtually impossible for anyone to know exactly what they were working on. Even teams were divided in such a way that you largely worked independent of each another."

The isolation was on purpose, one question had been answered. Josh remembered his earlier musings on how solitary his work had been while at the Assignment Building. As if reading his mind, Ambassador Omach suddenly mentioned the project.

"One of the last pieces to be initiated in the Cities was the design, testing, and building of the ventilation system. In fact, we are standing where the former SEH Morphing Division was based, and one of that division's brightest minds was assigned to this last stage of *Laja*. Mr. Josh Cunningham?" it was spoken as a question rather than a statement.

Josh's stomach tightened with hearing the ambassador call out his name. He was unsure what to make of it. Why the secretive invite if they were going to acknowledge him? He was tempted to step forward, but remembered his directive from the anonymous contact. *"Don't talk"* implied keeping in the shadows. He remained silent, but his eyes diligently watched the others in the room.

Heads turned this way and that as people looked for anyone to raise their hand or come forward in response to Ambassador Omach's inquiry. Nobody moved. Josh glanced to his left and saw where Carrie was standing. She was ignoring him, but then he saw her head turn slightly. For a fleeting moment, their eyes locked; she glanced away.

Something strange was going on. And while he now knew it was not Sehtym had summoned him to this meeting, the question remained – who had? Who arranged his flight? Who else knew about this secret meeting?

"Mr. Cunningham isn't here," Blair Leshief rose again, and walked over to the podium. "Unfortunately, while his contributions will always be appreciated in the engineering of the ventilation system, Mr. Cunningham lost himself recently and overdosed. We mourn his loss."

Murmurs of sympathetic expression went up around the room. A look of sadness crossed the ambassador's face. He thanked Leshief for sharing the news, and continued to talk about the scope of the project and the tremendous effort it required from people all over the world.

Josh was flabbergasted. His face flushed, and heart pounded. While the ambassador continued to talk, he was unable to listen. Unable to focus. Too shocked to even think.

Leshief says I overdosed? I'm dead? I'm right here, in the very same room, not dead! What is he talking about? How could he possibly know?

Ambassador Omach shared the cities were uniform. While the scope of each project varied as did the allowed occupancy per location, they were identical in shape, format, and protocols. Some of the world's most powerful leaders had been involved. Foreign nations once enemies were now working together towards a common goal – "for the betterment of us all," Derrick stated as he wrapped his presentation.

A hand went up. The ambassador called on the woman. She asked when everything had been completed. She was still working on her assignment. Derrick visibly struggled, thinking of how to answer her question. The ever-ready Leshief jumped up again, and leaned into the microphone.

"Ah, yes. Perhaps a little, good-intentioned misdirection. As you can see, all actual work was completed weeks ago. We've kept you occupied with busy work, though, until the time was right." There was a pause, and the gray-haired man gave a small sigh. "There is no simple way to say it, so I just will. The reason for this meeting was not to solely share details about your assignments these past several months. It is also because those in this room are invited to partake in *Laja*. Sehtym was able to secure passes for those gathered *here* to the refuge cities on the east coast. Most will be housed in New York City, but some of you will remain at the DC *Laja*."

A loud buzz grew in the room as people began to hear and process the Sehtym executive's words.

Sehtym is sending only some to the Laja cities? What about the rest? Those here scarcely make up all employees. Josh was confused.

Leshief was not finished.

"I must say this was highly classified, and until moments ago, was only known by a select few. In fact, at this very moment, a press conference is being held in our nation's capital." The man stepped aside, and nodded to an assistant off to one side.

The assistant saw the signal, and scurried over to a small tech table. He pressed a button, and giant screens flashed in the corners of the room. Josh watched as the place was encircled by flashing pixels. They focused and sharpened. He saw a woman – a Congresswoman from North Dakota – standing at a podium on Capitol Hill. All eyes in the atrium watched her.

"It is with great trepidation, and uncertainty, we announce the start of Operation Laja. With the number of infected cities rising every day, we are urging *everyone* to gather at the assigned medical outposts in your communities. You will be treated and protected. Please be advised, anyone carrying the Disease will receive no admittance. Based on calculations, our models are showing that in twenty-four hours the Disease is going to spike, and the rest of the world's population not inoculated will either contract it or be *attacked* by it. Stay safe, and follow the emergency protocols outlined in your communities."

Congresswoman Elisha Atkins' voice was resolute and rang clear. She did not hesitate as she outlined the safety precautions and security measures being implemented over the next twenty-four hours. Her demeanor was eerily calm, and it unnerved Josh.

His eyes scrutinized the live broadcast. It seemed surreal that this was actually happening. The world was to be evacuated; burrowed in the hopes of preservation. Survival of the fittest – if there ever was a definition.

But what are we surviving? What is actually coming? Josh thought of Luke and something the scientist had said at the Stone Arch Bridge. *Is this the New Day?*

Elisha Atkins finished speaking, and a solemn tone fell over the live audience on Capitol Hill. The climate in the atrium was scarcely different. Blair Leshief motioned for the screens to be shut off. The assistant quickly did so.

"We've been given twenty-four hours to take up residency at the refuge cities. It is your choice to accept, but if you are not in by then, you will not be able to *get* in. I advise extreme caution in dismissing this offer. Any further questions or details can be obtained at the info kiosks as you leave. Thanks for your help on this enormous undertaking. We have made a better tomorrow!"

Silence fell over the room. People were shocked and stunned. A single handclap broke out. Another joined in. It cut off as several people started talking at once, and then all around handhelds and devices came out as they tried to process what just happened. Everyone had questions. Josh himself had questions. He could not concentrate on any of them. It was hypnagogic – he was unable to *be* in the dream, but neither could he *not* see it.

"Can we bring anyone?" "What about our families?" "Am I allowed my therapy hamster?" "Will there be enough food?" "What should I pack?" "Are we allowed to return to our homes first to prepare?" "Do we just go there now?" "If I don't make it in time, what happens?" "What is this all about?" "What is going to happen outside?"

The questions rang out from all corners of the atrium. People were standing, shouting, imploring the digital kiosks for answers. The machines kept up with impeccable timing, almost as if the questions were known before being asked. Josh closed his eyes. The cacophony gave him a headache.

Suddenly, he felt a tug on his arm, and opening his eyes, saw Carrie next to him. Beckoning with her head, she motioned for him to follow her. They walked past the kiosks, past the newly renovated, overly welcoming guest center, and opening a door, left the indoors for the outdoor break area. It was used on pleasanter days, and while today it was overcast and drizzling rain, that mattered little. At least, they could talk in private.

"What was all that? What is going on? You acted so strangely at the airport. Wrote a cryptic message on your arm, no less. What do they mean you committed suicide? You are here, aren't you? Who invited you to this meeting?" Carrie demanded, angst in her voice. "I have an awful feeling about what *might* have happened were you still in Minnesota."

Josh stood still, conscious of the chilling sensation returning, and running down his spine and arms. The picture became more apparent, the focus sharper. As if what was seen dimly was in the *past*, yet, a mirage of what was *to be*, or was it what *could* be? He knew not.

*My prescription ran out days ago. The system fails, a mysterious package shows up, right when I'm at my worst. Impeccable timing? Did Sehtym know what I was feeling? Or…*the dark reality hit him. *I almost lost it yesterday, and how did they know? Was it always planned that way? Did someone else intervene?*

"I'm not sure," he stammered, unable to breathe. "I'm not sure of any of it."

The chills left, and he realized he felt quite ill. The question of what to do now permeating his mind. The enigmatic message with its scant details, had mentioned nothing regarding the *Laja* cities.

Am I to go to this refuge city? Why else would I be here?

"Josh, I've got a lot of questions myself, but c'mon, snap out of this." Carrie shook his shoulders. She noticed his sudden change and flushed cheeks; she sensed something was amiss. "What are they talking about? Twenty-four hours, and then we'll regret it?"

Josh shook his head. None of it made any sense. He was exhausted, and then, in a flash, he started to fall – or was he? A hypnotic feeling, as if he did not even exist, swept over him.

Carrie reached out, and caught him as he fell forward. She held him close.

"Hang in there, Josh," she breathed. "We have to get through this, and we only have a day to figure it out."

▪   ▪   ▪   ▪   ▪

An alert sounded, and a violent vibration on the tablet ensued. Dylan Knudson jumped back, startled at the noise, and stared at his device. Unsure of what was going on, Jim walked over and picked up the tablet. A digital clock displayed: 24:00:00 for one brief moment, and then it started to count down, one second at a time.

Jim had seen enough on the small TV at *Savannah Souvenirs* to know it was a doomsday clock. He instinctively knew it had *something* to do with the 'Golden Cities' Kaci had mentioned. Glancing down, he saw Dylan's curly mop of black hair hanging low on his brown-skinned forehead. The boy's olive eyes peered up at him, wondering what was going on.

"What is it, Mr. Jim?"

"We have some distance to cover, Dylan. We better be going."

The little boy respectfully nodded and slid to the ground. The soles of the ever-glistening *Ultimate Heroes* sneakers touched the floor.

The older man inwardly sighed. *How am I supposed to do this? Precious little time to travel all that way north – let alone trying to comfort this boy along the way.*

"You know, little man?" he spoke out loud; his words flowing naturally and honestly. "You are the bravest person I've ever met."

"How's that?" Dylan raised a small eyebrow, doubting Jim's sincerity.

"Because," the shopkeeper choked. "You're going with a complete stranger to an unknown place just because your mommy asked you to. I think that is incredibly brave. And you know what? Your courage gives *me* courage."

A little smile appeared on Dylan's face as he considered the praise from Jim.

"If my momma tells me that I have to be brave and help take you somewhere, I will. Come along, Mr. Jim."

A new chapter begins, Jim started trailing behind the small feet. *Another small child, hurt and alone, left to my care. Am I able to do this all over again? This time, a world hangs in the balance. Though,* a wry smile came over him, *maybe it's always been that way.*

FORTY-SIX

Josh surveyed the area around him. Trees with empty branches covered the landscape. Whispers of snowflakes from a light snow earlier that day dotted the vegetation. Most of the leaves fallen from the branches, had blown away – carried off to spend winter elsewhere. The remaining leaves swirled about, tossing to and fro in the air, briskly whisking by his feet. He realized he was sitting on a brick wall – a half-wall that ran around the borders of a small pavilion. Cocking his head, he became aware of the sound of rushing water nearby.

Glancing to his right, he noticed Carrie seated next to him. She smiled, and rubbed his arm in a friendly fashion.

"Where are we?" he asked.

"Great Falls Park. It's a favorite spot of mine. When I lived here, I loved coming. I'd sit and just look at the falls. Helped calm me, made me feel safe. Still does. Is that weird?"

Josh shrugged his shoulders. "Don't ask me what's weird. What do I know? How much time is left?"

"Less than eight hours."

"Don't you have anywhere else to be?"

The woman shook her head. "I don't have any family left."

"Really? From what you said about your parents I assumed they were still alive."

"They died. A few years ago – my mom from cancer, my dad from a broken heart."

"I'm sorry."

"Thanks."

It was quiet and then, not knowing what else to say, Josh quipped, "How about that old guy in Savannah? I thought you were pretty good friends."

"Ha! Jim? He is a good friend, but I haven't talked to him since my parents died. I hope he's all right. I know they had that incident with the woman on the wharf, and then a bad outbreak of the Disease." A look of concern appeared on Carrie's countenance. Her brow furrowed. "I hope he survives whatever's coming next."

"Are you going to the City?"

"Of course; what else would I do? And you?"

Josh bit his lower lip and shook his head. What *was* he going to do? Would any decision change the outcome at this point? Two days ago, he was ready to die. Today something inside compelled him to live. Still...

"I haven't been well for months. For sure, ever since SEH fell apart, probably longer."

He was surprised how easily he shared the feeling. Somehow it felt right. It had been tugging at him for some time. Carrie nodded understandingly as she listened.

"I mean with Jacobi's passing, Sam too – that definitely sucked. Forget about San Francisco and the events of...years ago." A faraway look appeared in his eyes, and he sat still for a moment. Then he shook himself and added: "To just be discarded by Sehtym, though, and then my room was broken into, I was attacked, questioned by some government agency..."

"Wait, what?" Carrie looked at Josh, her interest piqued.

"I was questioned by some dudes – and a lady," he remembered. "In black jackets. I don't know who they were with. NSA, I think?"

"No, you said your room was broken into?"

"Yeah, I was attacked. That's why I had a prescription in the first place..."

"Sure," Carrie cut him off. "But you were then questioned – like about the break-in, or?"

Josh tilted his head sideways. "No. I was interrogated about Sam and what I knew of him and...I don't know. Why?"

Carrie took his hand in her own, cupping it slightly. She looked deep into his eyes.

"Listen carefully, Josh, we have to go to that City. Something else is clearly going on here. None of what happened to you makes any sense. And there was something sinister in Blair Leshief's comment yesterday afternoon about your supposed overdose. Like he knew something all along – almost, as if he *expected* it."

Her words sank deep. Carrie was merely verbalizing his fears. The fear, of course, was precisely the worst part.

"You're right, Carrie. I thought the same thing myself. But that's just it…if I'm supposed to be dead, how am I ever going to get into the City?"

.   .   .   .   .

"All clear!" the baritone voice of Dr. Strong boomed out as he hurried out of the incubation bunker.

Danny Graves pushed on a large red handle, and the large glass doors moved together and sealed shut. Whatever was on the other side would be safe in their bomb and chemical proof hovel.

"Did you finish?" Tessa asked.

Luke nodded in reply. She gave a small smile in return, and let out a long sigh.

He was surprised at how involved she seemed to be. *Here I was just starting to think she was purely robotic and only cared about disrupting people's lives.* Even while he thought it, his conscience pricked him. It really was that she showed greater care and concern for the cause than she did for him.

"We don't have time to be standing still," Danny commanded. "Everybody move! The clock is ticking. Elisha Adkins said twenty-four hours in her broadcast. That time is fast passing!"

The small party began running down the corridor. At the end of it, they climbed up the narrow, metal spiral staircase to the next level. Then they burst into another quick jog as they moved to the vehicles parked at the end of the tunnel.

Luke clambered aboard a truck, and instinctively buckled in. It was an old habit, and habits die hard. Tessa flashed him a quick smile.

"I'm glad you joined us, Luke. We couldn't have gotten this far without you."

He nodded his head, appreciative of her words. The trucks started to roll out. It was then Luke noticed the growing concern and worried faces on some of his compatriots. Even Tessa seemed to tense up as the vehicles moved away.

It was quiet for a minute, then Danny cursed under his breath, and hit the side of the truck. Luke sat still, unsure of what was wrong. Dr. Strong and the other scientists remained quiet. Kelly looked back from her seat in the front.

"Chief says it can't be good. That was an encrypted broadcast."

"Meaning?" Dr. Strong was the one who asked for clarification.

"Meaning they lied to us again!" Danny shouted as he cursed, and hit the side of the truck again.

Luke cast a puzzled expression towards Tessa, unsure of Danny's reaction.

"Encrypted is a broadcast that is widely played, but solely picked up by designated receivers. Using the feeds they played on, it made it seem as if it were a nationwide broadcast, and everyone could see it – thus have a chance at surviving. Turns out, only a handful of outlets actually had access to it. We saw it purely because Jackson was able to hack it."

"I'd love to see one of those World Council mother—," Kelly cursed vulgarly. "Right now, I'd bury their ass so deep, dowsing couldn't find 'em."

"Who's decision was it to encrypt the broadcast?" Luke tried to rationalize. It made no sense anyone would deliberately choose to make a pretense of warning others, when in actuality ignoring them.

"Who knows? Does it matter?" Tessa looked at Luke, their eyes locked. "What is everyone else going to do? They have no idea what's coming."

Not knowing the answer, Luke merely shook his head. Tessa pushed a strand of the hair back, and tucked it behind her ear. Her lips slowly parted and spread into a warm smile as she tried to recoup her feelings. She took her hand, and placed it over Luke's. He could feel it trembling slightly, which he knew was no accident.

Feelings of empathy and love came over him. How strange the human mind is. That someone who was once an oppressor could now be the subject of admiration and even feelings of romantic love. How fickle are humans.

A tingle of excitement ran through him. It warmed his entire being, and made him feel more alive than he had ever felt. A sensation flooded him, one he had not quite felt in a long time – since his early college days perhaps. Somehow, he felt braver.

"What do you think is coming?" he asked Tessa, searching deep into her eyes.

"I don't know, Luke. But whatever it is, we'll face it together."

The truck suddenly stopped, and the back door opened. A woman stood there. She was wearing a freshly-pressed US Navy uniform. The bars of lieutenant displayed on her shoulders, elegantly trimmed by a golden thread. A smoldering cigarette was gently clasped between her forefinger and middle fingers. She flicked the butt of it as she surveyed the inhabitants of the vehicle, and gave a curt nod of her head.

"I'm glad you're all here. We have work to do. The health bunker was just one of many types of bunkers we've been monitoring and protecting these last several months. If my hunch is right, precious time remains until *New Day* hits. And from everything we've gathered, *New Day* means just that. Folks, it's the end of the world."

Luke locked eyes with those in the truck. They looked around at each other, taking in the moment. Everything they had been working on – some for months, some for years – was about to come to a horrifying climax.

"Let it come. We are ready, Chief." Kelly shouted.

Danny's eyes narrowed, and he nodded in agreement. Luke ran a nervous tongue over his lips, and looked back at the woman who led CDV. Chief's lips curled into a small, tight smile as she caught his glance.

"Are you ready, Luke?"

He lowered his gaze. His mind flashed through the events of the last year – which felt like ten years. Was he ready?

"No," he carefully responded, looking back at her. "But I will be brave, Chief."

The former Navy lieutenant tilted her head at Luke and nodded. A glimmer of courage shot through his veins as he met her gaze. She had a way of somehow inspiring – driving him to embrace courage and stand tall.

She swiveled and faced the cold wind outside. The gusts blew warm whispers of the cherry tobacco fragrance that cloaked her over Luke's face. Chief spoke, her voice firm as she addressed those behind her.

"We will all need courage for what is to come."

■　　■　　■　　■　　■

The hours seemed to drag on. The sunrise they had witnessed earlier in the day seemed as if yesterday. The noon hour approached. At precisely, twelve-noon, a chirp sounded on Josh's handheld. He pulled it out of his pocket. A message displayed.

ENTER CITY. AWAIT FURTHER INSTRUCTIONS. F2F

It was the anonymous sender again, but this time there was something else. Hands shaking, Josh held the device up to show Carrie. Her face brightened. Embossed behind the text of the message, was an encrypted passkey for entrance into the City. He could get in.

"Who is it from?"

"I think a security firm I've worked with in the past. San Francisco and…China." He suddenly thought of *Diabolus*, the entire reason he was in China.

After all of this, is it really so simple? Everything interwoven and connected to each other?

"The same people who contacted you about the meeting?" Carrie interrupted his thoughts.

During the early morning hours sitting on the wall at Great Falls Park, Josh had shared all the events of the last several months with Carrie. He felt compelled to – as if she were his last lifeline and security. Why not? The world was ending anyway.

He nodded in reply to her question.

"What do they mean? Await further instructions?" Carrie stopped her pacing, and slid back down next to Josh. The two of them sitting once more on the brick wall.

Josh closed his eyes, feeling the cold air of the wintry day in Virginia brush across his face. It caused his mind to travel. He could taste the sweet water of Colorado, smell the clean, fresh air, and see the majestic mountains – all part of the beauty in the Universe. If he listened carefully, he could detect the cries of a killdeer from Minnesota. He was on his futon, watching it fool a crow, and then realized all was as seen in a mirror. A paradox.

They were the crows, fooled by the trickster killdeer. A world that had caved to calamity and terror. Was it by choosing fear and discarding millenniums of previous thought and rationale? Light over dark now reversed? It seemed truth-seeking was a thing of the past. The clean smell, sweet taste, and beautiful view dissolved.

He was sitting over a rushing river – empty branches, bending trees, rustling dead leaves, and brown grass. It felt desolate. The truth mattered not in this new world. Only survival and those fittest would make it. He was long past that. His life was no longer his – he blindly followed instructions sent to him from an anonymous sender via text messaging.

How hopeless am I? Yet, even as he thought it, he felt as if there *just might* be a glimmer of hope.

"It's time," Carrie whispered, hugging Josh close, holding his head against hers. "We need to go."

For the second time that weekend, as if in a trance – following directions as if he were being controlled by someone else – Josh reached out and took Carrie's hand. Together they began making their way down the walkway to the parking lot below. Her red coupe was there. They would drive to the bus station.

The ride was short. Neither Carrie nor he spoke a word. The station was bustling as people clambered aboard and loaded the buses. Josh was not sure how many people were invited to live in the refuge city, but a quick glance around made it clear far more than just Sehtym employees. Thousands of people, perhaps tens of thousands. The loading process took another hour.

While the station was bustling with activity, the ride itself was quiet. Uncertainty of what might happen next escalated to a feverish pitch in the enclosed transportation vehicle. The tension was so thick one could cut it. Nobody said a word.

The bus pulled into a loading bay of sorts. Other trucks, coaches, and trailers carrying thousands of people bustled in and out. The bay extended quite a ways, and its roof was tall enough even the highest vehicle could enter. Josh raised his eyes, intending to better examine their surroundings, when a sudden fit of shakes overtook him. Lowering his gaze, he pulled his thin sports jacket closer. He felt something deep inside the right coat pocket.

Clawing and wrapping his fingers tightly around it, he pulled it out. At first, he was confused, then he realized he was wearing his *favorite* sports jacket. The same one he had worn the evening at Point Park. In his hand, was the small microchip given to him by the mysterious caller, supposedly containing all the research of what had been going on.

Does it even matter anymore? What does it all entail?

His curiosity gripped him. At that moment, he was oblivious to who might be watching or even what was going on around him. Grabbing his handheld, he started to insert the chip into the reader. Suddenly, a hand reached out, and firmly grasped his, stopping the action.

"What are you doing?" Carrie whispered sternly.

"Seeing what this is. Perhaps it holds the answers."

"Are you *crazy*? Whatever it might be, it's obviously contraband, and they won't let that into the City. Here, give it to me."

She took the device and expertly pried the protective lens glass off the camera on the back. Josh watched in bewilderment as she deftly stashed the chip underneath. Pressing the lens glass back down, he heard it snap into place.

"How did you…?"

The words died in his mouth. He stared astonished at Carrie, who merely handed it back with a shrug. It had been done hastily and not a moment too soon.

"Please have your passes ready!" a voice from the front of the bus shouted. A man with stripes of a sergeant climbed aboard. "Anyone without a pass will be removed!"

All of a sudden, a loud noise ricocheted through the air. It was a gunshot! Josh jerked upright in his seat.

Sirens blared outside; police and military escorts were moving the throng of people forward and inward. Josh's eyes scanned the area, trying to figure out where the shot came from. Another one sounded. Once more, his entire body involuntarily recoiled.

"That noise you hear," the sergeant shouted as he walked up and down the bus aisle. "Is what happens if you do *not* have a valid pass! I strongly suggest you give yourself up, and do not attempt to illegally enter. We have highly sensitive detectors, you will be caught. Only certain people have been chosen to live in these communities. Why would you jeopardize the world's future? There is swift justice for attempting to do so. However, volunteers will be left outside just *as you are*. That's a promise from the US government to you."

A hand went up near the front of the bus. Josh' eyes widened. Someone was trying to sneak in on their very bus?

A lady screamed, and the boy sitting next to her was ripped from his seat by two other guards. They carried him, kicking legs and all, and dumped the boy outside the bus. One of the guards pulled his sidearm and racked the slide. Josh was shocked. The sergeant had promised! He tried not to watch, but he felt compelled. People on the bus starting yelling and shouting to no avail.

The sidearm flashed down, and the boy fell over, knocked unconscious by the vicious blow. The lady in the front, who was the boy's mother, shrieked loudly. The sergeant stopped and said something to her, low and quiet. The shrieking dissipated. Only soft, controlled whimpers were heard.

Josh felt his eyes closing. He reached out his hand.

"Carrie," he whispered.

A steady, yet soft hand closed over his. Carrie sensed his fatigue, and grabbed his arm.

"Follow me, Josh. We've got this."

The two of them descended the bus, and started towards the entrance to the city. Josh had no idea where they were. The terminal was on the side of a hill, and he presumed the entire city must be below them. How deep or far it went, he knew not.

Sirens started to blare anew. A burnt orange color appeared on the horizon. Suddenly, a low plane swooped overhead. It was a military plane, an attack fighter jet.

"What in the world?"

Shouting erupted as others noticed the plane. There were more planes in the sky too – off in the distance – moving away from them. From the same direction, low rumbling noises could be heard. It was not the kind of rumbling a thunderstorm makes, but more like a crescendo of an explosion as it booms.

"It can't be," Carrie was breathless. "They are dropping bombs?"

Shrieks filled the air as others arrived at the same conclusion. Disbelief seized Josh. This could not be happening. It seemed foreign, incomprehensible – inconceivable.

"Whose planes are those?" "Are we at war with someone?" "I thought the fear was the Disease? Not guns and bombs!" "What about our families? Our loved ones?" "The Disease is our enemy. Death to the Unknowns!"

Josh and Carrie were pushed along by the throngs of people. Masses of humanity traversed along the terminal, awaiting their descent into the world below – to avoid the world above.

Josh felt like he was burning up. His body twitched, wanting to shake violently. He concealed it as best as possible. If he displayed any illness, he was sure they would not let him in.

Glancing back, he observed the horizon once more. The burnt orange color – was it because of bombs? Different explosions? Maybe a raging fire that started without the aid of ammunition. Whatever it might be, there was no doubt it was quickly consuming the world outside given the rapid spreading of the colors.

"Hold up your passes!" the soldiers screamed at the crowds of people.

All around, people lifted their hands, holding high the electronic passkeys. A scanner swung across the crowd, digitally scanning and filing each person as they entered. A sudden shout came from the front. The guards pushed forward, and grabbed a young woman. She turned and looked at her comrade – another woman. The latter started shouting and pleading, the guards shoved her down.

They pushed the first woman ahead. She protested and fought back. Grabbing her arms, they dragged her out toward the central bay. The woman left behind was surrounded by those standing near her. Burying her head in a stranger's jacket, she sobbed heartbroken. Another gunshot was heard. Near the bay's front, the first woman's body fell over, blood spurting from her head.

The crowds of people moved closer to each other. Huddling in small groups, trying to absorb the horror of what was happening. They had only their imaginations to provide commentary on the terror going on outside.

"This is what happens when we reject God and his son Jesus Christ."

"Shut up!"

"Who let the hater in?"

Josh peered, and saw the man who had spoken first, raising his hands in prayer. The others around him, shrugged their shoulders. "If there is a God, let him save him."

"What do you think is happening out there?" Carrie whispered to Josh.

"Maybe it's as some say – the Unknowns. Or maybe a new outbreak of the Disease; maybe because darkness has entered our world, and now all we feel is hopelessness." Josh thought of his old job. "We had to create truth verification teams because so many alternatives – false narratives were being presented and accepted as truth. If that's not broken, I don't know what is."

"Why do *we* get to survive? Who chose us?"

An alarm went off, warning those inside the bay that the giant steel doors were about to close. Josh spun around and watched, mesmerized as they slowly began to shut. Behind him, oversized elevators were running nonstop as people loaded onto them. The elevators would shuttle them to their destination – the City below.

"Oh my gosh," Carrie whispered as it dawned on her. "We were the last bus."

Her words sunk as if in muck on Josh's foggy brain. He heard them, yet the gravity of them did not register. Instead, he stood, transfixed by the orange glow outside as it brightened and continued to spread.

Inside, shadows grew. There was a glimmer of light poking itself in from the underneath the bay's entrance, the only illumination in the enormous elevator lobby. The interior lights did not come on. The giant doors continued moving closer to each other. The space where the light seeped in grew less and less. Visibility was low, and then worse.

The doors settled against one another with a dull, heavy thud. All was dark.

NOTE FROM THE AUTHOR

Word-of-mouth is crucial for any author to succeed. If you enjoyed the book, please leave a review online—anywhere you are able. Even if it's just a sentence or two. It would make all the difference and would be very much appreciated.

Thanks!
Caleb

ABOUT THE AUTHOR

Born in Michigan, raised in Wisconsin, Caleb Rocke has been storytelling and writing fiction since he was a child. His work has been featured through numerous mediums – print, film, online, and live performance. In 2011, he debuted as an author with the historical-fiction novel, *A Twilight in the Morning*.

When he is not writing, Caleb can be found playing softball and enjoying the outdoors. He resides in Saint Paul, Minnesota, with his wife and two children.

www.calebrocke.com
facebook.com/calebjrocke
twitter.com/calebrocke
https://www.linkedin.com/in/calebrocke/

Thank you so much for reading one of our **Sci-Fi** novels.

If you enjoyed our book, please check out our recommended title for your next great read!

Culture-Z by Karl Andrew Marszalowicz

In the year 2190, mankind has made great strides forward in the worlds of technology, science, and greed. However, when all three get together one last time, this oblivious generation may not exist much longer.